RANDOM HOUSE

LARGE PRINT

Hey, Cowgirl, Need a Ride?

Hey, Cowgirl, Need a Ride?

BAXTER BLACK

RANDOM HOUSE
LARGE PRINT

Published in the United States of America by Random House Large Print in association with Crown Publishers, New York and simultaneously in Canada by Random House of Canada Limited, Toronto. Distributed by Random House, Inc., New York. Design by Elina D. Nudelman

The Library of Congress has established a Cataloging-in-Publication record for this title.

ISBN-13: 978-0-375-72836-5
ISBN-10: 0-375-72836-8

www.randomlargeprint.com

FIRST LARGE PRINT EDITION

10 9 8 7 6 5 4 3 2 1

This Large Print edition published in accord with the standards of the N.A.V.H.

To all the old cowboys I've known,
like Al Belcher and Jon McCormick and
Casey Tibbs, who started with nuthin'
and ended up even.

They got their money's worth.

Hey, Cowgirl, Need a Ride?

You can talk about the glamour and the love
   of rodeo
The challenge and the heartbreak of the
   dally and the throw
Of the guts and luck and glory the leather
   and the sweat
The gristle and the power of the bull that
   ain't rode yet

And the get up-in-the-morning and the
   miles-down-the-road
And the bronc that stands awaitin' and the
   rope that ain't been throwed
The vision of the buckle worn by
   superhuman champs
And paid for in contusions, broken bones,
   in aches and cramps

And mothers in the bleachers and spouses
   back at home
Who keep the home fires burning while
   their darlin' loved ones roam

The siren's call of rodeo that beckons one
    last ride
The gamblers itch, the mountain top, the
    pinnacle, the pride
The reason they give all they have is
    measured in a score
A crowd, a millisecond, flag and timer, judge
    and roar
But for some the lure is simpler, the
    attraction that still pulls
Like me . . . just gettin' girls was the reason I
    rode bulls!

1

November 27, 1986:
Lick and Al in Camp

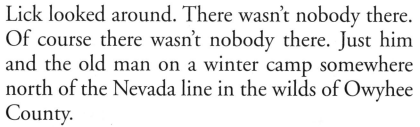

Lick looked around. There wasn't nobody there. Of course there wasn't nobody there. Just him and the old man on a winter camp somewhere north of the Nevada line in the wilds of Owyhee County.

The camp was a twenty-year-old, sixty-five-foot single-wide New Moon house trailer that the company had pulled out here in the middle of a piece of high desert called Pandora's Thumb. Good enough for two cowboys to bach and take care of four hundred cows on winter range.

The old man had a car. An old four-door Ford sedan that hadn't had a current emissions sticker in ten years and seldom ran without tinkering. The ranch manager brought them groceries every Wednesday from Bruneau, Idaho, a good two-hour drive. No phone, no fax, no electricity. No Kwik Chek, Wal-Mart, Denny's, Backyard Burger, Pizza Hut, roping arena, therapist, or tanning salon. No contact with the outside world except that weekly visit.

"What's the matter with you, Al? Ain't nobody here."

"Git my gun, kid. I think they're fixin' to overrun the bunker! Them Huns kin sure fight. I know. I've played cards with 'em. Drunk their whiskey, danced their women, and done their polka. And kid"—Al lifted his head conspiratorily—"I never did like beer. Took too long to git drunk. Like enterin' the Dixie 500 in a Ford Pinto. Ya spend all yer time just gettin' there.

"Did I ever tellya 'bout the time I shot down one of our own planes?" Al paused. A curtain pulled over his eyes. The old man's head crashed back onto the bunk and within five breaths he was snoring like a diesel.

Lincoln Delgado Davis, or Lick, as he was known, was a long way from his college degree, his failed marriage, and his fizzled attempt at rodeo. Thirty-four, single, and beholden to no one, he was ambivalent about his future. The word "career" wasn't part of his vocabulary. He'd signed on with this outfit because he wanted to do some ranch cowboyin'. He'd spent time in feedlots and figgered this would be different. It was.

Bein' stuck with the old man wasn't so bad.

In the two months they'd been together, first at the headquarters and now here, the old man had been through several hallucinatory spells like tonight. Wuddn't no big deal. Lick didn't know exactly how old the old man was. He was cagey about tellin'. Maybe he didn't know himself, but Lick assumed he was long past retirement age.

One thing for sure, he did look old. Al's gray hair was thin and about gone on top. His bare head had probably seen less sun than a Carlsbad Caverns bat. In the facial latitudes south of his hat brim his skin was as soft and supple as a welding glove. Years of toasting his ups and downs had left a road map of broken veins across his rosy cheeks and nose.

His eyes were faded blue and his fighting weight, which he claimed to have maintained since coming of age, was 146. We can assume that was fully dressed. He stood five foot eight when he enlisted in the U.S. Army in 1943. Out of kindness, one might characterize him as wiry, maybe spry. In the cowboy vernacular, he was just a pore doer.

Lick drew the covers up around the old man, turned down the propane lamp, and clanked into the kitchen. The wind whistled through the window edges where the duct tape had come loose. He put on his hat, coat, and gloves and headed out the back door to do the nightly check on the dogs and the horses. October had been mild. Fifty degrees during the day, twenties at night. But yesterday November had kicked Indian summer in the butt with a cold front that brought out the long johns. Low bruised clouds, sleet scraped off God's windshield, and wind that penetrated like taco grease on a cheap paper plate.

Lick looked up at the ugly night sky. The dogs were curled underneath the trailer on the leeward side where the skirt was broken. **Gonna be nasty tomorrow,** he thought to himself, **but so what, I ain't goin' nowhere.** He checked the two saddle horses standin' hipshot and dozin' up against the windbreak. They had three more horses in a fifty-acre trap down by the creek. Brownie and Bill, the old man's dogs, came sniffin' outta their hole beneath the trailer to help Lick make his rounds. He chopped a little ice in the horse tank with a short post and stood with his back to the wind, lookin' east. **I been worse,** thought Lick. **I been worse.**

A shot rang out! And it could dang sure ring out where the nearest neighbor was twenty-two miles away. The initial blast was followed by four more rounds. Lick raced back to the trailer.

"I think I got one of 'em!" the old man said as he stood in the doorway, obviously revived from his alcohol-induced blackout. He held a smoking .30-30 in his hands. "Rustlers, I reckon, or car thieves," he said.

Lick looked at the old faded turquoise Ford with renewed interest. It still sat like a tilted tombstone on the flat front tire. He thought he noticed a new bullet hole in the front fender.

"How 'bout some coffee, Al," suggested Lick.

The old man levered out a spent shell and pulled the trigger. The hammer fell on the empty chamber. "Might as well," he said. "I'm outta bullets."

"Don't forget the Milnot," reminded the old man when they were back in the kitchen.

Lick dug a can of evaporated milk out of the fridge door. "Got it right here." The fact that it was Pet milk and not Milnot never caused a problem. They sat at the Formica table with its sixties-modern aluminum tubular legs.

"Ya know, kid, I been thinkin'. Maybe I oughta go see some of my old friends. My old rodeo buddies, some of them fellers I cowboyed with. I used to ride bulls. It's a fact. I never won Pendleton or Calgary, nuthin' like that, but I had some good rides.

"Anyway, I ain't married to this oufit, although they've always treated me good. But I've got a sister somewhere. Washington, maybe, or Wisconsin, one of them 'W' states, I can't remember. But maybe I should just pop in and surprise her. I ain't seen her for twenty or thirty years. And I reckon I oughta do it 'fore I git too dang old to travel. Hell, you could go with me. I could be your guide. I got a little money, ya know. Lewis has been puttin' half my paycheck in a bank for me ever' month for however long I been here. Fifteen years, I think. Or twenty, or maybe it's fourteen. Anyway, it's a bunch."

Lick leaned back and let the old man talk. He himself was makin' eight hundred and fifty bucks a month plus board, food and horses furnished. He figured the old man to be making more. Maybe over a thousand. Lewis Ola, the ranch manager, always officially treated the old man like he was in charge. Lick did what he could to help and didn't worry about it.

He pried off his boots and propped his feet up on the extra kitchen chair. The winter wind and extended exposure had given his olive skin a sculptured look. He needed a haircut again. His thick black hair and his coloring were a gift from his Spanish grandfather on his mother's side. The heavy black moustache showed no gray but was looking ratty. He was an inch taller than the old man and twenty pounds heavier. He relaxed and tuned out the old man's ramblings.

Last payday they'd taken the old Ford and driven to Elko, Nevada, three hours to the south. The old man told him he'd gone to Elko every payday, once a month, since long before

Lick had come on board. "Like 'clarkwork,'" he'd said, "if the car's runnin'."

Lick had spent his last ten years on the rodeo circuit, so he'd had plenty of harrowing experiences on the road. He was better prepared than most, but he did get his eyebrows raised more than once riding in that old car with the old man driving. He found himself with his hands pressed against the dashboard more times than he could count. The track out to the highway was nothing but ruts and boulders for the first four miles. It had taken an hour. The next three or four miles wound through several hairpin curves and drop-offs before it leveled out and continued fifteen miles onto the blacktop.

Lewis always paid the old man the unbanked half of his check in cash. When they arrived in Elko, Lick cashed his check at the bank. The old man went directly to the Stockmen's Casino bar. Lick did a little shopping and a lot of looking at Capriola Saddlery. An hour later, he wandered into the Stockmen's looking for the old man. He wasn't hard to find. He was leaned against the bar in conversation with another cowboy and a woman.

"Hey, kid," barked the old man. "You need a drink!" It wasn't a question. He turned to the barkeep. "A whiskey and water for the kid and another for me and my friends."

Lick glanced at his watch. It read 1:00 p.m.

Which meant it was noon, Nevada time. For the next three days they only left the bar to play blackjack, eat the occasional scrambled egg, and venture across the railroad tracks. The old man would drink till he got tired. There was a corner booth with a padded bench where they'd lay him down sometimes. On at least two occasions Lick and Al slept in the car.

On the fourth morning, the old man reached over from the backseat and shook Lick awake. "Kid," he said, "I reckon we'd better head back, I'm outta money. I hope you got enough to get gas."

The old man pushed his chair back from the table. The scraping of chair legs on the floor brought Lick back to the present.

"Time for a little shut-eye, kid. I done checked the horses."

2

November 28: Teddie Arizona

The next day came in like a dump truck full of wet motel laundry. This particular sorry morning had stirred a few stinging raindrops into the brisk breeze. Yesterday's storm had blown through in a fury and left the dregs of an all-night party. The sky looked like somebody had spilt a lakeful of battleship paint on a glass ceiling. Lick and the old man were hunched against the wind riding to check the cows in Slippery Canyon. The cows had scattered bad. It was miserable work.

Lick was wearing a cap with earflaps. He had on long johns, a down coat, chaps, five-buckle overshoes, and ski gloves—and was freezing to death. The old man was wearing his usual "workin'" cowboy hat. Never covered his ears. As it got colder, he would add more shirts or vests under his jean jacket. On really chilly mornings, he would stuff wadded-up newpapers in the sleeves and around his middle. "Insulation," he'd explain.

They tipped over the edge of the canyon rim with the old man in the lead. As soon as they started descending, the wind gave up tormenting them. Stopping to rest their horses, they scanned the canyon that fell clear to the Bruneau River four hundred feet below and three-quarters of a mile away to the east.

"Not much movin'," said the old man. The navy could have been landing Phantom jets on the USS **Enterprise** a hundred yards away and the old man wouldn't have heard them. But he still had keen eyesight, particularly at a distance.

Lick continued to look for some movement or four-legged shadow that would indicate the whereabouts of the cows.

"Al, there's somethin' down there. At the bottom of that bluff just above the river. Somethin' movin', but it don't look like a cow. It looks like . . . maybe a person. Can't tell. Might be a horse, no, it's . . . yeah, I think it's a person."

"You mean a hiker?" said the old man. "Wouldn't surprise me. Doin' a nature hike. Lookin' for birds or cow pies. I don't know any fishermen dumb enough to try it this late, but they're not known for their good judgment and it's for sure no BLM guys would be out here on a day like this. Besides, it's too early in the day. They're still havin' their morning meeting."

"Well, let's ease on down and check it out," said Lick.

The old man kicked his horse down the cow trail and Lick followed. They lost sight of the figure several times as they crossed rims and washes along the canyon side, but every time they topped a crest, Lick could still see the person. After twenty minutes, they reined up with a clear view.

"Al, he seems to be workin' his way up the canyon but meanderin' a lot. I think we could cut across here and come down on his side. Whattaya think?"

"You reckon it's a rustler?" asked the old man warily.

"A fairly stupid one, if it is," observed Lick. "He's twenty miles from the road and afoot."

In a few minutes they rode up on the wandering pilgrim. When they were within twenty yards, they both reined up their horses.

It was a woman. She was wearing designer jeans, black rubber-soled boots, and a bulky, long-sleeved blue sweater. Her short, streaked-blonde hair stuck out crazily, like muddy wheat stubble with deer tracks in it.

The boys had made a lot of rock-clattering noise as they approached, but she paid no attention. They sat and waited, which was both their styles. She got within ten yards of the silent horsemen, then started to veer off again.

"Mornin' ma'am," said the old man.

The woman stopped, then turned her head slowly in their direction. She stared but didn't seem to comprehend. Lick dismounted and slowly walked toward her. As he closed the distance, he could see she was in a daze. Her sweater was torn, the right sleeve darkened. Her jeans were also torn in places. There was dried blood on the side of her face and her hair was matted above it.

When they got within touching distance, he could see that her eyes were glazed, almost metallic, like she had dimes in them. They were pale blue. Lick was put to mind of a sled dog.

He reached out to her like she was a spooky horse. The instant he felt the rough wool of the sweater on the tips of his fingers, she screamed! And connected with a wild roundhouse right that caught him square on the temple!

Lick's eyelids fluttered and light filtered onto the Technicolor screen of his retinas. A cold gray sky unfolded into his view. His body began checking in with his brain. **Flat on my back. A rock beside my left ear. Hands underneath my hip pockets. Cap's chin strap uncomfortably under my nose. Spurs splaying my feet. Blood pounding in my head. Bucked off again,** was his first thought. He lay still as the numbed neurons began to crackle to life.

He raised himself on one elbow with difficulty and looked around. A paper sack, which he recognized as lunch, lay nearby. There was silence except for the errant wisps of breeze that fell off the canyon rim high above. Within moments he was standing shakily and assessing his situation. The girl was gone. His horse was gone. His down coat was gone. A pretty selective mugging. **They took what they needed, laid me out like a corpse, and left me for** dead. **Who would do that?** Of course . . . the old man.

He studied the trail up the canyon. No sound or movement. He'd been unconscious for quite a while. With the dogged determination of a salaried posthole digger, he started up Slippery Canyon.

It was past the lunch hour when Lick finally saw their camp snuggled amongst the rocks and sagebrush like a machine-gun bunker. Walking into the wind hadn't improved his disposition. He'd worked up a pretty good sweat despite the cold. The old man's two dogs came out barkin' like hounds of the Baskervilles till he spoke to them, none too gently.

Approaching the trailer, he could see the old man peekin' out the window, alerted by the dogs. When Lick returned his gaze, the old man ducked out of sight. Lick strode resolutely to the door, pushed it open, slipped on the chunk of railroad tie that served as a step, and cracked his shin against the aluminum doorjamb. He fell halfway in, cursing and writhing.

"This had better be good, you old boar, or yer never gonna see Social Security! Leavin' me in the bottom of the canyon, stealin' my horse, stealin' my coat . . ." Lick was yelling. "What if I'd froze to death, or a cat come up or a boulder fell down, a landslide or an avalanche . . . maybe even an earthquake! I'd been swallowed up without a trace, sucked into the bowels of the earth . . . and without a horse! Did you lose yer mind, or what?"

The old man looked at Lick sprawled on the floor and said, "I left you lunch."

Lick gave him a long cold stare and reached down to touch his aching shin.

"Kid," the old man said with a hint of sympathy, "would you mind unsaddlin' the horses?"

Lick glared up at him.

"Yer already halfway out," the old man finished.

When Lick returned from putting up the horses, he had himself under control.

"She's in my bed," said the old man. " She's in pretty tough shape, I figger. Kinda zombie-like. Sure didn't fight much and once she lay there for a minute, she went plumb to sleep. Hasn't moved or made a sound."

Lick tiptoed down the narrow hall and peered in the door. The old man's room was orderly and picked up, as usual. The covers were up to the woman's chin, only her face visible on the pillow. She still had the dried blood on her face and in her hair. She was asleep but she didn't look peaceful. Her sweater and jeans were neatly draped over the old kitchen chair beside the bed. Boots and socks stood below.

Lick walked into the bathroom, washed his face, and came back to the kitchen.

"Coffee?" offered the old man. He'd already poured a cup and Lick could smell whiskey fumes coming off it. A special gesture from the old man, since they rarely drank liquor in camp, although they did keep a bottle of Jim Beam on hand for guests.

Lick sat down at the table and took a sip. "So what happened?"

"After she cold-cocked you, she sorta fainted-like. I got her up. She was shiverin', so I borryed yer jacket and helped her up on yer horse. I had to change the stirrups. I was gonna borry yer hat, too, but I didn't know how you'd take it, so I just borryed yer scarf and made her a bonnet. Oh, and we borryed yer gloves.

"We had to come outta the canyon pretty slow. I was leadin' her horse and she was hangin' on to the horn. Out on the flat she jis' leaned into the wind in a trance. When we got back I had to prise her hands offen the horn. She slid outta the saddle and I carried her in the camp here and put her to bed.

"She ain't said a word," he concluded.

"How bad you reckon she's hurt?" asked Lick.

"I didn't try to do no doctorin', but she's beat up pretty bad."

"Yeah," said Lick with a sideways glance, " I guess you got a pretty good look."

"Kid, there's not much in this ol' world I ain't seen. I drove an ambulance in the war for a time. Hurt bodies all look the same."

"So whatta we do now?" asked Lick, chastened somewhat.

"Wait. Maybe she'll have somethin' to say about it." Al shambled over to the sprung couch and lay down.

3
November 29: T.A. Wakes Up

The next morning they drew straws to determine who stayed in camp. Lick won and stayed behind. The old man rode out at 8:00 a.m. toward Slippery Canyon. Every thirty minutes, Lick checked on the woman still sleeping in the old man's bed. She rolled or shifted a couple times but never mussed the covers.

Lick was on his fourth cup of coffee and fixin' to heat up some SpaghettiOs when he heard a loud thump. He trotted to the bedroom.

She lay crumpled facedown on the floor beside the bed, the cover pulled partway off the bed over her head and still clenched in her right fist. She had on a black sleeveless tank top and white bikini underpants. On her left shoulder blade was a dark brown four-cornered spot about the size of a playing card. Lick leaned forward for a closer look. It was a familiar shape, but just what it was he couldn't quite recall.

She stirred and Lick stepped back.

"You awake, m'am?" he asked, and knelt at her feet. "We found ya down in the canyon and brought you here. Me and Al." He stopped, thinking he was babbling.

Slowly she began to pull the cover off her head, revealing a startling bluish-white eye, its black pupil a pinhole at its center. The left side of her face was swollen and scraped. She blinked, adjusting to the light, then shrugged the cover down around her shoulders. She looked toward the sound of Lick's voice.

"Me and Al brought you here. You were in shock, jis' wanderin' around like you were lost or somethin'."

The woman shifted position until she could see Lick with both eyes. There might have been fear in them, interest maybe, but not curiosity. Without dropping her gaze, she struggled onto one elbow.

"Yeah," continued Lick, "you were jis' wan- derin' around. We brought you here to camp. You've been sleepin' quite a while. You looked purty beat up, but we didn't try no doctorin', jis' let you sleep."

She stared at him.

"So," added Lick. "Here you are."

She studied him for another moment, con- centrating. "Who are you?" she croaked, rasping out the words.

"Lick."

"What kind of name is Lick?"

"Don't know exactly. Jis' what they call me."

She lay back down, exhausted. Within sec- onds, he could hear her steady, sonorous breath- ing. He eased up to see her face. She was fast asleep. Lick, still on one knee, picked her up and laid her back on the bed. **Not light, not heavy,** he noted. He unwound the covers with no protest from her, tucked her in, and returned to the kitchen table.

After SpaghettiOs and a chapter of Elmer Kelton's latest book, he went down the hall to check on her. He found her sitting on the edge of the bed, the covers rumpled behind her. She was staring at the curtainless window.

Lick watched her a few seconds till she real- ized he was there. She jerked slightly and reached back to pull the cover over herself. She gave him a suspicious sideways look.

"Sorry, ma'am. Didn't mean to spook ya. Can I get you somethin'? You hungry? Somethin' to drink? Strikes me you might be needin' a shower. Oh . . . I don't mean ya need a shower, that you, uh . . . just that yer hair and all . . ." He shut himself up.

She tuned him out, trying to make some sense of her condition. The side of her head was sore to the touch. She had a splitting headache. Her neck and shoulders were tender and painful. Her hands were cut and scraped. That much she knew already. She hadn't tried to stand yet.

"I could run a shower," he tried again. "I mean, we turn the water heater down every morning to save propane so I could turn it up and you could take a shower in half an hour if I turned it on now. I would've turned it on already 'cept I didn't know when you were gonna wake up so . . ." He studied her. She had a blank look on her face. "I'll just go do it now," he said, and turned back into the hall.

He returned a few minutes later. "Done. It'll be hot in about thirty minutes. Would you like some coffee?"

"No," she rasped, then paused for a ten count. "A glass of water."

"Great!" Lick said. He disappeared and was back momentarily with an old plastic glass nearly full. As she reached out to take it, the cover slipped off her shoulder.

"Whoa," he said, looking at her arm. "That's a pretty mean bruise. Listen," he went on, concern in his voice, "I'll holler when the water's hot. Then you can clean up and we'll git you somethin' to eat. It'll be a few minutes. You want another glass of water?"

She shook her head no. He left.

In a short while she heard water running. Then he reappeared in the doorway.

"It's hot now," he reported.

"You haven't got a robe or a towel, do you?" she asked.

"A robe?" His mind flashed back to Charlton Heston in a toga. "A towel, sure. Let me check."

He and the old man had two towels each. Bachelor towels. Hand-me-downs at least five years old. Thick as a co-op receipt and fluffy as a canvas tarp. They were closer to dishrags than bath towels. Neither man had ever bought a towel in his life. It would be as alien a thought to them as the gas mileage of a Lincoln Town Car would be to a Zulu tribesman.

Lick located the cleanest dirty towel and presented it like an offering to Cleopatra. She draped it over her shoulders. It barely covered her rib cage. She stood slowly, dropping the covers, and swayed precariously. Lick started to assist her but she caught her balance and he stepped back quickly.

"This way," he said. She followed him shakily to the bathroom and he quietly shut the door behind her.

He sat back down at the kitchen table, gripping the edge, and tried to stop his rapid breathing. Something inside told him that she was badly hurt and in need of compassion and comfort. Or at least somewhere in the back of his brain those thoughts occurred, but they lasted no longer than the glide of a shooting star. His last look into the bathroom as he closed the door had drilled a stealth shot into his chest. The escaping steam from the bathroom had smothered him like a bear hug from King Kong.

He squeezed his eyes tight. The lingering impression of long legs, silky smoothness, curvaceous circumscription, the grazing, galloping, sliding, sidling, fragile, fragrant flower of feminosity had floated within flaunting distance, and there, in that single-wide trailer hallway, momentarily disturbed the mutual molecules in the universe they shared.

A feeling as innocent as a snowflake and as complicated.

It reminded Lick of the time a no-good sorry feedlot horse named Scrap Iron had kicked him between the lungs.

Teddie Arizona was in the bathroom for an hour. Lick could hear the water being turned on occasionally. Adding more hot, he supposed. Finally he heard the tub draining and sounds at the little sink. He heard the bathroom door open and the bedroom door close.

After a few minutes, she walked tentatively into the kitchen, wincing with each step. She'd put her sweater and jeans back on and was barefoot.

"Ma'am, you . . . would you like somethin' to eat?" Lick stammered. "We've got SpaghettiOs, pork and beans, canned stew, peas, rice, canned pudding, some Snickers. There's some steaks but they're frozen, wait . . . and some . . . some, uh, I guess that's about it."

"You have any bread and peanut butter?" she asked.

"We do. We do have that!" He opened the refrigerator and took out both. "You want me to make you a sandwich?"

"I can do it."

He set the makin's on the table, fished a knife out of the sink, and put a giant economy-size jar of generic Concord grape jelly on the table.

She made her sandwich clumsily, ignoring the jelly.

"So, what's yer name?" he asked as she gnawed her way through the refrigerator-hard bread and stiff peanut butter.

"Teddie," she replied, and tried to swallow.

"More water . . . or somethin' else?" he offered.

"A gin and tonic," she answered.

He glanced at her in surprise, then slowly looked into her eyes.

Holding his gaze, she lifted her palms and gave an imperceptible shrug. "Just thought I'd ask," she said, with the tiniest sparkle.

For the first time, Lick relaxed a little. His relationship with women had always been frivolous and had soured after his last semiserious intimacy. This past year he'd been almost celibate and, though not content, was resigned. This woman, Teddie, had made him most uncomfortable. But now she had just cut him some slack.

"Sorry, water, coffee, or Milnot . . . canned milk," he explained after her inquisitive look. "We do have a little Jim Beam for medicinal purposes."

He got her another glass of water, served in a plastic cup that read, faintly, STOCKMEN'S HOTEL & CASINO. She finished eating and sat silently at the Formica table.

"Teddie what?" asked Lick finally.

"Teddie Arizona."

"Arizona? You sound like you're from Oklahoma, to me."

She stared at him a second. He knew he'd guessed right.

"Where am I?" she asked, changing the subject.

"On a cow camp in the wilds of southern Idaho."

"Y'all have a phone?"

"No, ma'am."

"I remember an old man."

"That would be Al."

"Where's he?"

"He's checkin' cows in that canyon where we found you. Me and him been here last few months with four hundred cows."

"Y'all are cowboys?"

"Yup."

"Well, cowboy, any chance you could get me to an airport or at least to a phone?"

"Nearest phone is fifteen miles—hour and a half of bad road from here. Nearest airport would be Elko or Boise. Four- or five-hour drive if we had a car, but Al's ain't runnin'. Lewis will be here on Wednesday with supplies. He could haul you out."

"Who's Lewis?"

"Lewis Ola. Ranch foreman. Actually, I think he's the regional supervisor over all the ranches this company owns in this part of the country. He checks on us every week. Brings the groceries. Are you in a hurry?"

"There's gonna be people looking for me."

"They're not gonna find you here. I guess one of us could ride outta here ahorseback and call your folks."

"No," she said firmly. "There's no one to call. These people lookin' for me . . . I'd just as soon they didn't find me."

4

November 29: They Get Acquainted

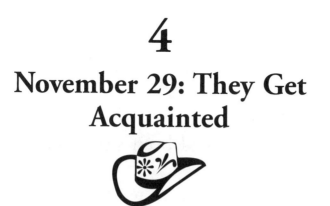

Teddie Arizona was still resting in Al's bedroom when the old man got back to the trailer late that afternoon.

"How's our little gal?" he asked Lick after peeling off his jean jacket, vest, two shirts, and the classified section from the **Elko Free Press**.

"Up and ate. She's restin' now. Her name's Teddie Arizona."

"Lemme tellya, kid, I found a wrecked plane half mile up the canyon from where we found her. Wing broke off and belly up. It slid into a draw beneath the lip of that big red rock, you know the one I mean. Hard to see."

"You reckon she was in the wreck?" asked Lick.

"I reckon we oughta ask'er anyways," answered the old man.

Neither Lick nor the old man was a gourmet cook. Lick was frying potatoes and planned on canned peas and bacon for supper. It was his week to cook. He was peeling the bacon when Teddie Arizona reappeared, rumpled, in the same dirty jeans and shapeless sweater. This time she was wearing her socks.

"Yer up," said Lick.

The old man had been sitting in the living room on the three-legged couch. When he heard voices, he came into the kitchen. "Say, little girl, how's yer head?" he asked.

"Pretty sore," she answered. "And you can call me Teddie Arizona." Lick mentally kicked himself for not inquiring about her health.

"Mine's Al Bean. Ya better let ol' Doc Bean have a look. Set down here in the light." The old man led Teddie into the living room and laid her on the couch with her head propped up on the arm. He raised the wick in the propane light on the wall above her head.

She had a laceration two inches long and nearly bone deep. It gapped in the center the width of a tenpenny nail.

"Whooey! This sure needs some stitches. It

was in '78 when a mountain lion took me outta the saddle. Sittin' in a tree, he was. Down in Arizona. I rode under him." Suddenly the old man stood, did a spin, and fell to the floor, thrashing.

Lick came running from the kitchen to find the old man grappling with a mountain lion on the rug. With a resounding thump, the old man dispatched the imaginary lion, then staggered to his feet.

"Yessir! Nearly tore off my nose. I had to sorta hold it straight with electrical tape but it grew back . . . just a little crooked but not so's you'd ever notice."

Lick had always wondered why the old man's face looked like Mount Rushmore after an earthquake. "Al, we got a first-aid kit," he said. "Lemme see if I can find it."

Lick returned to hear the old man discussing the options with his patient. "We just sprinkle some pinkeye powder in the wound and throw in a couple of sutures. But we're gonna have to shave yer head." Teddie Arizona was now sitting upright, pressed tightly against the couch as the old man leaned over her.

"Sit down, Al, lemme have a look." After the examination Lick said, "It is deep and does need to be closed. It's pretty nasty. I think I can clean it up with some alcohol and try to close it with these butterfly bandages. Might work. Short of goin' to a doctor. That's what I think. But we will need to clip part of your hair and shave the scalp to make the Band-Aid stick."

"Is it bleeding?" Teddie asked matter-of-factly.

"No," said Lick.

"All right then, clean it up. Put on some medicine, but skip the sewing and the Band-Aids. We're not cutting my hair."

There was a tube of triple-antibiotic ointment in the first-aid kit. Lick applied it liberally and pronounced her treated. "But," he added, "if you'd let me, I'd give you a shot of penicillin for infection. Got some for the horses and cattle."

She considered the suggestion a moment and replied, "Let's see if it gets infected. If it does we'll do the shot."

The old man got them coffee all around. At Teddie's request, he put a little Jim Beam in hers and, so she wouldn't have to drink alone, laced his own.

Lick pressed several questions on her: Where was she from? How did she get here? Should they try and get word to her folks? But she was evasive and very quickly learned to switch the conversation to the old man, who would ramble incessantly:

Lɪᴄᴋ: "Where are you from?"

T.A.: "Born in Oklahoma, but you guessed that. Al, have you ever been in Oklahoma?"

AL: "Yup, Fort Sill. That was in the summer of '42. Hot! You talk about hot. Had to be a jillion degrees doin' basic training, marchin' around like a bunch of puppets, but the humidity . . ." And he would carry on in this vein until Lick interrupted.

At eight-thirty, Teddie asked for five aspirins and excused herself. When Lick heard the bedroom door close, he addressed the old man. "So, whattaya think? Did you notice she never answered a single question?"

"Why, kid, we had a pretty good conversation. I guess she kinda warmed to me, bein' from Oklahoma and all."

"Tomorra I'll ride down Slippery and check out the plane," said Lick.

"You do what you want, kid. I'm goin' to bed." With that the old man fell back on the couch. "Oh, lend me one of yer blankets. The damsel in distress has mine."

Lick lay on the hard mattress in his six-by-eight room. He was thankful this night that the old man had seniority rights to the bigger room with the double bed. If it had been Lick's double bed, he might be sharin' it tonight with a man who slept like a two-year-old with the chicken pox.

Lick conjured up possibilities for Teddie's secrecy. He concluded that the most likely possibility was that she was smuggling drugs. Tomorrow he'd check out the plane. He dozed fitfully, engaging in gunfights with drug lords, women in space suits, and mountain lions. Too often his unconscious would flash back to a vision of Teddie standing in their little bathroom, steam rising around her as she leaned forward to test the water in the tub. Each time, his chest would tighten.

Dawn was a long time coming.

5

November 30: F. Rank Discovers T.A. Is Missing

"Whattaya mean, she's gone!" sputtered F. Rank Pantaker, irritated husband, and co-owner of Pharaoh's Hotel & Casino in Las Vegas, Nevada. He sat in his office suite, a complex complete with hot tub, exercise bicycle, and view of the strip from the top floor of the casino. Another man—tough, built like a goalie—stood nearby in the corner next to the wet bar. The woman took a small step backwards as F. Rank, six foot two, an ex-college football jock beginning to show signs of middle-age spread, stood and leaned over the desk toward her.

"Señor, lo siento, pero la señora, she tole me she was going shopping. An' she asked if I could pack her suitcase. It sounded funny to me, to take her suitcase shopping, but that was what she said, so . . . I deed it. An' dat was Jueves, in Turzday mornin'," answered Juana Sola Doce, personal maid of Mrs. Pantaker.

"That was the day after I left for Houston. She's been gone for—What time did she go?"

"It was at the noonday, **en la mediodía, en Jueves, como te dije, señor."**

"She told me she was gonna go flyin', get some hours in while I was gone, but she never said nuthin' about an overnighter," said F. Rank. "Okay, Juana, that's all, unless you can remember some clue she might have left as to where she went."

"Bueno, señor. I can't remember nuthin' but I will tole you." Juana excused herself and left the suite. F. Rank turned toward the man in the corner.

"Call the airport, somebody. See if she's . . . I don't know. If she left Thursday, that was three days ago," F. Rank mused aloud. "You'd think she'd keep me better informed. Not too much too ask, is it? I think I've treated that ol' gal purty dang well. Don't you think, Pike?"

"You bet, boss. Better'n you treat me." Although he was listed as an "Associate" on his W-2 form, Mothburn Pike was more accurately F. Rank's bodyguard. Nobody called him Moth.

"Well, you're not her."

"Whatever you say, boss."

"I mean, Teddie was a ski bum. Didn't have a pot to plant flowers in. Waitin' tables on stuck-up tourists. Livin' in a dump with drug dealers. I gave her a ring, a suite, a credit card, all my love . . ." Here F. Rank paused and considered. "Well, maybe not all . . ."

"Not all, boss," Pike agreed.

"Hell, I made her Missus Pantaker! Put her on my personal insurance. 'Course, maybe I'm readin' too much into this. Maybe she was kidnapped."

"With her bags packed, boss?"

"Yeah, maybe not kidnapped. But abducted while she was shopping. Have we gotten any calls asking for a ransom?"

"Not a one, boss."

F. Rank had returned in the early a.m. hours in a company plane from a three-day meeting with his father, S. Pry Pantaker, president of Pantaker Oil & Cattle Co.

F. Rank was his father's representative on location at Pharaoh's, where Pantaker O & C held 33 percent of the ownership. He was thirty-three years old, the third and youngest Pantaker son. A spoiled son, doted on by his mother, Pamela Lou Pantaker, and his father's sentimental favorite.

S. Pry had actually taken him fishing—once. When he was seven years old. It was a seminal moment in their relationship. F. Rank had caught a two-pound bass on a worm and reeled him in almost unaided. S. Pry was already talking about having the fish mounted when F. Rank removed the hook and tossed him back in the water.

S. Pry started in on a vehement lecture about starving children in China, waste-not-want-not, always watching your backside, hostile take-overs, how to use capital gains to avoid paying taxes, and hardball in general.

F. Rank withstood the barrage and calmly said, "I caught him, he was mine. So I let him go."

S. Pry spoke not.

"Besides," continued F. Rank, "he was dead anyway."

F. Rank grew up getting his own way.

"I can't believe she hasn't called," he said now. "I'll tell you this, Pike, I'll tell her where

the bear pooped in the buckwheat. She's not getting away with it, just disappearin' like that. All
I've done, I deserve some respect. Nobody pulls
that kinda stuff on me." F. Rank paused in mid-
rant. "Then again, maybe she's had engine problems and gone down somewhere between here
and . . . Hell, which direction did she go?

"Pike," he said, "Get Valter up here
right away. No, wait, call Allura. First I need a
back rub."

6

November 30: Lick Finds
Airplane Wreckage in Canyon

Lick was on the trail at daylight headed east
toward Slippery Canyon. It took an hour to
reach the spot where they'd found Teddie and
another forty-five minutes to find the red-rock
bluff that hid the wrecked airplane. The sun was
just reaching the bottom of the canyon when
Lick rode up to the crash site, the rays glinting
off something metallic.

The plane was a single-engine prop job with

the wings below the cockpit, although in its present position, upside down, they were above it. It appeared to be a six-seater. Lick hobbled his horse and approached the wreckage. The windscreen was broken and the frame bent out of shape. There were scorch marks and the greasy soot of a flash fire. The right-hand, up-canyon door was sprung open. Lick ventured inside.

Several magazines were scattered in the backseats along with assorted pop cans and candy wrappers. Lick found a backpack in the front of the cockpit. Maps and a logbook were strewn about. Around the back of the plane he found the baggage door and opened it. There were two matching suitcases, one big, one small. He extracted them.

Lick managed to tie the suitcases on either side of his horse and walked clear back up the canyon rim, carrying the backpack himself. On top of the ridge, he mounted his horse and carried the big suitcase in front of him on the pommel. It was nearly four in the afternoon when he hit camp. The old man's dogs welcomed him in. He unsaddled, then carried the bags to the trailer.

"By gosh," the old man said. "Where ya been, kid? Me and T.A.—that's what she calls herself—been talkin' over old times. She's takin' a break right now, restin'." Al took the backpack from Lick's arms. "Whatcha got there?" He opened it and peered in. "Buncha maps and books and stuff."

They heard the bedroom door open. The old man closed the backpack.

"'Scuze me a minute," Lick said to the old man, and walked directly to the bathroom to wash up. When he returned, the suitcases and backpack had disappeared into T.A.'s temporary quarters.

"I guess those were her suitcases," said Lick, commenting on the obvious.

"She grabbed 'em like they had her insulin!" answered the old man. "I'd say they was hers."

"Makes sense, if she was in the plane when it went down. All sorta adds up. Except why she doesn't want nobody to find her," said Lick.

"Maybe she's a Rooshun spy . . . ," mused the old man, his face taking on an espionogical glint.

"Or a smuggler," suggested Lick.

"Or a suitcase salesman." The old man brightened.

"None of the above," she answered from the living room entrance.

The old man and Lick looked at T.A. She'd changed into a fashionable, midnight blue long-sleeved knit shirt and clean jeans. Her dark blonde hair, shot through with light streaks and cut in a spiky shag, was still wet and hanging tight to her head. Her left eye was still a bit bloodshot, her left temple and cheek were bluish and swollen, but she'd put on little turquoise earrings. She wasn't the same woman Lick had run a shower for Saturday morning. He was developing a picture of her as more than just the "Venus in the Bathroom" image. It was her, all right, but a more solid version.

Teddie Arizona Mack was twenty-eight years old and stood five foot six. Lick took in her athletic, outdoorsy figure with its broad shoulders and an ample rear end that would have looked good ahorseback on the horse in front of you goin' down the trail.

She had brown eyebrows, a strong chin, clear skin that took a tan, no freckles, expressive hands, wide feet, and surgical scars on both knees from skiing injuries—these, of course, Lick couldn't see at the time. She also had, on her left shoulder blade, a birthmark the color of a coffee stain, which he had seen. Through her bruises and contusions he could see a large, pretty mouth with full lips that parted to expose her upper incisors and a slight overbite.

But it was her eyes that drew Lick's attention. When she smiled, they became less conspicuous, the color of old jeans, but when she looked at him directly and furrowed her brow, it was unsettling. The irises were so light they appeared silver, the color of a full moon. Each iris was edged with a dark ring.

The combination of those Siberian husky eyes, tan skin, and blonde hair gave her the coloration of a piebald palomino horse, Lick thought. The other thing, he noted to himself, was that she didn't look helpless.

"By golly, ya clean up good, little lady," observed the old man cheerily.

The pilot light in Lick's heart flared briefly. Nothing like the ventricle stopper of yesterday, but the interest was still there. The furnace didn't kick on, but it was put on notice.

Yup, he thought, **ya clean up real nice.**

7

December 1: F. Rank, Valter, and Pike Plan Search for T.A.

Paul Valter, head of security for Pharaoh's Casino, sat on a big white couch in F. Rank Pantaker's office suite. He held a thin manila folder. F. Rank sat opposite him on a matching couch, his handmade Lucchese boots resting on a glass-topped coffee table big enough to play hockey on.

Valter was a medium-size man, forty-six years old. He was wearing a custom-made suit, Gucci shoes, and a power tie. His light hair was thinning but he cut it short anyway. His head resembled a satellite view of a dirt path in the middle of a dead lawn. He was clean-shaven and had piercing blue eyes. Ex-military, obviously.

"So, where is she, Paul?" F. Rank asked, leaning back against the couch and running a hand through his dark, long hair.

As soon as Valter had received word from Pike that Teddie Arizona Pantaker had left town and not returned, he began a quick investigation. He questioned her personal driver and the manager and head pilot of Pharaoh's personal fleet. He'd had to wait until this Monday morning to track down the airplane mechanic and the tower. It was noon when he'd arrived at F. Rank's penthouse office suite to make his report.

"According to the airport manager, Mrs. Pantaker departed North Las Vegas Airport in a private plane, an NC 1077 Cessna Cherokee."

"Is that one of ours?" asked F. Rank.

"Yes," answered Valter. "It's the one she's been using to get hours on her Instrument Flight

Rating. Anyway, she left on Thursday afternoon at one-thirty. A flight plan was filed to Las Cruces, New Mexico. However, no plane of that description closed the flight plan in Las Cruces. We are also checking with Phoenix, El Paso, Albuquerque, DFW, Love Field, Oklahoma City, DIA, Salt Lake City, Reno, Los Angeles, and San Francisco. The range of that aircraft is seven hundred fifty nautical miles. We've checked intermediate airports and asked about refueling.

"Nothing so far. I've left my number in case they find anything. We also did a quick check to determine reported air crashes or Maydays. Nothing. Weather to the south was clear all the way to Texas the day she departed. To the north, northern Nevada, Idaho, Utah, and Wyoming have been overcast, with storms and turbulence, especially over the mountains. There was a big storm in northern Nevada and southern Idaho Thursday evening."

"Well," said F. Rank, "we have no reason to believe she went north. She's a good pilot. I know she made a couple trips last summer to Grand Canyon and Hoover Dam, sightseeing. One, at night, to Elko, I remember, workin' on her IFR." Turning to Pike, who'd been standing over near the window, he asked, "Didn't she take one of her bimbo friends with her sometimes?"

"Seems like one of the dealers went with her.

Lucy or Louise or somethin' like that. It was Thanksgiving, though. I remember that, boss. 'Cause she told you she'd had turkey enchiladas."

F. Rank gathered his thoughts. He had an odd and annoying way, at least to Pike, of looking skyward and raising his upper lip when in thought. It made him look like a bull who'd just sniffed a cycling heifer. Pike had grown up on a ranch in northern Nevada and was qualified to make that observation.

Regarding F. Rank, it would be fair to say that he was concerned about T.A., but not quite as much as he was leading others to believe. This was demonstrated by the fact that he hadn't yet called the police.

"Valter," F. Rank said now, "maybe you and Pike can find this Lucy, Lucinda, or whoever that dealer was. She might have a clue which way T.A. headed."

Valter and Pike waited expectantly while F. Rank did a little mental arithmetic. She'd been gone, let's see, Thursday, Friday, Saturday, Sunday, and today. Where was she? Had she crashed the plane somewhere? Was she doubting their relationship? Had she forgotten their deal? F. Rank pondered all these things in his heart.

His mind played back highlights of the last year and eight months. He couldn't conceive that she was out-and-out leaving him. Not with four months left on their agreement and his own promotion due in January to the position of Vice President in charge of Western Operations of Pantaker Oil & Cattle Co. Her timing didn't make sense.

F. Rank had met T.A. twenty months ago when he was on a skiing trip to Aspen, Colorado, with three of his college fraternity brothers, one of whom was the local prosecuting attorney. They were après-skiing and she had been their cocktail waitress. F. Rank wasn't quite handsome, not quite suave, but he was self-assured in a way that money allows one to be. He hit on her. She didn't do much to defend herself. Her shift ended at one in the morning. He waited, due in part to her tacit encouragement. He invited her to his $350-a-night hotel suite. She accepted. That night she lit him up like God's own weed burner!

F. Rank fell in LUV. Or, at least in FATCH-YOOASHUN! It might have been the snowy night, the chalet streetlights, his loneliness, her easy familiarity, the champagne, or . . . her short, streaked-blonde hair that bounced wildly when they did. Or her exquisitely soft skin that slid against him like a baby fur seal, her wide hips, prehensile toes, lusty aroma, femininity, unrestrained enthusiasm, or the startling moon-silver irises that pinned him to the mat the way a predatory wolf transfixes a starving caribou.

Being with her was like driving a Maserati for the first time, like seeing Halley's comet, or discovering that the chocolate really did go all the way to the bottom of the cone in a Drumstick. She'd illustrated a new chapter in F. Rank's Giant Book of Possibilities. And at the age of thirty-two, his book was already three-quarters full.

By 3:30 a.m. he was drained. He'd asked her to marry him. She'd declined. He gave her his card. She did not reciprocate.

He returned to the bar the next night and stayed till closing time. She was his waitress again. He wanted to take her back to his room. Shoot, he wanted to take her home, show her to his folks, start a family, have a scrapbook, throw himself in front of a moving train to convince her of his sincerity. Mostly, he just wanted to touch her one more time.

She declined. He wheedled and cajoled, he pleaded and cooed. She told him he was nice and that she'd had a good time last night, but she had other plans. He returned to his room with the intention of ending his life but instead watched the late movie on television and fell asleep.

F. Rank Pantaker, one disappointed Texas transplant, departed Aspen in his private jet the next morning and headed for Las Vegas with an unsatisfied yearning.

Two weeks later F. Rank received a phone

call at his office on the top floor of Pharaoh's Hotel & Casino in Vegas. It was from Loyal Nutz, his fraternity brother from the University of Texas, who was now the prosecuting attorney in Pitkin County, Colorado. The very same lawyer who had been hosting F. Rank the night he met Teddie Arizona.

"Remember the woman you met at the bar when you were here last month?" Loyal had asked.

"You know it, buddy," said F. Rank. "What I wouldn't give for another night like that!"

"She's in trouble," explained Loyal. "Seems her roommates are midlevel drug dealers here in the great Aspen underworld. We've had them staked out. I don't know how deeply she's involved, but I've procured a warrant for all three of them living in the house. We're planning to bust them this weekend.

"We've checked her as best we could. She's got a fairly decent reputation locally. Well liked, got a good job, but that doesn't mean she's innocent. We've not actually caught her dealing, but . . . circumstantial evidence, ya know. In the same house, easy access, and we know she smokes pot—"

"You think she's dealing?"

"Like I said, we don't know if she, herself, is a dealer, but her roommates are. Selling marijuana and cocaine, mostly, some speed—the usual recreational drugs."

"Is she an addict?" asked F. Rank, remembering her piercing eyes and snakelike writhing. The memory stirred him deeper down.

"I doubt it," answered Loyal. "Good job and all, but drugs are just part of the scene. She's definitely a party girl and it's likely she's getting it from her roomies. But even if she's not dealing but she knows her roommates are, that could make her an accomplice."

"Why are you telling me?" asked F. Rank.

"Well, if you really liked her as much as you said, and if she were to disappear before the warrant was served . . ." Loyal inserted a pregnant pause. "I suspect, since we have the goods on her roomies, we wouldn't be obliged to pursue her too far. She'd have to lay low. The warrant would still be good for five years. You could ride in like a white knight and, well, the warrant would give you a little leverage."

"How would I—?" began F. Rank.

"I could fax you a copy of the warrant, brother," said Loyal, "for old time's sake."

Upon receiving the fax, with her home phone conveniently included, F. Rank had called T.A. immediately and convinced her she was in danger. It took some convincing, since she figured his motives were suspect. She'd always been innately aware of her own seductiveness and its effect on mortal men. She allowed that his concern was flattering, of course. She never took affection for granted. But what he had interpreted as passion on her part that first night was merely a genuine exuberance. She was a natural-born lover.

But when F. Rank began detailing the tricky situation about to engulf her, she took him seriously. She hadn't thought about where Jeroba and Joanne, her roommates, procured the drugs that always seemed to be readily available. She herself didn't do drugs daily. But usually once a week she found herself smoking grass at someone's house, at a party, or in the kitchen having the occasional late-night hit with Jeroba and Joanne. She also drank liquor moderately, but she had stayed away from the stronger drugs. However, it wasn't impossible that her roomies were dealing, she admitted to herself. T.A. worked the late shift and they only crossed paths at home in the early afternoon. They led separate lives.

When F. Rank spelled out the particulars and told her he had a copy of the warrant for her arrest on suspicion of selling an illegal substance, it scared her.

"But I've never sold drugs," T.A. told him. "And how did you get a copy of the warrant in the first place? Who told you?"

"I've got friends in high places," he explained.

"And you're warning me," she said. "Why?"

"Because," he told her, "I want to marry you."

T.A. met F. Rank the next morning at the Aspen airport. They sat at a small table for two near the window in the airport coffee shop. He slid the fax across the table toward her. She scanned it quickly and asked, "What do you want out of this?"

"I told you. I want to marry you," he stated matter-of-factly.

She didn't say, "I'd rather go to jail, go down with the **Titanic,** move to Wendover, or have my fingernails pulled out one at a time," because that wasn't true. But she had no intention of marrying this man that she knew only in the biblical sense.

T.A. contemplated her chances of going to court and winning. There would be no one to testify that she had ever sold them drugs. Surely Jeroba and Joanne could defend her innocence. But would they? She decided to test out F. Rank's hand, "Frank—"

"F. Rank," he corrected.

"F. Rank, I appreciate what you're doing here. Warnin' me and all. But that's not reason enough for me to contemplate marriage. I hardly know you. You hardly know me. I might be better off just going to the police and—"

He interrupted, "They've had your house staked out for quite a while, as I understand. They've been building a case, and the arrest warrant and charges of selling narcotics aren't something they'd just do without cause."

"But I told you!" she protested. "I don't sell drugs! I don't really know if they do. We just live together."

"Well," said F. Rank, "something makes them think you're in on it."

"Who told you all this?" she asked, irritated. "Maybe someone's trying to set me up. I don't know why anyone would, but—"

"I can't tell you who gave me the information, I promised I wouldn't. But he thought I might be able to help you."

"This all sounds fishy to me," she said.

"Okay. Listen, I'll make you a deal."

"What do you mean, a deal?" she said curtly. "So if I don't marry you, you turn me in or something?"

"No, no!" F. Rank said, genuinely hurt. "Only a choice. You can make the choice. If you pick Door Number One, I get back on my plane and leave. Never see you again, or worry whether you're doing time in the women's prison, or waiting tables till you're fifty years old.

"You go to work tonight. Plan a normal weekend. Take a chance that what I'm telling you is wrong. But if I'm right and you wind up in the hoosegow, it'll be too late for me to help. Or, if you do believe me, you could just leave town, change your identity, and spend the next five years running from the law.

"Or," he said, with a grandiose sweep of the arm, "Door Number Two. You go home, right now, pack your bags, and get on the plane with me. You call any of your friends here next week or read the newspapers, or whatever it takes, and discover if your roommates are really and truly drug dealers and are in custody."

"What if I turned myself in?"

"Before you're arrested?"

"Yeah," she said.

"Do you want to spend the next year or two in the pokey, or on bail? Do you have a good lawyer, or will you be using the public defender? Do you want to spend the next two years being a suspect, or at least a material witness? Where you gonna live?

"And what if the prosecution thinks you're guilty, which they do, by the way"—F. Rank lied just a little, but he was making his point—"and they make a good circumstantial case and you're convicted?"

"But," she said, "even if I went with you, there'd still be a warrant out for my arrest."

"That's true," he agreed. "But as long as

you're with me, I guarantee that it will not be followed up on."

"How can that be! You can't do that, have that power over my life!" she protested.

"All I can tell you is, I can," he said, flat out.

The air hummed between them. Finally T.A. spoke. "It makes me sound like a slave."

"It's not that way at all," he explained, with sincerity in his voice. "You see, I do think—I know—that I love you already, but . . . it would also help solve a practical problem for me. I have . . . my family is . . . I've been told by my parents that I won't come into my position in the company, my proper inheritance, if you will, until I'm married, responsible, you know.

"Personally I blame it on my brother," grumped F. Rank. "He's older, stodgy, went to Harvard—big deal! He told them I'm immature! Not ready to be a manager, or whatever. Says I play the field, not stable, so they've still got me on this financial leash, if you know what I mean. So, I figger gettting married will show I'm ready.

"Listen." He leaned toward her. "I know this is sudden, maybe a little overwhelming for a small-town . . . I mean, a girl like . . . well, look, I do find you enormously attractive and, believe it or not, I think I really do love you, and that you could easily learn to love me—for the time being, it would work if you would just marry me . . . for the public perception."

"You mean," she said, "just be your wife so you can fool your parents?"

"Exactly," he said.

"What kind of people are they that you would do that to them?"

"They're good people," he answered almost indignantly. "They're just like me."

She let that personality self-profile sink in.

"But it wouldn't be so bad," he continued. "You'd move to Las Vegas, live in a penthouse on top of Pharaoh's Casino. You'd have money, room service, go to all the good shows, I'd take care of you. I'd be a good husband."

T.A. looked out the window at the Lear jet with PHARAOH'S HOTEL & CASINO painted professionally on the rudder. What did she have here in Aspen, anyway? Suppose she beat the drug rap. With no college degree or special skills, all she had in front of her was a lifetime of minimum-wage paychecks and a dwindling number of good parties as the wrinkles of time took their toll. Would she still be working for tips in ten years if she stayed?

Then the most revealing of questions slid into the back of her mind. The one she'd been avoiding since her mother died: Who'd care what she did?

The answer was what she'd expected. To put it painfully, there was no one she had to call.

The business side of her brain began to

calculate. T.A. looked back into F. Rank's eyes and gave him a good hard look. **A mail-order bride's dream,** she thought. **Maybe that's what I've become.**

"F. Rank," she began, "I would consider this if it were a business proposition, pardon the pun."

"What do you mean?" he asked suspiciously.

"I could consider marrying you for, say, two years. With a contract, in writing, five thousand dollars a month, my own bank account, flying lessons, and . . . a horse.

"Here's the deal: I pretend to be your wife. No one but you and I know that we aren't legally married. We just say we are. At the end of two years, we go through a fake but civilized divorce, for the sake of your folks. You pay me a bonus of . . . twenty-five thousand. I go my way, you go yours."

F. Rank hadn't expected this would be so easy—and so humiliating. He'd pictured himself as a white knight saving the damsel in distress. Maybe even love at first sight on her part, too. Alas, he was too smitten, too shameless to bargain. Maybe, he thought, as they grew to know each other, she'd fall in love with him, too, and they could be married officially. Of course, he brightened, that's how this would play out. In the meantime . . .

"And you'd play the part of my wife"—he paused, looking at her from the corner of his eye—"in all respects?"

She caught his drift. Then she nodded slowly and said, "In all respects."

Six weeks later, after a fourteen-day trip to Europe and the Mideast, they returned a "married" couple. The new Pantakers were feted by his parents at a large barbecue in their twenty-five-thousand-square-foot backyard in south Texas. Mrs. Pantaker, the mom, was disappointed that Sonny didn't let her throw a big wedding, but Mrs. Pantaker, the faux bride, was so charming that he was forgiven. F. Rank got a promotion, T.A. almost felt loved, Mom cried, and Dad was relieved. The newlyweds rode the company jet to Las Vegas to set up housekeeping at Pharaoh's, where they were supposed to live happily ever after.

T.A. had certainly lived up to her part of the bargain, in all respects, he admitted. But he eventually came to realize that she wasn't in love with him, in spite of their close quarters and intimacy. Their arrangement had lost some of its luster, but she was definitely great to have around. After almost two years, she was still a spectacular courtesan, though he never had the feeling that her whole heart was in it. Therefore, he felt he was in the right to have an occasional assignation on the side. He was discreet, well, fairly discreet, in order to maintain the public perception of a happy marriage. He expected to be made a full partner in Pantaker Oil & Cattle this Christmas. T.A.'s contract would expire in March.

He and T.A. had engaged in a little tiff in the days before he left for Houston. She'd become aware of his attentions to other women. It was just taking her a while to get used to his screwing around. Particularly with the spectacularly trashy massage therapist who had an office in the mall underneath the hotel. She hadn't actually caught him in flagrante with Allura Valura, the alleged therapist, but Allura wasn't very subtle and word had leaked out. Plus T.A. had smelled her on him.

She'd broached the subject indirectly, setting a trap as neatly as a tunnel spider spins her web. Just a hint, and F. Rank dove for it like a mall shopper torpedoing an empty parking space. He acted indignant and accused her of "acting like a wife." There ensued a couple days of stiffly formal communications and cessation of marital activities.

Now, some may think that T.A. might have been pleased or relieved that F. Rank was leaving her alone occasionally. Think of it as, "Take the day off, I'll drive the neighbor's

wife to work today." But people are funny critters.

Even forced relationships can create a mutual dependence and, therefore, a possessiveness that reveals itself in the green cloak of jealousy, e.g., kidnappers and their victims, drill sergeants and draftees, vegetarians and steamed broccoli, not to mention bull riders and bulls, dogs and pickups, or words and poets.

T.A. and F. Rank had grown to know each other beyond just the physical intimacy. He had actually fallen in love with her, but even that was not enough to overcome his own selfishness.

She, on the other hand, did not dislike him or even resent him in spite of her status as a kept woman. From being together constantly they had each become aware of the other's wants and needs, good points and shortcomings. And yes, she did enjoy his company sometimes. So his infidelity, straying from the intent of the agreement, so to speak, hurt her pride and she was salty enough to show it. He could have waited another four months.

She'd stopped short of accusing him and he'd stopped short of confessing, but his indiscretion was as obvious as a dead mule in a car trunk. She didn't berate him, but asked if she could take a couple days off and spend some time alone. He'd given her permission but made it clear that he expected her to fullfill her contract. He was even so crass as to mention the arrest warrant. She'd blushed. It had turned him on.

But now she hadn't come back. T.A.'s disappearance right now was a little worrying. F. Rank didn't want to rock the boat, he had other irons in the fire, as well. He watched Valter exit and called out, "Oh, and Pike, call Allura up here. All this thinkin' is giving me a headache."

"Right, boss."

8

December 1: Lick and Al Check Cows

By Monday at the camp, the weather had cleared. Lick and the old man rode hard all morning. They found the cows three miles downriver from Slippery Canyon brushed up in another little canyon that drained into the river. The cowboys hobbled their horses in a sheltered niche and ate their peanut-butter-sandwich lunch.

"So, whattya think, Al? 'Bout T.A., I mean."

"Not my type. Looks like the kind that counts her money and yers!"

"No, I mean her bein' so secretive, not wantin' to notify anybody about the wreck. What if somebody finds the plane?"

"Oh, they'll find it all right," said the old man. "There's plenty of traffic on the river in the summer. By then we'll be moved up to Yankee Bill Summit or over to Gold Creek and the little lady will be long gone."

"Lewis will be here on Wednesday," said Lick. "What's she gonna tell him? What are **we** gonna tell him? And if she's runnin' from the law, that makes us accessories."

"Kid, you worry too much," said the old man. He was laid back, soakin' up the sun like a lizard on a flat rock, his hat pulled down over his face. "Wednesday's a long ways off."

The old man drifted into slumber.

It was close to 6:00 p.m. when Lick and the old man hit camp. They unsaddled and fed the horses. Lick was mentally planning supper as they walked toward the trailer. Supper was on the old man's mind, too. "Sure be nice if we had a cook like the Basquos do," he said. "That Santiago can sure cook. An artiste with them sheep dishes. He can make mutton taste like prime rib. I've ate many a meal with them Basquos— in summer camp, anyways." They stomped through the door and were both hit with the mouthwatering aroma of fried meat.

"Well, strap on the feathers and take my pulse! This might be Heaven!" exclaimed the old man. "And yonder stands the angel in Gabriel's galley!"

T.A. turned at the stove and gave the old man a pained little smile. "I thought maybe I could cook y'all some supper. Hope it's okay."

"Okay?" answered the old man. "Okay? It's the kid's week to cook and he don't know how to make nuthin' but Hamburger Helper and that took him a month to learn. You ever eat macaroni that chipped your teeth? No sir, darlin', we don't mind one bit."

"I found these steaks in the freezer and thawed them out," she said.

"That's what they're for, little lady. That's what they're for," responded the old man. "We'll git washed up and be ready."

Lick was left standing in the middle of the room after the old man clanked into the bathroom and shut the door. T.A. slid the steaks around in the big frying pan with a wooden spoon. There was no spatula. She felt eyes boring into her and realized Lick was still there.

T.A. looked back at him over her left shoulder. He was unself-consciously posed. He looked like a movie star, or maybe what movie stars wished they looked like: big black cowboy hat, deep blue wool shirt, tan scarf, belt buckle, chinks, pointy high-top boots, blue steel spurs with silver rowels and a concho on each side of the spur strap.

Teddie Arizona didn't swoon, but a sudden weakness traveled the length of her body. The inside of her knees tingled.

Lick had been staring. Even as she turned toward him, his deep brown Latino eyes were unable to look away from her body. The long-sleeved shirt she wore was shapeless but the jeans fit oh-so-nice. His primal sense was pleased as she turned sideways, modeling for him, watching the left hip swivel in slow motion.

She waited a moment, expecting him to look up at her, maybe show some embarrassment at being caught. But he continued to drink her in. She realized he was in a trance.

"Lick," she said tentatively. It took him three or four seconds to raise his eyes. He seemed to be coming out of a coma. Finally he focused on her face.

"Lick?"

"What?"

"Are you . . ." She paused, trying to decide

what to ask. Okay? Under hypnosis? On drugs? Having gas pains? She finally said, "Hungry?"

"Well, if he ain't, I am!" announced the old man jovially as he clanked back into the kitchen drying his hands on a threadbare washcloth. Needless to say, the spell was broken.

9

December 2: F. Rank Discovers Money Missing

By Tuesday morning at ten-fifteen, F. Rank was strolling down the hallway of his private wing on the thirtieth floor of Pharaoh's Hotel & Casino, still wearing his flannel pajamas, monogrammed corduroy robe, and wool-lined slippers. Five days had elapsed since his wife had disappeared. He was beginning to worry about her safety, but he couldn't get rid of that gnawing feeling that she'd left him. Maybe not for good, but just enough to pay him back. He'd wait one more day. If he hadn't heard from her by then, he'd call the police.

The hallway outside his penthouse office was

adorned with paintings he'd chosen personally. F. Rank paused to look at his favorite, an enamel of Howard Cosell, "Dandy Don" Meredith, and Walt Garrison in the broadcast booth at the Astrodome. It had been a gift from his parents on his twelfth birthday. They had commissioned Marlin Oatly to paint it from a promo photo complete with autographs. The likenesses were very good despite the fact that Marlin made a living doing dog portraits.

F. Rank let himself into his office and locked the door behind him. Setting his coffee down on his desk, he sat, swiveled, and opened the false front of the bookshelf on the wall behind him, exposing a 2½ × 3 foot safe. He spun the combination, heard the comforting clicks, and swung the heavy door open.

He carefully lifted a large black box from the back of the safe and ran his hands over the smooth steel surface—a caress, almost. Then he spun the five-digit combination lock. The safe held his ticket to earning his family's respect. It contained five million dollars in cash. He'd placed the last down payment of five hundred thousand in the safe last Wednesday, before he'd left for Houston. In less than a month, he anticipated, the amount would double. His plan was in motion.

With a slight tingling sensation climbing up

his back, F. Rank opened the box gently, then rolled back the blue velvet cover. Inside he found only the complete works of Tom Clancy in hardcover. Heavy reading, approximately equal to the weight of fifty thousand hundred-dollar bills.

F. Rank F. Ainted.

10

December 2: Lick, Al, and T.A. Take the Afternoon Off

Meanwhile, back at the ranch, the old man and Lick spent all Tuesday morning checking the water holes and were back to the camp by noon.

Teddie Arizona had fixed a marinated steak with white rice and meat sauce. Canned vegetables and Bisquick biscuits rounded out the fare. The boys cleaned up, shaved, and got ready to eat like civilized persons for a change. Dinner conversation, though not at the level of the Yalta Conference, was stimulating.

"Do you guys ever take the day off?" Teddie

smiled at Al as she put a plate in front of him. She was looking better, though her bruises, now the color of vanilla pudding, would still stop passersby. She reached up to tuck a strand of hair behind her ear and winced as her fingers brushed her scalp wound, which was still tender to the touch.

"This is it," answered the old man, daintily wiping his mouth with the dishrag. "Half day Sunday."

"Today's not Sunday," said T.A., furrowing her brow.

"Well, we can make it Sunday just for you. Cows don't know the difference," said the old man.

"Well, thanks. I'm honored. It's pretty nice outside, considering," she said. "Maybe I'll take a walk. Is it too far to go see the Bruneau Canyon you told me about?"

Lick piped up, "Think you could stand bein' ahorseback? We could ride to the rim easier than walk. Be two miles one way. Can you ride?"

"Matter of fact, I can," she answered. "That'd be a great idea. Not much of a chance of running into anybody, is there?"

"None," replied Lick. "If they came by car, they'd have to follow that so-called road and it leads right here. If they were ahorseback, well, I've never seen anyone here but us. We're on kind of a peninsula. Like a giant thumb. There's deep canyons on the east and west sides that come to a point at the north end. They don't even need to fence it. It'd be a major ride to cross the river and come up the canyon side. Access to Pandora's Thumb is from the southwest end. But I've only been here since this fall, Al would know more. Ever see anyone up here, Al?"

"Not in the winter. Too far and too hard," the old man said. He was chewing methodically. He only had about half the normal complement of teeth, though those he had were good. He'd started brushing regularly twenty-five years ago and thought it helped.

"Good, then, we'll do it." She smiled.

"You kids go on," said the old man. "I allus take a nap on Sunday afternoon."

11

December 2: F. Rank Panics

F. Rank was F. Urious!

The coincidence of Teddie Arizona's disappearance and the missing five million dollars struck him like a kick in the stomach. Money and wife gone simultaneously. To his knowledge, no one who worked for him knew about that money. But T.A. knew.

He hadn't explained the details of his grand scheme to her but he couldn't hide his excitement as it all came together. It buoyed his spirits. She noticed and was pleased for him. He didn't try and hide the phone calls and conversations with Ponce de Crayon from her. It wasn't that he trusted her, so much as that he had taken her presence for granted. And she'd seen him put money in the safe on several occasions. But did she know the combination? He wasn't sure. He was sure of one thing, though. He wanted to talk to her, and right now.

Paul Valter, head of security, could feel the edge of the wet bar scraping his spine. "Mr. Unshakable," as he thought of himself, was getting his exhaust pipe reamed while Pike stood against the opposite wall blending in with the decor.

"Find her!" screamed F. Rank, inches from Valter's face. "That snipin' little snow bunny has robbed me! That ungrateful gold diggin', help-your-self hyena takin' money and splittin' like a thief in the dark of the dawn. That's why she's gone!

"You hear me, Paul! Gone, right under my nose! Actually"—F. Rank's voice turned menacing—"right under **your** nose!" F. Rank put his fat thumb against the tip of Valter's nose and pushed it like an elevator button. Valter made an ugly face.

F. Rank was shaking, spittle flecking his lips. "Get back to that airport and turn those slackers inside out. Somebody out there must know which direction she went, helped her gas the plane, fold her maps. Surely she didn't go alone."

"She was workin' on her IFR rating, boss," said Pike cautiously from the wall. "Could be she finished it. She's been flyin' solo for over a year. She took the Piper Cherokee. It's a twin-engine."

"Just track her down," said F. Rank. "And no Rescue Squad. It's important that we find her . . . by ourselves. I don't want anyone else knowing about this."

Valter started to speak and F. Rank cut him off. "Do what you have to, but I want an answer tonight! And Pike, you find out what happened to that dealer she hung out with. Now, go!"

F. Rank poured himself a quart of brandy and sank to the couch after he'd slammed the door on the two men. **That no-good, penny-pinchin', purple-eyed bingo bimbo.** Then he flashed on T.A. dressed in a fireman's helmet, body pinstriped red and white with yellow flames licking her chest and shoulders. "Come on baby, light my fire," she was saying.

I'll light your fire, you little pyromaniac,

when I catch you. You're one arsonist that's
flammable. Then he had a sudden sinking sensation in his chest. That five million was the
down payment on his dream. **I'll get it back,** he
told himself, **I've got to. Ponce will never
know it's gone.**

Ponce de Crayon was a self-made force.
Born in Wauchula, Florida, of a pliant Austrian-
immigrant trapeze artist and a smooth-talking
slick-back carnival charmer, he was christened
Heimlich Milhaus Tracker. The marriage had
started and stopped like an old car with conden-
sation in the fuel line.

Ponce, or Heimlich, as he was known then,
had taken up with the circus at fifteen and as-
sisted with the lion and tiger acts until he was
thirty-two. He was a natural and became a
skilled animal trainer. With an act involving
smoke and mirrors and wild beasts, he'd been
the highest-paid entertainer in Las Vegas for fifteen years, performing under the stage name
"Ponce de Crayon." He was a magician of majes-
tic breadth. He made elephants disappear, tigers
sing, and leopards hold lighted cigarettes between their teeth while he extinguished them
with a bullwhip.

At age forty-two, Ponce was tall and muscular, with a mane of black hair flashing one white
streak just off center from his widow's peak. His

right eye was a milky blue, the result of a tiger swipe, and his left was dark brown. He kept a trimmed goatee and moustache on his handsome face to obscure an asymmetrical smile pulled askew by more scar tissue. A cross between the Sheriff of Nottingham and a striking snake, he would have been utterly mesmerizing if it hadn't been for a single inconsistency: his accent.

Ponce's normal voice was sort of an Austrian drawl, a combination of his parents' clashing voice patterns. Although he was unable to speak any language but English, he could imitate many foreign tongues. When in the company of Australians, he found himself speaking Down Under. Russian, Scottish, Irish, Pakistani, French, Italian, Chinese, and German inflections would pop from his mouth unintentionally. Even rare regional accents imprinted on his brain.

Within one conversation, he might assume the intonation of a Mormon from Tremonton, a Cajun from Cypremort Point, or a Lutheran from Luverne. And to his everlasting misfortune, the accents imposed themselves on his daily conversations at their whim, often distracting the listener's attention. They became his Achilles' lip.

Nonetheless, he meant what he said, no mat-

ter how he said it, and F. Rank Pantaker was a
believer. And like F. Rank, Ponce had a greedy
streak in him, even though he was already filthy
rich. So when F. Rank had approached him with
a grand scheme, Ponce had pounced.

Ponce had used his vast wealth to pursue his
favorite hobby: exotic animals. His twenty-section
ranch, Ponce Park, an hour from downtown Las
Vegas, was home to an amazing assortment of
wild species. But his pride and joy was his private collection of endangered species, including
Sumatran rhinos, Indian tigers, Himalayan snow
leopards, California condor chicks, spotted owls,
pandas, koalas, bald eagles, Madagascar radiated
tortoises, musk deer, a Tasmanian tiger, wood bi-
son, mountain zebra, lowland gorilla, Mexican
grizzly bear, Mongolian antelope, Chinese sika
deer, ocelot, and orangutans.

Only a select few were aware of Ponce's trea-
sure. As soon as F. Rank learned of the exotic
collection, he thought, **Wouldn't that be a kick,
to shoot one of those endangered rhinos? Just
like bird-doggin' a covey of bald eagles, then
blastin' them outta the sky.** The more he
thought about it, the better it sounded. Imagine
inviting his friends to hunt endangered species,
or, even better, selling the hunting rights, like
Texas ranchers do in Texas for quail and whitetail. Offer an exclusive high-dollar catered hunt

only to those who could afford it. He dreamed about it for several days, came up with a guest list of amoral wealthy invitees, and got up the nerve to approach Ponce with his grand scheme. He was surprised and pleased to find Ponce receptive to the idea.

"You know, Vrank, I zometimes get an over-zupply," Ponce answered in the accent of his Austrian mother. "And, because of ze, shall I zay, 'informal' method of acquisition, I am unable to zell dem to ze public zooz, and ze like. It is not uncommon dat I vill have the occasional breast of spotted owl or condor egg omelet, but a hunt . . . yes, a hunt—"

F. Rank interrupted excitedly, "I'll betcha we could sell private hunts for a million dollars each! Five hundred thousand down to get your space reserved, maybe even make it a contest. Say the winner—the guy who bags the most—gets his million back. We could sell ten hunts at a time. They all come at once, no publicity, that goes without saying, and you and I split the remaining nine million. That would be . . . that would be, two into nine, no, two into eight goes, ah, I don't have my calculator, but it's almost five million each!"

"Vat, exactly, do you do for your half?" asked Ponce pointedly.

"Well," F. Rank said, somewhat hurt, "it was

my idea. And I know the kind of people who would be interested. I know the whales at the casinos. I know the ones that love to hunt and know how to keep their mouths shut. I'd invite them, take care of all the details, that would be my job. I get the guests. You fill their limit. I'll be handing you four or five million dollars on a silver spoon in your mouth," he finished, mixing metaphors.

Ponce's eyes narrowed. "And you vould never try and double-crozz your partner? Becauze, my young scoundrel, if you did, you should remember I can make more zan elephants disappear." Then he broke into song: "The hills are alive with the sound of gunfire"—a mutant version that set F. Rank's thoracic vertebrae rattling against one another. It was apparent that Ponce had a ragged edge.

But now it wasn't Ponce who'd been double-crossed. **Yes,** thought F. Rank, as he swirled the brandy in its giant crystal goblet and looked into the empty safe, **I'll find you, T.A., and you'll be sorry you messed with me.**

12

December 2: Lick and T.A. Take a Horseback Ride

An hour after they'd finished lunch, Lick and Teddie Arizona were mounted and headed northeasterly on a well-used trail. It had warmed up to fifty-five degrees and the wind was taking a break.

Lick had been pointing out the odd plant, a mountain range, or a cow track for T.A.'s edification. She didn't have much to say. He told her about Bruneau, a town at the head of the canyon, and Elko, the other direction.

"Where do you live? When you're not here, I mean," she asked.

"Nowhere, I guess. I just live here," he answered.

"Where do you go shopping?"

"We go into town for a few days once a month,"

"Which town?"

"Elko. South of here three or four hours. The Wednesday before we go, Lewis will charge the car battery, make sure we have a spare, and, most important, give us our checks."

"That old car doesn't even look like it runs. What if you get stranded?" she asked.

"Don't make any difference if we're late. Nobody's expecting us. Even the cows wouldn't miss us unless one of 'em got sick or upside down in a gully. You're only stranded if you're goin' someplace."

She pondered that observation, then asked, "How come you're a cowboy?"

"My dad's a cowboy. He's a pen rider in a feedlot in the panhandle. I did that summers in high school and college. Worked in the feedlots. Then I rodeoed, rode bulls mostly. I fell in with Al, met him in a bar, actually. I'd quit the rodeo by then, this was last year, and was kinda ramblin'. He told me they was lookin' for help on this outfit, so I says, what the heck. I hired on and here I am."

"Did you say you went to college?" she asked.
"Yup."

"Well, if you ask me, this job, I mean, living in a cow camp out here"—she swept her arm to imply the vast, empty landscape—"couldn't have been what you were thinking about when you graduated . . . was it?"

"There's a lot more to life than what you plan," he said. "Look at you."

She blushed. "Yes," she said, "I guess you're right."

Teddie Arizona didn't know if she could even lay claim to a life plan. She'd been born in Muskogee, Oklahoma, to Lyal Mack, a veterinary pharmaceutical salesman, and his wife, June, a budding community activist and real estate agent. They'd named her Teddie Arizona as the result of a strenuous birth, a bit of maternal postnatal amnesia, and a birthmark in the shape of Arizona on the left shoulder blade of a pretty, pale-eyed baby girl.

An only child, T.A., as they soon began referring to her, grew up wanting for very little. Dad bought her a horse when she was eleven years old and taught her to ride. She named the horse Superman. She participated in an all-girl equestrian drill team called the Muskogee County Rangerettes. The family didn't have a horse trailer but lived close enough to the practice arena that T.A. could go there ahorseback. For out-of-town performances, other Rangerette parents with horse trailers hauled the have-nots.

When T.A. turned fourteen, Lyal and June split the sheets. He took a job in Dodge City and remarried. The real estate market hit a slump and, although the child support payments continued on time, June was forced to tighten the purse strings. Superman had to go. To fill the void left by Superman and her father, T.A. discovered boys, beer, and pot her junior year in high school. At the same time, June fell in love with Hyram Himple, the husband of the middle school principal—a relationship that took up most of her time.

T.A. had an inner core of responsibility but a lack of moral direction. She was smart enough to keep out of "official trouble," but she was known to the local law enforcement as a party girl. She graduated with a B-minus average and a determination to have better than a B-minus life. She and a girlfriend moved to Sun Valley, Idaho, and became ski bunnies. Her girlfriend lasted there till Christmas, but T.A. loved it and stayed. She skied and waitressed in the winter and was a wrangler on a dude ranch in the summer. She soon graduated to men, tequila, and her faithful friend, marijuana. Not in excess, mind you, she rarely got out of hand, but she had a willingness to try most anything.

Two years later, she moved to the ski resort community of Vail, Colorado. She celebrated her twenty-first birthday on February 28 with her leg in a cast, surrounded by like-minded ski bums and bunnies.

That spring, her father died suddenly. T.A. borrowed money from her live-in boyfriend and

drove to Lyal's funeral. She didn't stay for the
wake. Her mother didn't attend. Two years later,
her mother was diagnosed with cancer. T.A.
moved back to Muskogee to care for her. June
lived another seven months. Any money left
from the sale of the house was absorbed by the
medical bills.

At age twenty-five, T.A. moved to Aspen,
Colorado, and became roommates with a couple
named Jeroba and Joanne. They were socially ac-
tive among the locals, the working class that
bussed the tables, parked the cars, ran the lifts,
and tended bar in the ritzy ski resort. Jeroba furnished her with joints when the party was on,
but with her job tending bar, T.A. was able to
pay her part of the rent and get by.

In February of that year she'd met a big, tall
Texan and a plan was hatched for her next two
years. Maybe it wasn't a life plan, but at the time
it looked like a start.

Alas, Robert Burns waited right around the
corner.

T.A.'s mind returned to the present, ahorseback on Pandora's Thumb. She and Lick rode on
in silence for a while. Eventually they reached
the rim of the canyon. A vast panorama spread
out at her horse's feet. Below her, a rugged
canyon wall sloped off to a winding river seven
hundred feet down. It was so unexpected it literally took her breath away.

Lick saw her reaction and smiled. "Not many people get to see this view," he said.

"Beautiful" was all she said.

Lick picked his way along a trail that started down the canyon. She followed. There was a noticeable stillness out of the breeze. In ten short minutes, they reached a small, level clearing with a steep wall behind them and the magnificent view beneath.

He hobbled their horses and they sat on a patch of dry grass.

"Oooh," she groaned. "I'm sorer than I thought." She stretched her legs out in front of her and lay flat on her back.

The sun was strong on this protected ledge. Lick sat with his arms wrapped around his knees, looking out over the canyon to the high desert country that faded away to the other side of the world. He felt toasty, inside and out.

"Lewis is coming tomorrow," he said without looking back at her. "He can take you out. Get you to a phone or at least to a town."

Teddie Arizona was quiet a moment. "He'll want to know how I got here. How come I'm so beat up."

"Yup, that he will. He's a man to do the right thing. Report the plane, get you to a hospital, all that."

"I can't do that," she said as much to herself as to Lick.

"Well, what do you figger on doin'? You got a plan?"

"Not yet. But I will. I'm just not . . . it's just that . . ." Her voice trailed off. In her mind she could see herself hiking out of here. She'd studied the topo maps at the camp and figured the route out to Highway 51 that led north to Mountain Home and Boise. She was a good outdoorsman. She could walk and shoot and ride. The hike to the highway and the hitchhike north held no fear for her.

She had brought ten thousand dollars in cash with her. It was safely stowed in her boots as she spoke, keeping her calves warm. The other four million nine hundred ninety thousand was in a storage rental in Las Vegas. She hadn't told anyone about taking the money and leaving. She wondered whether F. Rank knew it was missing. She'd charmed him the same way she'd charmed his family, his friends, and his business associates. She was charming. A charming, charming actress.

"Lick," she said, "would you mind rubbing my shoulders? Gently, please."

"Uh, sure," said Lick, a little surprised.

She got up stiffly and resettled herself in front of him, her shoulders pressing against his knees. It was warm enough to remove her heavy jacket, which she did.

Although Lick was as dysfunctional as any normal divorced, burned-out, girl-in-every-port, no-hope-no-plans-no-future emotional derelict, he was quite comfortable with the primitive physical aspects of the male-female relationship. He placed his hands on T.A.'s shoulders and began to rub gently. The heavy sweater padded her sufficiently to afford some protection. He did pull the collar down so he could get skin to skin on her neck.

She relaxed and he tried to think about baseball. Being pure of heart, he never suggested taking off her sweater or rubbing her calves—she was married, of course. But had she fed him just a little more line, he would have been on her like mud cat on stinkbait. Teddie Arizona knew these things and played him masterfully.

She hummed a feline purr. He slipped another microstep into her control. **I may need him,** she thought. **I'm not outta the woods yet.**

They had a nice ride back to the camp even though the wind had picked up.

"Invigorating," she said to Lick, with the first genuine smile of the trip.

13
Still December 2: Valter and Pike Report

F. Rank Pantaker felt a little more relaxed after Allura had given him a peach-juice rubdown. "Helps remove impurities from the system," she explained after pouring a can of peach halves in heavy syrup over his back and spreading it around with a rock especially selected from the head of the Arkansas River in Climax, Colorado. Allura surely applied herself, but trying to remove impurities from F. Rank was like trying to remove the H from H_2O. It would leave only hot air.

As F. Rank enjoyed his room service dinner of lamb chops and sweetbreads from the casino's famed Basque restaurant, he mulled over his situation. The missing five million dollars was the combined down payments of five hundred thousand each from the ten participants he'd signed up for the Million-Dollar Hunt Club.

The hunt had been so easy, such a good idea. He'd called them all personally. He'd sold them all on the ultimate thrill: the prospect of the rarest of rare trophies to display in their secluded, airtight, steel-walled galleries alongside their stolen Rembrandts, black market religious antiques, and compromising pictures of business competitors. If some of them didn't have those galleries yet, they at least had a trophy room full of gold records or basketball statuettes and the hankerin' for baubles only the rich could buy. It was a once-in-a-lifetime opportunity for those elite members of society who were able to make their own rules. Against the law? Whose? they might say. These were people used to making their own laws. They were only too eager to pay the high price that afforded them the ultimate protection from these laws. They knew that in his line of work, F. Rank had the contacts that could back it up.

The down payments were made in cash and hand-delivered in private planes. The international list of hunters included a celebrity trial lawyer from Chicago with homes and ex-wives in Maui, Malibu, Miami, and Aspen; a couple of Saudi sheik brothers; a mysterious Wall Street financier; an Iraqi general who did assassinations on the side; a Colombian drug dealer; a Thai drug dealer; a Texas oilman; a Southern California golden-boy NFL first-draft pick; and a lady rock star from the Big Apple.

Several people had declined F. Rank's rather vague feelers. His intuition guided him on how much to tell each one. It did not let him down. The last interested parties to finally decline were a pompadoured televangelist, a union-boss embezzler, and a wonder-boy computer wizard who had never fired a gun but imagined it couldn't be as much fun as video games. "After all," he explained, "when you've killed millions of virtual people, killing a real animal would be a letdown." So F. Rank quit at ten members, as he called them. Ponce had gotten excited and started planning the hunt right away. Each member was guaranteed a taxidermied trophy from the hunt on Ponce's own wildlife preserve—and a shot at the million-dollar refund. Ponce was guaranteed prestige in a very exclusive club.

Preparation had taken months. The only question now was, How was he going to get that money back?

Paul Valter and Mothburn Pike pounded on the suite door. F. Rank let them in and sat back down on the bed next to the leavings of his meal.

"So what did you find?" he asked.

"One of the maintenance men helped her load her bags and brought the plane up last Thursday at noon," said Valter. "Said she said something about flying to Houston with an overnight in Las Cruces. Said she did give him a nice tip, but that she usually did."

F. Rank grew impatient. "So, so? We know all that, where is she!"

Pike stepped forward. "I tracked down that dealer bimbo your wife used to hang out with. Ladonna. Turns out her mother lives in Mountain Home, Idaho. So I call there and, lo and behold, the daughter, Lamkin, Ladonna Lamkin, picks up. I asked if she'd visited with your wife lately. She said no. Had your wife planned to come see her? She said no. She asked if something was wrong. I said no. I think we were both lying.

"I checked the weather on the day that Mrs. Pantaker departed. Had she gone in the direction of Mountain Home, she'd have been caught in bad weather. However, Salt Lake and Boise Center are aware of no incomplete flight plans or pilot-in-distress signals. So I figure she either made it to Mountain Home or had trouble." Pike paused, waiting for a reaction.

F. Rank held a steak knife in his hand. He stared at Pike.

"He means," Valter put in cautiously, "it's possible the plane went down in the storm."

"Okay," said F. Rank, assuming a businesslike manner. "On the chance Ladonna is lying, call one of your security buddies in Boise and have him go to the residence immediately, reconnoiter, ask the neighbors, however you investigator people do it, and see if there's been any sign of T.A. In the meantime, meaning RIGHT NOW, draw a line between Las Vegas and Mountain Home, get a helicopter, and do a little search and rescue. I want you to go personally. Take Pike. With a pilot that's three. Surely you can find one little girl. It's"—F. Rank looked at his watch—"nine-thirty. If you leave now, you can make Mountain Home by morning. You might be able to do a little looking along the route. If she went down in the storm, there's a wild chance you might see the plane, but the odds are that she's in Mountain Home.

"I want her back unharmed, that is, of course, unless she was killed in a terrible plane crash, in which case, if you find THAT needle in the haystack, I want you to quarantine the wreckage. Regardless, when—and I said WHEN—you find her, get her isolated and call me. I want her unharmed, you understand? Or at least able to talk."

F. Rank stood up. Valter took a step back.

"Paul," F. Rank said, "this is life or death."

"Maybe she's not hurt," Pike ventured, touched by his boss's concern.

"Mine," said F. Rank coldly. "Not hers."

Outside in the hallway, Valter turned to Pike. "I've checked and if they were headed to Mountain Home, the only town on that flight path would have been Elko. We'll fly there first and do some asking. Busby should have the helicopter checked out by now. I called him before we went to Mr. Pantaker's office. He's got some gadgets that might be useful hunting for a downed plane. We'll leave at twenty-two hundred hours. Meet us at Pharaoh's private hangar."

Pike was disappointed when he didn't say, "Over and out!"

14

December 3: Valter, Pike, and Busby Meet Daniel Boon

Daylight was creeping west along I-80 and had just pushed back night's blanket on the tough little town of Elko, Nevada. The casinos were at their quietest. The registration-desk clerks were passing the missing microfilm and other valuable data from the thick-tongued night shift to the caffeinated morning crew.

Paul Valter and Mothburn Pike arrived by

helicopter just after the day's first scheduled commercial flight to Salt Lake City had departed. A short chat with the local airport munchkins revealed no knowledge of any plane answering to the description of Teddie Arizona's passing through Elko the week before.

Valter left Busby, the technofreak helicopter pilot, at the airport while he and Pike rented a car and drove the one mile to the Stockmen's Casino. "We'll ask around to see if anybody's heard anything about a plane or a wreck or the woman," Valter said. "Maybe some of the ranchers or miners have seen something. Gossip travels in these remote communities, ya know."

Pike, who'd grown up in these parts, knew.

They coffeed up at the Stockmen's, recoffeed at the Commercial, and then dropped into Capriola Saddlery.

"Nice place," said Valter, ingratiating himself with the lady behind the counter. He was a professional interrogater and knew how to schmooze.

"Something I can help you with?" she asked. Valter was wearing a down coat, lace-up L. L. Beans, and a baseball cap that read LAKERS. He did not look like a local.

"Yes," he replied with an engaging smile. "We're checking on a missing person. A woman, twenty-eight years old, medium height, medium build, sandy blonde hair, light blue eyes. She might have been in the area last week sometime. She's a private pilot. Her name is Teddie Pantaker."

"Pantaker?" the clerk responded. "Odd name."

"Not that odd," said Valter, a little defensive about his boss's moniker. "What's yours?" he asked.

"Kianne Two Foot," she answered.

"And you think Teddie Pantaker's odd!" he snorted. "Personally, I've never understood why so many folks name their children after towns in Wyoming: Cody, Douglas, Kaycee, Sheridan, Laramie, Jackson, Casper, Powell, Cheyenne, even Upton Sinclair! Nevada didn't do that. Do you know any kids named Pahrump, Jarbidge, or Gerlach? No, only towns in Wyoming. Drives me crazy!" Valter took a deep breath and looked at her a little sheepishly.

"Sorry," he said. "Sometimes I—"

Pike broke in. "He has a medical condition called Rand's McNally. It's like Tourette's syndrome, except he has the uncontrollable urge to inject geographical names into the conversation. It's brought on by stress."

"I see," the clerk said. "It's Kianne, like pepper."

Valter and Pike stared at her blankly. "My name," she said. "Kianne, not Cheyenne."

"Sorry," offered Valter. "You've got a fine name, Pepper. What say we start over. We're looking for a missing woman. We're worried about her."

"Are you the police?" she asked.

"Not exactly."

"Private detectives?"

"Yeah, sort of."

"Wow, cool," she said, impressed.

"So, have you seen a woman answering her description? She flew out of Las Vegas in a private plane Thursday night last week. We think she was headed for Mountain Home," Valter said.

"If she was flying through here the middle of last week, she came through a heckuva storm. Rain, sleet, a little wet snow. But the wind was fierce! We were out of power four and a half hours," Kianne said.

"How about north of here?" pressed Valter.

"I don't know, but Daniel Boon was just in here and he's from Mountain City. He could tell you 'bout up north."

"Daniel Boon?" asked Valter for clarification.

"He's prob'ly havin' coffee at the Stockmen's right now. He comes to town for a couple days, then heads back home. He said he was meeting somebody over there for coffee before he left."

"How will I recognize him?"

"If you're a private detective, it won't take you long."

"Thanks," said Valter as he and Pike headed out the door.

"By the way," she called, "what's your name?"

"Paul Valter."

"Shoot," she said with exaggerated disdain. "I jis' hate it when people name their pitiful kids after Olympic events."

Valter started to say something but Pike took him by the arm and swept him outside.

Exactly six minutes later, Valter and Pike stood by the cashier counter surveying the after-breakfast crowd at the Stockmen's Casino restaurant.

"That must be him," said Valter, nodding toward the only person in the restaurant wearing a coonskin cap, buckskin jacket, and powder horn.

"Very perceptive," confirmed Pike.

"Mr. Boon?" Valter asked the coon-tail.

Daniel Boon turned and, in a heavy Australian accent, said, "Righto, mate."

"We're looking for some missing persons and have been told that you might enlighten us as to the weather north of here last week."

Boon gave them a slit-eyed squint. "Maybe, maybe not. Yew buying?"

"Yeah, sure," said Valter.

"Folla me," Boon said, swooping up two paper napkins off the counter and pocketing them as he stood up.

"Not with the spoon, ya don't, Daniel," warned the waitress.

He returned the purloined instrument.

Ensconced in a booth in the corner of the gaming room, Daniel Boon asked, "What'll ya have, mates?"

"Coffee."

"Coffee."

Daniel spoke to the bartender: "Two coffees and a Tooheys."

"Mr. Boon," Pike began, "we're looking for a young woman."

"My gosh, at your age, you should be lookin' for a sheila who's a bit more seasoned, wouldn't ya think? More worldly, someone who's had her shots," advised Daniel Boon.

"No, she's gone missing. Along with her plane. Last week, Wednesday or Thursday, we think. We were told there was a storm—"

"Storm!" interrupted Boon again. "Storm! I thought Wild Horse Reservoir was 'avin' a typhoon! That Mountain City was 'avin' a hurricane! That Duck Valley was 'avin' a dance! It was the highest winds recorded since the spring of 1612 when the Nez Pierce was workin' their way ta Grangeville! Yessir, mate, it was a real main'sel snapper!"

Valter dove into the conversational gale when Boon took a pull on his Tooheys. "Any chance a small plane would've crashed between here and Mountain Home during that storm?"

"The royal question is, Is there any chance a small plane would have NOT crashed?" Boon stood and raised his beer can. "Therefore, my inquisitive friends, if you're lookin' for a plane that HAS crashed, you would be wise to hire a scout or explorer, a man knowledgeable of every canyon and cranny, every path and puddle, every buckaroo, beehive, Basko, and mo-bile 'ome between"—he paused dramatically, then lowered his voice—"heah and theah."

"Dare I ask," said Pike, "where one could find such a person?"

"Yes, yew dare!" replied the eloquent Boon of Owyhee County, formerly of Goondiwindie, Queensland. "And, kind sir, I . . . am your man! I 'ave the intricate network of contacts with their eye, ear, nose, and throat to the grindstone on the lookout for the dane and the mundane. If a plane crashed between Bruneau and Bangkok, Nit Creek and North Fork, Riddle and Reykjavik, Grasmere and the Ganges, these eagle-beaked, ever-vigilant nostrils of the American outback will know.

"I rest me case." Boon upended his beer can and sat back down.

15

December 3: The Chase Begins

As luck would have it, and sometimes does, Busby was hovering his blue-and-white Bell Ranger Model 3346 four-seater helicopter fifty feet above the wreckage of Teddie Arizona's Piper Cherokee by half past the noon hour.

With the expert guidance of the self-acclaimed Owyhee Wilderness Guide and Croc-odile Nabber, aka Daniel Boon, the search party had worked its way north along Nevada State Highway 225, continuing up Idaho State Highway 51, staying to the wild country on the east side. It was less populated in that direction and, according to their calculations, the wind would probably have blown any planes off course to the east. The search route took them over the edge of the Humboldt National Forest, then along the Bruneau Canyon.

"That's Mrs. Pantaker's plane, all right. NC 1077. It's a match," confirmed Paul Valter.

"Oi tol' ya we'd find her," said Daniel Boon, buckaroo guide and loose cannon. "Yessir, there she is, bashed into the side of the canyon, upside down, tits up, **bajo arriba,** belly to the sun, he sure is a sun-fishin' sun of a gun!" he concluded, singing the last line of that classic cowboy tune "The Strawberry Roan."

"Can you set down here?" Valter asked the pilot.

"Nope, Colonel, I need a flat spot. Too rocky and steep. Maybe down by the river or up on top."

"Okay," said Valter, considering. "Take her up."

Busby lifted the helicopter away from the canyon. By his altimeter they rose 310 feet and crested the rim. He rose up another 500 feet to look around. It was a bright, sunny afternoon. The top of the mesa was rocky and bare of trees. Sagebrush and patches of yellow grass spread out for miles. Eroded arroyos and small washes ran toward the canyon's rim like capillaries. Occasional water holes sparkled in the sun.

"Pandora's Thumb," said Daniel Boon. "A seventy-square-mile peninsula formed by the Bruneau River on the east and Goat Creek on the west. A natural cow pasture as long as the water holes stay full. You can see this last storm filled 'em up. A couple miles west is a cow camp. Usually has a cowboy or two on it in a good winter."

"Really," mused Valter. "I wonder if we should check with them first."

"It would sure be easier to ride down to the wreck if they'd lend us a couple of horses," said Pike.

"No horses!" said Valter, a little too quickly. He had an unnatural fear of horses, having fallen in front of a merry-go-round as a child. He still had dreams of being run over by a calliope stampede. "It's just a short walk down there. Besides, I'm wearing my hiking boots."

Pike looked down at his own brand-new ostrich-skin cowboy boots. "Maybe it would be wise to see if there's any cowboys there. They might have seen something."

Valter thought a moment. "No," he said. "Busby, land right here next to the edge. We'll go down and check the wreckage, then go from there. We might find a body or the baggage. No need to bother the cowboys."

Pike spoke up. "Remember, the boss said if we find anything, to call him first. 'Quarantine the site,' he said."

"Well and good," said Valter. "We'll reconnoiter the site, then decide our next course of action."

"Where did you leahn to talk like that, mate?" asked Daniel Boon.

"Twenty-five years in military intelligence," answered Valter. "Succinctness and clarity are essential for good communication."

"That's wot Oi look for in a wine," said Daniel Boon, ever the connoisseur. "That and a low price."

"Set her down, Busby," ordered Valter.

"Aye, aye, sir," the pilot replied.

* ★ ⋆

☾ ⋆ When Lewis Ola made his regular Wednesday morning visit to bring supplies to the camp, Teddie took her baggage and hid in the brush until he left at about ten forty-five. She'd persuaded the old man and Lick that she was in grave danger if anyone found out where she was. She'd exaggerated by saying the people she was running from would kill her—at least, she hoped she was exaggerating. She told Lick and the old man that she trusted them, but the less people that knew, the better. "Even Lewis," she entreated. "I'm sure he's a good man, but why place him in danger, I mean . . . he's probably got a family, that is . . . I mean, the two of you don't have . . . well . . . you know me. I feel safe with y'all. If I can only lay low for a few more days, the people looking for me might back off, go look elsewhere.

"Besides," she added, "it's so isolated here, the chances of them finding me are next to nothing."

None of these explanations seemed to faze

the old man, but Lick took pause to consider the deep end of the pool they were wading in. **Someone wants to kill her?** he thought.

After Lewis departed, they ate lunch, and then they all lay down for a postprandial snooze. They were startled awake by the distinctive thumping of a helicopter's rotors.

Teddie ran to the window in a panic and peered out. Lick and the old man ran outside and stood in front of the trailer, watching a helicopter hover over the edge of the canyon less than a mile away. It was easily visible on this clear, unusually calm day. It stayed aloft less than a minute, then descended below their horizon.

"It's them," she called out from behind the doorway, shaking uncontrollably. "I've got to get out of here. They'll search the wreckage and discover I'm missing and come right here. Right to your camp."

"I'd say yer exactly right," said the old man agreeably.

"Well, shoot, Al, give her a break!" commiserated Lick.

"It's true," the old man said, shrugging his shoulders. "She's dead meat unless we do somethin'."

"Al's right," T.A. said. "Let's see. They, uh . . . I've got . . ."

"Listen," said Lick, "take your suitcases out

into the sagebrush behind the camp and hide. Maybe farther out than this morning 'cause your friends'll be comin' in from above and will be able to see farther. Just wait till we give you the all-clear. We'll shape up the camp. If they come, we'll tell 'em nuthin'."

"You wait here with the ship," Valter instructed Busby. "C'mon gentlemen, let's check it out."

In forty-five minutes, Valter, Pike, and Boon were standing in front of the wreckage.

"Will you look at that," said Daniel Boon. "It's a wonder we found this at all. They must 'ave bounced and flipped."

The Piper Cherokee was upside down, pointing north. The tip of the right wing was torn off. The propeller and nose were a mass of twisted metal and prop. The rudder was sheared off, yet the fuselage was surprisingly intact.

Valter looked in through the open door. "This looks like blood. There's a women's magazine here." He carefully stuck his upper body into the cockpit. "No luggage," he noted.

Pike added from the back, "The luggage compartment's empty, too."

Valter backed out of the cockpit. "So, whattaya think happened?" he asked.

"Well," observed Boon, "she's gone and taken her luggage. Obviously this was not her planned destination."

"You see any tracks around here, horse tracks in particular?" asked Pike.

"No, but that trail down to here is still bein' used. Rain and wind since the wreck. 'Orse tracks? You thinkin' she was found—rescued, maybe?"

"Maybe we should pay a visit to that cowboy camp after all," said Valter.

* * *

"Here they come," said the old man. "I can hear it getting closer."

The helicopter landed thirty yards away from the trailer with a thunderous noise and whoosh, sending sticks, dust, and rocks pinging against the trailer wall.

"That low-life lit right out there by my car!" cursed the old man. "He'll ruin the paint job." He pushed through the door, saved his hat from blowin' off, and stomped out toward the visitors, stopping just beyond the edge of the prop while it coasted to a stop.

The door opened. Valter stepped out, crouched down, and walked toward the old man. He stuck out his hand.

The old man ignored it. "You low-down, blood-sucking tourists! Ain't you got no respect for a feller's domicile! Blowin' in here with that egg beater scatterin' rocks all over, sand blasting, seriously damaging the paint job on my classic vehicle I paid thousands of dollars for! Wuz you raised in a barn? No, I can see that ain't the case. You ain't got the sense of a country boy. You must be some kinda dude. Did your mommy buy you that little pair of brogans . . . and that looks-like-a-prison-haircut?"

"Al!" shouted Boon coming up behind Valter. "Al, hold on a minute."

Al peered at the man standing off to the side. "Well, Davy, as I live and breathe," said the old man. "I thought you died at the Alamo!"

The rotors went quiet.

"I didn't," Boon replied. "And the name's Daniel, mate."

"Well, you should have." The old man levered a shell into his Winchester Model 94 .30-30, still holding it across his chest and pointed skyward.

"Just a minute, sir," said Valter, backing up a step. "We're looking for someone. I apologize if we startled you. We'll pay for the damage to your car."

The old man didn't move.

"We spotted the wreckage of her plane in the canyon, but she's gone. We just thought you might have seen her," continued Valter.

The old man still didn't speak.

"Have you?" asked Valter.

"What?" asked the old man.

"Seen her."

"Who?"

"The woman."

"What woman?"

"The one from the wreck."

"What wreck?"

"In the canyon."

"What did she look like?"

"Pretty woman, twenty-eight, blonde hair, five foot six or seven— Wait a minute! How many women have you seen out here taking a stroll on this godforsaken rock in the last week!" said Valter, exasperated.

The old man swung his rifle around toward Valter. It now pointed at his head.

"What's the matter with you, Al!" said Daniel Boon. "These guys are just tryin' to find a sheila that's missin', that's all. They got money, mate. If you've seen her."

At that moment, Valter swept out his right hand and caught the barrel of the rifle, deflecting it. Accidentally, the old man pulled the trigger and the rifle boomed.

Back at camp, Lick was saddling the horses when he heard the shot. He led the horses behind the windbreak shed and tied them out of sight, watching from behind its cover as the procession marched toward the trailer.

He could hear the old man cussing his three captors. They were pushing him and talking roughly. Lick had grabbed the old man's .22 caliber nine-shot revolver and an aspirin bottle full of bullets from his sock drawer. He slipped up behind the trailer to better hear the interrogation transpiring inside.

"I don't know why you're being such a bonehead," Valter was saying. "We're only concerned for the woman's welfare."

"I never seen no woman," said the old man stubbornly.

"What's this, then?" asked Pike, striding back from the bedroom. He held up a bottle of mascara.

Al studied it. "What is it?" he asked.

"Mascara. Midnight Black. It doesn't look like your color, Al," said Pike.

"Must'uve been one of my dates that left it here," Al surmised.

"The bedroom and bathroom smell a might pretty for a cowboy outfit," added Pike.

"I try to keep a tidy camp," said the old man.

"No doubt she's been here," said Pike to Valter. "Or at least some woman, and recent, too. That back bedroom, the sheets don't smell like this rank ol' boar has been sleepin' in'em. Matter of fact, I'd bet that she slept in'em last night. Am I wrong, old man?"

"I'll bet she's hidin' out back somewhere. Just

ducked out when she saw the helicopter," said Valter. "Let's go take a look." Then he turned to the old man, "You here alone, ol' pardner?"

Suddenly Daniel Boon, who had been standing in the doorway watching them, pitched forward facedown and crashed into the crowded living room. His head hit a wrought-iron divider with a heavy clunk.

Lick vaulted into the trailer, stepping in the middle of Boon's back, pistol leveled at Valter, and said, "Nobody move!"

"By cracky, kid, I knew you'd come," cackled Al. "These snake bellies were fixin' to pull out my fingernails! By the way, they found your mascara."

Lick was looking back and forth at Pike and Valter. "Git your rifle, Al. And you," he said to Pike, "git your hands up. Cover 'em, Al."

Lick frisked Pike, then Valter, then Boon, who still lay facedown. Valter was carrying a standard army-issue Colt .45 semiautomatic pistol. Pike gave up a snub-nosed .38 caliber revolver. Boon was unarmed.

"Listen, boys," said Valter, "I take it you know about the girl. If she's dead or hurt, we don't hold it against you. If she's here or you know where she is, there's a big reward. Let's be reasonable."

"What girl?" asked the old man. "And if we

did know her, she might have just stayed the night and moved on."

"Walking?" asked Valter.

"Sure, she could have been an experienced hiker," answered the old man, reasonably. "We have 'em hike through here all the time. We have an apostle here."

"A what?" asked Pike.

"Apostle, one of the places like in Europe where hikers stay, like a bed-and-breakfast."

"Was she wounded?" asked Valter, the sly interrogator.

"Who?" asked the old man.

"The hiker. We saw a lot of dried blood in the cockpit of her plane," countered Valter.

"Not so she couldn't travel, that is if she came here, which, she just might not have. I'm just apostulating," said the old man.

"That's enough, Al," said Lick.

"You got it right, cowboy," said Valter, meanly. "You two boys are in over your heads. You're just inches—"

Pike interrupted, thinking this could still be done with sugar. "The other thing is that her husband is real concerned about finding her. He's not gonna quit till he finds her, and I, personally, would not want to be standing between him and her when he does."

"I'm too old to threaten, young feller. You

forget who's got the upper hand," said the old man. "You boys are just lucky we don't tie y'all to a sagebrush, cover you with cream of mushroom soup, and feed you to the coyotes. As it is, I think we'll just tape you together. Hold on a minute."

The old man went to the kitchen drawer and got two big rolls of silvery duct tape. "Take off yer boots. Now you, what's yer name?"

"Pike," said Pike.

"Pike, you git over here and stand back to back with Hermann Goering, here. Reach both arms around backwards in front of him. Good. Closer together."

The old man taped Pike's wrists together, then ran a strip through Valter's belt. He repeated the process with Valter, taping his wrists behind his back in front of Pike and securing them to the front of Pike's belt.

"Off with yer boots, Davy," said the old man to the groggy Daniel Boon.

He then backed Boon up against the left side of Pike and taped the three men together.

"You're not going to get far," warned Valter. "If she's payin' you, we can double it, triple it. You're getting involved in something more dangerous than you know."

"Danger!" said the old man. "Danger! I faced the panzers in France, I've looked down the barrel of a Nazi cannon. And the kid here, hell, he rode Kamikaze!"

"Was that you?" asked Pike incredulously. "I saw that! Two years ago at the Finals. I'll remember that ride all my life! I'd just like to shake your— Well, later. When this is all over maybe I could get your autograph."

"Sure," said Lick, temporarily beyond flattery.

"Okay, gents. Out here in the center of the room," instructed the old man. "Feet together." He encircled the six legs with four roundy-round circles of duct tape ankle high. "Now, we are gonna slip outta here, but first . . ." Using eight-inch strips, he covered their eyes.

"Al," whined Boon, "whattya doin'? I'm yer mate. I don't know these guys. I's just helpin' out. Bein' their guide, so to speak. Whyn't ya let me go. I'll high-step it outta here, won't tell nobody."

"Hold it, Davy," said the old man.

"It's Daniel."

"Really? I thought you wuz named after Davy Crockett."

"Nope. Daniel Webster, actually. My mother was a librarian but I—"

"Come on, Al," interrupted Lick. "Let's go. I've got the horses saddled!"

They grabbed their coats and bailed out the

door, leaving the seedy triumvirate like a three-dimensional jack of spades. Behind the horse shed they jerked the tie ropes loose and swung into the saddle. Immediately above them the helicopter roared across at fifty feet.

The old man's dogs jumped and the horses spooked! Two hundred yards out in the sagebrush they saw Teddie Arizona running at full speed. She was wearing her black ski jacket with yellow stripe accents. The helicopter had spotted her and was in full pursuit!

A helicopter can be a scary thing. From the ground it is like being attacked by a giant praying mantis. The powerful rotor wash can easily knock a person down and the noise can rattle your eyelids.

The old man and Lick kicked the horses into a hard run. Lick held his course straight toward Teddie. His horse, terrified of the helicopter, fought to turn off. The old man swung to the starboard side of the helicopter, unhitching his fifty-foot ⅜-inch nylon rope from its keeper on the swell. He shook out a loop.

Teddie Arizona was zigzagging, but Busby held the helicopter menacingly close. The old man rode up on the tailpiece at a dead run, swinging his rope. With the wisdom of mature plankton, he threw a beautiful loop over the tail rotor assembly, pulled back on the reins, and dallied in true buckaroo fashion.

The helicopter was twenty feet above the ground when the rope tied to the saddle pulled taut. It lifted the horse and rider straight up several feet before the tail section tipped down, plunging the old man and his horse back to Earth.

The old man could see T.A. was clear. The jerk had changed the angle and direction of the helicopter. He swung to the left and spurred his mount. Busby was frantically trying to regain balance and control—delicate maneuvers made even more difficult by the lunatic roper who now seemed to be riding in a circle clockwise around the floundering copter.

Busby felt a fleeting moment of control, pushed the throttle, and pulled back on the stick. The sudden jerk nearly pulled the old man's horse over backwards but he unpeeled his dally and pitched the slack just in time.

The old man's horse was in the "Trigger" position when the standing end of his best rope was sucked into the blades of the tail rotor. It sounded like stepping on a tin can. Maybe a lot of tin cans. Pieces of metal flew through the air. The helicopter, whirling like a slow top, crashed to the ground with a deafening roar. Dust, rocks, and brush filled the air.

As the copter breathed its last, Lick rode up to T.A., who finally got the horse's attention above the din. She grabbed the reins up next to the bit, slid back along the neck, and grasped the horn and the front of Lick's brush jacket, plunging her right foot in the left stirrup, which was swinging free. Lick got a handful of her ski jacket and pulled her up behind the horn onto his lap. To their everlasting good fortune, the horse didn't buck. He just wanted out of there! He leaped to a run in three short jumps. Lick managed to get the reins out from under T.A.'s torso, but she still had her right foot in the left stirrup, which pulled them hard to port. Lick leaned hard in the starboard stirrup to keep them upright.

Through some awkward banging and tugging he managed to get her laid across the saddle and his own foot back in the left stirrup. Within three minutes, they were far enough away from the battlefield to slow down. Lick trotted the horse, then walked him a short distance more. And short though it was, it was long enough to stimulate a primitive response in Lick's parasympathetic nervous system. Something had come between them.

She noticed his interest in her. She also noticed that she, too, had a funny tingle.

Lick stopped the horse, which was blowing hard. "Whoa, baby," he said, obviously talking to himself. T.A. slid down his leg off the left side.

"Quite a ride," she said, still a little rattled herself.

Lick gave her a quick, steady look to discern her meaning. She gave him no clue.

He looked back at the helicopter that now lay still. The old man was riding toward them.

"Climb up here behind me," Lick said, kicking the left stirrup free.

T.A. mounted behind the cantle and loosely put her arms around his waist.

Lick had not had so much as a kiss since summer. He didn't even miss women. At least that's what he thought. He'd kept his distance from Teddie Arizona, a married woman, except for that little back rub. But something had just happened. A spark had just fired in a long-dead cylinder.

The old man rode up beside them.

"Pilot's fine. Heard him cussing a blue streak. It's gonna take him a while to get himself out of that hunk of junk. Let's head to the Goat Creek winter camp."

Lick felt the warmth of T.A. pressing against his back and she tightened her arms around his waist as they crossed the country at a lope.

16
December 3: The Chase Continues

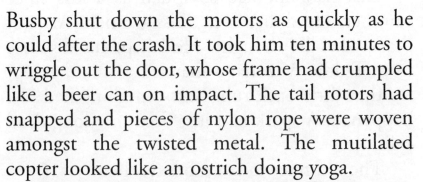

Busby shut down the motors as quickly as he could after the crash. It took him ten minutes to wriggle out the door, whose frame had crumpled like a beer can on impact. The tail rotors had snapped and pieces of nylon rope were woven amongst the twisted metal. The mutilated copter looked like an ostrich doing yoga.

"Aw, heck," said Busby in his former U.S. Navy training jargon. He squinted into the distance and saw two mounted horses loping across the sagebrush toward the south. "Oh, well, they can't demote me." Then he noticed muffled noises drifting from the trailer.

As he rounded the corner and stepped in the front door of the trailer, he heard loud, angry voices. A wooden chair was upended. A cheap coffee table lay on its side with magazines, matches, pencils, and accumulated cowboy paraphernalia scattered on the floor. Afloat on this landfill lay the three wise men duct-taped together.

"'Bout time," said Boon.

It took Busby several minutes to untangle and untape the captives. Valter had an ugly cut on one eyebrow that oozed blood. Pike's nose was beginning to swell. Boon had maneuvered deftly during the fall and had stayed on top. He was unhurt, though his arm was asleep.

Finally all four stood in the small living room. Valter fumed during Busby's description of the chase, helicopter roping, and escape.

"That road they're on," offered Boon, "takes 'em down offa the plateau here, across Goat Creek, and down to Highway 51. They'll pass by an old sheep station on the other side of the creek."

"So you think that's where they're headed?" asked Valter.

"Don't know," answered Boon. "If the sheila's tryin' to get away from you mates, they'd just keep goin'. But it's twenty miles on out to the highway—if they stayed on the road, of course."

"Okay," said Valter. "Busby, you see if that ol' car will start. Boon, if they stay on this road, how long before we catch up with them?"

"I've only been up here a couple times," replied Boon. "But the road up here on top is a real bush track. Horses can go faster than cars. But once we're on the other side of Goat

Creek, we'll hit a good gravel road. We'd catch 'em there easy."

They heard an engine roar to life outside. They stepped outside to see Busby at the wheel of Al's smoking Ford Galaxie four-door sedan, which Lewis the foreman had jump-started and charged the battery on that morning. From the helicopter they retrieved their travel bags, which included Valter's other .45 automatic and an extra handgun for Pike.

When Boon saw the guns, he balked. "I don't think I like the idea of shootin' at my mates."

"Don't worry about it, Mr. Boon," soothed Valter. "We don't plan on hurting anybody."

"I 'ope not. Friends are scattered far apart out heah."

They climbed in the car and turned back toward the road, which more correctly could be described as a series of ruts strewn with oil-pan-whacking rocks and bumper-dragging sage-brush. Skilled pilot though he was, Busby couldn't avoid all the rocks, ruts, and bumps. Valter, sitting in the passenger seat, with Pike and Boon in the backseat were thrown back and forth, knees to dashboard, hat against the head-liner, being whiplashed and snapped at a teeth-jarring, stomach-lurching four miles an hour.

"Busby!" screamed Valter. "Can't you make this hunk of junk go any faster? I could get there faster walking!"

"I'm pushing it the best I can," Busby said. "It's like driving a corn picker through a mine-field!"

Ten minutes down the road they passed the extra horses in a large fenced-in pasture called "the trap."

"What are horses doin' there?" asked Valter.

"Them's their extra mounts. They use'm to give their best horses a breather," explained Boon.

"Stop here, Busby. Let me think a minute," Valter instructed.

"There was a saddle hangin' in the tack room behind the trailer," remembered Pike.

"I saw it comin' back from the helicopter."

"All right, then," said Valter. "Boon, catch these two horses here, go back to the trailer, saddle one, lead the other, and follow us. Shoot, you might even pass us, good as this road is, and that way if they take out cross-county, we'll be prepared to follow them. Otherwise, we'll meet up down the road here at Goat Creek and make a plan. Got it?"

"Righto, mate," said Boon, getting into the swing of things.

17

December 3: Confrontation at Goat Creek

The sun was wan in the west and clouds were scudding in when the bargelike Ford Galaxie tipped over the rim of Pandora's Thumb and nosed down into the Goat Creek crossing.

"There they are!" said Teddie Arizona. "Across the creek. You were right, Al, they stole your car."

"I figgered that, bein' the common criminals they are," Al mused. "'Course, I wouldn't've been surprised if they'd stole our horses from the trap, too. Either way, they've got to come through here. It's our best chance to ambush 'em before we get to the highway."

T.A., Lick, and the old man were lying prone at the top of the rock cliff on the west side of Goat Creek. Beneath them, sheltered against a black sheet of vertical rock, lay sheep headquarters. It consisted of a stone house with a tin roof and beyond the house toward the creek an ancient stone horse barn, corrals, and a machine shed. Two saddled horses were tied to the corral fence. The saddled horses were bait in the old man's ambush plan.

The three of them watched as the Ford Galaxie slowly descended the steep road across the canyon from them. It drove cautiously to within fifty yards of the house and stopped. Two men got out of the car, one from the front passenger side, one from the driver's-side back door. Each was carrying a pistol. In the leeward silence of the cliff, Lick could hear the engine turn off and the car doors close.

Lick pulled back from the edge. In a low voice he said, "Al, there's two of 'em got out. Looks like the driver's stayin' with the car. I don't see the fourth one. Maybe yer right about them leavin' one back to bring our horses from the trap."

Al rubbed his chin. "'Course I wuz right. You don't reckon any of that bunch would walk? He might not be far behind, so let's git our plan goin'. I stay up here and stand guard. T.A., you slip down and let the air outta their tires. Lick, you slide around and grab our two decoy horses and we ride off, leavin' 'em stranded."

"What if that other one come ridin' up while I'm sneakin' the horses around?" asked Lick. "They've all got guns. I'm beginnin' to wonder if this decoy-horse plan was such a great idea after all."

"What's the matter with you, kid? You think I don't know what I'm doin'? I didn't get three stripes in Uncle Sam's army for bein' dumb. Wuz **you** ever in the army?"

Lick shook his head.

"Well, that's why. If you wuz, you'd know this wuz one of Rommel's favorite tricks. He'd park a camel tied to a palm tree out there in the desert and wait behind a sand dune for the Limeys to fall into his trap. That's how come he got to be a general."

Lick almost got snared in the logic, but gave up. "They've still got guns, Al," he repeated. "I'd be a sittin' duck."

"Have faith, my boy. We, too, are armed," the old man replied, patting the Winchester Model 94. "Besides, if we don't stop 'em now, they'll get T.A. fer sure." Al looked over at Teddie, who'd been listening. "Don't worry, little lady, we're gonna get you outta this mess, but it's gonna be exciting."

The old man stayed on top of the rim with his two dogs napping soundly behind him. Teddie took the .22 pistol and eased to the south, staying low because her black ski jacket with the yellow stripes was poor camouflage. Lick tucked Valter's co-opted Colt .45 into his belt and climbed down the north side above the corrals to reach the horses. His job was to lead them along the creek and up behind the car. There he would join up with Teddie, follow the road up out of the little Goat Creek canyon, and pick up the old man.

The sheep headquarters lay in the shadow of the cliff. For many years the old man had had poor vision, but with age it had improved, which helped his aim enormously. Unfortunately, his hearing had gone the other way. But he could still create a diversion should Lick or T.A. get in trouble. He could see the two pursuers cautiously inspecting the main house.

T.A. managed to get up behind the car more easily than she'd anticipated. She stayed low in a long ditch, then crawled directly behind it.

Busby, being a professional pilot, was used to long waits in the cockpit or log room while his passengers did their business. Waiting in the Ford Galaxie was no different for him. He had a pocket computer that played solitaire, a Louis L'Amour novel, and the patience of Job. At present he was actually asleep at the wheel.

Meanwhile, Lick was coming up from the north side of the horse barn, out of sight of the house. He crept toward the horses that Al had tied to the corral fence as a lure to draw in their pursuers.

The old man watched as Valter and Pike circled the stone house and eased slowly toward the horse barn. In the dim light he could see Lick coming in their direction. Now was the time for his diversion. He picked a spot a foot or two in front of the one closest to the barn and squeezed off a shot.

Teddie Arizona was on her back underneath the rear end of the car. She had just removed the valve stem cap from the right rear tire and was fixing to release the pressure when the shot rang out. Suddenly the key clicked, the crankshaft turned over, and the engine started.

T.A. pulled the pistol out of her waistband as the car began to move forward. Still lying on the ground, she fired one shot into the tread of each rear tire.

Busby froze as the car lurched beneath him and then he stomped on the brakes. He'd heard the shot in front of him, then two shots behind him. He could see Valter and Pike racing back toward the stone house and diving for cover. Who was doing all the shooting?

He noticed the sudden change in the angle of his craft. Should he get out? Should he drive forward to rescue the passengers? He mentally referred to the giant book of Pilot Obligations and Ethics regarding this situation. It was essentially the same as the giant book used by news photographers when faced with the dilemma of getting the shot or saving a life . . . ALWAYS GET THE

PHOTOGRAPH! The professional obligation was to get the aircraft (in this case, the vehicle) home safe and sound.

Busby scanned the horizon. Seeing no enemy in sight, he carefully opened the door and peeked out the crack. The left rear tire was flat. He pushed the door open and dove to the ground, rolling toward the back of the vehicle for safety. He slid beneath the left rear fender, still looking in the direction of the first shot. He exhaled deeply.

"Don't move a muscle," a female voice said intimately.

He didn't, other than his sphincter, which slammed shut.

Teddie Arizona crawled closer to him, gently placing the muzzle of the .22 caliber pistol behind his ear.

"You know what this is?" she asked.

"I, uh, assume it's a weapon of some kind," he stammered.

"Just big enough to make this the last conversation you'll ever have."

"I'm just the pilot," he whined. "I don't even know what's going on. You must be Mrs. Pantaker."

"Who's with you?" T.A. asked, pressing the pistol barrel against his skull. "Valter and Pike, right?"

"Right," he said.

"Just the three of you?" she asked.

"Uh, actually, there's another guy. Daniel Boon is his name. He's coming behind with some horses, I think."

Teddie Arizona looked over her shoulder toward the road that led back to Pandora's Thumb. It was empty. She pressed the pistol barrel into Busby's skull again for emphasis. "My friends and I are armed and prepared to shoot. Unless you want to put yourself in harm's way for F. Rank Pantaker, the world's largest orifice, I'd suggest you just lay right here till the smoke clears."

"No, ma'am, I don't! I'm just the pilot . . . with no plane. I don't even have a gun."

"Good. I'm gonna slide over to the side of the road, but I'll have you in plain sight. You understand?"

"Yes, ma'am."

"Cover your ears," she directed. He complied. She put a bullet each through the front tires on her way out.

Lick was sneaking along the west side of the horse barn, in plain sight of the old man up on the ridge. He stopped a minute to listen and to quiet his breathing. Not five seconds later, the old man fired his .30-30 again! Lick bit his tongue! The boom echoed against the canyon wall. He heard the clatter of footsteps out of sight around the corner of the barn. He sneaked a quick look. Two men were running toward the house at full speed. Thirty feet away to his left the two horses tied to the corral fence were pulling back on the reins.

Another shot boomed just behind Pike and Valter, and they disappeared behind the south side of the house. Lick slipped along the south face of the barn and under the big pole gate, creeping in the shadows toward the horses. He fingered the automatic pistol in his coat pocket. He'd never shot anything but a revolver. He pulled it out awkwardly and broke into a run.

"By gosh, Paul," Pike was saying as they hunkered behind the house, "these hayseeds sucked us into a trap. Lured us down here with these horses, then ambushed us."

"It sure seems that way," said Valter. "See if you can wave Busby up here. He can pick us up and we can get back on the high ground. Otherwise we're pinned down."

Lick took the opportunity to cross under the board fence, untie the horses, and lead them quietly down along the edge of the corral to the creek. He heard the .30-30 boom again, twice.

Teddie Arizona watched as Lick came up the creek with the horses. "Get in the car and drive down toward the house!" she yelled at Busby from her vantage point twenty feet away.

"But the tires are flat," he whined.

She leveled the pistol in his direction.

"Okay, okay," he said. He inched in through the left front door like a burglar and started the engine. Looking into the rearview mirror, he saw T.A. aiming the pistol at the back of his head. He dropped the old Ford into D. It crunched forward on its flat tires and slowly moved down the road.

T.A. ran across the marshy grass in a low crouch to meet Lick. They mounted up in the coming darkness and rode around to where the old man and his dogs still stood sentry.

"Al, I gotta hand it to ya," Lick said. "I woulda never believed it in a million years."

"Just like clarkwork," Al said. "Just like clarkwork."

Teddie Arizona stepped off the old man's horse and held it for him. She gave him a warm hug and a kiss on the cheek as she handed him the reins. "Thanks, Al," she said.

T.A. climbed up behind Lick, the old man fired two more shots at the house, then aimed one at the slow-moving car. "Good-bye, old friend," he said and shot out the windshield. They all watched as Busby bailed out the front seat and ran into the stone barn. "C'mon, dogs."

They trotted down the road into the dwindling sunset.

"Where to?" asked Lick.

The old man was feeling good. "I've got an idea," he said. "I've got an idea."

18

December 3: Romance Is Kindled

The old man stopped them as they approached a fork in the road. "These dudes will expect us to head directly north for Scotland, 'specially if Davy Crockett is doin' their scouting. He musta caught up with 'em by now with the horses. Besides, it's an easy trip and they'll all be tired and ready to go someplace civilized."

An odd description of Scotland, Lick thought to himself. He'd been there several times, since it was where one turned off Highway 51 to reach all the ranches and country that ran up against the Bruneau Canyon. The only thing there was a store that was like an 1880s concept of a Kwik Chek: just a bar, liquor store, pool table, junk food staples, meager hardware supplies, a post office, and a rusty three-hundred-gallon gas tank with a hose that dangled like a knotted rope.

"We go south, the opposite direction," the old man continued. "The hard way, 'cept it ain't any harder if you're well mounted. There's a ranch maybe fifteen miles from here. We can stop there if we need to, and if we don't, well, there's always Goose Valley or Mountain City."

Lick knew that they better find that ranch because it would take more than two or three hours to ride cross-country to Mountain City. With no food, and ice already formed on the still water in the creeks, it would be like running the Iditarod.

An hour down the road, they crossed Goat Creek again. They stopped and watered the horses in the moonlight.

"Better get a move on," said Al. "Don't want them catching up with us." They left the road, being careful not to leave an obvious trail, although the ground was frozen and even tracking a wounded diplodocus across the desert would be difficult tonight.

Two hours later, they connected to the gravel road that headed south. The horses were tiring, slowing down.

"Where's that ranch, old man?" asked Lick, shivering. "I thought you said it was right around here."

"Well, I'm not exactly certain where. Maybe two miles more, maybe twenty, but it's surely along here somewhere," Al said.

"Let's just find someplace to build a fire and warm up," said Lick. "I can hardly feel my hands and feet." Teddie nodded and sent Lick a grateful look.

They rode up a small draw and found a clay bank that was shielded from view of the dirt road. It didn't take long to get a small but toasty fire going. They loosed the cinches and hobbled the horses. The beasts found a few pickin's and started grazing. The old man laid back in a handy sagebrush and was soon snoring.

"Wish we had some coffee," Lick said to T.A. as they huddled together near the small fire and stared into the flames.

"I'm so nervous I'm still shaking," she said. "If Valter and Pi . . . if those guys catch up with us—"

"You know them?" he asked.

"Yeah, I guess I do. They work for my, uh, my fiancé, F. Rank."

"I thought you were married," he said.

"I am not officially married. It's a long story," she sighed.

"Maybe it's none of my business, but if you wanna tell me, I've got a few minutes," he offered.

T.A., out of habit and self-defense, had for years kept a very tight rein on her feelings. She had to mentally shovel off a layer of armor even to give Lick a civil answer. However, her nerves were frayed and her heart kept trying to raise its hand to ask permission to speak. It wanted to say, "This cowboy's gone out on a big limb for you. Don't you think a little of the truth would be in order?" For once, T.A. decided to listen to it.

"F. Rank's family, my ex-whatever's family, I mean, wouldn't give him an advance on his inheritance," she started. "If he wasn't 'stable,' as they called it. So he made me an offer a girl couldn't refuse." T.A. paused, waiting for Lick to react. He didn't. "That was twenty months ago. I only have another four months to go in our arrangement. Then we split, he cements his inheritance, and I get paid.

"Everybody thinks we're married. F. Rank and I are the only ones who know the real story. He and I, and now you. We act like we're married . . . in every respect," she added, so Lick would have no illusions about her deal with the devil.

"So that's why he wants you back . . . not out of love, but so the deal won't go sour?"

"That and something else. I, uh, took some money." She swallowed hard. "A lot of money," she whispered.

"Why didn't you just wait another four months and get your money then?" Lick asked.

"The money I took . . . it's not exactly just the money he would have owed me. It was more," she said.

"A little more?" asked Lick.

"A lot more than a little more," she said.

Lick waited for her to continue.

"I don't know if I can explain it," she began. "I'm not sure I understand myself. There's lots of reasons. Let's just say I got sick of it, of the arrangement, of him, of the game, of faking it, of myself, what I'd let myself in for. Then I found out he's involved in a scheme that's so horrible, so callous, so wantonly cruel, so . . . just so rotten I couldn't handle it. I know what I did was stupid, but I didn't know any other way to stop it. And now I've put y'all in danger, too." Her shoulders sagged. "Now he's got to catch me to find out where the money is. And he's runnin' outta time, has to have the money soon. So they're not gonna give up tryin' to find me."

Lick was staring at the ground.

"It's not drug-related, if that's what you're thinking. Well, not exactly. At least takin' the money isn't drug-related," she said, reading his mind. "It's . . . it's hard to explain. He and another rich Vegas big shot are putting on a big-game hunt and charging billionaires a pile of money to take part—the money I took."

"That's legal," interjected Lick. "Big-game hunting. We do that in Texas all the time. It's a big business."

"Yes, but F. Rank is selling the opportunity to shoot endangered species."

"What?" said Lick. "You mean like bald eagles or condors, spotted owls?"

"More like black rhinos, Bengal tigers, mountain gorillas, pandas, Himalayan snow leopards—and blue whales, if he could get a tank big enough."

"So, he's discussed this with you?"

"No, but his partner is the famous wild-animal trainer and magician Ponce de Crayon. You've heard of him, no doubt."

"I think so," said Lick, although he thought he was the guy who founded the YMCA.

"Anyway, they've been planning this for quite a while. I heard F. Rank plotting on the phone with Ponce. He's not very discreet. I'm just part of the furniture to him."

Bedroom furniture, Lick thought with a slightly green twinge.

"F. Rank and Ponce have already lined up ten hunters from all over the world. Each has paid a hefty down payment. Half down. Each is guaranteed a genuine endangered species kill. There's a lot of money at stake. So, to make a long story short, I stole his strongbox of down payments."

"How much money are we talkin' about?"

"Five hundred thousand," she said. "Each."

Lick had about seventy-five dollars in the money clip in his pocket. He was mentally calculating the difference. It seemed substantial. "When's the hunt gonna be?"

"On December thirteenth, during the big rodeo."

"The National Finals?" asked Lick. "In Vegas?"

"Yep. The National Finals. Out on Ponce's big ranch and wildlife preserve north of town. If I can stay out of their way and keep them from getting the money to pay out the hunters, maybe they'll have to cancel the whole deal. I wasn't being rational, Lick. I just thought if I took the money, it would stop them. I guess I didn't think it through."

"What'll they do if they find you?" Lick asked. "Don't they just want their money back?"

"I don't know if it's that simple. I might be able to negotiate with F. Rank. He's got something on me, he knows I can't go to the police. But exposing our fake marriage could make things messy with his family and inheritance.

"Ponce's another story. He's crazy. F. Rank's scared of him. He's liable to feed me to the tigers, money or no money."

T.A. hugged her knees more tightly to her

chest and looked sideways at Lick to see his reaction. He showed incredulity and concern.

Good. It was what she'd hoped for: sympathy. The practical side of her confession to
Lick was that she needed a bodyguard, a foot
warmer, and a backcountry guide to get away
from Valter and Pike.

This is the barter that often comes with
any relationship. One example: she's beautiful, he's rich.

But T.A. gave Lick more of the truth than
she intended. It slipped out like steam from a
cup of hot chocolate. It was not her nature to
be so forthcoming.

She'd been playing a role, acting. Even
through these last few days with the cowboys,
everything was done with her own selfish in-
terests in mind. The long-term effect on Lick
and the old man had never been a consideration.

Yet when she was telling Lick about her
arrangement with F. Rank and about stealing
the money, there was a physical sensation
accompanying each confession, like she was
peeling a scab, lancing a boil, pulling a
splinter . . . as if poison was being released
from her body.

She was a moment away from tears.

"I'm just so sorry I dragged you into this."

They sat in silence for a few moments.

"Warm enough?" Lick asked. His practical question broke the spell. Her tears receded.

That single question changed her back from vulnerable to vamp. From clay to rebar. From open to closed. From honest to opportunist. From relinquishing her feelings in a tender moment to regaining control of herself and whoever had what she wanted.

T.A. slid her arm under Lick's jacket with the smoothness of a snake crawling under the covers. He looked at her face in the firelight's glow. She had a wry smile on her face. Not what he expected.

"What?" he said.

"Just reading your mind, cowboy."

He raised an eyebrow, leaned forward, and kissed her lightly on the lips.

Her lips toyed with his. She gently ran her tongue along his upper lip under the moustache. He pressed his lips firmly against hers and slid his right hand inside her ski jacket.

With the deftness of a kangaroo rat unwrapping a Hershey's Kiss, he unsnapped her shirtfront and touched the rising topography. His fingertips followed the undercurve, sliding over the thin knit tank top encasing the straining swell that rose and fell. It was light as a grape, heavy as a melon, soft and resilient at the same time. A peach ripe for picking.

Her kiss became more aggressive, her tongue more curious, her lips more agile. Her left hand began exploring on its own. As it continued to search his tender places, his own right hand became more couragous. Inspired by its brother's boldness, the left hand took a dive into the abyss between her back pockets.

He fell back onto the rough ground. She rolled over on him, straddling his left leg. His left hand dove farther. He pressed with his palm. She squeezed with her legs. Their lips locked, their breathing became heavy, their chests were heaving, their exhaustion turned to frenzy, their bodies pushed hard against each other, then . . . released!

Silence settled for a moment, then silent tears . . . comfort . . . discomfort . . . sitting up . . . straightening up . . . a deep breath and . . . "I better wake up Al if we're gonna make that ranch before dawn. We'd make an easy target in broad daylight." Disentangling himself from T.A., Lick pushed himself to his feet, walked over to the sagebrush, and poked the snoring old man with his toe.

"C'mon, Al. Let's get movin'."

"Huh?" Snuff, snort. "Are the heathens bombin' us agin, Cap? Or is it Admiral Perry needin' supplies?"

"I'll get the horses," said Lick.

T.A. watched him in silence, a look of wonderment on her face like she'd just tasted a tantalizing new flavor of ice cream. "Ummm," she said.

There are those who might question the veracity of Teddie Arizona and Lick being able to engage in erotic exploration in the midst of a heart-gripping, life-threatening, environmentally inclement chase across the high desert at night.

To those of premature maturity and suppressed hormones: It has been shown that desire is sometimes enhanced by danger. It is a throwback to the frenzied mating of the mayfly in the face of an impending storm, or the blind groping of a macho black widower who somehow senses this is his last kiss, or the hyperventilating backseat teenagers swarming each other like termites as the clock on the car radio whirls toward curfew.

In truth, we are not discussing something as lofty as love. We are merely acknowledging that lust has been ripening on the vine and suddenly seems primed for plucking. Lust, that primitive preview of coming attractions that induces a sticky sensual static electricity. An uncontrollable force that strips you to the waist from the bottom up and blindfolds you

from the top down. The threat of danger engenders emotional instability, behaviorial insurrection, and desertion of the last shreds of self-discipline.

The effect is all heightened by the deep contention that life appears to be short, and there's nothing left to lose, so lust insinuates itself between two minds, which quickly degenerate into the live-for-the-moment mentality. And this is where our two hormonically charged characters now find themselves, not to mention the fact that the fervor helps them keep warm. In other words, some survival heavy petting was going on.

19

December 3: T.A., Lick, and Al on the Road

T.A. and the old man put out the fire while Lick rode to the high ground and looked back down the road whence they'd come. They heard the faint sound of steel shoes on the gravel. More than one horse, Lick realized as he listened to hoofbeats growing louder.

Lick raced back to the draw. "They're coming! At least I think it must be them. Down the road, maybe half a mile back. On horses. I can hear 'em talkin' and one of 'em has a flashlight. I guess they're trackin' us, but I thought the ground was froze too hard to leave tracks."

"Ol' Davy might be a tracker," observed the old man. "That Pike feller looked like he had a little cowboy in him, too. What say we ambush 'em? Leave their bodies for the coyotes."

"How 'bout we just hold 'em up and take their horses?" said Lick.

"They hang horse thieves," said the old man.

"Well, if it's them, where did THEY get the horses?" asked T.A.

"Prob'ly stoled 'em," concluded the old man. "From the trap. Okay, shoot 'em."

"No," said Lick. "Let's think about it."

Ten minutes later Lick and the old man were hidden on either side of the road across from each other at the top of a small rise.

"How cold you think it is?" Daniel Boon was asking.

Valter looked at his radon-illuminated all-purpose outdoor Apollo 7 chronometer. "Minus four degrees . . . centigrade."

"You cold?" asked Boon.

"No. I'm in a hurry. If you're right about these invisible tracks, we should catch up with them, or at least find them at this mysterious ranch you say is this direction. If we've been chasing wild geese, then we'll borrow a vehicle at the ranch and head back the other direction to catch up with Pike at Scotland. If it's where you say it is."

"How do you know they'll lend you a vehicle?" asked Boon.

"I'll just buy it, Boon. I'll make them an offer they can't refuse."

"What are you gonna do with the girl?"

"Take her home to her husband, that's all."

"What about the old man and the other cowboy?"

"Nothing. They just act smart, stay out of the way, and they won't get hurt."

"What if—" Boon was suddenly interrupted by Lick leaping from Boon's side of the road and grabbing his horse's halter shank from the off side. The horse reared in surprise. Boon, who had been riding bareback, slid right off the backside and landed on his duff, the flashlight flying from his hands.

Lick pulled the horse down hard and swung him around.

The old man had jumped a second later and jerked the left rein of Valter's horse, sending him crashing heavily to the ground. Lick swung around and took Valter's horse from the old man. Both pursuers sat in the road, dazed.

"Yer guns, you nickel-plated Lewis and Clark wannabes!" ordered the old man. He was pointing the .30-30 at them. He levered a shell into the chamber, cocking it.

Valter dug his pistol out of the shoulder holster under his air-force-issue bomber jacket and tossed it in front of his feet.

"How 'bout you, Davy?"

"It's Dan, and sorry, mate. I don't have one."

"All right," said the old man. "Before I pierce your ears and blow your kneecaps off, I wanna know where your two buddies are."

"What!" said Boon, alarmed. "You're not going to murder us! Why, we're, I mean, these guys . . . I'm just—"

The old man fired the rifle. Valter jumped out of his skin and Boon broke wind. The shot echoed briefly, leaving everybody's ears ringing.

"They took the fork north out of Goat Creek," Boon hastily answered. "We're going to meet them all at Scotland if we don't find yew first, which I guess we did, so I'm not sure what the plans are now." Boon hesitated. "Maybe you could ask Leftenant Valter here."

"Yer ridin' two of our horses from the trap and that's Lewis's saddle. Does that mean they have the other horse?"

"Yessir," said Boon. "Bareback. I'm not sure if they're riding double or afoot by now—the

way that horse was actin' they're liable to . . ."
Boon noticed Valter glaring at him and shut up.

"Is that right, Hitler?" asked the old man of
Valter.

"Except we're going to get the girl, sooner or
later," Valter said. "And you hillbillies might get
caught in the middle. You don't know who
you're dealing with. Best thing you could do
right now is just turn her over to me and be on
your way. She's nothing to you. She's in serious
trouble and you two heroes are likely to get hurt
if this goes on much longer. If it's a matter of
money—"

"That's enough, mister," spoke Lick from the
shadows.

"The trouble with you Nazis," said the old
man, "is you don't have a sense of humor. Nor-
mally I'd be content just to leave you here, take
our horses and go—"

"That would be fine, mate. I'd be glad—"
interrupted Boon.

"But," continued the old man, "I think I'll
just take your manly footwear, too."

"Aw, Al," said Boon. "I just bought these
Whites at Anacabe's. Two hundred and fifty dollars! They still hurt my feet."

"Off with 'em, you whiners! But to show my
sensitivity, so's nobody can say we didn't treat
you with that genyoowine cowboy hospitality,
you can each keep your right shoe. How's that?"

"Mighty generous, ol' mate, many thanks," spoke the shivering Boon.

"Kiss my—" spat Valter.

"Now, now," cooed the old man. "Let's not get testy."

"C'mon, Al," said Lick. "Let's go."

"You'll be sorry," warned Valter to the backs of the disappearing cowboys. "You'll be sorry."

T.A. led their two horses across the sage a couple hundred yards back up the road behind Valter and Boon. The old man and Lick joined her with their fresh haul of guns and the two left shoes. All three mounted a saddled horse, with Lick leading the fourth horse.

"Let's head straight for Scotland," Al said. "It's closer than the ranch, and it'll get us to the main highway faster. I got a friend, Stone Roanhorse, lives up on the Goose Valley Indian Reservation south on 51. We can give him a call from the store, have him pick us up." Al looked back at T.A. "You ready to go, little lady? We got to get there before those desperadoes. What time is it, kid?"

"Quarter to eleven," answered Lick, squinting at his wristwatch. "That's Cowboy Standard Time."

"Shank of the mornin', lad," chimed the old man. "Let's make some tracks."

At an easy walk a horse can travel five miles an hour. It was nineteen miles from the horse exchange to Scotland. Thus, allowing for potty breaks and another campfire stop to warm up, it would take them at least four hours, maybe longer. After a couple of hours of riding and napping, Lick raised his hand. "Hold up!"

T.A. and the old man reined in their horses and looked down the road to see if they could see what Lick was looking at.

"Over there, to the north of the road, the other side of Mary's Creek." He pointed. "Sort of a glare or somethin' on the horizon. Like a fire maybe. I'm thinkin' maybe those other two banditos had to pull over and build a fire to warm up like we did. According to Boon, they had one horse between 'em. Ridin' double, bareback, specially on Torpedo, could be a hazardous journey. We need to check it out. I don't know what you think, Al, but my guess is they'll be up and movin' again pretty quick. If we get to the store and they come up on us before your Indian buddy arrives . . . well, there's liable to be a shoot-out. I don't want 'em behind our back. If we can steal Torpedo while they're nappin' we'd buy a little time."

"Now yer thinkin' like that grand Indian general Sitting Bull," commented the old man. "Better make our move now. We get any closer and the horses will whinny and give us away.

Lick, whyn't you sneak around behind 'em and catch ol' Torpedo if he's there. Then ride him back toward the road. Me and Teddie will swing wide around to the west, cross-country, and see you on the other side."

"Let me go steal the horse," said T.A.

"You couldn't," said Lick quickly.

"Why?" she said.

"Well, yer . . . I've got . . ." he stammered.

"What? Better shoes?" she asked defiantly.

"No. It's just that, I, uh . . ."

"He's an articulate bugger, ain't he," said the old man. "Our camp has been a literary desert since he showed up. He's been reading one book, the same one, since September. I try and tell him the classics to upgrade his learnin'. I've done the epic poems for him, 'The Open Book,' 'Oh, My, You're a Dandy for Nineteen Years Old,' 'The Little Brown Shack,' 'The Castration of the Strawberry Roan.' He only knows one poem, 'Reincarnation,' but he can't even say it right."

"I can, too!" blurted Lick.

"Do it," said the old man.

"Uh, um," Lick cleared his throat. "What hath reincarnation . . . what hath re-in-car-nation done, a cowpoke asked his friend. It starts when they lay you in a box beneath your rendered mound. I mean . . . beneath your life's tra-vails . . ." Lick took a breath.

"Enough!" said the old man, "A travesty!

Cease and desist! You are to the spoken word what smallpox was to the Indians! I'm here to tell ya, if history was left up to him, it would begin with his last paycheck. How he ever got a college degree is beyond me. Maybe you can buy 'em now."

Lick took offense. "With respect to your twilight years, I don't see what difference it makes to you."

"Just trying to add a page to your book of knowledge, kid. You are—" Suddenly Al stopped.

"What's wrong?" asked Lick.

"Whose horse are you holding?" asked the old man.

Lick looked down at his left hand, being a lefty, and noticed that it held the reins of T.A.'s horse, which stood behind him, T.A.-less. He looked back over his shoulder down the road and into the dark sagebrush and ravines on the west side. The old man followed his gaze.

"Well, bite my lip and twist my toe in a knot!" said the old man, disgusted. "Ya let her git away."

"Sometimes, Al, you get on my nerves."

20

December 4: Horse Thief

Teddie Arizona was heading cross the country toward the small glow of the pursuers' campfire. The going wasn't as rough as it could have been. The moon had gone down but the starlight was strong. The sagebrush stood out against the lighter-colored ground. She fell down a couple times going over the occasional embankment but soon was within hearing distance of the glow.

"Git some more wood, Pike, willya, please. I'm freezin'." Busby was huddled next to the fire with his arms around his knees.

"Git it yourself. I'm nappin' here, can't ya see?"

Hidden in a low swale less than fifty feet away, T.A. heard Busby get up and stomp around in the brush. She spied the other horse on the opposite side of the camp, tied to a big sage by the lead rope. She waited till Busby had kicked up a couple pieces of deadwood and had headed back toward the fire, then she made a wide circle and crept up on the tethered horse. He saw her, smelled her, and snorted. Twin puffs of steam rose from his nostrils.

"What's the matter, boy?" she heard Pike say. "What did you do to the horse?" he asked Busby.

"Nuthin'!" Busby answered. "Anyway, I really couldn't give a rat's bicep for the evil bustard. Maybe it's a mountain lion gonna chew his head off. Suit me."

"Aw, yer takin' it too hard. He's just not one of those horses that rides double. Wasn't his fault. He's snorty, that's all. I rode him okay."

"Yeah, and I walked. My feet are killin' me."

"Well, my tailbone's killin' me. He's got a boney ol' spine."

Teddie laid low till they quit talking, then approached the horse cautiously. He watched her as she fumbled the lead rope knot with cold stiff fingers. She jerked it. The sagebrush rattled, the knot came loose, the horse pulled back, and T.A. froze.

Pike and Busby both rose quickly and looked back toward the horse. Teddie Arizona stood sixty feet away. The firelight showed her features.

"Where you goin', Teddie?" said Pike.

She didn't speak.

"You know you can't get away. F. Rank's never gonna let up. If you come with me we can think up some story he'll believe. I'll help you.

Better me than Valter. If he catches you there's no tellin' what'll happen. I like you. We've been friends, haven't we? I don't mean you no harm but we've come to take you back, so let the horse go and wait here with me." He stepped toward her. "He's your husband—"

"No, he's not," she said. Suddenly it seemed important to her to tell the truth.

"Sure he is," responded Pike.

"Not for real, only for show."

"He tells everyone you're his wife. You live with him. You wear his ring. Looks like a marriage to me." Pike continued stepping toward her, slowly, cautiously.

"Not officially, Pike. It's just a business arrangement for the benefit of his parents."

"If you say so, but—"

"Stop!" she shouted.

But he didn't. He broke and ran right toward her. The horse pulled back, but she jerked hard on the lead rope, grabbed the halter, then grasped the mane just in front of the withers. Pike was ten feet away when she heaved herself up across the horse's back, swung her right leg over, and kicked him hard in the flanks!

Pike's hand grabbed her left leg just as the horse wheeled into him, planting his left front size 1 Diamond horseshoe on Pike's left ostrich-booted arch. The horse swung across in front of him and pushed off against the size 12 starting block, tearing Pike's grip loose from T.A.'s jeans and doing serious soft tissue damage to Pike's metatarsal supporting structure.

Pike vented a flume of colorful epithets, erupting like a vituperative Vesuvius, and dropped to the ground with a groan.

T.A. and Torpedo, the equine beast, galloped across the high desert. Torpedo was running away and T.A. was going with him. She held her right hand tight in his mane and squeezed him with her legs as he bounded, ducked, and dived through the sagebrush and washes. She was a good rider and he soon realized that.

When Torpedo began to tire, T.A. had a chance to look around. They'd been running in a northwesterly direction, getting farther from the road but still headed toward Scotland. Finally Torpedo slowed to a walk. He was still jittery, but she managed to pull him to a one-sided stop with the halter rope. She dismounted, then took a few moments to catch her breath and assess her situation.

"Good pony," she said, rubbing his face. She had a fleeting thought of Superman, her old horse back in Muskogee. She recalled his face the way one would picture the childhood face of a close sibling, now grown.

She continued to talk to Torpedo quietly and

scratch that special spot right in front of his eye. Torpedo eventually took a deep breath and gave himself to her.

"Okay," she said. "Let's go find the boys."

Teddie Arizona was a horse person. It is a gift. There are people who never touch a horse, but they have the gift within them. It's easy to spot those folks. Whether very young or big enough to be cautious, they are instantly at ease around the beast.

Even more remarkable is that the horse is at ease around them. It's a wonderful sight to see horses and horse people communicate. And it's agonizing to see those without the touch try and gain the horse's confidence.

I've known cowboys who weren't comfortable around horses. I've wanted to ease over to them and say, "Ya know, maybe you'd be better at farming or sellin' hog wire." But I hold my counsel. They will concede soon enough.

T.A. was a horse person. She could ride, and that night she became "one" with Torpedo.

Teddie Arizona bore east on the big dark brown gelding they called Torpedo. When she finally hit the road again, she dismounted and quieted the horse, listening for the hoofbeats of Lick and the old man. She kicked into an easy lope and found them waiting a mile down the road for her arrival.

"Whoa, baby!" said Lick with concern. "You all right?"

T.A.'s eyes narrowed. "Yeah. You didn't think I'd make it?"

"No, it's not . . . I mean, yeah, I knew you could do it. I's just worried, that's all."

"Yeah, I'm sorry. I didn't mean to bark at you. I did okay. Ol' Torpedo here got me outta the storm, although we had a little scuffle. I made it out by the skin of my teeth." T.A. took a deep breath. "Good as Torpedo is, how 'bout givin' me back my horse."

She dismounted and stretched, then re-mounted the saddled horse that Lick had been leading.

"Should we just let these unsaddled horses go, Al?" proposed Lick. "They'd head right back Pandora's Thumb, wouldn't they?"

"I'm thinkin' we best hold on to them," said the old man. "The Third Reich might be closer behind us than we think. The horses would follow the road and would be easy to catch. I'd say we take 'em all the way to Scotland."

"If you say so," conceded Lick. "But Valter—is that his name?—" He looked at T.A. She nodded. "Valter and Boon are barefoot at least ten miles back and the other two carbuncles will probably wait where they are. But yer right, Al, I don't know that for sure, so we'd better keep the horses."

"Okay, then," said the old man. "Let's get goin'. Couldn't be more than five miles to go. You ready, Teddie?"

"Ready," she said.

21

December 4: Before Dawn

"My foot is about froze," moaned Boon.

"Keep walking," instructed Valter.

"I won't. I don't care if you don't pay me. I need to build a fire and toast my toes. You keep this up and you'll get frostbit. I've had it—frost-bite, I mean—and I know. It ain't fun."

"Listen, Boon. I've got a deal for you. You give me your boot and I'll keep walking. You can build yourself a fire here and wait till morning, or till springtime, for all I care. We're this close and I'm not about to let her make an escape."

Boon said, "My best guess is that we're still twelve miles from Scotland, which is the direction they're headed as best we can tell. That's a lot of walking in minus four degrees centigrade."

"I've got no time to argue with you, Boon. I'll give you fifty dollars for your boot."

"These are . . . this is a White's lace-up packer. Cost me an arm and a leg. How do I know that I'll ever see you again?"

"Boon, I'm outta patience and you're outta time. Pull that boot off before I have to pry the precious lace-up packer off your foot. And I will likely damage the ankle in the process. Permanently."

Boon tried to see Valter's features in the thin starlight.

"Do you doubt me?" Valter said with menace.

Boon waited a split second too long. Valter lashed out with his bare right foot and caught Boon a solid kick in the stomach. Boon went down with a whoomp and a whimper.

Valter unlaced the calf-high boot that covered the hapless Boon's right lower leg. It took a lot of unlacing.

"Build your fire, lightweight. Maybe the Salvation Army will be doing maneuvers in the area and they'll find you."

Boon tried to look up but his stomach was aching.

Valter stood up and tested the boot. "Thanks," he said. "It's been swell." He turned and began jogging up the road in the direction of Scotland.

Paul Valter had intense concentration, a fanatical dedication to authority, a high pain threshold, and a boss with the integrity of a magpie. At 0530 hours he trotted into the firelight of Busby and Pike's camp wearing two right shoes.

"On your feet, doughboys!" ordered Valter. "We're movin' out!"

"Oh, man," whined Busby, "you scared the bee pollen outta me! Where you been? The horses—where are they? And Boon?"

Valter ignored Busby. He spoke to Pike. "They ambushed us. Stole our horses . . . and our boots."

Pike and Busby looked at Valter's feet. He was wearing a size 9½ Sierra Club–approved right flat-heeled hiking boot with mud-and-snow-grip tread on his right foot and Boon's size 12½ calf-high lace-up right White's packer boot with 1½-inch riding heel on his left foot. He stood at a slight angle.

"I figger they're headed out to the highway, either to catch a ride or to call from that store Boon says is there in Scotland," Valter continued. "They think they left us stranded, but if we dogtrot all the way, we might catch 'em. If not, at least we'll be able to call and get a vehicle."

"How far is it to the highway?" asked Busby.

"Shouldn't be more than five miles," answered Valter, dismissing the subject of the missing horses. "I've been counting my steps and I've come approximately twenty-one miles in six hours. Boon said it was twelve miles from the Goat Creek fork."

"How many steps was it?" asked Busby, more amazed than curious.

"I can cover four feet per step if I'm striding, and I was striding. Thus, at my striding pace, that equals thirteen hundred steps per mile. I have twenty-one rocks in my pocket, one for each mile. I was at seven hundred forty-two when I cut off the road to get you." Valter looked around at their little camp. "I take it they must've snuck around you. I could see your fire a mile out."

"Didn't take much sneakin'," said Busby. "They stole our horse."

Pike cut his eyes at Busby. Valter saw the look.

"What happened?" he asked.

"They came in, caught us nappin', and took the horse. We had him staked out at the edge of the light," Pike explained.

"Was the girl with them?"

Pike glanced at Busby, then spoke. "Yeah, she was. It was a sorry horse, anyway."

"Well, you're an impressive bunch," said Valter with disdain. "I would've had better luck with a troop of baboons."

"I see you're afoot," said Pike in a neutral tone of voice. "I assume Boon is barefoot."

Valter looked at him coldly. "Put out your fire and let's go, I don't want to lose her."

In five minutes the three of them were trotting north along the frozen dirt-and-gravel road toward Scotland. The ground was too hard for them to leave a track, but it would have been a puzzle for a tracker if they had. Was it three men, one of them with two right feet, or four men, two jogging and two hopping on one foot, or two one-legged men, or a three-man sack race? Well, the possibilities are endless. Suffice it to say they left no track.

22

December 4: The Good Guys Arrive at Scotland

At 6:30 a.m. Lick, the old man, and Teddie Arizona rode up on the Scotland Stage Stop store

and bar. The predawn light cast murky shadows on this cold winter morning.

The proprietor, Fusion Byfull, was standing on the step of his rickety mobile home behind the store, shaking the dew off his lily. His diurnal hangover pounded in his head. A weak light shone through the open door behind him.

Fusion was typical of the pioneers on the Western outback: self-sufficient, suspicious, and not groomed in the social graces. These traits would have qualified him to be a prison guard, an NBA All-Star, or a clerk at the Motor Vehicle Bureau, but he preferred the isolation, loneliness, and lack of human interaction offered at the corner of Going and Gone on Highway 51, long miles either way from a traffic light or tanning salon.

"Fusion, you sorry excuse for a fellow human," greeted the ever-congenial old man. "Have you got the coffee on?"

"You boys are up early," said Fusion. "I assume something's wrong. I don't know why I feel that, but three cowboys"—he stopped and counted—"leadin' two ponies, ridin' outta the dark up to my busy intersection, seems to portend some dastardly deed in progress."

"You are absolutely right," said the old man. "An astute observation from someone so overestimated, yet . . . you have not answered the million-dollar question."

"Which is?" asked Fusion.

"The coffee, my slovenly friend."

While Fusion opened up the store, got the propane heater kicked on, and the coffee going, Lick unsaddled the horses and put them in a small old board corral amongst the disintegrating outbuildings. Fusion kept a few bales of hay, for which he charged ten dollars a bale, and a frozen water tank. Lick broke the ice in the tank and threw a bale in the corral for the tired horses. The old man scrounged up some scraps for his dogs. They watered with the horses.

Once the animals were taken care of, the old man tried to call Stone Roanhorse, who lived down the road in the burg called Shanghai on the Goose Valley Indian Reservation.

Fusion had the phone number of the tribal police office.

"You have reached the Goose Valley Indian Reservation Tribal Police Headquarters. Chief Highfoot is not here. But he may be at any time. If this is, uh, an emergency, please call Sherrill at three seven four two. She may be home then. You may leave a message, but I don't think anyone will, uh, hear it for a while because the answering machine is CRACKLE, SNAP, BEEP, DIAL TONE!"

The old man dialed the number. "Sherrill?" he said. "This is Al up here calling from Scotland store and I'm tryin' to find Stone. You wouldn't know his whereabouts, would ya?"

"Well, uh, I know he went to Glenns Ferry to a roping but that was three weeks ago, and I, uh, saw him at the reservation office, last week, I think. He was trying to fix his car. I think he must have done it because I, uh, saw him last night at his cousin's on my way home from work."

"I wonder if he's still there?"

"Just a minute and I'll look," she said and clunked the phone down on the night table. **Tick tock tick tock.** "It's still dark down here but the, uh, yard light is working and it looks like his pickup is still there."

"You reckon you could go get him? I'd sure be beholding. I need him bad and there's some money in it for him."

"Yeah, well, sure, I dunno, maybe, I guess, uh, because he could sure use the money, specially the part he owes me. You wanna hold the phone?"

"Yup. I do," said the old man.

Twelve minutes later, the old man heard a door slam through the receiver. Footsteps, clanking . . . "This is you, Al?"

"Stone!" answered the old man. "Sure glad you came to the phone. I hope I didn't get you outta anything."

"No. No, I was just visiting at my cousin's house. We were talking and having a glass of wine and, uh, playing cards."

"You reckon you could come and pick me up at Scotland store? I'd gas up your tank."

"Okay, I think I can come. We've just got a few more hands and she'll win. Then I can come. Where are you staying?" asked Stone.

"I'm calling from Fusion's right now. I'll ask him to make you some scrambled eggs if you get here for breakfast. I'll even buy."

"Humm, let me go see if the car'll start. If it won't, maybe I can borrow Sherrill's. You want to hold the phone?"

"Yeah. You go see if the car'll start and come tell me."

Fifteen minutes went by.

"Al, is that you?"

"Yup."

"This is Sherrill. Stone left already. He says you're buying him some breakfast."

"That's right."

"Maybe you could bring a box of donuts or something when you come down. That would, uh, sure be good."

"I'll see what I can do, you little dumplin'."

"See you soon, Al."

"Okay," he said, and hung up.

"My goodness," said Teddie Arizona, who had witnessed the extended phone call. "So, is he coming to pick us up?"

"Yup. But it's gonna cost us."

23

December 4: Confrontation at the Scotland Store

The dim morning preview of sunrise lit the sky weakly. Inside the snug little store at the Scotland Stage Stop, the smell of coffee filled the air. Fusion had made a mess of eggs, toast, hash browns, and sausage.

The old man ate sparingly while Teddie Arizona ate like a horse.

"Just out for a morning ride?" asked Fusion, his curiosity getting the better of him.

"Yup," replied the old man. "This lady here is a Hollywood movie star and she's scouting locations for a new Western movie starring an older experienced cowboy such as myself who is attacked by aliens trying to rustle cattle for cloning experiments. She plans on using locals for bit parts as well and I told her about you. How you had acting experience, and all." The old man winked conspiratorially at Fusion.

"Oh, sure," said Fusion taking the hint, "I've done lots of it."

The old man continued, "I know, and I've suggested she could model the aliens after you—take out yer front plate and show her that face you make where you look like a shark."

Fusion realized he should have left well enough alone. He furrowed his brow. "More coffee, anyone?"

Lick was staring out the window.

"Sit down and eat something, Lick," encouraged T.A. "Mr. Roanhorse will be here soon. It's already been nearly an hour since Al called him. You might as well eat while you can."

Lick was buzzing from exhaustion and caffeine. He paced back and forth from the stove to the window that looked out toward the road, nervously patting Valter's automatic pistol, which was still tucked into his belt.

"Like tryin' to talk to a post, ma'am," opined the old man. "He never listened to me none, either. I believe he could live on Vienna sausage and macaroni. Me, I prefer filet mignon with champagne, maybe some duck pâté like I had in France. I developed a discriminating palate over there in the big war. Lick here never had no chance to have a cultured tongue."

"I don't remember you havin' duck pâté, or duck soup, or duck nothin' in Elko. Seems like we mostly had Jack Daniel's and beernuts," answered Lick, a little surly. "Y'all don't worry 'bout me. I just wanna get outta here. You sure this Roanhorse is comin'?"

"He's comin'," said the old man. "He's comin'."

Suddenly a rock crashed through the front window. T.A. stood up, pushing the table back against the old man, who went over backwards. Lick raised the automatic pistol toward the front door, but before he could squeeze off a shot the door behind him exploded open, hitting him in the back.

Valter and Pike rushed into the room. "Stay right where you are," shouted Valter. "I don't want to see a muscle move or an eyelid blink."

T.A. froze, hugging herself, and spied Busby slipping in the back door. Fusion slowly set down his coffee and put his hands in the air. The old man was still sitting in the upended chair, flat on his back with his legs up in the air. He rolled his head straight back, smashing his hat, and looked up at Valter.

"You," ordered Valter, looking at Fusion, "I need some strong cord. Right now, or you're gonna be trying to get bloodstains outta the floor for the next twenty years."

Fusion looked at the old man and shrugged. "I'll see what I can find. Prob'ly baler twine is the best I got . . . but it's out by the hay pile."

"Go with him, Busby," Valter ordered. Busby followed Fusion outside.

"Soon as we get 'em tied up, I'm gonna call Mr. Pantaker," Valter told Pike. "Then we'll make some arrangements to transport her back to Vegas."

"You coward," T.A. spat. "You suck up to him and he takes advantage of everyone around him. Even you. I've heard him talk about you. Yeah, you. Calls you Robot Head. Thinks you're dumb." She wheeled on Pike. "And you, Pike. You think he enjoys your company. Huh! Bozo the Hayseed. He got you those ostrich boots 'cause he thinks you're a dodo bird."

"That's enough, Mrs. Pantaker," said Valter.

"Listen, you thick-headed screwloose. He's just using you the same way he's using me." T.A. paused, a little embarrassed. "I don't mean to cuss you guys. You both always treated me okay. I just had to get away. I've got no life there. It's like I'm a prisoner. I've got nothing he wants. He's just mad 'cause I can't stand him."

"Mrs. Pantaker, we're not gonna hurt you," said Valter. "He said to bring you back safe and sounds and that's what I'm doin'. I hope you don't do anything to make us accidentally hurt you. That's the last thing anybody'd want. Why"—he paused and slowly looked down at Lick and the old man—"I'd sooner cut off these two cowboys' fingers one at a time with a dull pruning tool, or pin their ears to the bar with tenpenny nails. I'd torture them within an inch of their life before I'd harm a hair on your head."

Lick's ears pricked up. For the duration of their hair-raising escapade, he'd been laboring under the impression that these men were going to kill T.A. if they caught her. The slippery thought slid by his wrinkled brow that maybe there was more to the story than met the eye.

Fusion and Busby came back in the store, stomping their feet and shivering.

"I can't believe we spent the night out there," said Busby. "It's cold enough to freeze antifreeze."

"Pike," ordered Valter, "tie her to the chair. Make her comfortable, but I don't want her to escape again. Then tie the old man to his chair. What about you, cowpoke?" he said, tapping his pistol barrel against the back of Lick's head. "You gonna give me any trouble?"

Lick didn't speak.

After T.A. and the old man were secured to their respective chairs and scooted up to the table, Valter enlisted Pike's aid to hog-tie Lick facedown on the floor, hands behind his back and legs flexed, boot heels in the air.

"Do I need to tie you?" Valter asked Fusion.

"Not if you want some breakfast," he answered.

Valter went to the wall phone behind the counter and dialed. Shortly he began, "Mr. Pan-

taker . . . Valter here. . . . Yes, we've got her right
here. . . . North of Elko. In Idaho, I think. . . .
No. No town. A place they call Scotland. . . . In
a store in Scotland. . . . No. No police involved. . . . Nope, none. . . . Nobody knows.
You're the first contact we've made since we discovered her whereabouts. . . . Yes, she's fine.
Seems to be. . . . Not very happy, no. . . . Yes, I
guess you could. I'd have to hold the telephone
up to her ear. . . . Well, we had to restrain her.
She's quite disturbed."

"Disturbed?" screamed T.A. "You sicko
lizardskin dog pile! You ain't seen nuthin'! Your
scam is—"

Valter held the phone out toward her. She
lunged at him, rising up, the chair coming with
her, shouting, "F. Rank, I know what you and
that wildlife weirdo are up to—"

Pike grasped her shoulders from behind and
pushed her back down. Valter pressed the receiver into her ear. "You'll never see your money
again," she continued. "I've got it hid. . . . You
cancel the hunt, you get your— You do and you
can kiss your cash— You wouldn't dare! Once
the press gets— Even if you stop me— Tell 'em,
I'll go to jail. . . . You can't—"

The blood drained from her face as she listened to his threats. Her eyes opened wide as the
air seemed to go out of her.

F. Rank's voice was audible, though his words were not discernible to the others in the room. He was ranting. Finally the phone went silent.

"You'll never get away with it F. Rank," T.A. said quietly, but by then Valter had removed the receiver from her face.

Valter spoke into the phone. "Yes. Yes, I understand. . . . Oh, yeah, well, the helicopter had mechanical problems so we're going to find alternative means. . . . If all goes well, we might be back as soon as this evening. . . . No. I don't think that will be necessary. Surely Pike and I will be able to do the job. . . . Right. We wouldn't think of it."

Valter listened for a while. Then he said, "The nearest airport would probably be Mountain Home or Elko. A helicopter could pick us up right here, I guess. . . . Listen, let me get Busby on this. He can call from here and see about arranging another helicopter. Soon as we have a plan I'll call you right back. Maybe within the hour. . . . Okay, yessir. Within the hour."

Valter hung up the wall phone. "Busby, get on this phone and see if you can find a helicopter to pick us up right here." He turned to T.A. "And you, little lady—"

"You know what he's gonna do, Valter? Money or not, he's going on with the hunt," she said. "I'm the monkey wrench in the works. Are you gonna do his dirty work? Look at me! I'm not going away and I'm not giving in. Are you willing to have me on your conscience?"

"You have made your own nest, my dear," answered Valter blandly. "I know nothing of any hunts or your theft. I only know that your husband wants you at his side and I intend to deliver you . . . any way I have to. If you can't act civilized, then I shall simply carry you, chair and all, into the washroom, where you will at least be out of earshot. I have no intention of putting up with your insubordination."

"Pike?" she said, looking over her shoulder at him, her eyes welling with tears.

Pike remained mute.

Surprising everyone, the back-door handle turned and Boon came mincing in barefoot. They heard the sound of a pickup driving off.

"Morning, men," he said cheerily.

"Mornin', Davy," said the old man cheerily. "Where ya been?"

"It's Dan, Al," said Boon. "Well, I hitched a ride into town with Jaybird. I'd built a little fire and spent the night toasting my bare feet. He picked me up and brought me here. Took about thirty minutes. I was gonna have him take me on in to Mountain Home, but I saw the horses in back and reckoned you blokes might need some help."

"You're a little late," said Valter. "We've already got it handled. We're making arrangements for transportation right now."

Boon walked around behind the bar and poured himself a water glass full of Wild Turkey. He saw the pile of weapons that Valter had taken from the captives. Valter's two automatic pistols, Pike's snub-nosed .38 revolver, the old man's .22 pistol, and the .30-.30 lever-action rifle lay on a table behind the bar. Boon surreptitiously slid one of the automatics into his waistband in the middle of his back.

"Anyone else care for a toddy?" he asked.

"I thought you'd never ask!" answered the old man, brightly. "Turkey," then, realizing his position, he added, "with a straw."

Boon ignored him and walked back behind the counter where Fusion was cooking. Valter was leaning against the counter, his back to the stove. He had stuck Pike's pistol in his waistband and was sipping his coffee.

"You got any coffee?" Boon asked Fusion.

"You know, I could use a toddy," piped up Busby.

"Busby," ordered an irritated Valter, "get on that phone. Find us a way outta here!"

Boon slipped up behind Valter, pulled the automatic out from the small of his back, and laid the point of the cool barrel against the right side of Valter's neck.

"I'd like my boot back . . . but very slowly," he said.

There are some words that can freeze a crowd, like "I just dropped my two-million-dollar diamond" or "Somebody just cut the cheese," but "I'd like my boot back" usually would not have that effect. However, under the circumstances, it struck a chord.

Everyone in the room immediately looked at Valter's feet. Valter spun hard to the left, and Boon pulled the trigger! The shot blew off Valter's right earlobe and he stumbled, tripping over his own feet—actually, over Boon's size 12½ boot—and fell, banging his head on the edge of the counter and knocking himself out cold. T.A., seeing her opportunity, pushed her chair back hard against Pike and toppled him flat.

Busby froze. Lick, still on his belly, didn't have a good vantage point, so he contented himself with staying put.

Boon leaned over the bar and looked down at the prone Valter, his face covered in blood and a pistol lying by his open hand. He looked quickly up at Busby, then down at Pike. "Don't be plotting any sudden moves, mates," said Boon. He picked up Valter's gun. "Busby," said Boon, "would you be kind enough to untie Lick and Al?" Busby quickly complied.

"And you, Mister Pike," he addressed Pike, who was flat on his back with T.A., still strapped to her chair like an ejected pilot, square on top of his chest, "I'd be grateful if you could just lie there for a moment until I have the whole situation under control."

Valter began to stir.

Lick was free. He stood up, stretching his shoulders.

"Lick," said Boon, "slide around behind the counter and collect those guns. And maybe you could aim one at Mr. Pike while I have a short talk with the head of security.

"Let's get a move on, Busby. Al probably doesn't enjoy bein' trussed up like a gladiator's calf."

"I dang sure don't, Dan—Davy," said the old man. "Although, next time I am captured and tied up, I believe I will request the reclining position. How ya doin', little darlin'?" he asked T.A. "Maybe we can get you unlashed, too."

Lick stood at Pike's head with a pistol while Al cut the baler-twine bonds tying T.A. to the chair. Freed, finally, she stood rubbing her wrists, then stepped over Pike and deliberately stepped on his ankle, the same foot the horse had mashed earlier that morning. He cried out! He tried to sit up, but Lick put a boot on his shoulder and pressed him back down.

"Stay put," ordered Lick. "Al, we need a plan here. What say we disable these characters and leave 'em here?"

"I might have somethin' to say about that," said Fusion.

"On second thought, Fusion, you might not," said Lick.

"Yer right. I've got nothing to add."

"T.A.," said Lick, "go get some more of that baler twine. We'll tie these boys up."

As they began to organize the retribution, Boon squatted down in front of Valter, who was now sitting up on the floor.

"I've got a bone to pick with you, ol' sod. It's not good etiquette to steal a bloke's only boot. By the way"—he turned back to the old man— "I hope you didn't throw away me other boot."

The old man shrugged. "Sorry," he said.

"Aw, fulminating wombat poop," Boon cursed. "I guess I had it comin' for signing up with this bunch of dunnybuckets. You could have shot me like I'm planning to do with this stiff-necked boot thief." Then, addressing Valter, he said, "Git my boot off and make it quick. Pike, what size of boot you wear?"

"Twelve," answered Pike.

"Perfect. Peel off them ostrich hides and let me try them on."

While Boon was reshoeing, T.A. returned

with enough twine to bale two hundred acres. She and the old man hog-tied Pike and Busby facedown.

"Your turn," said the old man to Valter. "Assume the position. T.A., darlin', grab one of those pistolas and point it at Hitler's head while I lace him up."

"It will be my pleasure," she replied.

Lick took Boon's elbow and led him out back where they could talk in private.

"Boon," said Lick, "we're leavin' here. We're supposed to have a ride comin'. You're welcome to come with us. You sure saved our skins. It looked like we, or at least the girl, was a goner."

"Let me ask you a question," said Boon. "Why don't you just let them take her back to her husband? They're goin' to a mighty lot of trouble to get her back. If these blokes are as serious as they appear, you and Al are just diggin' yourself a big 'ole."

Lick considered. "I don't think she'd be safe in their hands. I believe she's in mortal danger." Lick stopped short of mentioning that T.A. had admitted robbing her husband. "I couldn't sleep good if I just turned her over to these gunsels. Too many guns. Too much backup. She's kinda outnumbered and I never did like an unfair fight. I might cut and run when she's in the clear, but not now . . . not yet."

"Well, shades of 'enry Lawson, I'd be glad to have friends like you," said Boon.

"Well, you do," Lick answered. "What are you gonna do now?"

"I had all night to think about it and if Fusion's car is runnin', he and I can head down to Elko or up to Boise. We'll call Lewis. He can come pick up the horses. You three can go wherever you want. We can leave the three stooges here."

Fusion's car was running but Al had an amendment to the plan.

Before he could introduce the motion, Stone Roanhorse showed up in an official tribal police supercab pickup. He and the old man visited while Fusion cooked him some scrambled eggs.

"Those biscuits sure smell good," said Busby from his position on the floor. "It's been since noon yesterday that I've eaten. Could you spare a bite?"

"Sorry, lad," answered the old man. "You fell in with the wrong crowd. You should never bet a Nazi and a helicopter against two cowboys and a woman on the run." He turned toward Stone. "How are those biscuits, Stone?"

"Man, I sure was hungry. I didn't know it. I drank a beer and ate some Pop-Tarts. I didn't have time to put them in the, uh, microwave." He paused to chew and swallow. "Do you think he has some more bacon?"

"Anything you want," offered the old man. "Where did you find that snappy-looking vehicle?"

"It was parked outside the office on my way through town, so I thought I would just siphon a little gas, but then I noticed that the key was in it and decided, well, I could just, uh, borrow it and have it back real quick. It saved me some time."

"Stone, my good friend, while yer eating, we're gonna borry your truck to make a short delivery. We shouldn't be more'n half an hour," said the old man. He turned to Fusion. "Innkeeper, whatever the gentleman wants, please put it on our tab."

"I think a beer would be just right, thank you," said Stone politely.

24

December 4: Wickahoney Desert

Lick and Al loaded Busby, Valter, and Pike, hands tied behind their backs and tied to each other, into the back of the Goose Valley tribal police pickup with Al's two dogs.

"Just lie flat," ordered Al. "Eyes to the sky."

"What does it matter?" grumbled Busby. "I can't see anything anyway, with this tape over my eyes."

Lick and the old man jumped in the front of the truck and hit Highway 51. They drove north for less than a mile and turned back west onto a rough gravel road. It got worse the farther they went. They finally stopped after twenty minutes.

"This should be fine," said the old man. "We can strand them here and give ourselves a chance to escape."

"Where are we?" asked Lick.

"South of Wickahoney. You were actually there once when we worked cows this fall. Except we came in a different way. C'mon. Let's not keep these criminals waiting."

The old man dropped the tailgate.

"All right, gents, slide out here and stand at attention," he instructed.

"Couldn't we work out a compromise?" whined Busby. "You could just leave us at Scotland and we'd promise not to follow you anymore."

The old man poked Valter with a finger. Valter hissed like a Gila monster.

"I don't think your companion would honor our agreement," chuckled the old man. "Nope. Short of killing you or necking you to a mountain lion, this is the best I can do without having a weekend to think about it."

"What are you going to do to us?" Busby whimpered.

"Shut up, Busby," growled Valter. "Show some spine." He turned toward the old man, "You can shoot us all. You can leave us maimed and bleeding. You can pull our fingernails out one at a time and pour hot wax in our ears. You can carve your names in our raw and whiplashed backs. You can stick a screwdriver up our nose, and we will never, and I mean, NEVER, quit your trail—"

"A screwdriver up our nose!" screamed Busby. "You raving maniac! Have you gone completely mad! Pike! Are you gonna let this boot camp refugee speak for you? Do you really want to die out here of exposure? The coyotes tearing your stringy muscles from the bone and gnawing off your gnarled toes?" Busby's chest was heaving from his grand oration.

Pike remained silent.

"Are you done, helicopter pilot?" asked the old man sympathetically. "That was really good. I'm sorry it has so little effect on your partners in crime. Is there any message we could get to your loved ones if you don't crawl out of the wilderness in forty days or so?"

"Forty days!" Busby cried, then his shoulders sagged and he sighed.

"I guess not," remarked the old man. "Lick, bring the duct tape." He tore off a piece of the roll Lick handed him.

"I'm gonna take this personal," snarled Valter.

"I was hoping you would," said the old man, who then placed the strip over Valter's mouth.

Lick stood behind and held them as the old man did his adhesive artwork. It only took a few minutes.

The old man addressed Busby. "I take it you are a man of your word. Is that true?"

"Yes," said Busby with a hint of hope.

"Then I will give you the Pop-Tart from the front seat in return for a promise."

"What is it?"

"Lick has convinced me that we shouldn't leave you out here without some help. So, if you promise not to open your eyes until you count to three hundred backwards, then I will take off your blindfold. Yours, and yours only. You will be the periscope of this hideous insectoid mutant. Plus . . . you will get the Pop-Tart."

"It's a deal," said Busby, a little disappointed.

"Get the truck started, Lick."

The old man opened the Pop-Tart and fed it to Busby a bite at a time.

"Are you ready?" asked the old man.

"For what?" asked Busby.

"To not open your eyes."

"Oh. Yes, I'm ready."

The old man peeled the duct tape off the pilot's eyes. He walked backwards to the pickup. "I'm watching you," he said. "One false move, one wink or eyelash flutter and back goes the blindfold. You may begin counting."

"Two hundred ninety-seven, two hundred ninety-six, two hundred ninety-five . . ."

The pickup door slammed and off they drove down the bumpy road.

"Which way are they headed?" asked Valter.

"Two hundred ninety, two hundred eighty-nine, two hun—"

"You lily-livered pipsqueak! You couldn't have shined shoes in my outfit!" mumbled Valter through his taped mouth. It sounded more like a rap singer dropped in a well. He tried to kick Busby, but couldn't figure out how.

Lick looked back at the trussed trio. The old man had been creative, yet practical. Pike still wore his duct tape blindfold. A wide strip ran over the top of his head and down over his ears like studio microphones. "To protect them from the cold," the old man had said. Pike's arms had been duct-taped at the wrists behind his back His right arm was taped to Valter's left arm above the elbow and his right leg was taped at the ankle to Valter's left ankle.

Valter wore a duct tape ear-covering strip like Pike, a blindfold, and a mouth strip. His right arm was taped above the elbow to Busby's left elbow and his right ankle was taped to Busby's left ankle.

Busby wore duct tape earmuffs. Lick had fashioned them over his ears in cauliflower-like wads. He was neither blindfolded nor gagged.

It would be a job for Houdini to unpeel any of the bindings with teeth or fingers. Pike was in his stocking feet, Valter wore his own right Red Wing hiker boot, and Busby wore his tennis shoes. They could walk, in a three-man-sack-race fashion.

They were less than ten miles from Highway 51 in both directions and the weather was about two degrees centigrade. It wouldn't be their best day, but they would make it back to civilization.

25

December 4: Goose Valley

Lick had convinced Stone Roanhorse to let him drive. T.A. sat in the front seat next to him, with

Al and Stone in the back. They were all feeling fine after a brunch of two six-packs.

"I'm here to tell you, if ol' Dan hadn't showed up I'd'uve had to whip 'em all myself," commented the old man.

Lick laughed so loud he surprised himself. "Al, did anyone ever tell you that you are crazy as a bedbug? You're so full of hot air, it's a wonder you don't float off!"

"What? You don't think I coulda took those three bums? Why, all that time I was layin' on my back, I was thinkin'. One time back in Hunter, Kansas, I took on six big . . ." And the stories went on, each leading to another and another as the road stretched out before them.

There was no need to explain to Stone Roanhorse the reason they were being threatened by three other white men. Or why they needed a ride, or even when, where, or what was going on. Stone thought of chaotic situations, inconvenient laws, cars that don't start, gunfights, missed loops, empty wine bottles, electric bills, and incarcerations as safety cones in the potholes of life. Sometimes you swerve to miss 'em and sometimes you don't. A friend needs yer help, you help 'im.

After an hour they reached the outskirts of the town of Shanghai, Nevada, on the Goose Valley Indian Reservation.

"Better slow down," advised Stone. "They'll give you a ticket."

"Even in the company car?" asked Lick.

"The tribal police are having a fund drive to get Sherrill a new computer. Everybody's eligible."

26

December 4: Morning in Las Vegas

Allura heard water running in the bathroom. She lay back on the big pillow and took a long pull on her Diet Coke. She tucked the satin sheet up around her armpits and snuggled down.

F. Rank Pantaker stepped out of the bathroom with a towel around his waist.

"I believe you're losing weight, hon," said Allura.

"My ulcer is actin' up. I haven't been able to eat like I should."

"I can tell you're worried. Is it something you can talk about? Maybe I could help."

"No, I don't think so. It's just not fair, though. I work so hard . . ."

"I know you do, sugar. You work all the time," she consoled.

"I have this great plan with millions at stake and that no-good—" he stopped.

"Go ahead, sweetie. You know you can tell me. Get it off your mind. You'll feel better."

"I . . ."

"Is it personal? Something about us?" she asked.

"No. We're fine. Matter of fact, you're real fine. I don't know why my wife couldn't be as . . . as . . ."

"Helpful? Loving? Attentive? Thoughtful? Caring?" she said.

"Loyal," he said.

"You know I'm loyal. You could tell me anything—anything—and you know I'd never tell a soul. So come back here and lie down and tell Doctor Allura all about it. You'll feel so much better."

F. Rank Pantaker, complainer and potentially heinous criminal, studied Allura Valura. She had dark hair, olive skin, and the angular curves and hard body of a dedicated weight lifter. She could bench-press F. Rank, if it ever came to that. But right now he had this child's need to unburden himself. Release a little pressure before his ulcer exploded.

Allura had no ulterior motives other than to keep him happy and herself well paid. She worked at the casino's fitness center in the basement. Her specialty was massages, but she was delighted to be flexible to F. Rank's needs.

F. Rank lay back on the pillow and exhaled a big sigh. Allura started rubbing his forehead and the bridge of his nose.

"A large quantity of money was stolen from me little over a week ago. Right from under my nose. They figured out the combination to my safe, took the money, and ran."

Allura repeated the combination of his safe to herself. It was written on a piece of paper taped to his bottom right-hand desk drawer. She'd found it the second day she'd made a professional call to his office.

"Do you know the identity of the thief?"

"I'd rather not say," he answered. "But you know her."

"Humm," she hummed. "Go on."

"They're gonna have her back this evening if all goes well. But it doesn't stop my acid stomach. Those ribs and jalapeños we had last night are still comin' up."

"Well, if she's been caught, why are you still worried?"

"Fear of the unknown," explained F. Rank. "Does she have the money hid? Will I have to force her to tell me? Will she fess up before I have to strap her to the front of a speeding train and run her through a flock of migrating geese? Will I have to throw her in a cage full of mouse-addled rattlesnakes armed only with a slingshot? Or leave her in a walk-in cooler wearing nothing but a baseball cap and eye shadow until she begs me for a sweater? Give her truth serum by slow IV drip? Or . . . simply turn her over to our collection people, who know methods of eliciting confessions far beyond my simple imagination?

"And what am I going to do with the body, or her, after she tells me?" His eyes narrowed. "She just better give me the money," he said, adopting a low, chilly voice, "or she'll wind up as cat food. The chunky kind."

He turned to Allura and, for a two-second eternity, she saw the malevolence that lurked inside F. Rank's mind. And she knew that beneath his spoiled, self-centered, sometimes charming surface lay a devious, amoral, bloodred, uncooked center.

"So," he said, "that's why I'm chuggin' Maalox and walkin' the floor."

Allura pondered these things in her heart: baseball cap, plus addled rattler, speeding train, slingshot, and money equals Maalox. "I see" was all she said.

Oh, what a tangled web we weave
When the ill-equipped commence to thieve

And find out she is un-naive
And has her own tricks up her sleeve.
APOLOGIES TO SIR WALTER

27

December 4: Sherrill's House

Stone Roanhorse directed Lick to the parking lot behind the small police station. A Native American wearing jeans and a black down coat with a chief's badge came out the door to greet them.

"Boy, Stone, I'm glad you made it back. We had a horse get out down there by the Lake Road and Sam Will almost hit him with his pickup. It's a good thing he missed or we'd have to go get him and I sure hate to see a good horse run over." Translation: **Stone, tribal law allows me to flay your back with a skinning knife and stake you over an ant bed until the ants climb out through your navel for stealing my horse substitute. It's a good thing your sister is married to my mother's brother or I would have done a deep coup on the top of your head.**

"I have brought visitors bearing gifts," said

Stone. "You remember our friend Al from Scotland. He's brought his children." This ancient diversion of including family, practiced by indigenous tribesmen since the time of Chief Disappearing Hanky, assured that a formal acknowledgment of this important relationship would be respected. And, it gave the old man some time to think.

Al climbed out of the back and stretched his limbs. "How do," he said to the officer. Then he reached into the bed of the pickup and handed out two unopened cases of beer. He set them on the gravel. Then he retrieved a box of powdered-sugar donuts from the backseat. "For Sherrill," he said.

The officer appraised the offering, then looked back at Stone, who added, "And all three of his family would like to donate a hundred dollars to the computer fund drive"—he let the offer settle a moment—"plus another fifty for the Police Chief's Discretionary Fund."

"That would be very generous," said the Chief. "There is no need."

"I insist," said Stone.

"So do I," said the old man, who had fifteen cents in his pocket.

"If you insist," conceded the Chief, "but it's not really necessary." He picked up both cases of beer and walked over to load them in his personal vehicle.

Lick leaned out of the pickup window and said quietly to Stone, "Al and I don't have three hundred and fifty dollars. I've got maybe seventy, but Al doesn't have a dime on him."

"That is technically correct," added the old man.

"No problem, my friends," said Stone. "Please give me fifty and I'll take care of the rest."

Inside the station Stone spoke in the Shoshone tongue to a handsome thirtyish brown-skinned woman with beautiful black hair who was standing behind a waist-high check-in counter. It was Sherrill. He then introduced her to Lick and Teddie, explaining they were the old man's children.

"I am pleased to meet you. You, uh, look very much alike. It's nice to see white families staying with their parents past weaning. Al, you must be, uh, very proud to have them back home."

"Yes," replied Al, paternally. "It makes a dad happy to see his two kids appreciating how much their ol' pa has done to make their life a bed of roses. I've given them the best years of my life and they've made me proud. Junior here has gone to college to become a doctor and did missionary work in Africa, then worked on reestablishing the giant baboon population in Belgium.

"Sis, she was a nurse among the native

population in the wilds of the Amazon. Saved the lives of millions before she was struck with the Bamboo Plague, which caused her to become allergic to mercury and forced her to give up her medical career for lack of bein' able to take a temperature. Now she does volunteer work among the homeless in Scottsdale, Arizona."

T.A. listened with amazement, Lick with resignation, and Stone even raised an eyebrow at the mention of the giant baboons.

"Nice to meet you," offered T.A. "We thank you for helping Stone give us a ride."

Stone was magnanimous. "Sherrill," he said, "do you reckon we could find them a place to stay for a while?"

A while? A while, be it cowboy time or Indian time, meant only "Not forever." No one gave it a second thought.

"Al, your children can stay at my house if they want," Sherrill said. "I have an extra bedroom. Your son can sleep on the couch."

"And you can stay with me," Stone told the old man. "I'm living alone right now. Your dogs can keep us company."

Stone borrowed Sherrill's car and took "the children" to her house. Lick lay down on the couch. The radio was playing quiet country music. He fell asleep with his boots on. Teddy Arizona disappeared into the back bedroom.

28

December 5: Surprise

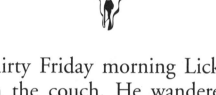

At eight-thirty Friday morning Lick rose from his bed on the couch. He wandered into the kitchen and peered out the window. The sun was shining weakly in a clear sky, but the wind had picked up. It looked pretty from indoors.

He drank a glass of water, ate a cold hot dog out of the fridge, and walked back to the bathroom, passing the closed doors of the bedrooms. **She's still sleeping,** he thought.

The bathroom was a converted utility room with a washer and dryer. Lick stood over the commode and raised bubbles in the murky water. He was in the process of making a circle around the bowl when he heard a short exclamation. He looked back over his shoulder, one hand on the towel rack and the other holding his light saber.

Teddie Arizona stood, one foot out of the shower, pulling a towel from the rack on the wall. He saw it all, like a radar gun zaps a passing car. A moment frozen eternally in time, a full-color centerfold memory to be recalled over and over as the ages pass until it's airbrushed into a fuzzy feeling.

Lick quickly looked back to the wall, stood straight, and tried to clamp it off and put it back, all the while getting at least one good doctor's-office beakerful on everything, including his pants.

"Uh, gosh, T.A., I thought you were still in the sack. The door was closed, I, uh . . . oh, shoot." He looked down at his zipper. "I'll get . . . I'll get out of here."

He walked to the door, assiduously avoiding looking at her. He grasped the door handle and pulled. It was locked. He punched the little lock button and tried again. No luck. He jerked a couple times and he felt the doorknob bend. He banged his shoulder against the door. It sounded solid.

T.A. watched from behind the shower curtain.

"Maybe I can take the handle off and . . . or, I could crawl out the window. I think I could get through it." Lick looked back over his shoulder to see what she was thinking. She'd wrapped the towel around her but still clung to the shower curtain.

"Why don't you just sit down over there and stare at the wall and let me find a robe or something," T.A. said. She had come into the bathroom earlier wearing an oversized tee shirt she'd found in Sherrill's closet. Her suitcases and backpack with all her clothing, makeup, pills, and personal totems were history. The only thing she'd managed to salvage during her escape was a small fanny pack—and the ten thousand dollars, which she'd divided into four envelopes and stuffed into her knee-high socks just before heading out into the sagebrush the day before. She rummaged around inside the dryer and came up empty. She also made a serious attempt to open the bathroom door.

Lick sat on the toilet lid and stared at the opaque bathroom window, which faced south. His mind kept flashing back and forth between the white of the window and the vision of Teddie Arizona, one foot out of the shower, like Venus stepping out of the seashell, like Lady Godiva with one foot in the stirrup, like all of womanhood displaying her plumage for the randy ruffed grouses, leering lechers, gasping gropers, and captivated caught-unaware cowboys to see.

It is, in fact, what it's all about, Alfie.

It can start wars. It can end wars. It can make you forget about wars. It can start fires, family feuds, fast-food chains, empires,

pilgrimages, hives, indigestion, heartbreak, heartache, ventricular fibrillation, and the collapse of kingdoms.

Lick had seen Victoria's secret.

Lick was suddenly a teenager again. Yearning, longing, lusting for . . . he didn't know what to call it back when he was seventeen, but it swarmed his whole consciousness like a black west Texas dust storm. He was in the middle of a long fall, he couldn't see down, he couldn't see up. He felt like he had a washtub in his chest, the white noise was loud in his ears. The vision of her was flashing in front of his eyes like a film on fast-forward. He was close to the edge.

She touched him on the shoulder. He jumped!

"You okay?" she asked.

"Whoa," he breathed.

"You, uh, you didn't answer me. I asked if you had any ideas. About getting the door open, I mean. Twice. You were kind of in a trance. Are you all right?"

He sat there a moment, then spoke. "Yeah, I'm fine. I just . . . You, uh, caught me off guard."

"I caught **you** off guard!"

"Well," he began, "this may be the perfect time to—"

"You're right," she breathed. She stepped in front of him still wrapped in the towel, took his face in her hands, and kissed him deeply.

What he'd intended to say was, ". . . the perfect time to discuss the next step." Would they drive down to Las Vegas? If so, would they want to leave Al here? Did she have any contacts at the casino? Did she have any money with her? But those thoughts were quickly obliterated.

For a fraction of a second, he was startled. Then he softened his lips to be more yielding. He raised his arms and put a hand on either side of her waist. He could feel the pliant skin beneath the damp towel, and the hip bones, his thumbs lightly pressing against her ribs.

She was an insistent kisser. An aggressive, pervasive, controlling kisser. Her lips and tongue were like a hearty handshake, a leg pressed between yours on a slow dance, a persistent breast in a crowded elevator, like riding a horse bareback. Physical, athletic, moist, and devouring.

At last T.A. broke the kiss and drew back.

With his hands still resting on her waist, Lick looked up at her, somewhat dazed. He made a couple of glottal catches. "Oh, my," he said.

"Gosh, Lick. I . . . it's just that . . . I didn't mean to do that," she said. Droplets of water clung to the strands of her hair. She had an odd look on her face. She shook her head, smiling.

Sunlight through the semitransparent window lent a luminous halo to her countenance. He thought she looked like a painting.

She stepped back, still holding his face in her hands. He raised his palms to her upper arms and tried to pull her to him. She kissed him quickly and firmly, then drew back. Her expression had changed.

"I would like to get dressed now," she said, not unkindly, "if that's all right with you."

He looked at her quizzically. **All right with me?** he thought. **I'm locked and loaded. I've cocked the hammer. I've armed the torpedoes. The coordinates are fixed, my basal ganglia have called for an air strike, the boulder is teetering on the edge of the cliff, the countdown has begun: Three, two, one . . .**

"Sorry," she said, "I shouldn't have . . . I, I just don't want to start anything. My mind is mixed up."

Wasn't it just last night—no, two nights ago—they were snuggling like octopi on the high desert floor? Wasn't there actually a laying on of hands? Lick couldn't remember exactly, but his fingertips did. They remembered the precise contours of the terrain the way a foot remembers a shoe.

Start anything? his mind asked. **Fast as you can pull the trigger!** screamed the army of testosterone coursing through his arteries, lighting his body up like a Christmas tree. It took him a second to gain some semblance of control.

"No, I guess not," he said, deflating.

She stood up in front of him and tightened the towel that formed a delightful decolletage, pink from the hot shower. She gave him a weak smile and turned to the sink and mirror.

Lick set about escaping through the bathroom window, which didn't take as long as he would have thought. There was no screen and three cinder blocks were stacked outside below the window. He was not the first one to get locked in Sherrill's bathroom.

He went around and opened the bathroom door. Just a little, so as not to intrude on T.A.'s privacy.

29

December 5: Another Romantic Moment

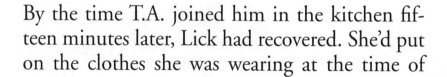

By the time T.A. joined him in the kitchen fifteen minutes later, Lick had recovered. She'd put on the clothes she was wearing at the time of their escape twenty-four hours before: jeans, the socks containing her cash, and the black knit tank top under a long-sleeved light blue denim shirt.

They both sat at the table with coffee and sandwiches.

"We need to talk," she said.

Lick didn't respond.

T.A. studied her stocking feet. How could she explain that in another life she would have jumped his bones like a frenzied goat! That beyond the physical attraction, she was beginning to admire his character? But something else was boiling inside her, making her skin crawl and the back of her throat constrict. It had to do with the confusing mix of her amorality, upbringing, and uncertainty about the future, a growing awakening that she might care for this cowboy—and fear of Ponce. Ponce de Crayon, the man she'd once considered a genuine hero, a shining light of integrity, an inspiration for her to rise above selfishness and serve the common good.

Ponce de Crayon, whose pedestal had crumbled like a machine-made taco shell when she'd learned of the scheme he'd cooked up with F. Rank.

T.A.'s first and only personal introduction to Ponce de Crayon had been through a fund-raiser at Ponce Park three months after she had moved to Las Vegas and in with F. Rank.

Ponce's personal cause célèbre was the preservation of endangered species. That night he hosted two hundred and fifty people, the froth on the Las Vegas latte, at his large wildlife park and refuge.

It was there he maintained and propagated spotted owls, black rhinos, Sumatran rhinos, snow leopards, pandas, Malaysian tigers, grizzly bears, black panthers, albino koalas, pinto polar bears, and a covey of bald eagles, just out of patriotism, or so Ponce said. (You never knew when a modern medicine man or tribal chief would need some authentic accessories for his breechclout or headdress.)

F. Rank, accompanied by T.A., responded to the VIP invitation. They were treated to a luxurious buffet of exotic foods and addressed by the host himself. Ponce was dressed like an English army colonel serving in India during the 1857 uprising, complete with white helmet, knee-high boots, jodhpurs, and a riding crop. He spoke with a crusty English accent, calling everybody "old chap" and "Corporal."

Ponce spoke like Moses from the Mount, like Kennedy from the presidential pulpit, like Billy Joe McAllister from the Tallahachee Bridge! He was capable of cutting through the glitz, the chrome and caviar, to the humanity that exists inside most human hearts, though not necessarily the cynical, rhetoric-proof, stainless-steel tickers that beat within the breasts of the Las Vegas elite. However, he did reach our heroine, whose heart happened to be empty at the time.

"During the Boer War," he was saying, "and my campaign in Inja, we shot tigers and elephants, lions, zebra, and termite mounds with a blasé disregard for the fragility of their place in the ecosystem. Serving on Her Majesty's ship the **Prince Reggie** during those heady days after our furious naval battle with Peru, we torpedoed sperm whales and took turns harpooning penguins. We would rope cute little dolphins and ski behind them.

"I shudder at the damage we've done, but"— his voice lowered—"times have changed. We now must act responsibly if we are to maintain and restore nature's balance. It is what I, in my own humble way, am trying to do here at Ponce Park.

"You may ask yourself what you can do. You may think to yourself, 'I don't have time to feed and water elephants, pick ticks out of rhino ears, take care of orphaned koalas, or care for condor chicklets. All I have is money. If there was only some way I could make a significant contribution to this monumental effort to save the planet, I would, just so I could sleep better at night knowing I made a difference.'

"Fear not, brave souls, you wonderful, compassionate, generous, anthropomorphic, zoophiles! By contributing to Ponce Park's Wildlife Outreach and Panda Fund, you can assure these magnificent animals their rightful place in the tapestry of life. Where they may exist in harmony with nature and outlive every man, woman, and child of you on this old mudball we call Earth, which, as we all agree, belongs to them as well as you and me and, yes, even the Royal Family.

"Pass the plate," Ponce spoke off microphone. "God save the Queen!" he boomed, and raised his wineglass in salute.

Ponce de Crayon had enchanted Teddie Arizona. She'd sat in rapt attention. His words were a 24-carat oasis in a desert of rhinestone materialism. She'd just begun to adjust to the dazzle of being part of the Lifestyles of the Las Vegas Rich and Famous. Her lack of faith in mankind was causing her to wonder if it was all as shallow as it seemed. It was the first time in many moons she'd experienced a moment of wrenching introspection. Like a quick shot to the heart, a kick in the solar plexus, it made her gasp out loud! Years of practice allowed her to slam the emotional door shut quickly, but not before one slippery tear escaped down her cheek.

After Ponce's altar-call conclusion and thank-yous to all who ponied up twenty-five hundred dollars per ticket to attend the fund-raiser, T.A. took a stroll through the Big Cat House. F. Rank remained at the bar with friends.

The Big Cat House held several of the jungle beasts that performed with Ponce in his spectacular magic act at Pharaoh's Casino. His act was the premier show in Las Vegas. Unlike zoos where a lifelike habitat was built to show off wild animals in their "natural" surroundings, Ponce Park kept the beasts in large, clean, airy cages. The climate-controlled buildings smelled of disinfectant and, faintly, of cat pee.

T.A. took particular interest in a large tiger. She watched the magnificent creature as he circled the perimeter. He plodded methodically, his massive paws padding silently on the cement floor. He never looked at her.

Watching the caged beast, T.A. whiffed an unpleasant analogy to her devil's bargain with F. Rank. She curled her nose.

"He thinks it's suppertime," said a voice behind her.

T.A. whirled around and found a guard in uniform watching her. "Does he do this all the time?" she asked, referring to the tiger's pacing.

"No," replied the guard. "Sometimes he forgets."

Me, too, she thought. **Me, too.**

Of the many things that drove T.A. to finally

pull the plug on her circumstances, the crushing disappointment of Ponce's betrayal had been the last straw. She'd never expected much from F. Rank, but Ponce had lifted her up. When he pooped in the buckwheat she fell hard. In the style of **The Flight of the Phoenix, Walking Tall,** and **Rocky III,** she picked herself up, picked up the five million, and set out to trash their party.

* * *

"Do you still think you can stop this big-game hunt?" Lick asked, breaking her reverie.

"Shoot, Lick, I don't know. It just seems like somebody ought to do something. After all, these bottom-feeders are going to kill endangered species. But I don't have any idea where to begin."

"I don't see why you can't just hold the money and call the police. 'Specially if all you want is to stop the hunt. Tell 'em everything. Give the money back," suggested Lick. "I think the law would understand."

"I can't go to the police," she said, almost whispering.

"What?" he said, not hearing.

"I can't go to the police," she said again, looking up at his face.

He studied her a moment. "If it's the money—"

"It's not," she interrupted. "It's more than that. There's a warrant out for my arrest." T.A. summed up the complicated details of the warrant and F. Rank's hold on her.

"Oh," he said as the confession sank in. "Well, how 'bout you just offer to give the money back to your husband, maybe in return for cancelling the hunt? You think they'd go for that?"

"No," she said dejectedly. "He made that perfectly clear on the phone back at Scotland. The hunt is going on, money or not."

"Yeah, but as long as you have it, you have some bargaining power, right?"

"I don't think they're in any mood to bargain. Right now I think he'd probably have me killed. I mean, I think he's capable of that. And I'm real certain Ponce de Crayon is."

"Why **did** you take the money? To spend it, to hoard it?" asked Lick.

"No, not really. It was more personal. I wanted to hurt F. Rank for treating me like a . . . well, you know, like what I was, a kept woman. And Ponce—I wanted to inflict some revenge on him for sucking all of us gullible animal lovers into his game. I guess I justified it in my mind by saying that it was to stop that horrible hunt. But it didn't work."

She stared out the kitchen window at the gray sky of northern Nevada and shivered.

"This is a mess," said Lick. He put some more milk into his coffee and stirred it. "Speakin' of messes, I should apologize for the . . . the bathroom deal. I just barged in—"

She held her hand up, shushing him.

"Last night, two nights ago, I mean, out there on the trail in the dark, it was just a spontaneous— I needed . . ." She hesitated.

"Me?" he asked. "Or just—"

She raised her hand again. "Don't say that. Don't go there. I didn't need 'just anybody.' But it was more than I'm prepared to deal with today. You and Al trusted me when all I've done is not tell you the whole truth, lead you on, use you. You've put yourselves in danger. Most normal people would have called the police, or a mental institution. If it hadn't been for y'all, I might be . . . I don't even want to think about what might have happened. The only feeling I should be allowed to have for you is gratitude. I'm not deserving of your kindness. Just know that I am truly grateful and I feel as rotten as . . . as . . . Ponce's shriveled-up heart."

Again, Lick was at a loss for words. "Wuddn't nuthin'," he said.

"And," she said, standing up as if to make a speech, "before you get in any deeper, I'd like to get Mr. Roanhorse to take me to the next town where I can get a car and you and Al can head back to the ranch. That's my plan." She looked at him.

"Then you go to Las Vegas and try to stop the hunt by yourself," Lick stated flatly.

"That wouldn't be any concern of yours," she said.

"And I never see you again," he said.

She shrugged.

He stood up, took her hand, and led her into the living room. T.A. watched as he took a blanket and two throw pillows off the couch and spread them on the rug in the sunny spot. He pulled her down.

"What is this?" she asked.

"A picnic," he replied.

She lay facedown.

Resting on his knees beside her, Lick started rubbing her shoulders. She closed her eyes. He slid her sleeves down and stroked and massaged her neck and arms. Then he turned her over. T.A. went limp.

Lick sat back and stripped himself to the waist. His forehead was damp from the exertion. He moved from her shoulders to her neck, forehead, and the bridge of her nose, then touched her lips with his fingertips. She moaned with pleasure but kept her eyes closed. He straddled her and lowered his lips to hers. When they touched it was electric. Very lightly he ran his tongue along her lower lip, then he delicately slid it in and explored the edge of her teeth.

Her tongue tentatively touched his, backed off, returned. Their lips pressed together gently. He lowered himself till their bodies just touched. He swayed over her, then slowly dropped down to his elbows, palms flat on the floor. She wiggled her chest into his. They kissed for several minutes . . . no hands.

Lick lifted himself back up to a kneeling position. T.A. opened her eyes and looked into his. He held her gaze for a moment, then hungrily let his eyes devour her body. Those steel gray eyes, malamute silver dollars under the partially closed eyelids. Creamy chest, blushing pink. The left shoulder strap of her black tank top had slid down, exposing the rise of a breast like a porcelain moon peaking out from behind a cloud.

Her belly showed between her tank top and jeans. As she breathed, the skin of her stomach rose and fell against the waistband of her jeans, opening and closing the entrance to paradise. Her left leg lay straight, her right leg slightly cocked. She smelled like cookie dough in a warm kitchen. It took his breath away.

Whew! Stop the world and let me off! Does life get any better than this? Anticipation is

half the joy, so said Captain Ahab. Lick has just eaten half a truffle, ridden the first four seconds, it's Christmas Eve, July Third, the day before Election Day, it's your first at bat, a new deal in gin, and that moment in time when you think all things are possible. It is true that most do not even have time to watch the moon rise, much less savor that split second between "And the winner is . . ." and "somebody else!" Lick was no different.

He gently ran a finger up under her tank top. On its own, it slowly inched its way north to Kilimanjaro. Just as it took its first step up the incline, her hand covered his and stopped the ascent.

Lick looked at her.

She shook her head.

Son of a scrofulous, wool-slippin', miscreant sludge scraper! May the magma of the *Titanic* bury me in six foot of Styrofoam peanuts up to my throbbing temples and put me out of my misery! My rocket has burst into a thousand pieces and lit the sky like a prison riot on "Just Say No" day! Shoot, chute, shute, ship, shap, sugar shack, shoop, stoop, and droop and jam it all to hail!

Aw, fudge.

Lick backed his hand out of the wishing well and she took it in hers. From her vulnerable position, that is, mouth-watering as barbecued ribs on a paper plate, she said, "Lick, for reasons that are too complicated for me to understand, I am no longer going to, uh . . . I have decided to, uh . . . Until I marry, I'm going to abstain from, you know, going all the way . . . so to speak."

Her composure receded like hot caramel sliding down the sides of a pecan praline sundae. It left her naked. She squeezed hot tears out of her eyes, looked up at him, and said with real anguish, "I am so sick of myself." She sobbed and covered her face with her hands.

Her emotional outburst was too much for Lick's simple testosterone-soaked brain to absorb. He felt like he'd showed up at a sword fight with a spatula.

His expectations deflated. They were not alone.

30
December 5: Sherrill and T.A. Talk

When Sherrill came home from work at 5:15 p.m., Lick was asleep on the couch and Teddie Arizona was browsing through the limited magazine collection: **American Hunter, Range** magazine, **Cosmo,** and the **Native American Political Journal**.

Sherrill unloaded her jacket and scarf and brought the groceries into the kitchen: potatoes, canned corn, and bread. "Hi, Teddie Arizona," she said. "I've still got some deer meat from that big doe my uncle killed down by the, uh, lake drainage last week. It should still be good. I've had it in the freezer. Do you like deer meat?"

"I ate a lot of it when I was a kid," T.A. answered. "It was okay."

"Did you come from deer country?" Sherrill asked.

"Eastern Oklahoma. Lots of whitetail."

"Oklahoma," mused Sherrill. "There are many

Native Americans living in Oklahoma. I, uh, have been there for an Indian Police Training course. They seem like very rich Indians in Oklahoma."

"It's the oil," observed T.A.

The two of them began fixing supper.

"Your brother is a handsome man," Sherrill said. "He seems to be part Mexican, yet you have hair the color of dry grass, I mean with shadows and streaks that pick up the sunlight. Did you have the same father?"

T.A. had a nimble mind. She changed the subject. "Did you go to college to become a police officer?"

"No," answered Sherrill, aware that her inquiry about Lick had been averted. "I went to, uh, the University of Nevada at Reno. I wanted to become a lawyer. I studied for three years but it is very hard. Then my mother fell and broke her hip so I, uh, came home."

"You have such beautiful eyes," said T.A. admiringly, "and your hair just shines."

"Like a crow's wing," said Sherrill, smiling. "It is what my mother calls me, Crow's Wing."

In fact, Sherrill was quite attractive. She was five foot five, with a round face, long, jet-black hair, deep dark brown eyes, and skin the color of peanut butter. At twenty-eight years old, she worked very hard to keep from getting overweight.

"So, you are visiting your father?"

"What?" asked T.A.

"Your father. Al," said Sherrill.

"Oh, yes. For just a while. I, uh, Dad and me, and Lick, . . . my brother, we, us, I mean, the family had some trouble—car trouble, I mean!" she blurted. "It was good of Mr. Roanhorse to give us a lift and of you to let us stop over. We'll be moving on soon."

Sherrill listened. **White people are no different than Indians when they lie,** she thought. **And it is not my business.**

"Wake your brother," she said, "and we can eat."

31

December 5: Three Stranded Bandits on Highway 51, Six Miles North of Scotland

Meanwhile, back at the corner of the Road to Nowhere and Highway 51, in the land of the star-nosed mole, the one-eyed man is king.

"Try to look casual," instructed Busby.

Hollywood Cratchet was returning home from her bimonthly visit to the Goose Valley Reservation Medical Clinic. She was sipping a diet pop and smoking a Kool filter. The Scotland store flashed by on her right at 72 mph. At the dirt road turnoff to Wickahoney, Juniper Mountain, and points west, she noticed a crowd beside the road. She slowed to 20 mph and passed them.

The crowd turned out to be small. Three, to be exact. Standing side by side like soldiers, but more shiny, like tinfoil statues. Was it some kind of practical joke? Nobody waved, but she had the feeling they'd been beseeching her. Although she didn't hear anything because the window was up and she was listening to Charlie Daniels at the top of his lungs, the feeling was strong enough to make her turn around, point south, and go back.

They were a strange-looking group. She slipped the compact .32 revolver out of her purse and rolled down the driver's side window of her Oldsmobile sedan.

The figure on the right was babbling. She couldn't understand him, he was talking so fast. Now he was trying to drag his trussed companions toward her car.

"No farther, Tin Man," she said, and cocked the hammer on the .32.

"This isn't the way it looks, miss," said

Busby, the only one who could see, hear, and speak simultaneously. "We're respectable businessmen. I'm a pilot and these gentlemen are in the employ of a large corporation that does a lot of work with the poor. Our plane crashed and we've been walking for several hours and we'd like a ride to someplace where we can rent a car. Or at least I would."

"I see," said Hollywood. "Are you seriously injured? It's hard to tell the way you're taped. I can take you to the Goose Valley clinic. It's on the rez, back down the road here. It's not far."

"No, nobody's hurt, not seriously," answered Busby. "But we'd really—"

"Were your companions blinded in the crash?" she asked in growing wonder. "Do you have multiple skin grafts on your legs and arms? Why does the big one have no shoes? Are they hearing impaired? You appear to be in need of some help but I'm not sure what I can do."

"A ride. Like I said, just a ride where we can call home and be on our way," Busby said. "And cut us loose, of course. This tape is killin' me."

"Boys," said Hollywood, still sitting in her car, "I can see you're in a bind and even though I'm a kindhearted soul, I fear that from your appearance there is more to your story than you're telling me. But I can't leave you here by the roadside in this condition. So I'll make you this offer: I'll give you all a ride to Mountain Home. I think the three of you will fit snugly in my back-seat. But . . . for my own safety I must leave you tied as you are."

"But miss, I don't know if I can make it to Mountain Home," whined Busby.

"Oh, you'll make it fine. Just a little tight is all," she reassured him.

"No. It's not that, it's just that we've been tied up since early this morning and I've got to go."

"I said I'd take you to Mountain Home," she said.

"No," he continued, "go, as in, to the bath-room."

"Oh," she said.

She looked into the agonized eyes of Busby, derailed helicopter pilot. There was no way she was going to let any of them get free. One could easily overpower her, release the others, steal her car, attack her, and leave her for the buzzards. However, the caregiver in her insisted that she help them any way she could.

"I refuse to untie you. But . . . I guess I could help facilitate the relief of your discomfort."

Busby's expression was one of pain, then concession. "If you please."

Hollywood got out of the car and stood before them.

"Maybe you'd like to turn with your backs to

the road? For modesty's sake," she suggested. They complied.

She stood behind Busby and placed the pistol in his back with her left hand. "Know what this is?" she asked.

"Yes," Busby gasped. "I won't do anything. I mean, I won't try any tricks. Now, please."

It wasn't easy with one hand. Getting the zipper down went pretty well but then she hesitated. Busby cringed, waiting for her to start digging around, but when she unsnapped his fly he realized that she had a better idea. Hollywood grasped his waistband from the back and slid his pants and jockey briefs down below his knees. Busby made several umphs and grunts until he finally broke free with a giant "Ooooooh."

"Anybody else?" asked Hollywood.

The blindfolded, earmuffed Pike spoke for the first time. "I'd appreciate it, ma'am. Although I wish it were under different circumstances."

"Well," she said, "a cowboy in the crowd. Let's see what I can do." She stood behind him and repeated the process. When Mr. Groundhog saw daylight, Hollywood said, "There you are, Studly."

While Busby and Pike were watering the lillies, Hollywood walked around in front of Valter, whose eyes, ears, and mouth were all taped.

"Why," she asked to anyone who was listening, "is this gentleman's mouth taped? It seems an extreme thing to do, unless, of course, he has a terrible injury to his lip. Does anyone object to my cutting the tape off his mouth?"

No one said a word. Matter of fact, neither was paying her any attention. They were in sweet relief.

Hollywood stepped over to her car and removed a Leatherman pocketknife from her glove box. After twisting and turning it several times in the waning twilight, she extracted a pair of tiny scissors from its innards. Then, as carefully as she could, she cut and peeled the tape from Valter's eyes and mouth. He blinked his eyes in the light.

"Can I help you?" she asked.

It was all Valter could do to remain civil. His intricate plan for Busby's slow, tortured demise was all that kept him going on the Wickahoney Death March. That, and how he would deal with the old man who had humiliated him so. Not to mention that buffoon Boon and the cowboy.

Right now he would like to do exactly what Hollywood was afraid they would do, but he was losing time. The girl was getting away. Sweet talk and cooperation were the best course. Ingratiating himself for the cause, he said, "If you don't mind, madam. If you are a nurse, then I hold your profession next to Godliness. I was in the military, wounded, and in the hands of your Sisters of Nightingale. You relieved my pain and suffering, and once again, you have come to my aid and I am grateful. In the name of the United States, the Army Nursing Corps, and the Marines, I place myself in your hands."

"That was inspiring, General, very inspiring. Alas, I still cannot untie you, but I'll do what I can to make you comfortable."

They heard a car whiz by on the highway, a screech of brakes, and the whine of transmission going too fast in reverse. A small four-door sedan parked across the road from them. A young Japanese couple got out and began taking pictures.

The taped trio was still in full flush, standing at parade rest, their blinding white buttocks in a tidy line like six shrunken heads on a cannibal's mantel. Hollywood stood to the side as an art instructor might when lecturing a class on the importance of asymmetry.

"What is it, honey?" asked the Japanese woman in her native language.

"It appears to be a folklore display by the natives," her husband informed her, continuing to focus his telescopic lens and snap. "I read about them at the Cowboy's Store in Elko."

"Should we pay them?" she asked.

Hollywood yelled at them to "git your scrawny little butts back in your scrawny little car and git the dadgum heckfire outta there before I duct-tape you to the hood of my car and run it through the Robowash!"

Although "scrawny," "duct-tape," and "heckfire" weren't in their vocabulary, "git" was. Kyoto and Saki hit the road.

Following the Olympic Synchronized Micturation, Hollywood did her best to pull the men's pants back up, but it wasn't smooth sailing. Not able or willing to negotiate the protrusions, she refused to get any more intimately involved and just left them at half mast.

"But you're a nurse," whined Busby, whose depth finder was chilly.

"No," she said. "I just do the accounting at the rez medical clinic. Do you want a ride or not?"

Hollywood helped them load in the back of her car. They sat humbly like three large angler fish on the bottom of the ocean. She covered each of their laps with a plastic grocery bag she found on the floorboard.

An hour or so later they were driving into the streetlights of Mountain Home, Idaho.

Hollywood pulled into the parking lot of the Mountain Home police station and shut off the car.

Valter spoke. "Ma'am, it would be just fine if you took us back to a car lot. Let us out, maybe cut our bonds. We'd be glad to pay you for your trouble."

Hollywood looked over into the backseat at her companions. "I could, but in the interest of the Ten Most Wanted victims' rights groups everywhere, I think it best that I leave you in the hands of a professional."

32

December 5: Lick and Sherrill Get Better Acquainted

In the dark of the night, Lick felt a finger on his lips. He'd been sleeping soundly on the couch and Teddie Arizona had been starring in his dream. In spite of the cold shower he'd taken after supper, their afternoon tryst was now replaying on the big screen behind his eyes.

They were in a meadow on a mattress. "Come into my arms, bonnie Jean" was playing softly. She lay before him, but the parts of her he ached to see had been airbrushed out, even in the shower scene, which cut in and out of the meadow, flickering fuzzily by in slow motion.

Lick began rising like a boogie board in the surf. Teddie Arizona's hair was floating. She was in a halo of bubbles. They were belly to belly and surfacing into a bright blue sky. He was about to explode out of his dream when suddenly he woke, confused.

The finger on his lips reached up and brushed across his eyelids, reclosing them. Then the hand slid down to his naked chest and started exploring. He lay still, as still as he could, as the light-footed fingers tracked across his body, peeling back the comforter.

CONTACT!

A welder's shower of sparks flew off the back of his eyes! The nearly full moon lit the room. Before him was a black-haired mermaid wrapped in an incandescent sarong, her tresses reflected in the watery moonlight.

She knelt and leaned forward till her skin was pressing against him. With her free left hand she began rubbing his right ear, the lobe, the helix, the conch. She ran her fingers under his neck and caressed his taut muscles. She tipped his head toward her and pressed the underside of her neck softly on his lips.

Lick involuntarily kissed her skin. She

moved her neck and chest and chin and cheek
and face and mouth over his quivering lips and
smooth moustache. She purred like a mountain
lion, rubbing and stretching and pushing against
him. She tasted like ginger and fudge. She felt
like velvet and smelled like liquid smoke.

Just about the time Lick thought he could no
longer stand the intensity, Sherrill licked his ear
and whispered, "Follow me."

33

December 6: The Morning After

The sun rose the next morning to see what was
going to happen at Sherrill's house. Sherrill had
to be at work by nine. She woke without the
alarm at six-thirty sharp. Lick's leg was touching
hers. He was breathing shallowly. His hair
smelled like sagebrush. It was a familiar aroma
on the high desert.

She slid from contact with him and stood by
the bed. **Men,** she thought. **Will I ever find a
good one?** She pulled a robe on over her naked
body and silently walked into the bathroom.

In the shower she soaked in the hot stream and relived the night. **He was good,** she remembered. **The second time was even better**. She scrubbed, shampooed her long hair, rinsed off, and stepped out onto the throw rug. Her body was steaming in the cool room.

Standing in front of the mirror, she could see herself from the waist up. "You're good, too," she said aloud, and smiled. "I could fall in love with me!"

The old man gave a quick knock on the front door and walked right in. It was eight-fifteen in the morning. There was a pale blue sky and a skiff of snow on the fields. Wind had plastered the white stuff to the west side of the fence posts.

The old man's racket stomping snow off his boots woke Lick from his boar's nest on the sofa, where he had retreated shortly after Sherrill had arisen.

"Good morning, Al," said Sherrill, stepping out of the kitchen to greet him. "Would you like some oatmeal? I put venison in it."

"Very authentic, my little Cherokee maiden," Al answered expansively. "Don't mind if I do!"

T.A. heard him arrive and came out of her

bedroom looking freshly scrubbed and ready for a new day.

"Good morning, children!" announced the old man, pleased with his invention of their new family arrangement.

"Hello, Daddy," T.A. said. "Did you sleep well?"

"Just fine, honey. And how about you, my faithful son?" the old man said, looking over at Lick. "And how did rodeo's answer to Minnie Pearl and Boxcar Willie spend the night? In sweet repose, I hope."

Lick lay under the wadded up blanket. He glanced at T.A. Did she know that he'd spent the night with Sherrill? Did he look guilty? Did he have any reason to feel guilty? Was there really anything between him and T.A.? After all, he justified, she'd spurned his advances last night.

T.A. waited for Lick to say something. He lay dumb as a post, with his hair stickin' up sideways and a bare foot pokin' out from under the blanket. He was looking at her with a strange expression, kinda hangdog . . . like a puppy that has pooped on the carpet.

Strange, she thought, looking at him. **I don't get it. Maybe he's embarrassed because he tried to follow his carnal instincts last night and I stopped him.** It irritated her slightly.

She glanced at Sherrill, who was radiant and was looking at Lick with a gleam in her eye. A fuzzy picture filtered into T.A.'s mind. She looked again at Lick, who was smiling lamely back at Sherrill.

No. It can't be, thought T.A. **What's wrong with me? I don't have time to think about this. I need to focus! I need a serious plan to save my life and, for sure, it would be a lot less complicated if Lick wasn't tuggin' on my** . . . Her mind started to say "heart," but her nerves said "elastic."

T.A. turned quickly away from Lick. "Looks like Brother's not quite ready to rise and shine."

Sherrill held her counsel. She knew all wasn't as it seemed, but as long as the platonic ruse was kept up, she would be the willing beneficiary.

Teddie Arizona was running on adrenaline. Complicating the fight-or-flight electrical charges sparking across her synapses was a smokestackful of emotions about a man she hardly knew. The high whistle of sex could be heard above the rumble of the steam engine. It was distracting.

Lick, college-educated animal-science major, divorced ex-never-world-champion bullrider, no longer prone to grand ambition,

thirty-three-year-old has-been, living a day at a time, had been spurned by a lady who actually pried open his heart a millimeter or two in the last week, but who now can't wait to unload him, and simultaneously smiled on by a Shoshone hula girl that he can't take his eyes off of. Mostly, he can't absorb it all right now, he just needs to go to the bathroom.

34

December 6: T.A. Reflects on Her Life

As soon as Sherrill left for work, T.A. called Al and Lick to the kitchen table.

"Would you, both of you, let me talk to you a minute?" she asked. She poured Lick a cup of coffee. "First, I want you both to know how grateful I am that you rescued me. I don't know what would have happened if I'd crashed across the canyon or in the river. I'm lucky to be alive, to have survived the wreck, and then to have wound up close enough to be found. Then, that you kept me and, well, cared for me until I could function."

"Wuddn't nuthin' else we—" interrupted the old man.

"Wait, Al," she contra-interrupted. "Please let me finish. And finally, what I am most grateful of all for, that you trusted me, fought for me, and have gotten me out of the clutches of my husband's—not really my husband—but his henchmen. For reasons of my own, I plan to return to Vegas to stop this crazy hunt he's got planned. Best I can figure, it's going to happen next week. Sherrill's going to help me get a ride to Elko, where I can rent a car and drive down to Vegas." She paused. "I plan to go alone."

There. She'd said it.

The old man started to protest. She held up her hand.

"Please, Al, I've made up my mind. I thought about it all night. It'll work and I won't be in any danger. And having three of us would just complicate it."

"How are you gonna get to Elko?" asked Lick.

"Sherrill has a friend who lives there, Olivia is her name. She's going to call and invite her to come over tonight. I can ride back with her."

The old man and Lick sat silent.

"It'll work, boys. You won't need to worry."

"We will, though," said Lick. "What about those guys we left out on the road?"

"They don't know where we are or they would have showed up already, right?" she said.

"Prob'ly," answered Lick with more conviction than he felt. "But I'd . . . we'd rest easier if we knew we could contact you to make sure, since, best I can tell, me and Al are the only ones on Earth who know the mess you're in. And if you disappeared, we wouldn't know where to start lookin'."

"If I disappeared, it wouldn't make any difference, I—"

"Hog balls!" said the old man. "Just who do you think yer talkin' to? Young lady, you got a short memory. Lick here, insensitive, wishy-washy burnout that he is, asked you a legitimate request. Just give us some way of knowin', 'cause if you disappeared it **would** make a big difference . . . to us."

T.A. blanched.

Lick was staring at the old man. He was surprised by his articulate ferocity and impressed by his argument, except for the "insensitive, wishy-washy burnout" part.

"What about Sherrill?" asked Lick.

"What about her?" said T.A., a little too quickly.

"We could use her as a contact. We'd check

in with her every day or so for a couple weeks. You could leave a message if you needed help," said Lick.

"Let me think about it," mulled T.A.

"Fair enough," said the old man.

"I'm gonna take a shower," said Lick, and rose to leave.

"If you want me to wash your clothes," offered T.A., "leave 'em on the floor in front of the washer. There's a big towel on the shelf above it. You can wear that till your clothes dry."

The old man and T.A. remained at the table.

"You sure you wanna do this?" he asked.

"You mean, stop the hunt?"

"Yup," said the old man. "There's nothin' more dangerous than stepping between a dishonest man and his money."

"It's bigger than me, Al." She struggled for the words. "These last few days with you and Lick I've had time to look at myself and I don't like what I see. For a year and a half, more than that, I've been living with this jerk—in our arrangement, he calls it—for money. For money, Al. I'm ashamed. I'm not sure if I'd have stayed much longer anyway, but when I discovered his plan to invite all these, these rich guys in to hunt the endangered animals that Ponce has at his wildlife park—illegally, I'm sure—something snapped! I have to stop them from killing those animals, but more important, I need to stop them to get my self-respect back. Hell, Al, I used to sing in the choir.

"F. Rank never even gave a thought that I would care. He discussed it over the phone with Ponce right in front of me. Like I was furniture. Which I was. Just the piece he took to bed and displayed when his folks came to visit. He'd already bought my soul. It was cheap. People like him and Ponce, they're so powerful they think they can buy anybody, that they're above the law. But they finally misjudged the depth of my self-esteem."

For the first time since the old man had found her, he saw beneath the surface. "Won't ya let us help ya, girl?" he asked.

"No. I've got a plan and I'm going to do it my way."

"All right. I see you've made up yer mind. However, you can't just sneak off durin' the night in true cowboy fashion without us biddin' you a fond farewell. Even the Lone Ranger had time to wave and leave a silver bullet. Stone said there's a big dance tonight at the Miner's Club down there in Mountain City. The Tindall Brothers are playin' and the booze is furnished by Misters Beam and Daniel. Seems the least we can do to thank Sherrill. Show her a good time, buy her a drink, spin her around the dance floor. How 'bout we make it a foursome?"

T.A. considered it, then shook her head. "I don't know, Al. I've got F. Rank's goons on my trail. I don't know if it'd be safe—for me or for you."

"But like you said, if they knew where you wuz, they'da found you by now. Let's have ourselves a good time, and then you can ride off into the sunset with Sherrill's friend."

T.A. gave the old man a weak smile. "Okay, Al, you win."

The old man got up, set his coffee cup in the sink, and said, "It's settled then. I'm goin' to town. Call Sherrill and let her know. I'll see you and Lick at the dance tonight. We'll say good-bye then."

"You going to walk to town?" she asked.

"Darlin', I live outside. This ain't nuthin'."

T.A. rinsed the cups and stared out the front window at the old man till he disappeared up the road. She heard the shower shut off and she knocked on the bathroom door.

"Lick," she said.

"Yeah?"

"Did you want me to wash your clothes?"

"I guess so."

"You're welcome to lay down on my bed while you wait. You couldn't have gotten much sleep on that couch."

Was she making reference to where he'd spent the night for a reason? Lick wondered.

Maybe she didn't know. "Okay," he said, "I am pretty sleepy."

In five minutes he was under the covers in T.A.'s bedroom, sound asleep.

35

December 6: Lick in Love

Lick slept for three hours. When he woke, his head was buried in a pillow suffused with T.A.'s pheromones. These little atomic messengers caught a ride via his nostrils to the primitive receptors in his brain. They woke up before he did. Lick sat up in bed.

T.A. knocked. "Can I bring in your clothes?" she asked.

"Sure," Lick answered.

She walked in carrying a tidy bundle. "I ironed your shirt but your jeans aren't quite dry. I might've ruined your scarf. It must be fifty years old."

She set them on a dresser by the door.

"Thanks," he said.

"You want some coffee?"

"No," he said, "I'm fine. Except . . . well, I

wish you wouldn't leave. You and I have just gotten acquainted, ya know."

"I'm all mixed up," she said. "I'm not going to be very good company for a long time. I've got a lot of self-examination to do."

"Well, 'bout you wanting to wait till after you're married, that's fine. I hope you didn't think that would affect my opinion of you. Making out doesn't have to be all or nuthin'."

"What brought that up?" she asked.

"I dunno, I got the impression that you thought I was bein' too forward, maybe. Expecting too much, too soon, on our first date, so to speak."

"Well, you were, weren't you?" she said.

"Of course." He smiled. " But"—he raised his finger—"maybe we could establish some limits. Draw some lines, put up some Danger! No Tresspassing! signs."

"Like where?" she asked.

"Come over here and I'll show you."

T.A. walked over to the bed.

"Limits shall be defined as no touching below here." He placed a finger right in the middle of her chest. "Along a line extending east and west to here." He traced a convex curve over each breast to the armpit. "Or below here." He traced a straight line from the point of one hip to the point of the other.

"But," he continued, pulling her closer to

him, "this," he said as he kissed her neck, "is legal, as are hands and toes and knees."

"No knees," she said. "I'm ticklish."

"Okay, then, the small of your back." He pulled her even closer and slipped his right hand under her sweater in the aforementioned lumbar area. A warning bell went off in her brain. His touch felt so good.

A surge of sexual anticipation coursed through her body. **Oh, no,** her brain sighed, but she let him pull her down anyway and take her in his arms. She melted. She was a basket case. Lick was calm waters in a stormy sea. He held her as they kissed deeply. The sweater scratched against his bare chest as they caressed each other. He fell back on the bed and she crawled on top of him. Passion ran through them like electric current. Each little touch seemed to generate sparks. They squeezed hard, then he pushed himself up on his elbows. Both were breathing heavily. He had a sleepy-eyed grin.

"You feel so good, Lick," she said, her eyes misting. Her heart fluttered like a captured bird. Her skin felt like it was on fire. "I wish I could just stop the world right now, but I—"

He put a finger to her lips. "Shhhhh. Close your eyes. Relax. I'll stand guard."

Within two minutes she was breathing softly and drifting off to sleep. He gently maneuvered around until they were side by side, a blanket in between them, her head resting on his shoulder.

Lick got his passion under control. He hadn't had anything more than superficial attraction to a woman since he'd divorced six years earlier. He'd been riding bulls professionally most of that time. The women in the collage of those he'd known were all nice, some were wonderful, some even loved him, but his heart was galvanized, protected, impenetrable. A reaction, psychologists would say, to an unhappy marriage, an insecurity, and an unwillingness to clean out his closet of hang-ups.

Even making the National Finals Rodeo two years ago and riding the unrideable Kamikaze didn't open him up enough to feel love.

Last year he'd gone back on the circuit, but without his traveling buddy, Cody, it wasn't as much fun. He'd had a lackluster year, didn't make the Finals, and in April this year had quit riding bulls.

He went to a doctor, who told him he was depressed and prescribed some pills.

Lick never had the prescription filled. He eventually wound up in Idaho and started working for Lewis Ola. He hadn't had so much as a date for six months. Mostly, he was in emotional hibernation.

Being in the proximity of Teddie Arizona for

the last few days had slowly perked him up a little. Then the flirting and the tentative body contact began to stir him physically. Those feelings were exacerbated during the excitement of the chase two nights ago. Now, holding her as she slept, he began to feel a tightness in his chest, like something was trying to get out. Tears welled up in his eyes. Pressure mounted in the back of his head, a heaviness. It required a lot of willpower to push it all back down.

She's leaving, he thought. **I'm not going with her. But . . . so what? I mean, why should I worry that she's leaving? I'm doin' just fine out there on the Thumb. She's got so many problems. I can't deal with that. Besides, there's Sherrill. I like her. She doesn't expect anything. I don't need the baggage. I can barely take care of myself.**

He looked at Teddie Arizona sleeping, and a big ache rose in his heart.

Oh, no! Lick is falling in love! He doesn't know it, of course. Here's a man that hasn't faced an honest feeling since his dog died fifteen years ago.

The fact that the object of his affection has a cinder block in each hand and one foot off the end of the pier doesn't compute in the equation of blind-can't see your heart in front of your face-stumbling love.

In Lick's case, the combination to his lock has just clicked through the last tumbler, exposing an emotional eclipse that had been blocking out the sunlight of reason, revealing only the naked corona of pure-innocent-unquestioning-undefinable-intimate-angelic-lust-yearning-compassion,　head-over-heels, dyed-in-the-wool forever-after

> L is for the loins I've girded for thee,
> O is for the Oh, My! in my heart.
> V is for the button in your cleavage,
>   E is that I don't know where to start!

As we draw back and take a long view from the ceiling, we see a man and a woman side by side on a bed in the guest bedroom of a small house on an Indian reservation on the Idaho-Nevada line.

She is sleeping, he is wide awake staring up at us. His expression is one of agony. You can feel the heat from the conflict going on between his heart and his mind. But he shouldn't worry, because he may have less influence on his own future than even he knows.

What has happened to Lick is a common occurrence in those rovers and wanderers who keep moving to stay ahead of emotional attachment. Because when the heart and soul finally get exhausted and give in to love, they fall hard. And usually, it's with whoever is standing in front of them!

So it behooves the eligible rambler, cad or damsel, forever after, to watch where you're standing.

* * *

T.A. slept for an hour, rose, kissed Lick on the cheek, and went to fetch his jeans.

"Sherrill is a sweetheart," she told Lick when she returned. "I don't want to involve her, so if you'll play along with this brother-sister act, I'd appreciate it. When she gets home from work, we're going over to the tribal store and pick up a couple things I need. Then we can grab a bite in a restaurant and go to some dance Al found out about. It means a lot to him that we all go, say our thank-yous to Sherrill for her hospitality. And then . . ." She paused.

"And then you leave," finished Lick.

"Lick," she consoled, "after it's over, Vegas, I mean, maybe we could get together."

Lick stared at her dejectedly. "T.A.," he said, "I can't let you go. I mean, I don't want to let you go. I think I'm . . . I know you've got . . . Listen, whyn't we just leave here right now? Tonight. You and I. We can move to Lubbock, or Rapid City, Lethbridge, who cares. It doesn't matter. We just go. You can send them their money back. We'll hide out until they cool down and leave you alone and we could . . . There's absolutely no reason that makes any sense why you'd go back to Vegas. Come with me," he pleaded. "You don't have to love me, just let me . . ." He couldn't quite say "love." "Just give me a chance. I'm afraid if you leave, I'll never see you again!"

It had been a long time since his soul had been so bare.

She was reluctant to hug him or even take his hand. He was opening and she was closing.

Being loved is a burden if you can't reciprocate. He's tossed her an egg and all she has to catch it with is a brick pot holder. It's a messy situation.

"I'm going, Lick," T.A. said firmly. "I'm sorry, I have to. But I do promise that I'll call or write when the smoke clears, and maybe we can meet under better circumstances." She paused and he remained silent. "Okay, then, for now," she continued, "let's you and I go to the dance, have a good time. I'm not sure I should ask, but do you have any money? I know you spent yours helpin' me get away. I could lend you some."

"Naw, I've got money," he lied. "Got a little stashed in my boot, just in case."

"Okay," she said, but she didn't believe him.

"But I'm buyin' supper tonight." He nodded.
He was now as messed up as she was. Funny
what love can do. He would have been better off
catching the chicken pox.

36

December 6: The Miner's Club

When Teddie Arizona and Sherrill stepped inside the restaurant that adjoined the Miner's
Club in Mountain City that night, with Lick
trailing behind, all eyes turned to the two
women. Sherrill looked especially spiffy in her
stonewashed jeans and black tee shirt with a picture of Geronimo on the front. Dangling
turquoise earrings set off her raven hair.

T.A.'s trip to the tribal store had been fruit-
ful. She'd replaced her baggy turtleneck sweater
and hiking boots with more stylish attire: black
jeans, a thin beaded belt, black Justin ropers on
her feet, and an off-white long-sleeved knit
pullover a size too small with a scoop neck. The
three rhinestone stars emblazoned up each sleeve
and the silver filigree earrings she wore com-

bined geometrically with her starlight-bright eyes and made her look like a constellation.

Between Sherrill and T.A., Lick was taken aback and afront.

By the time the old man and Stone arrived, it had begun to snow.

"If this keeps up, I don't know if Olivia's gonna make it up from Elko," said Sherrill, looking out the window at the flakes beating against the panes.

"I'll worry about that when the time comes," said T.A. "Worse comes to worst, I'll make other arrangements tomorrow."

"Okay, but you run into any trouble, you call me, okay?" Sherrill said. "You know my number, right?"

"I got it, Sherrill, thanks." T.A. wasn't planning on any trouble she couldn't buy her way out of. She surreptitiously patted the cash in her pocket. She had nearly ten thousand dollars in her boots. One hundred hundred-dollar bills were split evenly into two envelopes and snuggled tightly beneath her tube socks next to her skin.

Stone headed into the barroom when it was time to eat. Sherrill snugged in right next to Lick at the table right at the edge of the dance floor. She'd insisted on him riding shotgun with her in the front seat on the ride over, too. Fair enough.

It all worked with T.A.'s plan, even though Sherrill's continual references to "your brother" and "your sister" irritated her.

Lick was aware of T.A. putting on a "happy face" for the occasion. He was trying not to wear T.A.'s rejection on his sleeve. The old man was oblivious to the electricity between Lick and the two women. Matter of fact, when the waitress gave Lick the old man's venison burritos and Al got Lick's enchiladas, extra spicy, they never even noticed. T.A. did, but decided to not say anything; she was dealing with her own demons.

The heavy air at the Miner's Club was filled with laughter, music, conversation, and the aromatic mixture of workingmen, strong perfume, and beer. The smell of sagebrush, diesel, and leather that penetrated the pores of those who worked on the high desert rose from their bodies, hair, and clothing like steam off hot biscuits.

The bar was busy and a crowd was gathering. Al excused himself to join the crowd.

Dances were common at the Miner's Club, since the nearest town with even a supermarket was Elko, eighty-three miles away. Although the dance wasn't formal by any stretch of the imagination, the club was still a family place. Ranching families whose lives revolved around cows might be two months at a time between visits to a big town like Elko or Boise. At the Miner's

Club, you met with your neighbors like in any suburban neighborhood, except the distances were measured in miles, not blocks.

Most people knew each other through school functions or brandings or church. Children who were homeschooled or bused to schools with twelve kids in six grades played with other kids in the dining area or sat at tables playing cards. At dances on warm nights they played outside.

One lady in town ran a "nightcare" facility in her house for dance nights, taking in nursery school and grade school children. Wee babies accompanied their mothers into the bar. The sheriff's deputies knew that the kids were under eighteen and that some of the guests were illegal aliens, but this was still the frontier, and sometimes the law accommodated the need for company.

The Miner's Club was a place where you left your guns and your prejudices at the door. Single men, cowboys, miners, ranching families, Indian families, Mexican families, ranchers' daughters, forest rangers, trappers, dropouts, and alcoholics all mingled. It was a place where loneliness could be fought off for an evening. An aura of civility reigned in this most uncivil of places. You were allowed to get drunk but not to turn into a foul-mouthed bully or bother the nice girls.

The Tindall Brothers had been playing their music at the Miner's Club for as long as anyone could remember. They were from a family who ranched on the west side of the Bruneau Canyon and were the "local music." Now their sons and daughters were playing. Terrible Tindall played the piano; Teresa, who'd married into the family, played the guitar and sang; Tinker played the drums; and Take Out played the fiddle and sang. Much of their music was fifties, sixties, and seventies hard-core country songs with a generous smattering of Bob Wills, Lefty Frizzell, and old-time fiddle. They sang anything from Jimmy Rogers, the Mississippi "Blue Yodeler," to Merle Haggard. The one thing all the songs had in common was that they were danceable. What the band lacked in accomplishment and harmony was compensated for in rhythm. Tinker could really pound the drums!

The band was on a two-foot riser at the far end of the room fronting the dance floor. The dance floor was usually full, the shot glasses tipsy, the dancers sweaty, and the conversation loud. A man was allowed to ask any woman to dance as long as he was on good behavior. She was allowed to decline. Sometimes a hard look from a daddy's eye would prevent some rambunctious cowboy or borderline psycho from asking a sixteen-year-old high-desert debutante for a dance.

Lick was drinking Black Velvet and water. He was keeping up with the old man, which was dangerous because the old man was a professional and in shape. Somewhere around nine-thirty or ten, Lick switched to tequila. Not the good Reposada or Añejo, but the clear-varnish kind that the Mexicans use to blue gun barrels or put around the baseboards to poison ants. Lick was trying to drown any concern he had about T.A.'s departure. From a distance, one would think he was handling it well. At one point he found himself dancing with T.A.

"You okay?" she asked lightly.

"Yeah. Doin' fine, havin' a time, steppin' out with my baby, and how, I don't mean maybe," he chimed.

She looked into his face and raised an eyebrow. He was no longer connected to reality. She guided him back to the table and Sherrill pulled him down beside her. "I'll take care of him," Sherrill said. T.A. turned and walked to the bathroom.

Sherrill put her arm through Lick's and slid close. "Your sister seems nervous tonight, Lick."

"Well, she's planning to go back to her home, and maybe she's thinking about missing us," said Lick, carefully enunciating.

"That's pretty lame," observed Sherrill.

"What?" he said defensively.

"I don't think she's your sister. But if that's the way you want to play it, it's fine with me."

"What do you mean, she's not my sister!"

"Is she?" Sherrill asked.

"Dang right. Of course!" exclaimed Lick, true to the end.

"Well, okay, that suits me fine," she said, squeezing him tighter.

"You've got her a ride to Elko, right?" he asked.

"Yep. Olivia's not here yet, but she said she'd take her back when, uh, she left the dance tonight."

"So, there you have it," said Lick.

That's her story and he's stickin' to it, and that's the name of that tune. He had reached the point of fluffy comfort. He was warm on the inside and Sherrill was warm on the outside. It had the makin's of a "no tomorrow" night.

Lick's gaze eventually settled on a ruckus at the bar. He squinted enough to focus on the old man, who was standing at the bar challenging anybody within shouting distance that he could stick his head up through the ceiling fan without getting hit. Bets were being taken. A crowd had gathered. The old man was waving a handful of five-dollar bills. Shouts for a demonstration welled up from the crowd. The old man signaled for Lick to join him. Lick stood shakily and walked to the bar.

The old man spread his arms and proclaimed, "I have invited one of America's greatest Almost-World-Champeen Lovers, Fighters, and Wild Bull Riders to be my assistant in this daring feat of Cowboy Head Bobbing. All the way from Pandora's Thumb, our own, the one and only, the gorilla in our midst, known only to us as Lick the Magnificent!"

The crowd cheered. Lick smiled.

"Now if you will, Señor Lick," said the old man, "climb up on the bar and switch the speed setting to slow."

Lick put one leg up on a swiveling bar stool and stepped up. The seat spun like a lazy Susan. Lick whirled out and away. His undextrous pirouette sent him flying horizontally into the outstretched arms of two lady miners from North Fork. They clutched him like the answer to their prayers. He had fallen as manna from Heaven. All their preparation in anticipation of the dance tonight was worth it, including the hour they spent over the makeup counter at the drugstore in Elko trying on lipstick, each selecting a fluorescent flame-colored smooch paste. They had practiced planting lip prints on their arms, the glass countertop, and the attached mirror so they could admire and evaluate their labial signatures.

Knowing how precious and passing was their gift, the lady miners attacked Lick like paramedics administering CPR to a drowning man. When the cowboys finally grabbed Lick's hind legs and pulled him out of the sirens' grip, his face, neck, and exposed chest were covered with kisses. He wore a crooked grin. The crowd heaved him back up on the bar and helped him get to his knees. Lick crawled down the bar and stopped in front of the old man.

"The informed of you," the old man intoned, "know that I can stick my head up through this ceiling fan as it revolves round and round and never touch a hair on my head. My reflexes are so quick, so catlike—as many of you know who have seen me cheat at cards—that it would not be fair for me to take your money."

Lick had a mental picture of the old man's bald head.

"But—and I do mean but—we have one in our presence, in this very bar, one who has tried time and time again to beat me in private competition. One you have seen on TV, and in **Western Horseman, Outdoor Life,** and **Good Housekeeping,** the vice-champion fan-dodger of all time, standing before you as we speak! Lick, take a bow!" shouted the old man.

The crowd cheered enthusiastically.

"Who in here believes that Lick can successfully stick his head up through the fan five consecutive times and not get hit?" the old man asked.

Nobody responded.

"Three consecutive times?" he asked.

No one spoke.

"Wait a minute!" preached the old man. "I have told you that he is the vice-world-champion fan dodger of all time. Is no one willing to bet that the vice-champion could do it once? Even once? And to sweeten the pot, I will give you odds of a hundred to one!"

Even in a sober crowd, it's hard to pass up hundred-to-one odds. But in a herd now functioning at the mentality of a turkey barn, the odds were irresistible.

Thirty-two people put up $5 each, betting that Lick would be able to make at least one head insertion without getting hit. The old man had $153 in his fist. Someone was light.

T.A. furrowed her brow as she watched from the table. She slipped through the crowd up to the old man and asked in his ear, "You're not gonna hurt him, are ya?"

"No, no," said the old man, "I've done it a million times. It dudn't hurt much . . . 'specially if yer drunk."

T.A. put a hand out to Lick, who stood

stooped on the bar beneath the fan, watching it re-volve. "Lick, you don't need to do this," she said.

He looked down and gave her a foxy grin and a large theatrical wink. She couldn't tell if he was in control or uncomprehending.

 The injury wasn't serious. The fan wasn't broken. The gauze bandage around Lick's head looked dashing and the blood melded beautifully into the collage of lipstick. The only downside was that after he came to, he was nearly sober.

37
December 6: T.A. Is Kidnapped

"There she is," said Valter.

He and Pike sat in a delivery van they'd stolen from the parking lot behind a plumbers' wholesale store in Mountain Home, Idaho. It was now idling in the parking lot outside the Miner's Club. Green lights shone on the dash and the heater hummed comfortingly as snow fell heavily on the windshield.

"Drive up closer," instructed Valter.

T.A. stood hugging herself in the cold crisp Nevada night. She'd stepped outside into the parking lot for a breath of fresh air. It was 11:30 p.m. and Olivia, her ride to Elko, hadn't shown up. No big deal, T.A. told herself, she'd buy a car or hitch a ride tomorrow.

She looked up at the stars and shivered; the knit top didn't offer much protection from the cold. Her resolve had strengthened as the evening had worn on. Any doubt she had about herself and what she must do had vanished. She looked back in through the open door and caught a glimpse of Lick waltzing across the dance floor with Sherrill. It looked to her like an old photograph: the snow, the light shining through the open door, the starry sky. She sighed and relaxed her shoulders. **It will work,** she thought to herself. **I'll worry about him another day.**

Lick had noticed T.A. standing outside as he two-stepped by. After the song ended, he excused himself and went in search of her. She was standing at the edge of the bright porch light, on the snow-covered gravel. She seemed lost in her thoughts.

"Howdy," he said, as he stepped up behind her.

She glanced over her shoulder and grimaced at his looks. He was wearing his hat over the bandage but the bruises were coloring like burnt crust on a hot roll. "How you feelin'?" she asked.

"Okay," he answered. "This ain't nuthin'. I been hurt worse than this takin' a shower."

She laughed. Snow frosted her hair. She looked like an angel.

"How 'bout you? Still gonna save the world?" he asked.

She smiled. "Yep. That's what I'm gonna do."

"I hope you're doin' the right thing," said Lick.

"I'm doing what I have to." She paused. "Although I admit, meeting you hasn't made it any easier."

Lick wasn't sure what she meant, which was nothing new. He often didn't have a clue what women were saying between the lines. He touched her neck with the back of his hand, let the touch linger a long moment, then turned and walked back inside.

T.A. felt his touch, then felt it disappear. She heard his footsteps fade. Then she felt his hands on her biceps. She started to look back at him but he pushed her forward, roughly.

At once, a big arm wrapped around her body, pinning her arms to her sides. A hand was clapped over her mouth and she was lifted off the ground. She couldn't scream, the hand was too tight. She kicked both feet out forward, trying to shake loose. Then she saw Valter in front of her, grabbing at her legs. She connected with a kick to his knee. Valter groaned, then actually smiled.

"Keep it up, sweetie—I like it!" he said.

Pike was squeezing her tightly. She kept thrashing but he managed to drag her to the back of the van and get the door open.

Once he was inside the bar, Lick turned for one last look. Pike and Valter were trying to push T.A. into the back of a van!

He wheeled and raced through the door! He hit the step on a dead run, his heel shot out from under him, and he sailed, feet first, into the parking lot. He lit on his back and elbows in the heavy gravel and slush.

He heard the van door slam, looked up in time to see Valter one step away, mid-kick. The lights went out.

Five miles down the road headed south, T.A. finally quit fighting. Pike was still sitting on her chest, pinning her arms to the floor. He, too, was breathing heavily.

Valter, in the driver's seat literally and figuratively, sighed. "Whew. I'm glad you stopped to take a breath, little lady. How ya doin', Pike?" he asked. "I'll bet your ears are ringing!"

"Just holdin' my own," Pike panted.

"Stay where you are," Valter said. "We

should overtake Busby soon. We'll tie her up then."

* * *

It didn't take long for someone to find Lick in the parking lot. They helped him inside. The band even took a break so everyone could get a good look. Sherrill was wiping the blood off his face. The kick had split his lip and rattled a couple teeth, but no broken bones. His eye was puffy.

The old man was leaning over him. "What happened, Lick? What were you doin' layin' down in the driveway? Makin' snow angels, and somebody drove over you? I've told you time and time again not to be playin' in the street. You're worse'n a car-chasin' dog."

Lick's brain was still foggy. He managed to form the word "Por . . . um."

"Por Um?" repeated Sherrill.

"I think he's tryin' to say something in Spanish," volunteered an onlooker.

"He does speak Spanish, that boy. I heard him talkin' to some of them backcountry exchange students on their way north," confirmed the old man. "Or maybe he's havin' a dream."

"Let's get him to the clinic," said Sherrill.

Luckily, the tribal ambulance had just arrived in the parking lot, making its routine

Saturday-night rounds. Even though Mountain City wasn't on the reservation, the ambulance and medical facilities were made available on dance nights. They slid the unconscious Lick in the back and slammed the door.

"We'll follow you in a minute," said Sherrill to the paramedic, guiding the old man to her car. She laid her hand on the door handle and paused. "Where is T.A.?"

"I reckon Lick would know," answered the old man as he looked at the thickening snow.

Sherrill set the old man in the front seat of her Buick. "I'll be right back," she said, and ran back into the bar.

38

December 7: Goose Valley Reservation Medical Clinic

Lick regained consciousness on the gurney as the paramedic rolled him into the small Goose Valley Reservation Medical Clinic. The paramedic parked the gurney in the hall and went to inform the night nurse who was assisting the Physician's Assistant, who was the head of the clinic.

The old man and Sherrill arrived at the clinic ten minutes after the ambulance. They found Lick still strapped to the gurney in the hall. Lick opened his eyes and looked up at them.

"Whee-ooo!" said the old man. "Bad lip."

"Are you okay, Lick?" asked Sherrill, concerned.

"Bine," answered Lick.

"Where's T.A.?" she asked.

Lick looked at her. In his moment of lucidity, he had concocted the beginnings of a byzantine explanation to protect T.A.'s secret—to assure Sherrill that T.A. was all right so that Sherrill wouldn't mobilize tribal, state, and federal law enforcement officers to pursue her. Because if they did, the police would surely find out there was a warrant for T.A.'s arrest. Ad-libbing, he feigned unconsciousness. He fluttered his eyelids and rolled his head.

"He's passed out again," said the old man. "Just when we need him."

"Let me check what the PA's up to," said Sherrill, heading down the hall.

"Al," whispered Lick urgently. "Al, lissen to be!"

"Why, glory be, you're alive! You were just

playing posthumously!" said the old man, mangling his marsupials.

"Right! Lissen, dey got her. But we candt tell Sherrill pecause if de police catch her she will go to chail pecause she's got a warrant for her arrest so jus' do wot I say. Let me esplane it to Sherrill and you jus' agree. Okay?"

"T.A. will go to jail? You mean she's a criminal? We've been aiding and abetting a serial killer or ax murder or horse thief?" said the old man with mock horror.

"No, no, it ain't dat bad, but it's bad enouph. It has to do wit' drugs, she was framed but . . ." He could hear footsteps coming back down the hall. "Jus' trus' me, Al. Lemme do d' talkin'."

"It will be a while," said Sherrill returning. She looked at Lick. His head was clearing and he could look her in the eye. "Lick, can you talk? Your sister is missing. I made a quick pass through the bar to find her when they discovered you in the parking lot. Nobody had seen her."

"Yes," said Lick. "I can esplane. You don' haf to worry. She caught a ride with a truck drifer goin sout'. She tol' me to tell you. She had to make a quick decishion and since your friend hadn't come because of the bat wedder she said she would take a chance. She said to say t'anks for effert'ing."

Sherrill gave Lick a long look under furrowed brows.

"How did you get hurt?" she asked.

"Slipped on de step," he replied.

She held his gaze.

"Dat's wot happened," said Lick weakly.

Sherrill looked over at the old man.

"I don't know," he said. "Lick knows his sister better'n I do."

"We can take him now," said the nurse from down the hall. "Sherrill, could you wheel the patient in, please."

39

December 7: South from Goose Valley

"There he is," said Valter, almost gleefully.

A white Chevy Suburban with tinted windows sat with the motor running in a large pull-off ten miles south of Mountain City near the Wild Horse Reservoir. Snow was falling.

Valter pulled in beside the Suburban. Then he climbed between the two bucket seats into the back of the van. Pike was still sitting on Teddie Arizona's chest, pinning her arms to the floor. His back was aching.

Valter brandished a roll of duct tape. "What's good for the gander is good for the goose," he said, looking down at her.

She gave him a fierce look.

"A word of advice, my dear," said Valter menacingly. "Just cooperate and you can make this trip in relative comfort. Easy or hard, it's up to you." He grasped her right arm. She jerked it away, grabbed his jacket collar, pulled him over on his knees, and banged his head against Pike's.

Pike grabbed her wrist and slammed it to the floor. His left eyebrow was bleeding.

Valter drew a hand back, saw the look of challenge in her eyes, then relaxed. "I told you I like pain, didn't I? Thanks." He smiled.

"Yeah, I noticed how satisfied you looked after walkin' all night in two right boots. That kinda pain musta made you laugh out loud," she spat.

"Mr. Pike," Valter said, "I believe our journey will be a lot more pleasant if I put the first piece of tape over her big fat mouth." With that, he slapped the sticky gag over her foaming lips. "Turn her over, kind sir, and I will secure her hands behind her back."

It took them a few minutes to truss her

ankles and wrists. Pike sat her up and leaned her against the bank of drawers that formed the wall of the van.

Valter went to speak with Busby, who was waiting in the Suburban. Then he opened the back door of the van and addressed T.A. "Now, Mrs. Pantaker—" She interrupted with muffled cursing and puffing of her cheeks. "Sorry," Valter continued, "I didn't understand you, but we are in a bit of a hurry here, so . . . here's the plan. We're going to transfer you to the back of the car next to us. It should be comfortable, although you will be sitting on the floor. So let's move it!"

Pike was behind her holding the back of her pullover with one hand. Valter stood aside as she slid feetfirst out onto the snowy ground. Just as her feet hit the ground, Pike released his grip. She braced the back of her legs against the bumper and rammed her shoulder into Valter. Valter staggered, recovered, then kicked her feet out from under her. She fell forward, face-first into the snowy roadside.

"Feisty little vixen," said Valter, none too pleasantly.

Pike reached down to pick her up.

"Hold it, Pike. Let her rest there for a moment. You clean out the van. Make sure we didn't leave anything. Keep wearin' those gloves and that stocking cap. I'll keep an eye on our passenger."

Valter squatted down next to T.A.'s head. He could see a little blood on the snow. He said, "I'm trying not to take this personally. But it has been a frustrating—no, a challenging last two days. Your companions did a valiant job, but alas, I've got the benefit of professional training, a motive, and"—he leaned closer to her face—"I never give up. You have a choice. If you continue to resist, I will wrap you like a mummy, put you in a duffel bag, and tie you on the luggage rack. Or . . . you can act like a lady.

"I will pull over every couple hours for a 'comfort stop.' It won't be in town, just along the road somewhere so that you can . . . well, do your business. There is no way you can change the course of events, so you might as well make it easy on yourself."

T.A. glared at him.

"Busby, if you will help me, please, I think Mrs. Pantaker is ready to accompany us."

They lifted T.A. into the back of the Suburban.

"Relax and enjoy the flight," he said to T.A., and shut the doors. Pike took the backseat, with the job of keeping an eye on her.

Valter climbed behind the wheel of the Suburban. "We're just ahead of the storm, heading south, so I'm going to be pushing hard till we hit the freeway. They might have got a call out to the police, but odds are that it'll take a while.

Besides, they won't be looking for a white car. All aboard," he said grandly, and pulled onto Highway 225. Elko was seventy-five miles away. He made it in less than an hour.

40

December 7: A Call to Cody

Lick sat up in the hospital bed. It was 8:00 a.m., just turning light outside. Ten inches of snow covered the valley. The power had come back on at about 4:00 a.m. The clinic was bustling.

Lick's lip had been sutured, and so had the ceiling-fan injury on his forehead. The Physician's Assistant had given him a sedative and a local anesthetic to do the treatment. He'd also insisted that Lick spend the rest of the night in the hospital to ensure there were no concussion repercussions. The old man had slept in the chair next to his bed. It was the old man's snoring that had finally woken the patient.

Lick was pulling on his boots and he accidently banged the chair where the old man lay honking like a rooting sow.

"Whoa!" said the old man, sitting straight up. "Alowishus Sitting Bull Bean, Corporal, U.S. Army 305 02 3470."

"It's okay, Al! It's jus' me, Lick."

"I ain't talkin'! You can tie me to the stake, make me do the bunny hop or eat brussels sprouts! I ain't talkin', you Nazi scum!"

Lick shook the old man's shoulders. "It's me, Al. Lick. Wake up!"

The old man shook his head and his eyes opened. He blinked. "Lick," he said, "what are you doin' here?" He looked around. "What am **I** doin' here? Am I hurt bad? Maybe it's just a flesh wound. Randolph Scott always had a flesh wound. He could still keep firin'."

The old man's mind began to devolve from his bizarre dream into reality, like a Laundromat dryer full of soggy thoughts slowly winding down.

"T.A. got caught last night," Lick began, his enunciation still impaired by swollen lips.

"So you said," acknowledged the old man.

"Yes. By those guys who chased us across de desert. Now listen, I've got a plan."

"I remember," said the old man. "You said we couldn't get the police involved because she was a drug dealer."

"No. No, she's not a drug dealer but she does have a warrant out for her arrest, so she's on de run. Her husband, dot really her husband, but her husband, de guy that sent de goons after her that chased us, he knows about de warrant and if she gets caught by de police they will check her ID, or worse, find him, and she'll go to jail. So, that's why we can't tell Sherrill that's she's been kidnapped."

The old man looked into Lick's eyes. They were the eyes of someone not pondering the consequences of life's stupid choices.

"Like a chew?" he asked Lick, as he shredded a stomped-out, half-smoked cigarette, ate the paper, and stuffed the burnt shreds of some-body's old Camel Light in between his cheek and gum.

"You know I quit last month. Besides, it ain't Copenhagen," said Lick disgustedly.

"Well, son, I agree we can't just let those goons get away with this. She is part of our family now, your sister. And if we can't call the Rurales ourself, then we better mount a posse. 'Course, there are some obstacles. . . . We don't have a car, we don't have any money, you look like a poster for Revolutionary War bonds, and we don't know where they're takin' her," said the old man.

"Wrong," said Lick. "We do know where they're takin' her: Las Vegas, Pharaoh's Casino."

"What about a car, and some cash?"

"I've got an idea about that. Bring me that phone over there . . . please."

He dialed.

"Cody . . . It's Lick."

★ ★ ★

☾ "So, you rodeoed with this Cody feller," said the old man after Lick hung up, "and he still said he'd come? He must not have much sense, or doesn't know you very good."

"He's comin' right away. They've done worked their cows and are jus' feedin' and fixin' machinery. He's got a nice crew cab, pretty new—"

"Did you ask him about a little jingle, a little travelin' money, a little wampum to foot our expensive tastes?" asked the old man.

"No, of course not. What kind of person do you think I am? Besides, he'll have some. He's one of them responsible types."

"So, when does he git here?" pressed the old man.

"If he leaves today, I'd guess he'll get here tomorrow night at the latest."

"What do we tell Sherrill?"

"Jus' what I've said. We stay here today, Cody comes tomorrow and we thank her and leave."

"You gonna stay at Sherrill's tonight?" asked the old man.

"Guess I have to," said Lick. "Just to keep the story straight. You could sleep on the couch."

"Naw, I reckon I'll stay with Stone again. What say we have some breakfast?"

"You got enough to pay for it?" asked Lick.

"Yessir," he said. "Propeller money, son. 'Bout twenty dollars left."

Lick looked at him quizzically.

The old man reached over and tapped the gauze bandage that was wrapped around Lick's head.

Lick nodded with recognition.

Eight hundred miles away, Cody Wing was explaining the plan to Lilac.

"He must be in trouble," she said.

41

December 8: Cody Arrives

Cody Wing pulled up into the parking lot of the Goose Valley Tribal Police Headquarters at nine the following night.

The snow was deep, but the roads were snow-packed or clear. He shut the diesel engine off and dismounted the two-year-old, high-wheeled, four-wheel-drive three-quarter-ton ranch pickup with a front-mounted grill guard that looked like Godzilla's face mask. He stretched, then walked into the building.

Lick and Cody shook hands warmly, coffeed up, and visited about civilities. Then Cody asked, "So, why am I here?"

There are philosophical ramifications in the answer to that question, since Cody had interrupted his life, left his pregnant wife on the spur of the moment, and driven endless hours in inclement weather, simply because Lick said he needed him.

It would help to know the history of their relationship, but that would require reading the prequel to this novel, *Hey, Cowboy, Wanna Get Lucky?* So, suffice it to say they had been rodeo travelin' partners for several years and had developed a closeness that transcended even blood relations. They were interdependent, each other's sounding board, counselor, critic, fan, and friend during high imes and when the cards went the wrong way.

And it's no surprise that a lonely, lost man like Lick called the only person he felt close

to. That, and the fact that Cody was the only one Lick trusted who had money and a car.

Lick led Cody through the whole story from the discovery of the girl in Bruneau Canyon to his black eye and loose teeth from the parking lot kidnapping the previous night.

"So, the reason you haven't called the police is . . . ?" posed Cody.

Lick had thought this out. "I don't want to tell you," he said, "'cause if I do then it makes you an affiliate."

"You mean accomplice," corrected Cody.

"Yeah, accomplice. But it's nuthin' big, it's just that there's a warrant out for her arrest."

"You mean like for a parking ticket?"

"No. But still, just trust me on this. That's why we haven't told Sherrill everything," said Lick.

"Because she's a policewoman," cognited Cody.

"Right."

"And it's your plan to go and rescue the damsel in distress, find the money, stop the endangered species hunt, and marry her," summed up Cody.

"Marry her! I didn't say anything about marryin'," protested Lick.

"Then I don't understand why you're getting mixed up in this whole mess to begin with. What you have described is a four-alarm, third-degree, double-trouble, titanic train wreck that will take all of you to the bottom of the San Andreas Fault and swallow you whole. I mean, if it all worked out, which I can't see how, how are you gonna explain harboring a thief, sleeping with another man's wife—"

"She's not really his wife," interrupted Lick.

"So she says, but maybe she's just using you. Hell, she already has. You're protecting a fugitive and you helped her escape. Now you're going to risk your life to save her from the claws of the mobsters, so if you're not going to marry her, why in the name of Jim Shoulders, Casey Tibbs, and Larry Mahan are you risking your neck?"

It was not a rhetorical question.

"Are you through?" asked Lick.

The two stared at each other as Lick tried to think of something to say. He looked away, shuffled his feet, and cleared his throat.

"It's the right thing to do," he said with a sigh.

Cody continued to look at his old friend, who still lived in a single man's black-and-white world.

"Okay," he said positively. "Where do we start?"

* *   *

(* Lick and Cody climbed into Cody's pickup and slammed the doors. Cody waited for the plug light and cranked the engine. He let it idle a few seconds.

Lick spoke. "Man, Cody, you're soundin' as cynical as I used to be. The ranchin' life don't suit you?" Lick was referring to the split-up of their traveling rodeo partnership two years ago, Cody's return to the family ranch and marriage to Lilac. Cody was now twenty-nine years old.

"Well, I'm sorry, but that's the way I am," he answered curtly.

"Hey," said Lick, "I don't mean nuthin', pardner. You just used to be more laid back. I was always the one lookin' for the dark side. You kept me goin', remember?"

"I'm sorry." Cody sighed again. "It's the way things turned out. Dad got prostate cancer last summer, he's not been himself. Takin' radiation, maybe surgery. His heart sorta went out of the ranchin'. Mama's fine, but it's a lot for her to handle, too, Dad bein' depressed and all. Kaycee, my little sis, in her teens and drivin' us all crazy. Younger brother's in college and my older brother took a teachin' job in town. He still helps at the ranch on weekends, puttin' up hay, brandin' and all, but they've got kids and things goin' on. You know how it goes."

Lick had no clue how it went. He'd never had kids. His first marriage had been a long, drawn-out bust. When it ended, he didn't lose anything he cared about. Since then he'd lived hand to mouth, rodeo to rodeo, paycheck to paycheck, no emotions spent. He had let his vessel go empty. Cody was as close to him as anybody, and he hadn't seen him for over a year.

"How's Lilac?" asked Lick.

"I'll tellya, she's my savin' grace. She sold her city clothes, married us all, and never looked back. She is so good. She can do anything she sets her mind to: drive a tractor, saddle a horse, shoot a deer, stack hay, make jerky. Plus she's so good with Kaycee, Mama loves her, Dad thinks she's the best thing since sliced bread, and, to top it off, she still loves me!"

"So what's buggin' ya?" asked Lick.

"Responsibility, I guess," Cody answered. "I thought I was ready to run the ranch, but now that I have to, I don't know if I've got it in me."

"You don't like it?"

"Sure I do. I love it, it's just hard lettin' go of the travelin' life. You and I had such a great time rodeoin'. Before I traveled with you, I had some good pardners, too. I read the **Rodeo Sports News** and keep up. We even made it down to Frontier Days last summer. I saw Loball, and Frank. I miss it, that's all."

"You could still ride in the rodeos around you, Livingston, Cody, Cheyenne, Pocatello, Red Lodge. Wouldn't be too hard to enter up and go over," suggested Lick.

"I did, actually, the first year I went home.

Rode in Cheyenne and Denver, but it wasn't the same. I'd got rusty. Besides, I think about gettin' hurt now. Didn't used to, but now with the ranch to run and Lilac bein' pregnant and all—"

"You're gonna be a daddy!" Lick interrupted. "My gosh. I can't believe it." Lick looked out the window at the snowy tribal police station parking lot as a gust of wind shook the pickup. A monumental moment passed, wherein he saw the chasm that had developed between them. "Maybe you shouldn't have come," he said.

Cody looked at him and smiled. "Nope, Lick, I needed a break."

✦ ✦ ✦

☾✦ On the drive out to Sherrill's house Lick brought Cody up to date on Al Bean.

"I don't know how old he is, but he's dang sure a cowboy from the old school. But he's not quiet and he doesn't mind stickin' his nose into other people's business, or his foot into your mouth . . . or his. Anyway, he always seems to land on his feet. And he does like to take a drink. And he's quicker on the wit than you might expect, so don't underestimate him. He can be slippery and windier than a sack full of whistlin' lips."

"So how did y'all get hooked up with Sherrill?" asked Cody. "Is she Al's girlfriend?"

"No, she's just . . . We met her when we got here and . . . she was Stone's cousin or somethin'. Al told everyone that he was our father, so that made Teddie Arizona and me brother and sister, so that's what Sherrill thought, though I think she figgered it out, but T.A.—Teddie— and I played along, and I've been playin' along, only 'cause Teddie thought it was prudent, so, I've been like, oh, I took Sherrill to the dance and . . ."

"And?" Cody asked.

"And nothin'. Except that she sorta thinks that she and I are . . . Sherrill does . . . I mean, that she and I have a relationship," ducked and dived Lick.

"Do you?" asked Cody.

"What?"

"Have a relationship?"

"Well, sort of."

"Let me cut to the chase here," said Cody. "Are you and Sherrill sleeping together?"

"Sleeping together?" responded Lick innocently.

"I don't know what you call it when you are doing it with a police officer. Conjugal visits? Penal colonizing? Mounting a Royal Canadian? But are you having sex with Sherrill while T.A. is sleeping on the sofa?" asked Cody.

"Actually, I was sleeping on the sofa. . . . Aw,

Cody. I don't know what to say. It's complicated. But it doesn't change anything. I'm going after T.A.—me and you and Al. And we're gonna save her, 'cause these crooks that kidnapped her are for real. And they're playin' for high stakes and she's in the way. And I don't know any more than that. We're the only ones who know how much danger she's in, so, for whatever reason, she's been dumped in our hands. And you're here, so . . . I know that if anyone can git her out, it's us. After that, who knows. But right now it's one step at a time."

It was quiet in the big pickup cab.

"Take a right and it's the first house on the left. You can see it up there," said Lick, pointing.

Cody took a right.

42

December 9: Rancho Seco

F. Rank Pantaker drove his Lincoln four-door sedan through the unremarkable entrance to the Rancho Seco twenty-two miles northwest of Las Vegas, Nevada. He crossed the cattle guard and followed the dirt road another four miles to the headquarters.

He pulled up in front of the ranch house and parked next to the white Suburban with an Idaho dealer sticker in the rear window. He stepped out, slammed the door, hitched up his pants, and went in.

"Howdy, boss," said Pike.

"Howdy" was the reply.

Valter strode into the big main room. "Glad to see you, Mr. Pantaker."

"Everything okay?" F. Rank asked.

"Yes, sir. Cargill and Loretta have taken good care of us. Mrs. Pantaker is still in the master bedroom. We took the precaution of searching it. Cargill is watching the bedroom and bathroom windows from a respectful distance. Busby is sitting outside the bedroom door. I've unbound her wrists and ankles, but she is a serious escape risk. And not averse to trying it," explained Valter. "I wouldn't take her outside that bedroom without a leash."

"Has she said anything about the, uh . . ." F. Rank didn't want to mention the stolen money. "About why she left, at all?"

"No. She hasn't said two words since we pulled the tape off her mouth."

"Okay. Well, let me see her," F. Rank said.

He followed Valter to the bedroom door,

nodded at Busby, who stood at attention, and went in. He shut the door behind him.

T.A. was lying on the bed. When the door opened, she sat up and swung her legs over the side. She was wearing a dirty white pullover, dirty black jeans, boots, and one silver filigree earring. Her hair was a mess and her forehead had a red scrape across one side.

"Glad to see you back," said F. Rank, without expression.

She glared at him. Those malamute eyes were piercing.

"I'll get right to the point," he said. "You have my money and I want it."

She remained silent.

"As best I can piece together from the stories I've heard this last week, you've left a trail of destruction worthy of the Mexican army. A wrecked helicopter, a string of bullet holes, loose horses, marauding Indians, stolen cars, and lovesick cowboys from here to the Idaho line."

"You didn't mention the footsore, barefoot, disarmed three blind goons," she added defiantly.

"I guess I haven't heard all the stories yet. Maybe you can catch me up on this after we get the money back."

"What money?" she asked innocently.

"You know what money. I won't even dignify

your question. I would appreciate it if you would not take me for a complete fool. Now. Where is it?"

She stared into his eyes unblinkingly. "Does Ponce know it's missing?" she asked.

He didn't answer.

"He doesn't, does he?" She smiled.

He returned the smile, then drew his hand back to smack her.

She leaped at him like a striking snake! Her fist mashed his nose to one side. He swung wildly, missing. She ducked under his arm, came up with a bedside stool, and cracked him on the back of the head. He crashed over the bed, unconscious.

"Everything all right in there?" asked Busby tentatively through the closed door.

"Don't hit me again," T.A. cried loudly. "Ungh," she grunted. "Okay, okay, I'll tell."

Busby winced and sat back down. He hadn't exactly hired on to be a kidnapper and accomplice to assault. But he knew these guys were pretty touchy, so it wasn't the time to ask for a leave of absence.

T.A. nervously studied the situation. She searched F. Rank. No gun . . . dang it. Not even a pocketknife. She did take his wallet, though, and his car keys. She knew that F. Rank wouldn't remain down long. She edged to the curtain and spotted Cargill, the ranch caretaker, under a tree, staring at her window.

A plan, a plan . . . , she thought.

In the ceiling of the closet was a trapdoor. She pulled a chair from the bedroom, pushed the trapdoor up, and pulled herself into the attic. During the remodeling of this old ranch house, the contractors had installed air-conditioning ducts in the ceiling. Lots of blown insulation covered the attic floor. There was an attic fan in the wall at the north end of the house.

Stepping on the trusses, T.A. made it to the attic fan. She managed to bend one blade back and poke a hole in the outside screen. Soon she was out on the porch roof and moving to the side away from Cargill's outpost. The pitch was steep. She eased to the edge, lay belly down, and peeked back under the roof. The porch was deserted.

T.A. carefully hung down till her feet touched the porch rail, then she dropped down to the dirt. There wasn't much cover between her and F. Rank's big Lincoln parked out front.

Then she heard F. Rank's voice from inside the house: "She's climbed through the attic, you morons! Check out front!"

She broke from cover like a jackrabbit in front of a speeding car's headlights. She was opening the car door when the shouting became louder.

Jump in the seat. Hit the electric lock. Turn the ignition. Step on the gas.

The car was still pointed toward the house when it moved out smartly. She wheeled hard to the left, sending Valter skittering sideways. He was waving his gun and screaming something.

Suddenly an arm shot across her left shoulder and grabbed the front of her pullover! The cloth knotted up in the big fist. She pulled back, simultaneously bowing her head and swinging her arms toward her attacker. The pullover peeled off slick as a whistle! F. Rank flew backwards, landing hard on the loose gravel, his gun coming loose and sailing into the brush.

T.A. grabbed the steering wheel, regained control, and turned hard to the right in the big dusty driveway. She stomped the gas, fishtailed, and threw gravel and sand all over Valter, Pike, Cargill, and F. Rank.

"Shoot the tires!" shouted F. Rank.

The volley sounded like the 13th Vermonters defending Cemetery Ridge from Pickett's Charge at Gettysburg. Bullet holes blossomed on the Lincoln's trunk. The rear window shattered. The rearview mirror exploded inside the car.

T.A. ducked as low as she could, peeking up periodically as she drove to see if she was still in the ruts. She felt a sharp pain on her right cheek. When the speedometer hit sixty, she sat up

straight and looked back through the damaged
rear window. She could only make out jumping
figures in front of the house.

It was four miles to the blacktop. T.A. kept
the pedal to the metal, hitting seventy when she
could, headin' for the highway!

**That means, by my calculations, she had
less than three minutes to decide her course
of action. To the right, Las Vegas; to the left,
Death Valley. They'd be following, she knew.
She wasn't worried about losing her life. She
knew where the money was buried, but . . .
her pursuers could be intimidating. She
couldn't outrun them, so she had to outsmart
them. Good plan. Famous last words.**

43

December 9: Gas, Bait, and Gospel

At the blacktop, T.A. swung the Lincoln hard to
port. The road was a two-lane with the occasional dip that at 90 mph lifted the whole vehi-

cle off the ground. **A phone,** she was thinking. **I've got to call Sherrill.**

Fifteen miles from the ranch turnoff, she spotted a service station on the right side of the road. There was a single-wide mobile home planted a short distance from its back door. Nary a tree lent ambience to the unpainted cinder block and gravel. A fading sign read GAS, BAIT, AND GOSPEL.

T.A. slowed and pulled around behind the station, hiding her car from the highway. She gently opened the car door and took a step toward the back porch step, which was a reincarnated forklift pallet.

A cold gust of wind sent goose bumps up her arms. With a start she realized that she was nearly topless; her flimsy bra didn't offer much in the way of thermal protection or modesty. She turned back to the car and searched the backseat. She even looked in the trunk. Nothing but a greasy gunnysack with snow chains inside.

Shivering, she tried the back door. It clicked open and T.A. peered through the crack. A rough-hewn but handsome rancher stood at the counter talking to a man behind the cash register.

"Velbert," the rancher was saying, "you need to get some new pumps. That Civil War model you have out there takes half a day to fill up my tank."

"Well," the gas man replied, "then I'd have to charge you more and you already gripe 'bout the price."

"You gotta admit you're a dang sight higher than Las Vegas."

"So is Paris, but you don't see them tryin' to keep up with Sin City."

"Okay," said the rancher, "could you just come out and unlock the nozzle? That's a pain, too."

"Just self-defense against them ne'er-do-wells that gas up and leave without payin'," the gas man explained.

"I know, I know, but I gotta get goin'. I've got a cow in the back."

The two men walked out through the front door toward the pickup and stock trailer parked by the gas pump.

T.A. didn't waste a second. She quickly slipped inside, found the phone, and dialed Sherrill's number. The answering machine picked up after five rings. T.A. spoke quickly. "Sherrill, please get in touch with Lick and Al. I need their help. Have them check in at Pharaoh's Hotel in Las Vegas as soon as they get here. I'll be checking with the registrar every hour on the hour. They can register under the name of—" The answering machine clicked off.

The two men were walking back toward the station. T.A. quietly replaced the receiver. She grabbed a stained white butcher's apron from the wall and let herself out the back door.

She suspected her former captors were going both directions from the ranch in hot pursuit. They would surely spot her in the big Lincoln. She made a decision and ran around the side of the gas station closest to the parked pickup and trailer.

The trailer, a sixteen-footer, was divided crossways into two eight-foot sections by a swinging cross gate. A half Bramer, half Hereford horned cow, barren and big as a bull elk, stood in the front section. T.A. unfastened one of the tailgate doors and slipped inside the back section. Her presence did not please the cow, who banged into the steel sides and spewed a stream of green soup tail-high on the inside trailer walls and, of course, T.A.'s apron. None too soon T.A. heard the rancher and the gas man coming her way.

"Thanks, Velbert. I'll see ya next time."

"Okay. Take care."

T.A. shrank back into the corner of the trailer as the rancher checked the hitch and peered in at the cow. "Okay, mama," he said. "Yer gonna like where I'm takin' you."

T.A. heard the pickup door open, close, and the engine crank. They pulled out on the highway headed south toward Las Vegas. She was very uncomfortable and very cold, but convinced she was on her way to putting Ponce and F. Rank Scumbag in jail, or at least on notice. It gave her strength and she began plotting her next move.

Dear Reader,
I have come to believe, not in fate, but in forks in the road: choices we make with no knowledge of the outcome. You step off the curb in one direction, you get run over. You step off in the other direction and you meet someone who changes your life.

And in spite of all our effort to make the right decisions, they are often out of our hands. Like now, in Teddie Arizona's case. She thinks she has outwitted her foes and is now in control. But wait . . .

"Pull over there," pointed Valter to Pike when they spotted Velbert's GAS, BAIT, AND GOSPEL. "Circle the station. Yeah, around here. . . . Well, if it doesn't look like our little butterfly has landed."

Pike stopped the car. The two men got out quietly. Valter pulled his pistol and gave a quick glance into F. Rank's big Lincoln. It was deserted.

"You ease around front, I'll go through the back," ordered Valter. "Count to twenty-eight and I will, too. Synchronize our efforts. One . . . two . . . three . . .

"Twenty-eight—Go!" They burst through the doors of Velbert's shop. Instinctively, the savvy proprieter pulled a sawed-off shotgun from beneath the cash register with a practiced movement.

Pike's boot heel slipped on the greasy wood floor. His feet flew forward and his head flew backwards just as Velbert's 12-gauge exploded a glass fixture just above the entrance. The glass showered down on Pike.

"Don't move!" shouted Valter.

Not only did Velbert move, he pulled the trigger on the other barrel. The shot went into the ceiling, but one stray BB bounced a glancing trajectory off Valter's thinning regulation flattop. Valter fell backwards, convinced he'd been hit. Which, of course, he had. Drywall and stucco rained down on him from the ceiling.

Velbert peered over the countertop, smoke rolling from his double-barreled baby.

Both invaders lay on their backs, groaning. Velbert grabbed two shotgun shells from the drawer and started reloading.

"Wait!" shouted Valter. "Don't shoot! Here,

look." He raised his right hand and let the pistol drop from it.

"You, too," said Velbert to Pike. Pike just groaned.

"Listen," said Valter, "we work for F. Rank Pantaker, owner of the Pharaoh Casino. He's also got the old Rancho Seco place back down the road. You know it. I've been in here before. That's his Lincoln Town Car parked behind your building. The car was stolen. We assumed the thief was in here. That's why we came charging in, so if you've seen her—the thief, I mean—"

"It's a woman?" asked Velbert.

"Yes. We don't mean her no harm, she just stole some stuff and we—"

"Her car's out back?"

"His car, actually," corrected Valter. "Go look for yourself. Did you see her?"

"In here?" asked Velbert.

"Well, her car, his car, the stolen car, I mean, is parked behind your place, so I thought she might be in here," explained Valter, trying not to become impatient.

"No girl or woman came in here," said Velbert.

"You mind if we take a look?" asked Valter.

"Well, you can pretty much see it all from where you're layin'."

Valter sat up and gazed around the station. "How 'bout the house trailer out back?"

"I keep it locked. I doubt if she could get in," said Velbert.

"Could my colleague take a look?" asked Valter, indicating Pike, who was now sitting up and rubbing the back of his head.

Pike gathered himself up and went out back. Valter was questioning Velbert when Pike returned to report that the trailer was empty.

"No one but Slake Radokovich," Velbert was saying, "A local rancher. He was haulin' a cow."

"Could she have gone with him?"

"If she did, I didn't see her. I was with him the whole time. Even walked him to his rig to relock the gas tank—ne'er-do-wells, ya know. Steal gas."

"What kind of car was he driving?" asked Valter.

"Fairly new Chevy pickup, pullin' a stock trailer."

"What color?"

"The pickup, the trailer, or the cow?"

"All of 'em, and how long ago did they pull out?" asked Valter, exasperated.

"White truck with his brand on the side door. Looks kind of like a chicken foot to me. Three stickin' up, one stickin' down."

"What?"

"The toes—stickin' up, stickin' down." Velbert saw the quizzical look on Valter's face. "The brand, I mean. Looks like a chicken foot to me."

"A turkey track," interjected Pike.

"I couldn't see the cow," said Velbert, "but you could be right."

"How long was the trailer?" asked Pike.

"Long enough, I guess," said Velbert, clueless.

"Okay, okay!" said Valter, raising his voice. "How long ago did he leave?"

"I was putting his twenty-dollar bill in the register here, when y'all came crashin' in the door, so you must'uv passed him on the road if you were comin' from the south," said Velbert.

"I do vaguely remember a truck and trailer pass us. He was really crawlin' and we were doin' a hundred," said Pike.

"Let's go!" said Valter. "Sorry for the mess," he told Velbert. "Send a bill to the ranch."

Pike threw gravel as he wheeled out onto the road headed toward Las Vegas. They didn't pass a car for ten minutes. Pike had the motor screaming and they were doing over 100 mph. Five miles beyond the ranch turnoff, they saw the back end of a stock trailer in the lane ahead of them. They were soon able to pull alongside, and they noticed the turkey-track brand painted on the side of the door. Pike slowed to 55 mph and maintained his position while Valter scoped out the inside of the pickup.

"I can't see anybody in the cab with him," said Valter. "Or in the bed of the pickup, but I can't be sure. Make him pull over."

Slake Radokovich had been loading his lip with a fresh pinch of Copenhagen when he noticed a white Suburban with tinted windows pull up beside him. The passenger was signaling for him to pull over. Slake thought about it for a second, gave Valter a little wave, and reached beneath the seat for his Ruger .357 Magnum.

Pike slowed down and pulled in behind the truck and trailer when it swung off onto the shoulder. "Get out your deputy sheriff's badge," Valter told Pike. "We'll try and look official here."

Slake opened the door and stepped out, standing beside the open cab. The .357 lay unsheathed and cocked on the seat beside him. He leaned against his truck.

"What can I do for you boys?" he asked.

Valter stood in front of him while Pike came to the other side of the pickup bed. Slake gave Pike the eye. "I'd be a lot more comfortable if you came over here with your pal."

Pike pulled open his coat, showing his deputy sheriff's badge.

"Where is she?" asked Valter.

Caught red-handed. This was the seventh of

his neighbor's cows Slake had hauled off into the boondocks. Montrose Galt's spread bordered Slake's for three miles. Montrose had a starve-out desert rancho. His cows were always hungry. Slake had some good pasture and he tried to save it, but Montrose's cows regularly passed through the common fence and spent a good deal of time eating Slake's grass. Each time Slake went to repair the break, he found that the fence had been mysteriously cut, pushed down, unstapled, or unwired.

Slake accused Montrose of deliberately letting his cows get onto his property, but Montrose claimed it was Slake's fault for improving the pasture. But mostly he just stonewalled, knowing there was nothing Slake could do legally.

Taking matters into his own hands over the last two weeks, Slake had pulled his trailer out into his pasture and loaded up one or two of Montrose's cows. Then he'd dropped them off at places like Death Valley, the municipal golf course in Las Vegas, Nellis Air Force Base, the Indian reservation, and the city park. Montrose's brand was an MB on the left rib and easily readable. It didn't take the local constabularies long, with the help of the State Livestock inspectors, to identify the owner and give him a call to retrieve his wandering cows. Montrose spent a lot of time driving long distances to retrieve his livestock.

This particular afternoon, Slake was on his way to a gated community in the swank part of town. He planned to drop this cow off and then go have a beer. But, Slake thought to himself, Montrose must have been waiting to nail him and called the Livestock office. It didn't look good. Stealing cattle was a primo offense here in the Wild West. The cow had a big MB on her left rib.

"Where is she?" asked Valter again.

"Officer, can I explain?"

"There's nothing to explain," said Valter, hearing the guilt in the rancher's voice. "Is she behind the seat?"

Slake raised a quizzical eyebrow.

"Get her out here, right now, cowboy," barked Valter.

"You mean right here on the road?" asked Slake.

"Right here, right now," stated Valter.

"You got a rope or somethin'? She's pretty wild. She ran me over tryin' to load her," said Slake.

"Here's the deal. Hand her over, then you get in your truck and leave," said Valter.

"You mean you're not gonna arrest me?" asked Slake.

"Nope."

"And you don't need a rope or tranquilizer, or nuthin'?"

"Get her out here," ordered Valter.

"She's in the trailer. She's all yours, Officers."

Valter showed a small smile and nodded in acknowledgment of the cowboy's clever thinking. He and Pike walked back alongside the stock trailer. Slake slid in behind the steering wheel, appreciating his good luck. He uncocked the pistol and pulled the pickup door shut. Either these two policemen were tougher than shark-hide boots or dumb as a cedar post. Regardless, Slake wasn't going to give them time to change their minds. He started the truck and dropped it into D. Then he waited.

Valter and Pike couldn't see into the trailer from the side, so they walked around instead. Pike grasped the handle of one of the tailgate doors and lifted, then he and Valter each swung a door wide. Inside the trailer, T.A. unlatched the middle divider separating her from the cow and pulled it open just as Valter and Pike stepped into the breach. The cow bellowed and charged right over the top of them! The thundering herd of cow walked Valter like a foot log and knocked Pike back against the open door.

T.A. took her best shot, leaping out of the trailer and over Pike, who was still flailing. Pike's sweeping hand caught her butcher's apron in midair, clotheslining her. Her feet sailed out in front of her and she crashed back onto the gravel shoulder.

While Pike was pinning a screaming T.A. to the ground, the pickup and trailer rig peeled out onto the highway, leaving them locked in mortal combat. Valter lay flat out on the highway and dryin' in the sun. The cow had trampled his leg, stomach, and shoulder, then left a stream of guacamole down his crumpled body.

It took Pike a few minutes to handcuff T.A. into the second seat of the Suburban and lay Valter out in the back. He gave T.A. a final shove before jumping back behind the wheel.

"Hey, that hurts, you jerk!" she fumed.

Pike looked back at her expressionlessly, then started the car, hung a U, and headed back toward the ranch.

44

December 10: Back at the Ranch

Meanwhile, back at the ranch, T.A. turned in her sleep and her manacled wrist pulled against the bed frame, waking her. She sat up against the headboard and rubbed her eyes with her free left hand.

She was sore all over. Scratches and welts burned. Her eyes and nose felt gritty. She noticed she was wearing a khaki shirt with the sleeves rolled up. It was at least two sizes too big for her. They'd pulled her boots off but left her dirty tube socks, she saw with relief. She still had the nearly ten thousand dollars in those socks. She spied Pike, who'd been dozing in an overstuffed armchair by the door.

"Pike," she said, "why are you goin' along with these criminals?"

He didn't answer.

"They don't give you much credit, ya know. Valter would sell you out in a New York minute and F. Rank treats you like a shoeshine boy. I thought you were a cowboy—a buckaroo. I've

heard you talking when you get around some of
the cowboys that come in to gamble. I just want
to know what kind of cowboy you are.

"I know you know what F. Rank's up to.
You're gonna let him and that maniac Ponce de
Crayon shoot a bunch of endangered animals?
Just to impress a busload of cheezy billionaires?

"You wanna meet a couple of real cowboys?
Get to know those two who saved my life. I'm
honestly surprised at all they did. They've risked
their lives against low-life weasels like Valter.
And why? To save me! They don't even know
me, Pike. How ya like them apples? They don't
even know me, and yet they put themselves between me and people who want to hurt me.
Does that make any sense? I'll bet they don't
even know why. Real heroes. How many times
do you get to be around real heroes?

"And look at you, taking money to go out
and ruin people's lives. You're not much of a
cowboy, Pike. You're a hood. A dirtbag. Scum.
I'll bet your mother's proud of you." Pike had remained silent throughout T.A.'s tirade. Now he
slowly turned toward her.

"I saw him ride Kamikaze," he said without
emotion.

"Who?"

"He rode into the arena naked on a camel,
borrowed some spurs, a bull rope, a hat, climbed

on the back of that man-eatin' son of a bad dream that had never been rode—and punched his clock."

Naked? thought T.A.

Pike continued, "It was absolutely the greatest thing I've ever seen at any rodeo, hell, at any sport, in my entire life."

"Did you use to rodeo?" asked T.A.

"When I was—" Pike started, then caught himself. He stared at her with a flicker of awareness, then shut down.

"Did you?" she persisted.

"There's a bedpan under the bed," he answered. "I'll leave the room for a moment if you need to use it."

T.A. threw him a pleading look, but before she could say another word, he'd closed the door gently behind him.

45

December 10: F. Rank's Confession

Ponce de Crayon was pacing like a coed waiting for the results of her pregnancy test. He hadn't taken F. Rank's confession that his wife had stolen their five million dollars in down payments well at all. He ranted and raved and blistered F. Rank with a fusillade of insults, castigations, and demeaning comparisons in metaphor and simile.

It was nearly a quarter hour before the lava flow began to harden. Ponce's eyelids became slits. His left eyebrow crinkled down; his right one would have joined the scowl if it hadn't been for scar tissue.

"You," he rumbled, "are ze stuff vot collects in ze bottom of a tool drawer dat hasn't been opened zince ze carpenter died! You are ze grease stain on ze carport, ze rust on ze anchor of a ship lost at see during ze Spanish American Vor! You have ze visdom of a barnacle, ze insight of a mayfly, and ze imagination of a lobotomized brussels sprout!

"How I ever managed to let you talk me into anyzing is beyond my ability to appreciate. You have zuch good judgment. You vall in love vit a vaitress, hire her to fool your doting parents. Now she takes our money—and hides it!"

Ponce's eye began to twitch. "Thank gootness, it is only your half of de money that was stolen. You find it or you may find you and her both pushing up codfish."

"No way," F. Rank said, crossing his arms like a pouting child. "We both take the risk.

Anything we make we still split, even if it's only the second five million."

"You impotent little shrimp!" screamed Ponce.

F. Rank cringed but still held his ground, "Half! I get half, whatever it is!" He stuck out his lower lip.

"You chiseling little weasel! You find that money," threatened Ponce. "If you don't, I'll stuff you in a culvert and plug both ends—vit cement. You bring me zat voman. I vill make her talk."

Both ends? Of me? mused F. Rank. **Or both ends of the culvert?**

Ponce de Crayon spoke into the intercom on the wall. "Pierre, prepare **le Habitation Napoléan pour le nôtre** houseguest," he instructed in a perfect rendition of Maurice Chevalier mangling the Queen's English.

"Oui," answered the wall.

46
December 12: Cowboys in Vegas

"Pharaoh's is right up there." Lick pointed.

Cody eased the pickup into the right lane. They'd parked Al's dogs with Mr. Roanhorse back at the rez until the old man returned.

"Where you reckon we should park?" Cody asked.

Al answered, "Valet-park it there, right in front. Them boys'll take care of it. Sure is a nice truck, Cody. I had one this color once when I was riding pens down there in Nebraska. I run it through the truck wash out on I-80. They had some big sprayers they used on aluminum trailers. Said it cut through the dried stuff on the floors and sorta polished the aluminum. Peeled the paint right off that baby! I'm tellin' you, it turned this color in fifteen seconds. By the way, what do you call this color?"

Cody steered up next to a doorman shivering in a Cleopatra hat and a toga.

"I'd like to valet-park my rig," Cody told him when he got the window down.

The shivering Egyptian handed him a ticket. Cody turned back to Al.

"Primer," said Cody. "I call it primer."

* * *

❈ As luck would have it, and as I've said, it sometimes does, which makes the story go smoother, the Cowboy Reunion, better known as "the Turtles," was having its meeting at Pharaoh's. These were the original professional rodeo cowboys dating back to Leo Cremer, Yakima Canutt, and Bill Pickett, who represented the first three books of Pro Rodeo's Old Testament.

There were lots of seventy-plus-year-olds in the large ballroom on the second floor of the casino. Most were still ambulatory and able to tell plenty of tall tales. Some were old enough to remember the first big rodeo in Boston Gardens, where the cowboys had a "strike" for a bigger part of the gross in 1936. They remembered the great broncs like Midnight, Five Minutes to Midnight, Descent, and Tipperary. They could still picture the great rides: Casey Tibbs on Necktie or Freckles Brown on Tornado. There wasn't a story to be told that someone couldn't stand on a chair and tell a taller one. This annual gathering of the Stove-Up Cowboys Association was overseen by Sunny Day, who'd been a rodeo wife and secretary for more years that she could remember. She was the glue that held the living scrapbook together.

They were also given special treatment in the Gold Card Room at Thomas & Mack Arena, a place set aside during the National Finals Rodeo for venerable professional cowboys. Membership required that the cowboys be at least fifty years old and have participated in the sport and won sufficient money. The "Room" was actually a bar where the blue collar royalty of rodeo mingled. A place where you didn't have people asking you what it was like to nearly be a champion, or how it felt to get bucked off, or be required to listen to a fan tell you about how he almost rode a bull . . . but a sandstorm hit, he lost his shoe, or his mother wouldn't sign the paper.

The Turtles were the founders of professional rodeo. They are the elite. The old man was a Gold Card member and a Turtle.

The Turtles spent their daylight hours meeting and visiting at Pharaoh's. In the evening some would venture over to Thomas & Mack to watch rodeo performances. They might slide by the Gold Card Room to put in an appearance. They had a certain cachet, these septuagenarian vaqueros, but remember, dear reader, that Al Bean was a typical member of this group, so you can see it wasn't like a reunion of college presidents or secretaries of state.

* *

It didn't take Al long to find the Cowboy Reunion on the second floor and get into the thick of the reminiscing. However, he was in the midst of his contemporaries, who could remind him when he deviated from the acceptable lie.

"Gosh, Bean Brain, I ain't seed you since you rode that buffalo through the lobby of Howard Johnson's back in—"

"It weren't a buffalo, it was through the boathouse at Evangeline Downs—"

"Evangeline Downs weren't even built in '56—"

"Were, too. Yer thinkin' of Johnson City, not Howard Johnson—"

"Harry Johnson, you mean? Cow boss in Bruneau for a hundred years—"

"I had a dog named Bruno. Blue heeler. Mean as a snake—"

"You mean the Snake River Stampede? That's where I met her. Brunette. Almost bucked me off."

Lick and Cody soon glazed over. They took their drinks and free food and went downstairs to the casino.

"How about it, cowboys," invited one of the blackjack dealers. She was a fair-haired, pink-cheeked, blue-eyed, cocked-and-loaded pistol. Her long blonde hair was pulled back into a shiny waterfall and her smile was a dentist's dream.

Cody and Lick looked at each other, contemplated, then shrugged "Why not?"

"Till we finish our drinks," said Lick.

Lick only had ten dollars, so he got ten one-dollar chips. Cody had over three hundred in his pocket, so he bought one hundred dollars' worth of fives and ones.

Lick had an easy way with strange women. The dealer smiled at him and minded her own business. He was out of money in three minutes. "I knew I shouldn't have split those sevens. You ready to go?" he asked Cody.

"Not quite yet, my friend," said Cody without looking up. He peeked at his bottom card, then scratched the table with his cards. The dealer placed a four of spades faceup on his pile. "Twenty-one," said Cody as he rolled over his cards.

Lick discreetly studied Cody's pile of chips, which had grown taller. Roughly three hundred dollars, he figured.

Cody placed twenty dollars' worth of chips in two piles to his right and left. The dealer dealt him two down in each pile. "Blackjack," said Cody, rolling over an ace-ten under his left hand. He peeked underneath the two cards by his right hand, then looked into the dealer's sweet steely eyes. He slid his two cards under the stack of chips to indicate he would stand pat.

The dealer rolled hers over: 3, 6, 2, 3, ace, pause, 9, bust.

Cody counted out three hundred dollars' worth of chips from the table and put them in his jacket pocket. That left two hundred sixty dollars on the felt.

He bet two hands at a time, split about every third one, and won 80 percent of the time.

Lick kept looking at Cody quizzically, a great big smile on his face. The waitress, dressed as Cleopatra, complete with a snarling asp rising from her widow's peak, kept the boys' refreshment glasses coming. Cody was too deep in concentration to drink much of his complimentary beverage, so as to avoid offending Cleopatra, Lick was finishing it.

Lick didn't mean to break Cody's run of good luck, but his raucous hooting—yee-haws, right ons, blow me downs, and "Git this sailor another tequila!"—was drawing a crowd.

At the end of the deck, the blonde dealer dunked the cards and stepped back. Another dealer slid into her spot.

"Here, darlin'," said Lick as he reached into Cody's pile of chips and picked up what looked like a couple hundred dollars, and gave them to her.

"Thanks," she said to Lick, and wished Cody good luck.

"So," Lick said to the new dealer, "think you can stop the lucky streak? Take yer best shot. Why, I've seen him win twenty times in a row. He sits at home day and night playin' blackjack. He's autistic, ya know. A genius, an idiotic Seville, an Einstein in sheep's clothing. Belongs to Menstra. He's figured out the system. He knows the secret!"

Lick was rising to a crescendo. "And you wanna know what it is?" He turned to the gathering crowd. "Do you wanna know what it is?"

"YES!" yelled the enthusiastic audience in unison.

"Get twenty-one every time!" With that explosive expulsion of wisdom, Lick fell over backwards and the crowd cheered.

The dealer waited till Lick's interruption subsided, then dealt Cody two hands. Cody won. He won the next thirty of thirty-eight hands through two more dealers. Cleopatra kept bringing him drinks. Lick kept protecting Cody by drinking them, keeping him out of harm's way.

After two hours, Cody had won nearly five thousand dollars and Lick was still upright.

Then Cody lost three in a row. He looked at his pardner leaning on the table and pushed himself back. "I'm done," he said. He gave the dealer a hundred and looked at Cleopatra. She offered him a fresh drink.

"Thanks," he said.

"Anything else you'd like?" she asked innocently.

"Yes," he replied. "Directions to the men's room."

"What a run!" said Lick. "We haven't done that good since we placed in the money eleven rodeos in a row back in . . . whenever that was."

Cody and Lick were side by side in front of the upright porcelains, each one unilaterally occupied.

"Two years ago, Lick. That's when it was. 'Cept eight of that eleven were yours. We sure smoked 'em that year." He paused and looked at the wall, "Wonder what ol' Kamikaze's doin' these days."

"Aah, they are turning him out to pasture," answered Lick. "Emerald Dune, the announcer, bought an interest in him. They're gonna use him as a breeding sire. Gonna make a killin' sellin' his calves. More power to 'em."

"I'm sure you know," said Cody, "they was afraid he'd kill somebody else. He just got meaner and trickier. Did you know Manly Ott drew him at the Finals last year? Turned him out. I saw it. Lilac and I went. Manly straddled him in the chute and when they pulled the gate, he just stepped back up on the rail.

"Nobody booed or nuthin' like that, but it was a strange moment. That was Kamikaze's last rodeo. The conglomerate got together and started promoting him. Sellin' semen. Only thing they couldn't say in the advertising was UNRIDDEN." Cody looked over at Lick, who smiled.

It had only been two years since these two "once professional" rodeo cowboys had concluded the most exciting year of their lives, culminating with Lick making the National Finals Rodeo in the bull riding. At the Finals, the top fifteen money winners of the year competed in ten rodeos, ten days in a row, the "Super Bowl" of rodeo. Lick really had no chance to win the PRCA world championship, and was a long shot even to do well at the Finals, but by the seventh go-round he was still in the running to win the average.

However, gamblers intervened and kidnapped him in an effort to reduce his
chances. But Cody and Lilac rescued him in
time to compete in the last go-round.

The bull Lick had drawn was the unridden widowmaker Kamikaze. With horns like
an upraised preacher, the look of Lucifer in
his eye, and malice for all who climbed on his
back, he was Darth Vader, Black Bart, and
T. Rex all rolled into one.

Lick made a ride that tore the roof off the
stadium, melted hearts, and made grown men
cry. It was a no-hitter at the World Series, a
Hail Mary for a touchdown to win the game,
the last step in a walk across Texas.

Lick left his mark on the sport he loved.
Cowboys would talk about it forever.

That chapter in their lives lay beneath
Lick and Cody's conversation like the ocean
under two survivors in a rowboat. It's funny
how friends can pick up where they left off.
Not necessarily on the outside, because the
outside changes with time, but on the inside,
in those private places where memories don't
get worn out by overuse and the constant
scrutiny of revisionist doubt.

Emotions well out of some deep pot as if
they've been simmering quietly. Yet when you
tip the lid even slightly, they billow forth like

steam clouds, smothering you with sights and sounds and aromas of memories as fresh as your last breath.

For a precious moment, these two friends were in the arena that afternoon when Lick slew the dragon, rode Kamikaze, and Cody got the girl.

Lick and Cody placed another hopeful phone call to Sherrill at the Goose Valley tribal police station. She still hadn't heard anything from Teddie Arizona since the first call three days ago.

"I'm worried," said Lick. "I figger she's one of two places. Here at the casino, out at Ponce de Crayon's rancho, or hid someplace else. And since it's gonna be tough to figger out where that someplace else is, we're best off checkin' out Ponce's and the casino."

"I've got an idea," said Cody. "Let's see if we can get up to her husband Pantaker's office or his penthouse suite."

"Not husband," reminded Lick.

"Whatever the story is," said Cody. "But we start up there. Talk to the help, get a lead, so . . . here's my idea. . . ."

47

December 12: A Massage and a Message

Lick and Cody had cornered a bellman.

"So you see, we want to be discreet, not make a scene and all, but her ex-mother-in-law is quite ill back in Tulsa and we're sure she'd want to know, but we would rather just tell her privately, so as not to make her uncomfortable in the presence of her husband, Mr. Pantaker." Cody took a breath. "Does that make sense?"

The bellman raised a crooked eyebrow and studied Cody. "Ya know, I heard truer stories when I was a bailiff," he said.

Lick looked at Cody and said, "He's right. You can't be subtle with a man with such acute acumen. Let me just tell him the real story and see if he'll help us. Mrs. Pantaker's old uncle Horatio from Nowata died and left her a potful of money. He hired me and Lemkooler here to find her and deliver it. However, we must do it anonymously and directly . . . that is, lay it in her hands. He also gave us plenty extra to lay in the hands of whoever helps us do the deed. Do you know any hands that can help us get in touch with Mrs. Pantaker?"

The bellman held out his own hand. Cody laid a hundred-dollar chip in his palm. The hand remained extended.

"That's a big hand," observed Lick.

Cody placed another hundred in the out-stretched palm. Then another.

"That's good, Lem," said Lick. "Let's see what this fine feller can tell us."

"First off," said the bellman, "I can tell you we haven't seen her for a couple of weeks. There were a lot of rumors about her disappearance, but nothing definite. But for one more chip, I can take you to the person who knows what's going on, if anybody in this casino knows."

Cody slid another hundred-dollar chip into the bellman's hand.

The bellman made a quick call on the house phone, then returned to the boys. "Follow me," he said.

Two floors down, in the casino cata-combs, they entered the Spa, Fitness Center, and Tanning Salon. The bellman left Cody and Lick in the waiting room while he disappeared down one of the hallways. The cowboys sat and admired the pictures of fit people flashing brilliant smiles in action scenes, frozen in midair playing volleyball, the tamborine, or roulette. In a few minutes the bellman returned leading a curvaceous dark-haired woman wearing a knee-length robe with **Toga Time** embroidered on the left side, above her heart.

"This is Allura," introduced the bellman. "The best masseuse in Las Vegas."

"Gentlemen," she said, "I understand you would like a massage, facial, and tanning bed?"

"No, we—" started Lick.

"You betcha, ma'am!" interrupted Cody. "And, like he says, you're the best."

"Will that be cash or credit card?" she asked politely.

"Cash," replied Cody.

"No offense, gentlemen, but may I see?" she asked pleasantly.

Cody pulled out two handfuls of hundred-dollar chips.

She smiled. "Who's first?"

"We'd like to go together," said Lick.

"Oh, really?" she said, scrutinizing them. An errant thought crossed her mind, but she reconsidered quickly. **Oh, well, I'll know soon enough.**

"Follow me, gentlemen."

✦ ✦ ✦

☾ ✦ They entered a well-lit room with a tanning bed, Jacuzzi, salon chair, and two massage tables. She handed them two robes. "There are changing rooms behind those curtains. Please take off your clothes and put these on."

"All of them?" asked Lick.

"Yes, but don't be concerned. I'm a professional," she assured them as they headed down the hallway.

Lick looked at Cody and whispered, "Why don't we just ask her what she knows and git outta here."

Cody looked around. "Playin' all that blackjack made my back ache. I want a quick massage. Plus I figure crossing her palm with more silver might entice her to tell us more."

"Whatever," said Lick, and he stepped behind Curtain Number One.

Our heroes, in their quest for information, have stumbled innocently into the eye of the tiger. Unbeknownst to them, Allura (real name Tawanda Fonda, of the Portland Fondas) has suffered much consternation in the last three days. F. Rank Pantaker (her Olympic event) has been ignoring her. Busby, the company pilot, has been consoling her, saying it's not personal with F. Rank, it's just that his wife has been found but is still not cooperating, and the missing money will be needed no later than Saturday night, following the big hunt.

Since Allura is no fool and F. Rank still doesn't know the meaning of being discreet, she's pieced together the crux of the ongoing adventure. Based on the bellman's explanation about these two cowboys, she's figured out that they are the very ones chasing after Teddie Arizona and that they're not here to pay her a social call. She's caught between loyalties and, as usual, will come down on the side of truth, justice, and Allura Valura.

She knows that if Teddie Arizona comes back into the picture, or if F. Rank goes to jail or has to face the wrath of Ponce de Crayon, her future might not include regular trips to the Riviera or the Bahamas, not to mention fresh diamonds.

She takes Teddie Arizona's behavior personally and is seething below the surface. Our heroes, as usual, have no clue.

When the boys came out in their robes, they found Allura stripped down to a string bikini. Statuesque, sculpted, and six-packed, she looked like a Michelangelo action figure.

She gestured toward a twelve-by-twelve tumbling mat on the floor. "Lay down, boys, face to the floor."

They complied. Lick spoke from his supine position. "We are looking for the whereabouts of

F. Rank Pantaker's wife. She's come into some money and—"

Allura straddled him in one swift leap and sat heavily on his back, knocking the wind out of him!

"F!" grunted Allura. "Umph!—Rank!—Umph!—Pan!—Umph!—Taker's!—Umph!—Wife!—Umph!"

Lick was grunting in counterpoint.

She reached under his chin with her left hand, gripped the back of his head with her other hand, and turned his head around till he was looking up her nostrils. His cervical vertebrae made a sound like Bigfoot walking on bubble wrap.

"That little conniving—umph!—money-grubbing—umph!—who's just selling her precious little—umph!—to that low-down, whimpering—umph!—of a sorry excuse for a—umph!"

Cody sat up, grasping the robe tight around his throat, while Lick was being pummeled and bounced.

"Lie down!" she commanded Cody. His eyes flicked nervously toward the door, and Allura sprang from Lick's wheezing form, applying a flying scissors lock around Cody's waist, dragging him back to the mat. She squeezed with her powerful thighs till Cody felt nauseous.

"She's — ooph! — not — ooph! — his wife! Ooph!" Cody gasped.

Cody's outburst worked. Allura suddenly released her death grip and stood up.

"Whattaya mean, she's not his wife?" With a practiced motion, she whipped the robes off their cowering bodies. "Gentlemen, let's talk. First, who in the shades of Mahatma Larkey are you? And what do you already know? And no cowboy crapola or I'll show you the oblique groin lock I learned from a Tahitian busboy."

"To make a long story short," started Lick nervously, "she run off from this husband of hers, although he's not really her husband, it's just sort of an arrangement—"

"What do you mean?" asked Allura. "They're not married? He thinks they are. He tells me that all the time."

"Nope, they're not. Anyway, she run off and he sent these goons after her and I think they've caught her or are tryin' to—"

"'Cause she still has the money, right?" said Allura.

"Yeah, somethin' like that," Lick said. **So, she knows about the money,** he thought. **What else does she know?**

"So what are **you** doing here?" she asked Lick.

"I don't know exactly, ma'am," Lick admitted. "Just that she needs help and—"

"He's in love," added Cody.

"I am not! It don't have nuthin' to do with that!" said Lick.

"So let me get this straight," said Allura. "You want to rescue her and take her away from all this. And you say she's not married, just shacking up . . . and what about the money?"

"I don't want the money. She don't want it either, she just wants to stop them from pulling off some wild-animal hunt, shooting endangered species."

"I know all about that. How was she gonna stop them?" she asked.

"She had a plan, but I think they've caught her, 'cause we were supposed to meet her here, sort of. . . . It's all mixed up."

"So, what are you going to do about it?"

"Step one is to find her, which is why we're here . . . being grilled by Wonder Woman's stunt double, who we are willing to pay, by the way, for some information, if she'd quit pounding a couple of good ol' boys, who wouldn't harm a flea, into masa. So, if you know anything that can help, tell us. If not, be prepared for a full frontal attack. Now, gimme my robe!" Lick's impatience was showing.

Allura smiled. Not the kind of smile that invites intimacy, but the sly kind a fox makes when she realizes someone left the door open to the henhouse. She relaxed her threatening posture.

"I can tell you this," she said. "I don't know

where she is right now. I do know that the day before yesterday there was a big ruckus in F. Rank's office. Valter and Pike were holding her at the Rancho Seco. But that was two days ago, Wednesday."

"So you think she's still at that ranch?" asked Lick.

"Knowing F. Rank, he might have had her taken out to Ponce's place to help convince her to tell them where she hid the money," she told them.

Actually, F. Rank had summoned Allura yesterday. He'd told her he was distraught about having to confess to Ponce and thought having his wife there would help dilute Ponce's fury. Allura had made him feel better by explaining how it was all Teddie Arizona's fault. But why was the two-faced cad still claiming he was married!

"Also," she continued, "several very special VIPs arrived at the casino yesterday and more were expected today. And tomorrow's the big day, as best I can tell. It's going to be at Ponce de Crayon's Ponce Park. Therefore, if I was a gambling woman, which I am not, I would search for her at Ponce Park."

Allura leaned over the two men, her grin broadening. "For your information, and this is strictly personal, I would be quite pleased if Teddie Arizona disappeared from F. Rank's life. I'd also be real happy to split up the money if she knows where it is and knows what's good for her, and . . . if you two can afford another hour, I'd like to show you a real Toga Time tag-team match. Still want the robes?" She snapped one of her bikini strings.

"I'm married, ma'am, and he's in love. Maybe you could just hand us the robes," said Cody wistfully.

"Too bad," she clucked. "You boys don't know what you're missing. I have a black thong in the art of Martial Love. I have participated in a study of the Qwagelin Love Triangle, Sustained Ebullience. My personal best: sixteen hours." She reached behind her and untied her bikini top. It hung loosely from the neck straps.

"Oooh." The air went out of both gentlemen. Their eyes locked onto curtains number 1 and number 2.

It has been said that the greatest measure of character is the resistance to temptation. Had they been offered a million dollars apiece to shoot someone, they would have refused immediately. Or the chance to win a bronc-riding buckle by cheating, they'd have punched out the messenger. But in a circumstance where they had the time, no one would be hurt, and none would be the wiser . . .

"How many hours?" asked Lick.

"Like I said," repeated Cody, "I'm married and he's in love."

Allura gave them a respectful smile, hesitated, and tossed them their robes.

48

December 12: T.A. in the Tower

Valter wasn't taking any chances. He duct-taped T.A.'s ankles, wrists, and mouth before loading her into the back of the Suburban for the hour-long trip out to Ponce Park. He sat in the back-seat with T.A. while Pike drove.

Upon arrival Valter gripped T.A.'s elbow and escorted her up the spiral staircase that led to the Napoleon Room. This was Ponce de Crayon's version of Rapunzel's tower, a turret that rose three stories above the Big Cat House in Ponce Park's animal facility. The hexagonal room had glass windows on all six walls, offering unobstructed views of every acre of the sprawling grounds. It was sparsely but tastefully furnished with a queen-size bed, a desk, a chair, throw rugs, and a lamp. A bookcase and filing cabinet stood in one corner. A topo map of the entire property adorned one wall, while paintings and posters of Ponce and his wild beasts crowded the others.

Valter had allowed T.A. to go to the bathroom downstairs before taking her up to the tower and shoving her inside. He handcuffed her right hand to the headboard of the bed without even untaping her wrists.

"I'm taking no chances, Mrs. Pantaker. You cannot be trusted. Thus I am leaving the gag on as well as the ankle tape."

She looked up at him, then back down at the floor.

"I'm going to get your husband now. If I were you, I wouldn't push these people too much more. They are quite serious and"—he leaned closer to her face—"no one knows you're missing. By not cooperating, you have brought this upon yourself." He turned to Pike who had followed them up the stairs.

"Leave her tied just the way she is. No bathroom calls without my permission, no conversation, no nuthin'. Remember, don't make friends"—he looked back at T.A.—"because you might be the one taking her on her last ride."

Valter turned and descended the stairs.

T.A. looked over at Pike and raised her eyebrows questioningly. He looked away.

* * *

(T.A.'s resolve was waning. She fought back tears. **Is this all a big joke? Am I just a joke? Why would I be so stupid? I can't believe what I've done, what I'm doing! I'm bruised, battered, and bewildered; Lick and Al are walking on thin ice, probably out of a job; I'm screwing up a sweet deal with F. Rank—and for what? To save a few animals from some lowlife's perverted scheme to make money. And they're willing to do anything to pull it off, including** . . . She didn't want to think about it. She began to cry.

Pike heard her snuffling. Her nose was plugging up. There was nothing he could do.

* * *

(Twenty minutes later, footsteps clattered at the bottom of the stairs. The trapdoor fell back and F. Rank ascended into the Napoleon Room.

He saw T.A. on the bed, trussed and with her mouth taped. She looked completely bedraggled, her hair filthy and matted. Her clothes were as rank as a tannery. He felt no swelling of the heart, no rush of emotion welling up behind his eyes. F. Rank was shallow as a shot glass. What he did feel was relief that she hadn't escaped—although, of course, he was scared poopless of Ponce de Crayon.

"I hope you've decided to cooperate," he said.

She looked up at him.

"Listen, babe, this is really important to me," he began again, adopting a conciliatory tone. "You know I love you, I'd still like to marry you. You could be a part of all this. All you have to do is tell me where the money is. No big deal. We'll go back to normal. The way it was. Remember how happy we were? You shopping, me . . . businessing, a little roll in the hay, then a round of golf, a trip to Miami. The good life. How 'bout it?" He smiled a nervous smile.

She stood, sliding the handcuff along the vertical bedpost. She turned as best she could and faced F. Rank. Their eyes met, his in expectation, hers with a dash of pity. It wasn't about the hunt or the money now; it was about her self-respect. She slowly shook her head.

F. Rank's countenance fell for just a moment; then it began to harden. His beady eyes became slits.

"If you do this, it's out of my hands. You'll force me to tell Ponce, and he **will** make you talk. My hunt **will** still go on. And you . . .

you look like something they'd feed to the tigers."

She stared at him unblinking.

"Look at you, backwoods trash. I can't believe I ever paid you a dime." He left the room without another word.

T.A. slowly sat back on the bed. She was shaking uncontrollably. Her emotions were frayed, she was exhausted, her muscles ached, the bindings hurt, and the duct tape on her face chafed. She had to concentrate on breathing and fighting off the bursts of panic that flashed through her mind occasionally. She stretched out on the bed as best she could. Pike sat silent as a stone.

An hour later, they both heard the footsteps on the staircase below. The trapdoor opened and in climbed a man dressed in a handmade purple velvet suit with fluorescent orange piping. A black-and-silver tiger was embossed above the breast pocket.

Ponce de Crayon made an intimidating entrance. He was one of those people who change the level of the water when they enter the aquarium. T.A.'s eyes were immediately drawn to the striking white streak in his dark, wavy hair. Then she noticed he had one blue eye, like an Australian shepherd she'd once owned.

Ponce walked to the bed. She slid her feet

onto the floor and stood up awkwardly, scraping the handcuffs on the metal headboard. She could sense the muscular power beneath his suit. He reached out a big hand and hooked his right index finger under her chin. She winced. He firmly pulled her head to face him.

"So, you are ze little flower zat is causing me so much trouble." His voice was low and modulated, with a French accent. Of course, he always spoke Frenchly in the Napoleon Room.

"I hope I can convince you of ze error of your ways, but first I must apologize for our wretched hospitality. We do not treat even our animals like zis. But your husband, he is not skilled in ze social graces. Allow me to arrange to make you more comfortable so zat we may have a more civilized conversation. I will call for you at five."

He turned to Pike. "I will be sending a maidservant to assist Madame Pantaker with her toilet. Please extend her the courtesy of some privacy. However"—he looked back at T.A. and smiled his crooked, snarling smile—"I will still hold you personally responsible for her, shall I say"—he inhaled through his nostrils for effect—"security."

* * *

☾ Within fifteen minutes Chi Chi Leblanc, Ponce's wardrobe designer, seamstress, fashion counselor, and French-accent coach, was in the Napoleon Room to help Teddie.

She had come prepared.

49

December 12: Lick and Cody Go to Ponce Park

"This would've sure been easier in the daylight," said Cody, peering through the windshield down the two-lane road. "What time is it?"

"Quarter to six," said Lick. "How much farther is it?"

Cody looked down at the odometer. "Another fourteen miles to the turnoff," he said.

"You don't think Allura gave us bad directions, do you?" asked Lick.

"For two thousand dollars in chips, I don't think so," said Cody.

Out of the black night two headlights suddenly pointed at them from less than a hundred yards away.

"Quick," said Lick, "pop the hood! I'll duck in the brush." He scurried out of the car while

Cody stood in front of the pickup, hand on the grille. He was frowning in feigned concentration when the vehicle slowed and stopped beside him. It was a limousine.

The driver powered down the window and leaned over. "You okay?"

"Not sure," said Cody.

"Are you headed to the party?" asked the limo driver.

"Uh, yeah. This the right road?"

"Yes. But it doesn't get paved until you reach the main gate, which is another eight miles. I can't pick up riders, sorry, but I expect there'll be others coming back and forth tonight."

"I'm supposed to wrangle some horses tomorrow, but I don't know exactly what's goin' on."

"It's kind of hush-hush," said the driver, "but they've got a group of VIPs going on a wild-game hunt."

"You mean celebrity types?" asked Cody.

"Not your run-of-the-mill celebrities. These are the stinking-rich types. The kind that you don't see their pictures in the paper. Only on the Forbes Zillionaire 500. I'm making another run back to the casino to pick up a lady rock star. You'll see others coming by here in limos. Plus, lots of kitchen help, locals. And, I can tell you, the security's pretty tight. Hope you've got your name on the master list or you won't get past the first gate. Good luck to ya, buddy. I've got to go."

"Thanks," said Cody, "we'll see you down the road, I guess." The limo drove off.

* * *

They topped a ridge and suddenly a little valley spread out before them. A mile away they could see two or three cars stopped along the road, and another mile beyond was a cluster of lights.

Cody killed the engine. "That must be the main gate. Probably got a checkpoint, guards and all," he said.

They sat in silence for a minute, then Lick spoke. "You got any bright ideas?"

"How important is this?" Cody asked in a neutral tone.

"Well," said Lick, "I've been layin' under the wagon scratchin' fleas and lettin' life pass me by. And I'm thinkin' even if I don't love her, or care about savin' endangered species, or want to rid the world of the evil twins F. Rank and Ponce, or . . . give a rat's patoot where this chapter ends and my next one begins, I am ready to do somethin' . . . and there is nobody that I'd rather do it with than my ol' pardner. So I say, let's crash the party."

"Do you have a plan?" asked Cody.

"I will, compadre. By the time we get there, I will!"

50
December 12: The Limousine

The limousine driver had never heard of Anakra Nizm, the intensely private Wall Street warlock with considerable influence on the Federal Reserve Board and president, chief stockholder, and beneficiary of more banks than the James Gang. An international financier, counselor to anybody who could pay the commission, and a private collector of art, artifacts, and rare specimens.

The limo driver knew only that the man in the backseat looked like a model for menswear. In his sixties, with wavy gray hair, blue eyes, and a stern expression, the financier radiated confidence. He was accompanied by a stenographer/niece/daughter/trophy wife/rental/anybody's guess, and by an officious right-hand man sporting a briefcase and a nervous smile.

The limo's headlights shone on a large dually

pickup in the middle of the dirt road. The driver hit the brakes. The assistant lowered the partition separating the driver from the passengers.

"Why are we stopping? What's that in the road?" the assistant asked the driver.

"I can't tell, sir. There are two men standing in front of the vehicle and it's blocking the road."

"Better see what it's all about," ordered the assistant, glancing at Mr. Nizm to confirm he'd made the right decision.

"Just make it quick," said Nizm. The man in the down jacket and cowboy hat approached the limo. The second man stayed by the pickup, legs spread, hat pulled down, holding a rifle in the parade rest position.

The driver rolled down his window. "Is there a problem?" he asked.

Cody stuck his head inside and peered into the backseat, where two figures sat in the dark. "Sir, we are undercover for the FBI," he said to the driver. "We have reason to believe that a mass felony, the destroying of endangered species, a violation of the Endangered Species Act and punishable by fines of a hundred thousand dollars and fifteen to twenty years in the penitentiary, is going to be committed tomorrow morning. We also believe that, in addition to the perpetrators, conspirators have been invited to participate in the crime. Now, allow me to speak to the persons you are transporting. Roll down the back window, please."

Before the driver could respond, the rear window buzzed down. Cody could feel the warmth from the heater in his face as he leaned in.

"Good evening, gentlemen," he said. "We will appreciate your cooperation. I will need your invitation, code, or whatever information is required to get through security. Also some means of identification—a business card will be fine.

"It's obvious you aren't going to the party to bus tables. My proposition to you is simple. You leave me the clothes you're wearing. You will take my vehicle, return to town, go directly to the airport, and depart on the next flight. Your identity will remain unknown, at least in my written records, and you will be saved enormous embarrassment, not to mention probable jail time. I expect you to say nothing of this to anyone if you wish to remain uninvolved.

"Do not return to the hotel. If you never hear of this again, count your blessings and thank your lucky stars it was you we stopped instead of the next limo. Is this perfectly clear?"

Anakra Nizm studied this imbecile. Obviously not an FBI man, but whoever this cowboy was, he did know about the hunt and he was certainly right about the publicity. Nizm abhorred publicity. He paid a private PR expert a six-figure salary to keep his name out of the papers, his photo off the society pages—or any pages—and his whereabouts and background unknown.

The other thing that gave Mr. Nizm pause was that though he himself was a master of deceit, he practiced his skills on ambassadors, princes, politicians, and dictators. They were civilized. This fellow leaning in the window didn't look like a fool; he looked like he fit right into this godforsaken Hell's half section in the middle of nowhere. And that gave the cowboy an edge. Nizm thought of asking about a refund of his half-million-dollar down payment, but realized it was not the proper time to discuss it. Besides, he'd get it back. He had too many connections to allow these Las Vegas hustlers to scam him.

He made his decision. "Would you be kind enough to give me some clothing to wear to the airport?" he asked.

"I just happen to have some in the back of my vehicle," said Cody, "and we are in a hurry."

While the exchange was being made, Cody took the limo driver aside.

"You're in on this, too. We can get you five to ten on aiding and abetting, and I can personally guarantee that your life will be in danger if you alert anyone outside of this vehicle about this exchange." Cody appraised the limo driver's uniform. "I'm going to need your shirt, coat, and tie immediately. Here's five hundred dollars for your trouble." The limo driver swallowed and began to unknot his neckwear.

As Lick emptied their stuff from the pickup into the limo, Cody looked down at the nervous driver. "If you're worried about getting in trouble with your boss, I can guarantee you this hunt tomorrow will be a disaster and you'll be thankin' us from the bottom of that five-hundred-dollar bill. Now, get 'im to the airport, leave the truck in long-term parking, unlocked, with the key under the floor mat. I'm takin' your ID so I can write you a thank-you note."

Lick and Cody watched the truck turn around and head back toward Las Vegas. The assistant was hunched down in the pickup bed, shivering. Lick shook his head and gave Cody a big smile.

"By gosh," he said, "you have flat become a first-class talker and confidence man! The FBI, I am impressed! I take it you're gonna be the big game-hunter and I'm the driver."

"Yup," said Cody. "Might be somebody in there who knows you, and that would spoil our sneakin' in. Sorry that the jacket and shirt are so big, but we only need to get through the check-point. This will get us in." He handed Lick a gold coin the size of a silver dollar. It was minted with the Pharaoh's Casino logo on one side and a picture of a panda on the other.

"Solid gold, I bet," said Lick.

Whether it was solid or fool's, it did the trick.

51

December 12: Pass the Poi, Please

It was close to six when Chi Chi, Valter, and Pike escorted Teddie Arizona to a large second-floor office and accompanying suite that ad-joined the Big Cat House. A small room-service table was set up, with white linen, candles, and Limoges place settings. A bottle of a particularly exquisite Napa Valley reserve waited in the cooler.

"Wait here," said Valter. "And remember, we'll be guarding all the exits." The trio filed out, closing the door behind them. Teddie walked to the window. Beneath her spread a vista of cages, outdoor animal-confinement areas, vast high-desert landscape, and the remnants of a weak sunset.

She saw something reflected in the glass and did a double take. For a moment she thought it was a reflection of a painting on the wall behind her, or a hologram that moved when she did. The reflection was of a beautiful woman. T.A. was stunned and actually raised her hand to her cheek for confirmation. She hardly recognized herself.

Chi Chi had been a showgirl herself and then a makeup artist for the showgirls. She knew how to make flowers bloom.

T.A.'s dramatic eye makeup would have made Cleopatra envious. Her thick streaked-blonde hair had been trimmed, layered, and styled into a shining mane. Small gold earrings shone on her lobes and a pearl choker glowed around her throat.

She was wearing a floor-length evening dress made of sheer ivory fabric held up by spaghetti straps. Delicate sequins decorated the deep-cut neckline. The elegant length was a compromise, Chi Chi had said, because although she'd wanted to show off T.A.'s shapely legs with a higher, more flattering hemline, alas, she thought it best to cover the ankle cuffs. They were actually horse hobbles that Pike had found in the tack room. Valter had insisted. Chi Chi sighed, and let T.A. wear her tube socks and cowboy boots under the concealing hem. "Stilettos and shackles don't mix," she said.

T.A. shuffled around the room, vaguely aware of being watched. She finally spotted the miniature security camera in the corner.

She heard the doorknob turn. Ponce de Crayon walked in alone. She could feel the electrical charges within the confined space realigning to make room for his presence. He now wore an ascot and a red velvet evening jacket with satin lapels.

When he opened his mouth to speak, a flat New England accent emerged; it was like listening to a tape of President Kennedy give his inaugural address. "Good evening," he said. "Sorry to keep you waiting, but we're having a reception for the hunters tonight and I've been overseeing the last-minute details." He pulled one of the chairs back from the table. "Won't you sit down?"

She sat awkwardly, hampered by the ankle cuffs and the flimsy, revealing neckline.

"You look lovely," he said, admiring her. "Chi Chi does such a wonderful makeover." He picked up the bottle. "A glass of Chardonnay?"

She gave him a cold stare.

"Very well, then, I will dispense with the pleasantries. I was hoping I could persuade you to forgo your desire to disrupt our wonderful weekend. And, of course, there is the issue of the money. What will it take for you to pull this thorn out of my paw, so to speak?"

T.A. looked at him levelly. "What I'm having trouble understanding is how you, a professed animal lover and trainer, could actually kill these endangered creatures. You were one of the bright spots of my life when I moved to Las Vegas. I envisioned you as a man of integrity. Your Wild Animal Refuge, your efforts to save endangered species . . . I actually looked up to you. When I began to understand your intentions, when I overheard F. Rank talking to you on the phone about killing them, I . . . It just drove me over the edge."

"Ah, but you see, my dear"—his accent began to dive Down Under—"they are not really endangered, my little sheila. I raise them, I buy them, I keep them from becoming extinct. The wilderness is being paved! It is the legacy of our techno world. The people who make all the decisions live in cocoons. They spend their lives in front of a screen. They have no intention of going to India or Africa or China to see pandas, tigers, or white rhinos. Condors, spotted owls, snow leopards, even dinosaurs are saved on their computers forever, and that is enough for most people. They think Jurassic Park is real!

"Soon all the real wild animals will be raised

in private parks like mine. It is capitalism. If you want to stop poachers, you don't deal with them, you shoot them. You cannot reason with poachers. They are competition. If a Chinese potentate needs powdered rhino horn to keep his wife happy, he can come to one of the private suppliers, like myself. That is what most people don't understand. I, and others like me, will be keeping the endangered species alive, but of course we expect to make a profit doing it. Not too much to ask, is it?" He smiled an innocent smile.

"Are you serious?" she asked incredulously.

"Deadly so," he replied. Then, picking up the bottle, he asked again, "Wine?"

T.A. considered her options. Belligerence. Acquiescence. Duplicity. She had to assume that her only hope, Lick and Al, hadn't gotten her message, or if they had, they had no way to find her. Even if they did find her, what could they do? Whatever was going to happen, she was going to have to do it on her own.

She still was the only one in the world who knew where the money was, but would they be able to force her to tell them? Deep inside, she was afraid they would. Yet she was pig-headed enough to think that she could still find a way out of this, save the animals, and reclaim herself. She'd done a lot of things she wasn't proud of for money. Maybe she was capable of doing some unsavory things for the greater good. She decided to play along with Ponce's flirtation.

"Maybe just a little, please," she replied, extending her glass.

Ponce poured. "I have an excellent selection," he said. "Actually, three cellars. I pride myself on surrounding myself with only the best. I'm sure you will agree with me, it takes a certain kind of person to appreciate the finer things in life.

"I suspect you have gained a taste for the good life. F. Rank needs someone with your sophistication to guide him in his search for quality. That is why I think you and I are much alike."

He sipped his wine. She was expressionless.

"Regardless," he continued, "someone with your compassion for the endangered species could be very valuable within my organization. Once you grasped that the endangered-species harvest is essential for raising money to preserve them, you could help legiti— uh, promote my operation. It could be a lucrative arrangement for you. Provided, of course, that you turn over the money.

"It's not the money," he explained. "It's the principle. You can see how this makes me look in front of my employees and business associates. Surely you can understand?"

He waited for her to respond. "Well?" he said pleasantly.

The half glass of wine she'd drunk had begun to stir small bubbles of indigestion. She winced slightly as rising acid flooded the back of her throat.

"Well?" he asked again.

She waited a few seconds, then said, "I'm thinking."

"I've ordered some poo-poos," said Ponce, switching to a Hawaiian accent. "Ees good, brudder. Ah, here dey ah."

A waiter dressed in a Hilo Hattie shirt brought in a tray of treats. There were pineapples, mangos, mandarin oranges, sushi—abalone, shrimp, octopus, and squid—even a dish of purple poi.

T.A. had never seen poi. Ponce saw her scrutinizing it. He picked up the bowl and held it out to her. She looked at him quizzically. He nodded for her to try it. She extracted a chip from the tray and collected a sticky thumb-size glob on her Tostito.

Poi is an acquired taste, like Vegemite or lutefisk. There is no way to prepare oneself properly for that first bite. It's like licking your fingers after applying deodorant cream.

T.A. didn't see any way to just take a nibble, so she opened wide and crunched the whole thing. Her shock at its taste was overwhelmingly unexpected. It was as if she'd bitten into a gall-bladder, or sprayed her tongue with Easy-Off! Her immediate reaction was to expel the offending substance without delay!

Ponce was positioned—maybe poised would be an appropriate pun—approximately two feet from her, face to face, across the table. Even with his catlike reflexes, he was unable to save himself. Think of a 12-gauge, full-choke, 3-inch Magnum load, fired at point-blank range. The poi was expelled so fast it vaporized into BB-size globules, which splattered Ponce's expectant up-lifted countenance.

T.A. was horrified! She stared wide-eyed at the frozen face of Ponce de Crayon, waiting for him to explode. He simply stared at her. She watched the purple poi coalesce and begin to slide down his cheeks, carrying miniature ice-bergs of Tostito chips in its glacial progress. A drop formed on the end of his nose. It looked like his face was melting.

Without direction from her brain, her mouth began to lift into a grin. She squeezed her lips together to hold them in a straight line, but her eyebrows began to raise. Then suddenly, in a rush, she broke into a huge guffaw, an explosion of mirth that filled the air between them with a microscopic mist of purple pinpoint poilets.

She pushed herself back from the table, unable to quit laughing. Twice she gained control, then looked at Ponce and broke up again. Finally, weak, wheezing, eyes watering, nose running, and body depleted, she sat back.

"Sorry," she said, and breathed a deep sigh.

Ponce wiped his face with a linen napkin and glared at her. "It is obvious that you do not take me seriously," he said. "For a moment I entertained the thought that you vere lady enough to come to my party." He now spoke in his best KGB accent. "I even vondered vat someone like you could have in common vit dat bellicose oaf vat you are married to. I realize now that you two belonk together. You are an uncouth barmaid fitting his style."

A spontaneous wave of fury rose up inside her. "I've seen bouncers with more class than you," she said, her malamute eyes burning into his good one. "I'm just sorry I couldn't see through your cheap con from the beginning."

He reached across the table to grab her but she avoided his hand. He straightened his shoulders, stood up, and said in a low growl, "You haf just dug your own grave."

52
December 12: T.A. and the Tiger

Ponce called for Valter, who'd been waiting outside the door. "Please escort Mrs. Pantaker to the practice cage in the arena."

Valter led the hobbled T.A. down a series of halls into a two-story room the size of a basketball gym. At one end of the arena was a steel cage the size of a two-car garage.

Ponce arrived a few minutes later. His hair looked freshly combed. He'd washed the poi out of his ears and was wearing a tight sleeveless body shirt that revealed his rippling muscles. He was carrying a twelve-foot whip.

"Welcome to my office," said the spider to the fly.

T.A. shivered.

Ponce went to the cage, opened the door, and stepped in. "Bring her here, Herr Valter," he said in his Prussian best.

Valter shoved T.A. into the cage with Ponce.

There were three large stools. The top of the cage rose sixteen feet above the sawdust floor. Ponce gave her a malevolent glare.

"Do you smoke?" he asked.

She shook her head no.

"Indulge me," he said with menace. He placed a cigarette between her lips and lit it, then turned her in profile.

"Stand right here and don't move a millimeter."

He stepped back from her ten feet and cracked the whip. She winced.

"I suggest you do not move. Put you hands behind your back and stand up straight."

T.A. closed her eyes and said a quick prayer. She heard the swish of the whip, the crack of the popper, and opened her eyes. The lit end of the cigarette was gone. Her knees buckled but she caught herself.

Suddenly a low door opened at the back of the cage and in slunk a huge orange-and-black tiger. He was nearly ten feet long and weighed over six hundred pounds. The tiger slipped up on one of the stools and sat.

"This is Khyber," Ponce said, reverting to an East Indian accent. "He is a fourteen-year-old Siberian tiger. Very rare, only four hundred thought to be living. They are the biggest cat in the world. Isn't that right!" he cried, and cracked his whip at the tiger. Khyber roared. T.A. took a step back.

"We feed Khyber whole lambs. Alive. We keep a flock just for this purpose. When they reach about one hundred pounds, we shear them and serve them with mint jelly, ha, ha, ha, ha!" Ponce laughed a hideous cackle.

"What is it you weigh, my dear?" he asked innocently. "I'd guess about one-twenty? Not much more than a yearling ewe. Come. Stand in front of me," he ordered.

T.A. stayed frozen in place.

"Come!" he shouted and cracked the whip inches from her face.

T.A. hobbled over to him. He grabbed her by the arm and swung her in front of him, face to face with the big beast. He engaged his fearsome whip again, snapping the popper in front of Khyber's nose. The huge cat swung a big paw and roared.

Although she was eight feet away from the tiger, T.A. pushed back into Ponce's hard body. She could feel the heat from his skin, smell his pungent male animal scent. He pushed her closer to the tiger and cracked the whip again.

Again the tiger roared and swiped at the whip. T.A. struggled to get away but Ponce held her tightly in his grip. He pushed her forward toward the tiger, cracking his whip and tormenting the magnificent predator, who growled and roared and stood on his hind legs clawing at the air and baring his ferocious fangs.

All the while Ponce de Crayon was laughing and shouting, challenging the tiger to charge and attack, then dominating him. Suddenly, he stopped. T.A. crumpled to her knees. She was less than an arm's length from the head of the massive animal. Ponce stood over her, eye to eye with the tiger.

"You would like to eat this little lamb, no?" he crooned to the beast. "She would be very tender, you think. Not all covered with wool like the others."

Ponce grasped T.A. by the hair and gently tilted her head back so the tiger could see her face. "Not very pretty by tiger standards, I guess. But she does have a backwoods beauty, and . . . as you know, presentation is half the meal. Good night, my friend." Ponce nodded and an unseen hand lifted the back door of the cage. The tiger never took his eyes off Ponce. Ponce counted silently to five, then whispered, "Sic."

The tiger whirled off the stool and departed. The door to his underground tunnel clanged behind him.

Ponce pulled T.A.'s head around to face him. His face was inches from hers. "Are you still so certain you don't want to tell your master where the money is? The next time, I may just let Khyber have a little bite. Maybe start right here," he threatened as he placed his right hand around her neck and squeezed.

Still looking into her frightened eyes, he released her and she slumped to the floor. He stepped out of the cage and locked it behind him.

"Let her stay here and think about it," he told Valter. "If she yells, tape her mouth. That is all."

53

December 12: Party Crasher

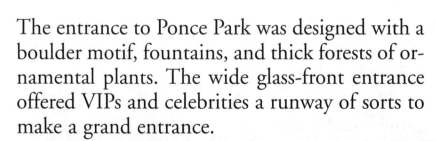

The entrance to Ponce Park was designed with a boulder motif, fountains, and thick forests of ornamental plants. The wide glass-front entrance offered VIPs and celebrities a runway of sorts to make a grand entrance.

Lick turned to Cody, who sat in the back of the limousine wearing Anakra Nizm's tailored suit and shoes. "You look like you could pass for a businessman or fancy lawyer or whatever that guy was. Except for the tie. I don't think you've got that right." The boys couldn't get the tasteful handmade silk tie to lay flat, especially with a granny knot at the collar.

"I'm gonna drop you off at the front door," Lick continued. "You're gonna have to wing it. If Pantaker's henchmen are there, they'll recognize me for sure. I'm gonna park this rig and explore around behind the scenes. Let's say we meet at the front door each hour on the hour. If one of us misses, we don't sweat it, we just be there the next hour."

Cody was getting nervous. "What if they have pictures of that guy? What if somebody knows him?"

"Cody, my boy, the coin is coded. It has a number. That's all they need. Besides, we're wingin' it. What can I say? Would you rather sneak around the outside with me? Might be safer."

"I reckon it would be better if we split up. Be a better chance of hearin' something about the girl," conceded Cody.

"Teddie. Teddie Arizona. T.A. She's got a name," said Lick.

"Sorry, I know, I'm just—"

"Listen, Cody, you can do it. If you could pull off an FBI undercover agent, you can dang sure do this. We gotta take our best shot. Okay, here we go. I'm gonna drop you off right up here and it looks like there's a bunch of limos parked over there to the left. That's where I'll leave this rig. See you in . . . forty-five minutes."

As Lick pulled the limo to a stop, a doorman stepped forward promptly and held open Cody's door. Cody flashed his gold coin.

The doorman said to Cody, "Please go by our reception desk on the left after you enter the foyer. They are waiting for you."

Lick stepped into the foyer and paused a moment to take in the scene. Sequined velvet curtains in sherbet colors offered a clashing backdrop to a magnificent display of mounted wild game. The style could be characterized as "Elvis meets Tarzan." Taxidermied animals abounded: a polar bear eating a seal, three wolves attacking a bull elk, an anaconda swallowing a tapir headfirst.

Through the glass wall on the opposite side of the room he could see the pool area. It was populated with attractive, well-dressed people mingling, munching, drinking, and talking.

"**Boa noite, senhor.** May I help you?"

It was the . . . well, in a hotel it would have been the concierge, in a café it would have been a waitress, in a dark room during a burglary it would have been a surprise. Here, it was Isabella Reyeno, organizer, formerly of Portugal.

"Uh, yes," said Cody, handing her the gold coin.

Isabella studied the coin, checking the unique code number. "Ah, yes, Senhor . . . Nissum," she said, checking his name on the guest list. "Welcome. How would you prefer to be called? Many of our guests have chosen to be called under an alkali, a false name, if you understand what I mean. To protect your privates."

"Excellent idea," said Cody. "How about . . . Count, uh . . ." He paused a moment. He had an uncle by marriage that he'd always liked although the man didn't fit into the "ranchy" part of the family. His name was Milsap Downs. He claimed he was related to Hugh Downs and that the racetrack in Lafayette, Louisiana, was named after him.

"Downs," said Cody.

"Countdowns?" confirmed Isabella.

"Yes. Count Downs," said Cody, enjoying the sound of his new title.

"Muito bem, excelente, senhor," she said. "Ah, here is your personal escort tonight, who can answer your questions and introduce you to the other guests . . . if you wish."

Cody felt a presence beside him. He looked around, then up. His escort stood an inch taller than he in her medium heels, and he was six feet in his borrowed tasseled loafers. She had pale ra-

diant skin, golden hair, light blue eyes, and a
long face with a strong jaw. She was wearing a
dark single-breasted suit jacket secured by one
brave button two inches below her solar plexus,
with no blouse beneath. The hemline on the
matching skirt was halfway up her thigh.

She wore two gold bracelets on her left wrist,
and a solid gold, inch-wide neckband that came
to a graceful point right above her angle of
Louis. She wasn't necessarily beautiful, but absolutely striking—a Nordic princess. The kind
you see striding down the concourse by the
dozens in the Minneapolis airport. Cody felt the
tug of sexual tension, the uncontrollable surge
that makes your knees weaken: what some
would call the estrogen wash.

"This is Chrisantha," introduced Isabella
pleasantly. "She will be your escort for the party
this evening. Here is your gold panda," she said,
returning the coin.

"Chrisantha, this is Countdowns."

"Count Downs," Cody corrected.

"Ya, I'm very glad to meet you. Come vit me,
Countdowns."

They walked a few steps, then she stopped,
turned around, and faced him. "Allow me to fix
your tie, Countdowns. It looks like a Laplander
vas trying to strangle you." She smiled and retied
his tie, then led him outside to the veranda.

As a Norwegian foreign exchange student, Chrisantha had completed a masters degree in chemistry at North Dakota State U. in Fargo and had come to Las Vegas with a classmate after graduation. Her classmate/roommate, a math major/physics minor who was working in the counting room at Pharaoh's Casino, had recommended Chrisantha for the escort job.

The men and women who were serving as escorts had been informed that their VIP guests were paying big bucks to be a part of a "special tour." The escorts should be prepared for unusual requests from them, and peculiar behavior. These guests were very powerful people and might have eccentric tastes. The escorts were under no obligation to do anything more than offer professional service. They were not informed as to the specific occupations or backgrounds of the VIPs, although some were obviously more conspicuous than others. The two Saudi sheiks wore their traditional robes and thobes. The Colombian drug dealer looked the part, as did the Iraqi assassin aka general, and the Texas oilman. Eager readers of **People** magazine might recognize the lady rock star, the California beach boy all-pro football quarterback, or the celebrity trial lawyer. But the grandmotherly Thai opium smuggler or the secretive Wall Street power broker whose clothes Cody was now wearing could easily have faded into the lunch crowd in any New York City restaurant.

Chrisantha was aware that most of the guests were probably not acquainted with one another. All these factors made her quite comfortable in retying Countdown's tie. For all she knew, he could be a recipient of the Nobel Prize in Physiology. Although he was much too young.

They strolled around the landscape. "Vud you care to sit?" She pointed to a small round white table with four chairs. A candle in the shape of Ponce holding a torch was the centerpiece. He was already burned down to the elbow.

"Sure," Cody answered. He pulled her chair back, seated her, then himself. He felt a twinge of guilt just being in her presence. Things seemed to be getting out of his control. His mind seemed to blank out that Lilac was back at the ranch and pregnant with their first baby. And that almost exactly two years ago today, he and Lilac had been married at the National Finals Rodeo where Lick had ridden the unrideable bull Kamikaze and won the average. Or that he was spending his second anniversary sitting next to every schoolboy's dream.

Cody's skin flushed. He couldn't help looking at Chrisantha. The front of her jacket had gapped open and he could easily see the dark shadows and seductive curves of breasts on parade. Her skirt naturally rode to within a handsbreadth of forbidden territory.

Chrisantha noticed Cody noticing. She was very comfortable with inspecting eyes, as sensual women often are. Being admired is part of their life. She rippled the air between them slightly by signaling a circulating waiter.

"You would like a drink, no?" the waiter asked.

"Only if Christina—"

"Chrisantha," she corrected.

"Chrisantha. Only if Chrisantha will have one with me," he said, looking at her.

"Ya! Sure I'll have one vit you, Count-downs."

"I'll have a . . . glass of wine," said Cody, thinking it wouldn't do to be reducing his inhibitions whilst Lick was circling the compound like a man with one oar and Teddie Arizona could be nearby in mortal danger.

"**¿Y usted, señorita?**" asked the waiter.

"An Oslo Iceberg, please," enthused Chrisantha.

"**¿Perdón?**" asked the waiter.

Cody looked at Chrisantha quizzically. "The bartender vill know," she said. "Vodka on the rocks with a sardine on a stick."

"**Regreso muy pronto, señor,**" said the waiter.

Cody looked around the stone-floored

atrium. It was a jungle with a pool, surrounded on three sides by rooms that opened onto it. It seemed to be open to the night sky until Cody realized it had a glass roof. The temperature was warm, slightly humid, and conversation was steady but muted.

"So, who are all these people?" asked Cody.

"Vell," she said touching his arm, "they don't tell us vat it is everybody does. But I am sure they are all good peoples. Vould you care to visit the hors d'ouevres table? The presentation is very special."

"Okay," said Cody.

She led him to a bountiful table. The chef stood behind it in sparkling white. He was wiry, with a thin moustache. "**Ah, monsieur, bienvenue.** We have a splendid array of very special, even rare, selections. Allow me to introduce you to them, all home-raised and harvested here at Ponce Park.

"First, we have pygmy owl sautéed in lemon butter and chives, minced snail darter with Vidalia onions, snow leopard tartare, condor-egg soufflé sprinkled with powdered rhino horn, and broiled African elephant tongue, very tasty."

"What's that?" asked Cody pointing at a tray of skewers.

"Ah, yes, barbecued gorilla fingers. Very, very good, but piquant."

Cody wound up filling his plate. The Bengal

tiger tri-tips were excellent, as were the musk ox cheese curds and panda chips. He made a second trip to the hors d'ouevres table to try the blue whale pâté, which the chef admitted had been imported.

Chrisantha ate heartily as well. Soon she was picking food off of his plate and he was eating out of her hand. A second glass of wine. Their knees were touching. She was facing him, leaning over occasionally, allowing him a free peek.

He was aching.

"Vould you like to come vith me? I seem to have lost my contact." She smiled.

"Where?" he asked with a stupid grin.

"Give me your hand and I'll show you," she tempted.

He turned toward her just as she swung her long leg between his and touched him. It was electric.

"Oooh," he groaned. "Stop!" he said breathlessly. "I can't do this." He wasn't sure if he had said it aloud or to himself.

"What?" she asked innocently. "This?" and she pressed her knee into him.

He backed away enough to break the physical contact. "I can't." But this time he knew he had said it only to himself.

It has been said, I believe earlier in this very book, that resistance to temptation is the

true measure of character. Most encounter this dilemma while trying to diet or quit smoking. Not necessarily frivolous goals, but insignificant in magnitude compared to selling government secrets or cheating on love for lust.

So far as we know, Cody has been faithful in mind, heart, and body to the woman who swept him off his feet two years ago. He has probably had no desire for anyone else, and living in the outback of the United Western States has helped reduce his exposure to the opportunity.

Yet here, far away from the chance of discovery, the siren comes calling. Cody has no one to tie him to the mast. He must wrestle with the Devil alone. And you know, friends, he's not accustomed to saying no.

"I didn't mean right now," she said, "but venever you vant. Or vatever you vant. Are you having a good time?"

Cody was afraid to speak, not trusting himself. He stubbornly gathered his composure and resumed picking at the food on his plate. As he was sucking the last morsel off of a gorilla finger, he felt a buzz go through the crowd. Ponce de Crayon was making his entrance.

"Who is that?" Cody asked quietly.

Chrisantha leaned close to him. She smelled

like a wet snowsuit, which reminded Cody of his Wyoming home, and of his sweet Lilac who was holding down the fort. "That is the Ponce de Crayola, our host here at Ponce Park, and behind him is Mr. Pankaker, the owner of Pharaoh's."

Ponce found a central location where he could address the crowd, most of whom were seated. The man was a formidable presence who immediately drew the attention of every man and woman in the jungle atrium. The jacket he was wearing was made from a jaguar pelt. The pants were tights fashioned from the skin of a thirty-foot anaconda. The boots were Malaysian crocodile with spotted lemur tops. A red silk scarf wrapped twice around his neck and ran through a keeper made from the vertebra of a lynx. His jet-black hair with its jarring white streak, the scar running down one side of his face, the lone blue eye, and the black goatee made him look like the Devil dressed up as Santa Claus.

One barely noticed the taller, less garishly dressed man behind him, who could have been mistaken for an overweight high school football coach.

Ponce smiled his crooked smile and began in a vaguely Eastern European accent, "**Bienvenue, bienvenidos, willkommen, bonavida,** and welcome to my most honored guests. I hope the accommodations at the Pharaoh's Hotel and Casino have been up to your standards. Most of you have met F. Rank Pantaker. He has made the arrangements with you all to be here.

"I am Ponce de Crayon, a simple animal trainer, magician, and lover of exotic dining and sport. This is my modest facility." He made a sweeping gesture with his hand. "Our plan for tomorrow is for you all to gather here by nine a.m. for a weapons fitting, guide acquaintance, gear acclimation, and attire, transport accommodation, and sporting preference.

"Each of you will have your own guide who will know how to outfit you perfectly for your special needs. All the big game is within a fifty-section fenced area here at Ponce Park. The perimeter fences are eight feet high and electrified to prevent escape and the invasion of unwanted visitors, man or animal.

"Since we only have one or two of certain species, you may express your preference to your guide. We will all depart the compound together tomorrow, before the noon hour. You will all be equipped with heat-sensitive laser scopes, the latest in movement sensors, and skilled guides.

"Everyone is guaranteed to succeed and is

entitled to his or her trophy. We have suggested, in the spirit of international relations, that a portion of the meat be set aside from each catch so that we may prepare a sampling for the banquet tomorrow night. Arrangements will also be made to flash-freeze the edibles from your trophy, as well as perform any taxidermy you would like done. All with the discretion you may expect from Pharaoh's and Ponce Park.

"As specified in our agreement, the remainder of the fee will be due at the completion of the hunt. Now," Ponce said dramatically, "as a token of my appreciation and respect, I would like to invite you all into my theater for a private show. Your escorts will guide you and I will see you momentarily." He turned quietly and disappeared, leaving F. Rank to mingle with the crowd and go over the details of tomorrow's hunt.

Cody glanced at his watch. It was almost eight o'clock. He pushed back from the table. "I need to go outside for a bit," he explained to Christantha.

"I'll go with you," she insisted. She got as far as the entrance before he stopped her.

"Please wait here," he said. "I need to talk to my driver."

"If you need protection, I've got some in my—" she offered.

"No, I'll be just fine. I mean, what can happen in a parking lot?" he said, dumb as a post.

54

December 12: A Disappearing-Tiger Act

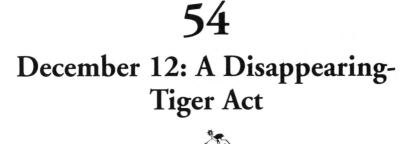

Several limo drivers were sitting in a comfortable waiting room. It had a television, pay phone, house phone, soft drinks, sofas, card table, bathroom, and daybed. A large window gave them a good view of the limo parking area.

They'd seen Lick's limo pull in. Two of them recognized it. They wondered who was driving LV 224 tonight. It wasn't a tight-knit society but, like cabbies, they were casually acquainted with a million drivers. When Lick got out, they didn't recognize him, but all agreed he needed a better-fitting suit.

Lick saw the other drivers watching him through the window. He waved. They waved back. They went back to their business, waiting for him to join them, but he didn't. Instead he reconnoitered around the sides of the building and found that, as far as he could see, the whole complex was surrounded by eight-foot Cyclone fence with razor wire. He saw no guards, and the pole lights were in the usual places, i.e., in front of buildings, on walkways, in the outdoor arena. Still, it was tight as a drum.

He spotted what looked like a hog-confinement shed, also some very fancy barns. He spied an observation post. It was a stone castle with windows facing all around like an airport control tower. A dim light shone from the room at the top of the tower.

Lick explored the compound from his position on the outside and found three large, gated, lighted entrances along the way. All were locked and/or manned by a guard. He stayed well outside the range of the lights, walking through the sagebrush and washes.

At five minutes to eight, he was lurking in the parking lot. On the dot of the hour he saw Cody coming through the automatic sliding front door, accompanied by a tall, striking blonde woman. Cody spoke to her. She seemed to cling, then turned and walked back into the lobby. Cody waved good-bye, then started toward the parking lot.

"Man, Cody, she was shiny! What's her name?"

"Chrisantha."

"Chrisantha? What kind of name is that?"

"She's not from here. North Dakota, I think," said Cody.

"Oh," said Lick, as if that explained it all.

"Listen, Lick, I got the scoop. Everybody arrives tomorrow morning at about nine. Somewhere around ten they start the hunt. It sounds like it's going to be like the Oklahoma Land Rush! Everybody takes off at once. Each hunter has a guide. Best I can tell, some will be on horseback, some in army tanks, four-wheelers, on motorcycles, camels—"

"Camels?" interrupted Lick, remembering his own camel ride through downtown during the National Finals Rodeo two years ago.

"It's gonna be pretty exciting."

"Have you got any leads on whether Teddie's here?"

"Not really, although F. Rank Pantaker is at the cocktail party right now, along with Ponce de Crayola—"

"That's Cray-ON," corrected Lick.

"Cray-ON," repeated Cody. "I would think if she's here—Teddie, I mean—sometime during the evening one of them is going to go check on her."

"Not necessarily, but if that's our only shot . . . ," answered Lick. "We can keep an eye on them, I guess, but two eyes are better than one."

"What?" said Cody, momentarily puzzled, picturing a pirate with a patch.

"Two eyes are . . . I mean four eyes . . . Aw, shoot. You could keep an eye on them, both eyes, and I'll try and check out the compound. Trouble is, I can't get in the dang thing. They've got this place tight as a Tijuana drug dealer's medicine cabinet. You need to get me inside somehow."

"We're all going to see a show that Ponce is putting on," said Cody. "Probably his magic act. He's got a theater in here. Then I'd guess most would be going back to the hotel after that. Security is tight. I don't have a plan yet, but Chrisantha might help. I can't quite figger her out, although she's hittin' me up pretty hard."

Lick gave Cody a cross look.

"Don't worry," assured Cody, "nothin's gonna happen. It's just if she can help us find Teddie . . ." He paused. "Let me think on this a minute. I don't know if she would help me sneak you past the door or if she'd blow the whistle. Whattya think?"

"How dumb is she?" asked Lick.

"Pretty smart, actually. She's acting the part of the professional hostess, but she doesn't know what's goin' on, about the hunt, I mean. I think she's just workin' by the hour," answered Cody.

"You got any money left?"

"Less than a thousand . . . in chips. Listen, let's check back again in an hour or sooner. I'm not sure how long this show is gonna last." Cody patted Lick's back. "And about Chrisantha, let me see what I can stir up."

Lick didn't like waiting. The longer he waited the harder he thought about Teddie Arizona. His mind was clouded as to his motive for trying to carry out this rescue. Every time his heart said, **It's the right thing to do,** his mind legitimately asked, **Why?**

That was when the flood of emotions swarmed him, filling his chest with anxiety and causing the blood to pump in his temples. **I gotta think!** he told himself. Al would say, "Pilgrim, you've come this far and here you are, still on the outside. Do somethin' even if it's wrong so you'll be able to face yourself tomorrow when you shave."

Lick walked into the drivers' waiting room and asked if there was a phone he could use.

"On the wall," one driver said.

He looked up the number of Pharaoh's Casino and put in a quarter.

"Yes, registration please. . . . Yes, could you

connect me to the Old Timer Cowboy Reunion that's holding their meetings there?"

A voice with a drawl picked up the line: "Old Timer Cowboy Nap and Sleepover, Sunny Day speakin'."

"Sunny Day," said Lick. "Sunny, I'm lookin' for Al Bean."

"Who is this?" she demanded.

"Lick," he answered. "Clyde's son."

"Well, I'll be dipped! Honey, where are you?"

"I'm here in Vegas, but—"

She interrupted, "How's your ol' daddy? Last I heard he was ridin' pens in a feedlot in the panhandle somewhere. He could rope, that boy. I remember one time in Guymon—"

Lick interrupted back, "Sunny, sorry to rush you, but I'm in a bind that I can't explain over the phone. I need to talk to Al."

"He's left, honey. Him and Cherokee Bob and the Texas Kid went to the rodeo. Don't know if they got tickets, but they've all got a Gold Card. So at least they could get out of the cold."

"Al's got a Gold Card?" asked Lick.

"Yup," she answered. "He used to ride broncs. Couldn't keep his mind on business, though, too smart for his own good. Always claimed he wanted to be a rancher, own purebred cows and raise good quarter horses. I hadn't seen him for years. He's still crazy as ever. How'd you get messed up with him?"

"It's a long story, Sunny, none of which matters right now. Can you get a message to him?"

"I reckon. I've been married to Cherokee Bob and the Texas Kid, and I would'uv married Al but he never asked me, so I reckon they'll find me tonight or in the morning."

"Tell him to gather an army and be at Ponce Park by ten tomorrow morning. Tell him we're going into battle," instructed Lick.

"Am I allowed to ask what this is about?" asked Sunny.

"I'd try and explain it to you but it's so complicated it would take too long. It's just that me and Al have got tangled in a problem and it's startin' to go sideways on us."

"Let me guess," she said. "There's a woman involved."

"Well, yes, but it's—"

She cut him off. "It's okay, honey. You don't have to say any more. Lemme get this straight. Bring the army to Ponce Park at ten tomorrow mornin'."

"Right."

"Does Al know where this park is?"

"I don't know, but he'll figger it out. Sunny, I know this sounds strange, but it's important, life or death, and I wouldn't ask you if it wasn't."

"Can I come?" she asked.

"The more the merrier. 'Bye, Sunny. I gotta go."

"By the way, they're retiring Kamikaze tomorrow night at the Finals. He'll buck out and that will be it. Off to the stud farm. They're gonna have a short little ceremony."

"Don't know where I'll be tomorrow, Sunny. I gotta get through the night."

"Okay, boy. Take care yo'sef," she said.

"'Night. And thanks." Lick hung up and walked outside to wait in the shadows. He exchanged the oversized chauffeur's cap and jacket for his own cowboy hat and coat. Restless, he decided to make another reconnoiter around the perimeter.

He headed in the direction of the observation tower, west, as well as he could figure. He heard voices. He eased up next to the fence and stopped still. Then he saw a parade of people walking toward a building. **That must be the theater,** he told himself.

Lick was suddenly struck with a micturation urge; scientifically speaking, he had to take a whiz. He pushed his way to the center of some bushes and made sweet relief. As the torrent splattered on the ground a bare patch of concrete began to appear in its wash. **It must be an old sidewalk, or septic, or well, or something,** he thought. Lick absentmindedly continued to expose more concrete as long as he was able. Then he scraped around in the loose dirt with his boot. Soon he'd cleared a spot as big as a car window, found the edge, and cleared the lip.

It was a lid. Curious, he got both hands under the lip and lifted. The warm smell of animals and straw rose to his nostrils. He slid the heavy lid to the side to reveal the edge of a hole. There was a faint light emanating from some kind of tunnel. Without a firm plan in mind, he decided to investigate and squeezed through the opening.

A square pit at least four by four with cinder block sides descended eight feet. Rebar handles were attached along one side to form a ladder. At the bottom of the pit a tunnel four feet tall headed in the direction of the fence.

Lick crouched and headed into the tunnel. He counted his steps and was sure he was past the fence. As he progressed, the height of the ceiling began to increase. Another twenty feet and his tunnel connected to a much larger tunnel. It was six feet tall and eight feet wide. But the entrance was blocked by a steel gate with shiny bars four inches apart. The door built into the gate was chained shut and padlocked.

There was a foot-tall gap between the top of the gate and the ceiling. Swinging his right leg up across the top bar, he began to squeeze through the space. He hooked his nose, buttons, belt buckle, and one family jewel in the process, and for a moment was wedged like a shim under a table leg. He nearly lost his hat.

He was startled by a sudden rush of air and a blood-curdling roar that literally made him bang his head and his tailbone simultaneously. He heard the sound of movement deep inside the bigger tunnel, the crack of a whip, a command that sounded like "pinhead," and another growl. Before he could turn his head, something passed below him in a hurry. He stayed stock-still. Soon he heard the slamming of a door. Then silence.

Relieved to be alive, Lick dropped to the floor. He saw that there were actually two tunnels. Below his feet, running beneath the tunnel, was another passageway covered by steel bars, with a slim boardwalk running down the middle. He guessed this was the way animals were driven from the barns to the theater. He started in the direction of the theater and soon reached a stairway that led up to a door. The animal alley continued on underneath the floor like a culvert passing beneath a low bridge.

Lick could hear noises now. Low growling, someone humming, crowd murmurs, laughter and applause. There was music . . . bullfight music, it seemed to him.

He leaned down over the alleyway but couldn't see anything. He could smell strong animal odors. **Like a cat box,** he thought. He tried the handle on the door gently. It gave. Slowly he opened it. It was pitch-black on the other side of the door.

Suddenly there was an explosion of applause! Lights seemed to flash above him. He slipped through the door and plastered himself against the wall. He was backstage in the theater. Two men on the other side of the stage behind the curtain saw him.

Lick's eyes were adjusting to the dark. Behind him was a ladder in the wall that led to the catwalks above the stage. He grabbed a rung and scrambled up. Beneath him he could feel and hear commands from the stage, roars from some jungle beast, and excitement from the crowd. He started across the stage on one of the catwalks. One of the backstage men was coming up the ladder after him. He looked in front of him. The other stagehand had climbed up the opposite side and now blocked the other end of the catwalk.

Lick slid off the catwalk onto a four-by-eight platform that seemed to hang suspended over the stage.

Both his pursuers stopped still. One waved at Lick to get off the platform. Then he froze and put his finger to his lips, indicating Lick should be still.

Suddenly a huge billow of smoke accompanied by blaring music assailed Lick's senses. Then, the platform dropped out from under him!

55

December 12: Tiger Act

Cody and Chrisantha sat third row center in the eight-row theater, which was elegantly appointed in gold-leaf décor and rich velvet curtains. To Cody's left sat a small Asian woman who introduced herself in proper, though accented, English as Ms. Narong, from Thailand. She showed Cody pictures of her grandchildren. "They live in Singapore and San Francisco," she told him. "Very good grandchildren."

Behind him the lady rock star named Qpid d'Art and two large men were whooping it up. Qpid was a voluptuous black woman. Her deep red leather vest was festooned with feathers that matched the plumage in her hair. The two gentlemen with her were almost cartoonish in their suit coats, one lime green, the other fluorescent orange. Black satin lapels, rakish fedoras, and heavy gold necklaces completed their ensembles. They were loud, and they were drunk or high or very happy, or all three. In her exuberance, Qpid kicked the back of Cody's seat, causing him to jiggle his drink.

"Sorry!" Qpid giggled, then accidently slipped and whacked him again. "Oh, man! Sorry, we're gettin' screwed up!" She leaned forward between Lick and the Asian woman and said, "Sorry, Grandma," then had a laughing fit accompanied by lots of pounding and gyration. As she was gasping to recover, she leaned forward one more time, her scarcely contained expansive breasts elbowing themselves between Lick and the old woman, "Sherry, shorry, sorry," she giggled and wiggled.

Quicker than the Lone Ranger could get the drop on Black Bart's acting coach, the sweet little Asian grandmother drew a .44 automatic pistol as big as a ham hock, and stuck it under the straining halter top on the north face of the closest Teton.

"That's awright, missy," said Grandma. "I think it won't happen again. If it does, I will let the air out of one of your life rafts."

Qpid sat back contritely.

Cody was too surprised to speak. If Qpid's

left 18 CCL (half of a 36 D) had been unable to stop the .44 shell, he would have been hit in the shoulder. Grandma just smiled sweetly at him. The pistol had disappeared.

Chrisantha took it all in and gave Cody room to move. Everybody faced forward as if nothing had happened.

From the booming speakers in surround sound, Beethoven's Fifth Symphony suddenly rained down upon the crowd. Timpani thundered, cymbals crashed, cellos laid ground cover while violins strafed the theater. Now and then a flute or piccolo would ricochet across the room.

The startling noise caused Chrisantha to grab Cody's leg forcefully just above the knee. He'd once rescued a poisoned great horned owl. In a moment of Saint Franciscan compassion, he'd set the stunned, unmoving creature in his lap. Guided by some deep instinctual roosting behavior, the beast roused itself from its coma and sank all eight talons into the meat of his thigh. That memory returned instantly.

Cody stood straight up, breaking Chrisantha's grip. She screamed! He screamed! Mercifully, the stage suddenly filled with smoke and the small crowd turned its gaze from the screaming couple to Ponce de Crayon as he stepped out of the cloud to center stage. Cody sat back down. Chrisantha scooted away from him.

Another cataclysmic explosion of lights, music, and smoke was followed by a wave of Ponce's magic cape. A six-hundred-pound Siberian tiger appeared like magic on the stage next to Ponce. He put the tiger through his tricks like a conductor decorating a cake. The tiger roared, stood on his haunches, batted the whip, even rolled over and curled up on a giant throw pillow. Ponce lit a cigarette and held the still-burning match up in front of the tiger. The tiger blew it out.

It was a splendid display of animal magic. The crowd was awed and appreciative. With a flourish, Ponce swirled his cape again. The stage flashed with thunder, lightning, and smoke. The master of Ponce Park stood downstage imperiously, like Red Adair, master fire snuffer, in front of an oil well fire.

The smoke gradually dissipated, leaving Ponce in all his glory, the tiger replaced by a dazed cowboy behind him, stage left. The cowboy's hat was crushed, his nose bleeding, and his moustache askew. He looked like he'd just dropped in—from ten thousand feet. He struggled to stand up straight.

"Lick!" Cody said in surprise.

"What?" asked Chrisantha.

Cody considered what he'd just said. "I mean, look!"

Ponce de Crayon stood smiling and unaware

of his supporting actor onstage until Busby, who was sitting in the back row, shouted, "That's him!"

"Who?" asked F. Rank Pantaker, who was one row in front of him.

"That cowboy! The one who rescued Teddie before we got her back," answered Busby.

Cody could hear it all clearly. He looked back at Lick, who was regaining his senses. Ponce still didn't realize he wasn't alone on the stage.

The crowd had now fallen silent.

"You sure?" asked F. Rank.

"Yessir!" affirmed Busby.

"Get him!" cried F. Rank, springing out of his seat.

The two stagehands raced for Lick. Ponce saw F. Rank and Busby charging the stage and heard the noise behind him. He turned. Lick reared his head back to stop the bleeding and fell over backwards just as the stagehands descended on him from opposite sides. The one coming from backstage left hit Ponce and knocked him into F. Rank, who was just mounting the stage in a single jump. It was a midair collision! The stagehand entering from the right missed them altogether and sailed off stage left into the audience like a sailor being buried at sea. Lick staggered back up to one knee in time to see the divers recovering and crawling back onstage in his direction. He turned and weaved to the door. Down the stairs he stumbled, falling flat on his face. He rolled over on the grid that formed the top of the tiger alley.

His hand hit a latch pin. He pulled it, rolled off the trapdoor, and dropped in. The barred lid closed on him. He was now in the darkened tiger tunnel. He heard his pursuers banging through the stage door above him, clattering down the stairs, and racing away down the upper tunnel.

Back in the theater, the audience sat in silent confusion. They didn't know if it was all planned or if they themselves were in danger. Cody leaned over and whispered to Chrisantha, "Get up and tell everyone it's part of the act and the show is over."

She looked into his eyes quizzically.

"For me," he whispered, and kissed her on the lips.

She smiled, stood up, and strode to the front. Cody started clapping. Soon everyone joined in, smiling.

Chrisantha gave the speech of a career diplomat. "Ladies and gentlemen, I hope you all enjoyed our evening's entertainment. And now ve vill all rebound to de main veranda for drinks, good-nights, and socialisting. Follow me, please."

As he joined the crowd filing out of the tiny theater, Cody hoped he could dig himself out of the sticky tar pit of temptation he'd just stepped in.

56

December 12: In the Tiger Cage

Lick was in the tiger tunnel that led from the theater stage back to the animal cages. He crawled farther under the stage and listened while the crowd departed. As his eyes adjusted to the dimness, he could see the mechanism that allowed the tiger to appear and disappear onstage. The barred tunnel ended with a ninety-degree turn into a three-sided, clear, hard plastic elevator that was eight feet high and had a black ceiling, a black floor, and hydraulic rams underneath.

The roof of the elevator was now level with the floor of the stage. When the elevator was raised, its floor pulled even with the floor of the stage. The roof was hidden by an overhanging curtain. During the rapid ascension and fall, smoke and lightning hid the mechanism.

Lick debated crawling back up through the overhead door to gain access to the upper tunnel but deemed it too risky. **They'll be back,** he thought. In the tiger tunnel an I-beam lip ran lengthwise along the top corners. Maybe he could flatten himself against the inner wall and escape detection.

He worked his way cautiously down the tiger tunnel, which smelled like the kennel room of a veterinary clinic. It forked and the upper tunnel crossed over him left to right. He opened a heavy barred gate and entered the left fork. Soon the tunnel connected with a large round cage twelve feet high and forty feet across. The cage itself was inside a big room with painted cinder block walls. A few chairs were scattered around the room. Lick lifted the barred sliding door and entered the cage quiet as a cat. His eyes adjusted to the darkness. Nothing but straw scattered all around and a lion tamer's stool. Then he saw her.

He knew immediately it was Teddie Arizona. She lay in the fetal position on the sawdust floor, like a fallen angel in her ivory dress. He approached her slowly and laid a hand on her shoulder. She gasped and swung a hard backhand, catching him square on the jaw, knocking him off his feet! Then she sprang.

In another instant, T.A. was kneeling above Lick's prone body. "Oh, Lick, I'm sorry. Are you hurt? Did I . . . ? I was so . . . I hope I didn't—"

Lick moved his arm and looked back over his shoulder cautiously. "T.A. Are you all right?"

She looked like a wildcat. Her hair was sticking out at odd angles and was sprinkled with sawdust. She had several red scrapes and welts on her face, shoulders, and chest. The flimsy dress she was wearing couldn't hide her heavy breathing. She unconsciously lifted the spaghetti strap that had fallen off her shoulder. She bent over Lick to touch his face and he looked right down at her heart. Neither of them noticed Valter, who had slipped in and was now watching them from outside the cage.

"Who is this interloper!" demanded Ponce, rushing into the training arena a few moments later, trailing a winded F. Rank.

Valter realized that F. Rank had never seen the cowboy. "This is one of the cowboys that Mrs. Pantaker was with when we found her in Idaho," he said.

"So," said Ponce, eyes narrowing. He whirled and marched out the door. F. Rank turned back to T.A. and Lick, who were slowly rising from the sawdust.

"What a mess you've made of everything, Teddie," said F. Rank, shaking his head. "It's out of my hands now. I hope you know what you're doing."

There was a loud clang as a large Siberian tiger blew into the cage with a roar! Valter recognized him as the one who had been onstage with Ponce.

Lick and T.A. stumbled back against the bars, hearts pounding. The tiger skidded to a stop ten feet in front of them. His eyes bored into them and he roared again.

Ponce reappeared on the other side of the bars. He spoke in a soothing voice. "The time has come to make your last call, to shine your last shoe, to have your last meal, to make your last stand. Prepare to meet Custer!"

"I have kissed my last fool!" T.A. whirled around, shouting through the bars at Ponce, who stepped back in surprise. She had both hands on the bars and fire in her eyes. Her diaphanous dress clung to her curves like a wet tee shirt on the Statue of Liberty. Dust rose from her hair as she shook it.

"I have tolerated my last indignation, and cooed my last dove! You bunch of pompous, pretentious pretenders to the throne of celebrity have condemned yourselves to the shallow landfill of weak sisters, also-rans, and runts of the litter. Look at yourselves!" she demanded. "Look at the company you keep. You're like something I'd have to scrape off my shoe before I came in the house. What a lame excuse for the best America has to offer! You want your money back? Not a chance! Not as long as you go on with this charade you call a hunt. You think I'm afraid of this tiger? Gimme that whip. I'll show you who's afraid!"

Teddie Arizona stood there like Joan of Arc charging into the locker room of the Oakland Raiders at halftime. All the men were stunned into silence—including Lick.

Ponce recovered his composure and drew his pistol. F. Rank gasped.

Suddenly the tiger took a step toward Lick. Then another step. They were big steps. Lick put himself between T.A. and the four-legged beast. He raised his arms and shouted at the tiger. The tiger backed up, startled. Lick dove to his left and reached for the lion tamer's stool. The tiger made a movement toward T.A. Lick swung back and cracked the big cat behind the ear with the leg end of the stool.

The tiger pivoted and swiped a pawful of bared claws toward Lick. Then he pounced. Lick went down on his back, hard, the seat of the stool pressing into his chest. The stool legs drove into the six-hundred-pound striped beast, one under each front-leg armpit, and two into the soft underbelly.

The tiger screamed in pain! T.A. grabbed the tiger's tail and pulled the off-balance animal backwards off of Lick. The tiger turned on T.A., holding his right front leg tight to his body. Lick clambered to his feet and swung the stool down hard, seat first, on the tiger's rump. The tiger paused in confusion.

A shot rang out!

Everyone jumped. The tiger turned tail and limped through the low door and back down the tunnel.

"This iss absolutely enough!" yelled Ponce, holding the smoking pistol. "Get them!"

Valter pulled his gun.

"Shoot HIM if you want," said Ponce. "I want HER in chains."

"You heard the boss, cowboy. Is this the hill you want to die on?" asked Valter.

"Lemme tellya, you dog dumps. I don't really care," answered Lick, surprised at his own answer.

"No, Lick," T.A. said calmly, " you're not gonna die for this. You're worth more than all these professional lightweights put together. This is my battle."

"Now you tell me," he said.

She relaxed her stance. "I'll go with you," she said to Ponce.

"Well, I'm not leavin' without her," said Lick.

Ponce studied Lick. The brim of his hat flapped loosely on one side and he was covered with sawdust. He looked like a breaded muskrat.

"Get some rope," instructed Ponce. "Tie them good and take them to the tower. We've got a big day tomorrow. And after tomorrow, I will be generous and give Mrs. Pantaker one last chance to tell us where the money is. After that, we can decide their fate." He paused before departing, then smiled his crooked grin and added, "That should be fun."

57

December 12: Cody and Chrisantha

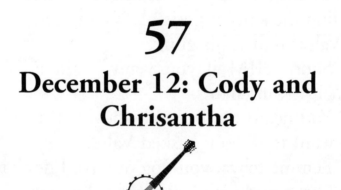

The party had begun to break up by 11:30 p.m. Neither Ponce de Crayon or F. Rank Pantaker returned to the veranda. Several of the guests were gathering their wraps and entourages, and working their way to the limos for their ride back to Pharaoh's Hotel. Cody watched the beachboy–all-pro quarterback disappear down the hall with Qpid d'Art.

"Where are they going?" he asked Chrisantha.

"There is guest rooms here at the Park for those who vish to freshen up, or stay later . . . or stay the night," she explained. "You vould like me to take you?"

Cody's first thought was, did it cost extra? But then he remembered that, for a million dollars, some perks were to be expected.

His second thought was, if he was going to help Lick, i.e., save his life or help him find T.A., he needed to find a way to remain inside the park as long as possible. Lick hadn't showed up in the parking lot for the 10:00 p.m. check-in, and Cody was starting to worry.

And, his third thought was, what to do about Chrisantha, who was already misinterpreting his intentions?

"Sure," he said.

He trailed her down a hallway with rooms named after jungle animals: Lion, Tiger, Leopard, Panther, Cheetah, Jaguar. She stopped in front of the Ocelot room and inserted the plastic card. The green light flashed. Into the den they entered.

"Vould you get me a drink, please," she asked. "Vodka, ice."

Cody began to fiddle with the ice bucket. "Chrisantha, I've got a big problem and I either need to tell you about it or ask you to leave. I'm not who I am. Or who I seem to be," he said, turning back toward her.

"So?" she said.

"I mean, I'm not this rich guy that you think I am."

"So?"

"You think I have money, right? I don't."

"I've already been paid. I don't care," she responded.

"No, not that you want money, I don't— What I mean is, I'm not even here for the hunt. I'm not even supposed to be here."

"So?"

"Well, so you can leave. I have things I have to do."

"You have my drink."

"I know, but—"

"Countdowns," she said, "I don't care. I don't care if you're rich. I don't care if you have things you have to do. I don't care if you're not Countdowns."

"What do you care about?" he asked, like a mastodon sliding into La Brea.

"You. You are a man. You look like a man, you feel like a man, you smell like a man, and I need . . . a man . . . right now."

He was starting to say something when she hooked her thumbs on the sides of her freshly unbuttoned suit jacket, swept them apart, and placed both her hands on her hips. The fluid motion was the equivalent of Superman spreading his cape and baring his **S**.

Cody was caught in the headlights.

Cody began to stir. He felt the pillow beneath his head, the bed under his back, the lips pressed against his, the heaviness of her body weighing on his chest. He smelled wet snowsuit. The fist of remorse squeezed his heart like only a Judas could know.

The memory of a flashing bilateral areola borealis caused a rush in his loins. A wave of shame rolled over him, in spite of the heart-stopping thrill that literally pulled his head back. The lips separated briefly from his own, then pressed hard again . . . and blew into his mouth. He inhaled involuntarily and coughed.

"Talk at me, Countdowns. Are you all right? Can you hear me?"

The voice was coming from above him. It was very faint and far away. He felt a rough wet rag rub across his face, a cool palm touch his forehead, and a throbbing on the side of his head. He opened one eye.

Chrisantha swam over him. She appeared to be looking through a porthole. Her eye was large and fishlike.

"What . . . where?" He paused and watched her come into focus.

"You fainted," she said.

Fainted? he thought. **Were we boxing and I faked a left hook and she poleaxed me?**

"You fell and hit yur head on the table there," she explained.

"Why were we kissing?" he said, still foggy and confused.

"I vassn't kissing you, I was givin' you the Hammerlick Moldover," she elaborated clear as day.

"Isn't that where you squeeze somebody from behind?" asked Cody, suddenly locating her plane of thought.

"I don't think so. Der vass no squeezing of behind, just the blowing of airs into yur mouth."

"That's artificial brespiration," he slipped, Freudianly.

"They are not artificial," she said, affronted.

Cody slowly raised his hand to stop this spiraling miscommunication. "One question," he said. "Did we . . . did we have, have we been . . ."

She stared at him uncomprehendingly.

"No," he said aloud, but mostly to himself.

"No, we couldn't have or surely I would remember and . . . I'm not undressed and you're not nak—, uh, . . . not undressed, either . . . like me, if we were, undressed, I mean, which we would be if we'd been . . . Besides, if we had and I didn't remember, I don't know if that would be a greater tragedy than not doing it and remembering. What do you think?" he asked sincerely.

Chrisantha frowned in genuine consternation. "I think you should see if you can get up and . . . But maybe you have amnesty and your brain is damage. Let me hellup yew." Facing him, Chrisantha leaned over and hooked her elbows under his armpits and lifted. He nearly smothered before he stood erect.

"There," she said as she steadied him.

Cody weaved a little and felt a momentary blackout. It passed. He shook his head and sat back down on the bed. "Lick," he suddenly said.

"Lick?" she asked. "The same Lick who appeared out from of the clear blue sky at the tiger show?"

"Wait," he said, waving his hand to stop her talking. He rubbed his eyes. "No. Lick is— This is what I need to talk to you about. I either need to tell you or you need to leave."

"Vat about us?" she asked, spreading her arms and shrugging her shoulders.

"They are . . . beautiful," he answered,

assuming she was speaking for herself and her accessories, which, of course, she wasn't, but it was an English-language nuance that escaped her.

"Yes, ve could be beautiful. Ve have the wine, the satin sheets, the protection, the room, and tomorrow vould be a great day for the hunting, ya?"

"No," said Cody, steeling his nerve. "I am married. I cannot have . . . relations with you."

"You do not like me?" she asked, sliding by the concept of "cleaving to no other till death do us part."

"You need to understand something," said Cody. "And you can, because you're smart, I can tell, and you've seen a lot more of the world than me. So you know it's not because I don't like you, or find you attractive, or—"

"But no one vould know," she interrupted, puzzled. "I don't even know yur name, vat could possibly harm it? Besides, I'm so . . . how do ve say it, thorny."

"Thorny, yeah," he agreed. "But I've got bigger fish to fry. Bigger fish to catch," he corrected. "No, skip the bigger fish, I've got a serious problem and I need you to do me a favor and it has nothing to do with fish."

"Vell, I don't know. I don't think it's happened before," she said.

"What?" asked Cody.

"Somebody vat turned me over."

"Down," he said.

"Turned me overdown."

"Best I can tell you is, don't take it personally. As tempting as you are, I am married to a woman that I would climb mountains for, swim oceans for, crawl through twenty-six acres of broken glass just to sniff the tracks of the wagon that hauled her laundry. I love her . . . and she loves me. So, you see, even if you were Mona Lisa, Marilyn Monroe, Cleopatra, the Venus de Milo, or the African Queen, you would still not be able to break the love barrier. As I said, it's not personal between you and me, it's personal between her and me." He stopped and looked at her pleadingly. "Chrisantha, the right thing for me to do would be to walk out the door right now, but my friend is in a terrible bind. He needs my help and I could very much use your cooperation . . . your assistance. It would make what I have to do so much easier."

"Vell," she said after a moment's consideration, "vat is it I vould be respected to do?"

Cody sighed with relief. "I need to look around the compound, the park," he said. "I need to do it secretly and I need you to cover for me. To stay right here in this room all night. And . . . not say a word to anyone."

"Are you goin' to give me a raisin?" she asked.

"A raisin?" He pondered a moment. "I imagine they have snacks in the little refrig there, the minibar."

"No, no, a raisin . . . to stay and hellup you and not tell Mr. Pankanker and da Crayon vat it is you are doing. Vitch is, vat it is, I don' know . . . anyway."

"Oh," said Cody, nodding his head. "Yes, staying here for no raisin except to help me."

"Do you vant it is that I should know?"

"Tell you what, Chrisantha. I assure you I'm not going to hurt anybody. And you won't get in any trouble, you have my word. So, for right now, the less you know, the better it is . . . for now, I mean. If you can live with that," he finished.

"If I can live vit that, I can. And maybe you might change your mind? If I had a good enough raisin . . . who could know?"

Cody stepped out into the hall thoroughly vexed.

58
December 13: Searching for Lick and T.A.

Cody made his way outside and past the animal pens. He advanced toward a big machinery shop. A large halogen lamp lit the maintenance yard.

The crew had gone home but Cody suspected that a night man might be about, so he stayed to the shadows. Several pieces of large machinery were lined up like dinosaurs at parade rest. Front-end loaders, a road grader, two backhoes, a tractor, three semi trucks, and assorted flatbeds, pickups, and cement mixers.

Light shone from the shop windows. He eased up to one of them and peered in. What he saw looked like a heavy-metal video game. Several elaborately customized four-wheel-drive vehicles sat like lions waiting to be released on the Christians in the Roman Colosseum. Mad Max meets Bigfoot. Two of the vehicles had flying bridges behind the windshields; tomorrow's hunters would be able to stand and look out over the top of the cab. Another vehicle had a turret like a tank. A .50 caliber machine gun was mounted in front of the manhole. The shooter would have a 180-degree field of fire.

There was an open-topped Suburban that resembled a touring bus. An obviously rebuilt World War Two jeep sat proudly amongst the others. Cody could see it had headers and dual exhaust, and the chassis and axles had been altered to accommodate twenty-four-inch truck wheels. It had no windshield. Shoot at will, Cody guessed. There was a dune buggy that could have been owned by the Sheik of Palm Springs. Two motorcycles were partially hidden, but they appeared to have vented rifle barrels protruding from either side of the center post on the handlebars like guns on the wings of a P-51 Mustang.

What a collection, Cody thought. It was every redneck monster-truck driver's dream. Every smash-'em-flat, dogfight, diesel dirt bike, three-eyed super Harley, good ol' boy, with Technicolor tattoos, head reared back, shirttail out, three sheets to the wind, and burnin' like a house on fire.

Man oh man. Cody could almost smell the smoke.

He tried the steel door to the big shop. It was locked, as were the back two doors and all the windows. He made a pass around the five animal enclosures. He found signs denoting the residents: WHITE RHINO, BLACK RHINO, PANDA, PO-LAR BEAR, and GRIZZLY.

Where's the tiger? he wondered. The one Ponce had used in his act. He continued to explore and found an enclosed aviary where Ponce had stashed two California condors with their wings clipped, at least twelve bald eagles, and an assortment of spotted owls, pygmy owls, and a covey of whooping cranes, along with some crowned lemurs and koalas.

Finally he worked his way around to the Big Cat House. He tried the door. Locked tight. Another steel door. He peered through the glass in the door. He saw that it opened into a large, well-lit concrete alleyway with cages on both sides to his right. To the left were workrooms, offices, and a hallway. Suddenly he heard people coming down the hallway from the left. Cody stepped back and plastered himself against the side of the building.

The door opened and two men came out. One was large, with a buckaroo moustache and hand-tooled cowboy boots. The second was smaller and wiry. Both had on baseball caps and jackets.

"Whattaya think they're gonna do with 'em?" the smaller man asked as they passed outside.

"I don't know. It's not our deal," said the big man.

"She's not gonna talk, ya know."

"It's not our deal, Busby. Just let it go."

"Well, they can't just . . . I mean, if she tells 'em or doesn't tell 'em, seems to me it's the same outcome. I don't know whether I wanna be mixed up in this."

"Don't think about it. Just do what you're told. It ain't our deal to worry about. We've just got to make sure they don't escape on our watch."

"But—"

"Knock it off! I don't wanna hear any more. I'm tired."

"Okay, but—"

The big man stopped and looked at his companion. "No more," he said. "No more." They walked toward the atrium in silence.

Cody let out his breath and was about to step out from the wall when he heard a new set of footsteps coming confidently his way. Ponce de Crayon strode out of the darkness heading for the same door the other two men had just exited.

Ponce paused at the door long enough to unlock it, then entered. Cody broke from the shadows and tried to catch the door before it closed. No luck. Only a scuffed knee. He looked up at the tower. **They must be in there somewhere,** he thought, **but what do I do now?**

He looked down at his watch. It was long past midnight. Cody's coach had become a pumpkin.

59

December 13: Prisoners in the Tower

Three stories up in the tower, Lick and T.A. each stood on a straight chair, trussed hands suspended upright at chin level, elbows bent. Their faces were less than twelve inches apart.

The two were immobilized through a devious figment of Valter's ingenuity. They were tied to opposite ends of a polyethylene ski rope, which ran up and over a large iron chandelier hanging from the twelve-foot ceiling. The rope was so short that when one sat on the chair with arms stretched above his or her head, the other was forced to stand on the chair with arms stretched overhead. Only when they both stood on the chairs could they lessen the pressure on their arms. Valter kept an eye on them from the bed.

The only thing that lessened the indignity was that T.A. had been allowed to change back into her dirty jeans and khaki shirt before being locked in the tower.

T.A. leaned in to whisper to Lick. "Do you think I should tell them where the money is?"

"I don't know what I'd do if I were you," he responded quietly. "There's no tellin' what'll happen, even if you tell 'em."

"That's what I'm afraid of," she said. "I don't think F. Rank would harm us, but I have little doubt that Ponce and Valter here would do us in, in a heartbeat. My problem is," she said, "you."

"Me?"

"Yes. I couldn't let them . . . I can't even say the word . . ."

"Murder," he suggested.

"Yes. I couldn't let that happen. I would have to tell them on the condition you were let free."

"**We** . . . **we** were let free," he whispered with a flash of anger.

"Having a lover's quarrel?" asked Valter lazily from his sitting position on the bed.

Lick mumbled an unintelligible retort.

"Watch your lip, Two-Bit," laughed Valter. "You're not speaking from a position of strength."

"Yer pretty tough, all right, **pendejo,**" sneered Lick in frustration, "with a gun in yer hand, six guys at yer back, and a girl between us."

Valter rose from the bed and in one swift movement kicked Lick's chair out from under him. Lick fell hard, his back hitting the floor, which jerked T.A. off the chair she was standing on. She cried out in pain. Then Valter kicked the chair out from under her dangling feet. She hung suspended, all her weight on the joints of her shoulders. She screamed in agony.

"Valter!" an authoritarian voice boomed as the door to the tower flung open and Ponce strode in. "Wot are you dooink! Yew moost not get zo ekzited. Yew moost ekzercize control. I yam a liddle sewerprize-ed. Yew alwaze zeemed zo profess-see-own-al."

"Sorry, sir. I was—"

"He was tormenting the girl," Lick lied in a disgusted tone. "He was teasing her and touching her—"

"I was doing no such thing!" exclaimed Valter, his pride wounded.

"A little jealousy? Do I detect indignation from the inept Sir Galahad?" observed Ponce.

"The truth is," he continued, the Eastern European accent morphing into the vocal clarity of an Iowa native, "I couldn't sleep knowing you two were alive and kicking. So I have brought a solution. Valter, it will let you rest easier, too."

Valter looked uneasy. Although he was good at using it as a veiled threat, he had never been asked to commit cold-blooded murder and didn't know what he would do if the occasion arose.

Ponce produced a small valise and from it drew a bottle and a disposable plastic syringe. He carefully broke the seal on a 20-gauge needle and attached it to the syringe. He made a big production of filling the syringe from the bottle.

Lick's eyes widened as he looked up from the floor. T.A., her head down, was spinning slowly by her tethered arms.

Ponce looked over at Valter. Valter froze his expression. He looked like a still frame of a candidate who had just broken wind as he was being presented for baptism.

Ponce smiled his crooked smile. One side of his moustache quivered like a wounded bird. "This will put them to sleep for several hours. After the hunt is concluded we will use more effective methods to elicit the location of . . . MY MONEY!" He whirled on T.A. He drove the needle through her jeans right above the left hip pocket. She screamed! Ponce pressed his left hand against her belly and held her steady as he pushed the plunger, emptying the syringe. Finished, he retracted the needle swiftly and let her go.

Lick scrambled to his feet, which lowered T.A. She wobbled slowly, her toes touching the ground, arms still stretching upright. Her head fell. Her knees buckled. She was out cold. Lick's arms stretched even tighter against the dead weight.

"Your turn, buckaroo," said Ponce refilling the syringe and fitting a new needle. Lick kicked out at Ponce. Ponce deftly dodged the attempt.

"Now, now. Do you want to remain in this position all night, or would you like to go to sleep peacefully? Do you think she looks comfortable?"

Lick grimaced and looked down at T.A., who was breathing regularly but hanging in an awkward position, all the weight of her body pulling on her arms.

"Maybe this would help her," said Ponce. He grasped T.A.'s side of the rope and hung on it, pulling it down until she lay crumpled on her knees, relieving some of the tension. Lick's feet were now twenty-four inches off the ground. He hung and swiveled.

"Make up your mind, cowboy," said Ponce.

He waited for ten seconds, then ordered Valter, "Pull his pants down around his knees."

Valter walked behind Lick carefully. Ponce still held the rope but stood back from Lick's hanging body. He held the syringe up so Lick could see it.

"I should give this intramuscularly, but I could go directly into the peritoneal cavity if I was just stabbing in the dark," warned Ponce. "Of course, there are other ways to induce slumber if you choose to make this difficult."

Lick tried a swift kick but was off target. Valter threw a hard kidney punch, which took Lick's breath away. Valter then reached around from the back, undid his buckle and zipper, and pulled his pants down around his boot tops.

"Turn him around," ordered Ponce.

Valter moved Lick 180 degrees.

With one hand Ponce stuck the needle through Lick's white jockey shorts and injected him with the powerful anesthetic.

60
December 13: Late-Night Reconnoiter

Cody walked around the perimeter of the tower. No windows were openable and no other doors except the one he had seen Ponce enter. He checked his watch: 2:10 a.m. Ponce had been inside twenty-five minutes. At last the door opened and Ponce emerged. He paused at the sound of footsteps. As Cody watched from the shadows, F. Rank Pantaker rounded the corner, heading for the tower.

"Where do you think you are going?" asked Ponce.

"Oh, I just thought I might try and persuade her one more time to tell us where the money is," answered F. Rank.

"It won't do any good now. I've given them both a little sedative cocktail, which should last until morning. Besides, I'm afraid we are going to be much too busy to worry about her while we've got guests to attend to."

"Oh," answered F. Rank, who was sinking into a deep depression.

"Do not weaken on me now, F. Rank. We have a magnificent day ahead of us. I have paired you with the Wall Street banker, who has asked to be called Count Downs. He has chosen to hunt the clouded leopard using the machine-gun motorcycle. A good choice, a worthy adversary."

Ponce put his arm around F. Rank and steered him back toward the atrium and their rooms.

Cody followed them at a safe distance. When he reached his room he inserted the key card, took a deep breath, and opened the door. The pungent, tangy smell of a women's aerobic class assailed his nostrils.

61

December 13: Morning of the Hunt

Day broke over an anthill of activity at Ponce Park. A Cessna-eye view showed a large field buzzing with vehicles, horses, and people in quasimilitary uniforms crawling over the landscape.

Large outside lights burned bright holes in the gray of morning.

Cody and Chrisantha walked down the hall into the atrium. He was wearing, as per his wardrobe request, khaki hunting pants, an insulated shooting shirt with suede elbows and shoulder patch, a baseball cap, and his own boots. She was dressed in army issue desert camouflage pants and shirt, and was wearing black lace-up army boots. A matching bill cap and mirror aviator sunglasses completed her trappings. They looked ready to invade Normandy.

"Something to eat?" he asked.

"Vel, shure," she said, smiling. "I'm really quite hungry."

They picked and tasted their way through the exotic breakfast buffet, trying the Galapagos-turtle-egg soufflé, dolphin tongue, and a side of cured, smoked Przewalksi's horse meat.

"Vat do you think?" she asked, savoring the tenderloin of San Joaquin kit fox.

"Lick taught me you can eat anything if you put enough Miracle Whip on it," he said, slathering a dollop on a fillet of short-nosed sucker.

F. Rank Pantaker spotted them at their table and came over.

"How y'all doin' this mornin'?" he boomed.

"We're fine," said Cody.

"I'll bet you are," smiled F. Rank, leering at Chrisantha. She smiled back.

"I'm sorry I didn't get to come visit with you personally, but what with you bein' in Zurich and Antwerp and Wall Street and all those places hangin' out with them socialist foreigners, I couldn't keep track of you! Ha, ha! Just as well, you sendin' the money. Hope everything is to your likin'," he said, winking toward Chrisantha. "Oh, and we got the clouded leopard lined up. All the way from Borneo, I think. They're little boogers, no bigger'n a coyote. Pretty fast, but if we can get him up a tree it'll be a snap. Anyway, the whole fifty sections is fenced, so, worse comes to worst, we can corner him. We got radio collars on all the big cats anyway, so trackin' him won't take all day. . . . I see the little lady is goin' with ya, right?"

Cody nodded.

"Good. When yer ready, we can go over to the staging field and pick up your mode of transportation."

"I'm ready," said Cody.

"If you gentlemen vill excuse me, I vill join you in a few minutes," said Chrisantha, rising and wiping her lips.

"Shorley, ma'am," said F. Rank graciously. "Follow me, Count," he said, and they headed toward the staging area.

62

December 13: Pike Peaks

T.A. stirred and the pain of her bruises and scrapes came to life. Her arms had been untied and she found herself lying on the bed. Lick lay beside her under his own blanket, tied to the bed frame by his neck and ankle. He was snoring peacefully. She sat up against the head-board with some difficulty. The room was getting light. There was a clock on the wall: 9:01 a.m.

T.A. looked around the room. She saw Pike sitting in a straight chair beside the top of the stairs. He was watching her.

"What now?" she asked Pike. He made no reply.

Ten minutes later, there was a knock at the door. Pike rose and opened it. A tall blonde woman dressed in army fatigues stood in the doorway, a large tray in her hands.

"They sent me here to see if you vould like some brakefest." She smiled and looked at T.A. "You and the nice lady."

"Yeah, sure," said Pike. "Put it there on the table."

Chrisantha strode across the room. "Monsieur de Crayon hopes you all had a very good night's sleep," she said.

"You saw him?" asked Pike.

"Ya, I yust delivered him some cappuccino in his office. He vas talking vit a man vat looked like Saddam Hussein. Anyvay, he vants you all to eat something." Chrisantha uncovered the large tray she was carrying. A smell of bacon and cinnamon rolls filled the air.

"Who vould like caffe?" she asked, holding up a large pot.

"Well, I dang sure could use somethin' for a headache," observed Lick, now awake and trying to push himself into a sitting position. The rope around his ankle prevented it, so he lay on his side.

"I think you better go," said Pike. "I'll serve the . . . these people."

"You don't have to vorry, mister. Ponce has told me they are being detained for the authorities," Chrisantha explained.

"I'm not sure you should stay," said Pike, worriedly.

"Vell, if you don't vant me here, I can go. Vould you like some caffe? You look tired." She poured a cup. "Cream and sugar?" she asked Pike.

He studied her a moment. "No. Black," he said.

Chrisantha served a plate of breakfast to both Lick and T.A.

"Reckon you could untie either my neck or my ankle, so's I could sit up?" Lick asked Pike.

"Nope," answered Pike.

Lick and T.A. ate with gusto and each drank two bottles of water. Lick had to use the chamber pot as well. Chrisantha offered Pike a sweet roll. He declined, choosing to drink his coffee and watch the others.

"Are you two man and wife?" Chrisantha asked the couple tied in bed.

"No questions," instructed Pike. He continued to stare at Lick.

"Why don't you ask him, Pike," said T.A.

"What?" asked Lick.

T.A. looked at Lick and said, "Pike there thinks you're a hero."

"You never told me that."

"He said you rode that bull."

"Don't amount to a hill of beans now," Lick mumbled.

"You can't say that," T.A. said. "Tell him, Pike. He can't say that, can he?"

The pause hung in the air.

"Nope," said Pike. "He can't. Nobody that did what he did can say it didn't matter."

Lick's forkful of Denver omelette hung in the air. He took a hard look at Pike and spoke. "Look at me now, Pike. Two years ago I was king of the mountain, now I'm workin' on a cow outfit on the edge of nowhere, prob'ly not now, they've done fired me, I'm sure. Bein' chased by a bunch of thugs that I don't even know. Maybe two friends to my name, if I could think of another one, and not knowin' what I'm gonna do tomorrow whether I get outta here or not. That buckle don't mean diddly-squat if ya don't have yer act together. I couldn't even buy this breakfast if they handed me the check. How's that for a hero?" Lick concluded matter-of-factly.

T.A. stared at Lick. "Well, aren't you the whiner."

"Hold on, Mrs. Pantaker," said Pike.

"You shut up, Pike," snapped T.A. "I've got more invested in this man than anybody here, and if he's a world champion—"

"He only won the average," interjected Pike.

"If he's a world champion, that doesn't say much for the sport of rodeo. You probably don't deserve that buckle," she said to Lick.

"Yes, he does," said Pike, curtly. "He deserves it. I don't care what else he does, or is doin', or has done, he rode Kamikaze. He rode him like he owned him. He gave us all a day in the sun.

Every fifty-dollar-a-day puncher, every gunsel, every wannabe, everybody that's doin' day work at the feed store or drivin' a truck 'cause he can't afford to be a cowboy. Say what you want, Missus, but you can't take that buckle away from him. No sir. He earned it—the hard way. I know. I saw him do it."

The room was stunned to silence. T.A. stared at Pike openmouthed. Lick was blushing.

Chrisantha knelt down beside Pike's chair. She put her hand on his leg and looked at his face. She had tears in her eyes.

A volley of gunshots broke the mood. Several big booms and some smaller fire continued. The sound of vehicles rumbling and engines being revved added to the cacophony. An unintelligible voice over a loudspeaker crackled in and out.

"They're moving out," said T.A. "Let us go, Pike. There's enough decency left in you to do the right thing."

"What do you know about the right thing?" asked Pike, still irked at her criticism of Lick. "'Member, I've been watching your act for . . . what, two years, now?"

"You're right. You're absolutely right," she answered. "And that's the reason for my stealing the money and escaping F. Rank's prison. It was never about the money. Heck, I'd give it back right now if they'd stop the hunt. But they won't.

I'm just trying, for once in my life, to do the right thing. So I can look at myself in the mirror and not be ashamed. I'm ashamed for you, too, Pike. I think there's a good man, a good cowboy, still inside you somewhere. And if I can find the grit to change my life, you can, too."

Chrisantha was kneading Pike's leg gently and still looking at him. He placed his hand over hers. She stopped kneading. He didn't lift his hand. He seemed frozen in thought.

Finally Lick said, unrhetorically, "You wanna know what I think?"

Pike, who'd been staring into the space behind them, focused his eyes on Lick and answered, "Yeah. I would like to know what you think."

"I think she's a better man than either one of us . . . that's what I think."

Pike stared at Lick. All the posturing and pride washed out between them as they held eye contact. Lick's last humiliatingly honest observation sank to the naked heart of Pike's discontent. He took a deep breath and exhaled. "I couldn't have said it better."

Chrisantha leaped onto Pike and knocked his chair over backwards! She had her arms around him and was kissing him like a toilet plunger doing CPR!

63
December 13: Charge!

Pike and Chrisantha untied T.A. and Lick and found their boots. They all ran downstairs and raided the workers' locker room. Lick easily found a nice down jacket with a fur collar and some work gloves. Somehow his cowboy hat had made it to the tower. T.A.'s choice was not as wide. The lockers were used mostly by men.

Pike ran back upstairs and returned in a minute. "Maybe this will fit!" he said, holding up a red-and-black matador's jacket elaborately embroidered with silver brocade. "It was in Ponce's costume closet. There's a cape, too!"

T.A. had been holding a long white lab coat. "Let me try it on," she said, taking the heavy chaqueta from Pike and putting it on over the khaki shirt. "A little long in the sleeve but warm enough, especially with this here," she said, pulling on the lab coat.

"Take these," said Lick, handing T.A. a pair of work gloves.

They were ready. The four of them headed

for the door. They could hear the roaring and revving of engines getting louder.

✦ ✦ ✦

🌙 Meanwhile, on the staging field, Cody had chosen one of the motorcycles. F. Rank preferred to ride in one of the big pickups. He switched on the handheld receiver that would monitor the signals from the radio-collar transmitter on the clouded leopard. He was also in radio contact with Cody through the custommade headset built into the motorcycle helmet.

"We're moving out, Count Downs," F. Rank crackled over the walkie-talkie on channel 7.

"Go ahead," Cody responded. "I've got to run behind the barn!"

"I'll wait," said F. Rank.

"Just drive slow," said Cody. "It'll just take a second!"

"Okay," said F. Rank. "They won't release the leopard until we give them the signal."

Cody wheeled his big dirt bike back toward the tower building. He dismounted and raced to the door. Just as he reached for the handle, the door swung open, knocking him back. The helmet he was wearing absorbed the blow but he still staggered.

As T.A. pushed through the door she shouted, "Grab him, we'll take his motorcycle!" Pike fol-

lowed her through and delivered a hard punch to
Cody's stomach. It doubled him over. The air
went out of his lungs as he dropped to his knees.

"Vait!" cried Chrisantha. "It's Countdowns!"

"Who?" yelled T.A.

"Countdowns, I mean, Rory! Cory! Colby!
Your friend! Vat's his name!"

"Cody?" asked Lick.

"Ya! Cody! Countdowns, the hunting
poster," she confirmed, not understanding the
fine line between poster and imposter.

Lick helped pull the helmet off while Cody
gasped for air.

"The . . . hunt's begun," Cody wheezed.
"Why did you hit me?"

"I didn't," said Lick. "Pike did. Why were
you wearing a helmet, anyway?"

"That's enough!" shouted T.A. "Is this your
friend, Lick?"

"Yeah . . . Cody," Lick explained. "He and I
intercepted one of the official hunters. Cody
took his identity and—" Then Lick remembered where he had seen Chrisantha. "And you."
He looked at Chrisantha. "That's what you've
been tryin' to tell us, that Cody's—"

Chrisantha interrupted, "Ya, that's Countdowns, I mean Coty, he's already unfiltered the
hunting trip and is waiting for us to escape, so
you can rescue the girl, this girl here."

"Did he tell you that this girl here, Teddie, is going to stop the hunt?" Lick asked.

"I don't know," she said questioningly. "I think ve vas mostly to save the girl."

T.A. dove into the breach. "Boys and ma'am, I have been through hell and Mountain City to stop this hunt. There is still time. I am going to take that horse and with a gun or a knife or my fingernails I am going to mess up Ponce's day. Any help would be appreciated. Where do you stand, Pike?"

"I'm with you, Mrs. Pantaker," he said.

"You may call me Teddie," she said politely.

"And I," spoke up Chrisantha, sliding up next to Pike and putting her arm through his, "am vit him."

T.A. looked back toward the field and the cloud of dust beyond. Two company pickups were still parked in the staging area along with a gas truck, a beer wagon, and an ambulance. "Okay," she said, "Pike, you—"

They all heard the noise at the same time. It was a distant rumble, the sound of vehicles at high speed. Horns honking, but in the opposite direction of the staging hunters.

Lick ran over to the Cyclone fence gate that allowed big trucks into Ponce Park. It had a lock the size of a ham hanging on an equally over-sized chain. Lick peered through the fence to see the cause of the uproar. It was a conglomeration of pickups, horse trailers, U-Haul trailers, cars, and at least two semis in procession.

The first pickup came speeding up to the main entrance. The driver suddenly swerved to his left and came directly toward Lick. Lick's first thought was to turn and run, but then he saw a body lean out of the passenger-side window. It was waving a beer. It was the old man.

The car slid to a stop sideways in front of the gate.

"Al! It's you! I'd fergot all about you!" said Lick in surprise.

"Yessir, my young rodeo mongrel, I have arrived with reinforcements!" exclaimed the old man. "When does the party begin?"

"They just left, Al. We're fixin' to chase 'em and muck up the hunt," replied Lick.

"Well, open the gate, pawdner, we'll just go with ya!" said Al.

"She's locked," said Lick.

"Stand back, take the women and children, and cover yer eyes!" proclaimed the old man.

They watched while the old man directed his chauffeur to back up along the line of vehicles that were idling in the immediate area.

Suddenly T.A. and Lick heard a diesel engine rattle and catch. They turned back toward the staging field to see the gasoline truck, a ten-wheeler, swinging in their direction. Before Al could give the command, Pike, behind the wheel of the gas truck, put one right down the center.

It tore through the gate! Great screeching noises accompanied the blowing apart of the wire, aluminum, and steel. Pike had a smile on his face. Chrisantha squeezed his knee.

Within ten minutes all the old man's army had passed through the mangled gate and were in the staging field. They quickly commandeered the two pickups and the ambulance.

"This fine assemblage," the old man was expounding to Lick, Cody, and T.A., "is the Old Timer Rodeo Cowboys Association, the Turtles, along with a few specialty acts and . . . the Rodeo Clown Reunion. If lies, exaggerations, broken bones, forgotten rides, and just-outta-the-moneys were flammable, this bunch could heat London for a fortnight! Just tell us the battle plan, General Custer, and we will charge the beachhead, swim the Ganges, scale Mount Olympus, and defeat the foe, five, and six of 'em! All ye need do, Fair Miss, is purnt the way!"

"Cody," T.A. turned to him and asked, "have you got a plan?"

Cody considered his answer, then spoke. "They all left this point right here and fanned out. Each hunter has his prey preselected and the guide can find their particular beast by tuning in to its radio-collar transmissions. The birds, too, I reckon, have a collar, but they have their wings clipped so they can't fly too good, anyway—"

"Listen, Cody, my son," suggested Al, leaning out of his pickup window, "what say we just sic the cavalry on 'em and go fer broke."

He pointed to the crowd behind him. Cowboys and cowgirls were unloading horses from the back of the open-topped semi trailers. Some were lugging tack from their vehicles and saddling the beasts. Others were unhooking their horse trailers.

Lick took a harder look at the enthusiastic crowd. It looked like a potty break at a seniors' picnic. "Ain't a guy there under seventy, Al. They're liable to get hurt," he said.

Al gave him a cold stare. "Lemme tellya, tenderfoot, there's boys in that bunch who could still do a day's work on horses you couldn't saddle," he stated, quasi-quoting a line from a Larry McWhorter poem.

Lick was chagrined. He climbed up on the cab of one of the semis and whistled the crowd to attention. "I am going to assume," he shouted, "that Al Bean, here, has told you what's goin' on. If he hasn't, there's no time to explain. Out there in that giant piece of desert is a bunch of high-rollin' lowlifes, takin' a bunch of big-money mafia types on a hunting safari. It's all a setup. Shootin' fish in a barrel. Every critter they're hunting is illegal to hunt. These folks think they own the world. They think they're tough. I say, they don't know what tough is. We'll hunt down every last one of 'em and pee on their fire! Grab a horse, a car, or climb in the back! If you've got guns . . . shoot low! Let's move out!"

Lick climbed down from the semi and dropped in front of T.A. Their eyes locked. He saw passion rise in the malamute steel-grays. She grinned. Sparks crackled between them. His heart was pounding.

"It's time," he said.

"I'm grabbin' a horse," she said, and started to walk away. Then she turned back, put both hands on Lick's upper arms, and kissed him on the lips. They held eye contact for a humming-bird's heartbeat. Then she spun and ran back to gather a mount.

Lick climbed on the motorcycle behind Cody. With the snap of an ankle and the twist of a wrist, they were off in a roar! Within the next ten minutes, an army of assorted cowboys and cowgirls rolled out across the sagebrush flats, spreading like cheap wine on a white tuxedo.

64
December 13: The Hunt Begins

"I see you," said F. Rank into the walkie-talkie. Count Downs's motorcycle had appeared in the rearview mirror of his pickup.

"Good," said Cody. "I see you, too."

The truck slowed as Cody approached. "The leopard is about two miles to the northwest," F. Rank said over the two-way. "In quadrant twenty-two, if you remember the map. Best way the guide says to handle it is for you to get within half a mile. Then we'll give them the signal to release the leopard from the cage. He'll hear you comin' and you should have about three-quarters of a mile to get in behind him with your scooter and line up on him with the machine gun. Pull alongside me so you don't have to ride in all that dust."

Cody didn't respond, just stayed the course. Lick was hunkering down behind him, with his eyes shut tight against the wind and sand and his hat pulled down tight over his ears. He looked like Gabby Hayes in the wake of a B-52.

F. Rank was puzzled why Cody hadn't pulled up next to him yet. "What are you doing back there, Count! Answer me! I can't see you for the dust. Can you hear me?"

F. Rank stuck his head up through the sunroof in an attempt to see the trailing motorcycle. They were only going forty miles an hour, but on rough ground it made for a bumpy ride. Cody pulled within two car lengths of the pickup and F. Rank could make him out.

"What are you doing, Count? Everything okay ?" shouted F. Rank into the handset.

"Pull over right now, Pantaker, or I will blow up your truck!" shouted Cody.

"What are you talking about? Are you crazy?"

"Pull over, Pantaker! This is your last chance!"

F. Rank leaned over to his driver. "Take a hard left!"

The pickup swerved to the left, Cody leaned with it, lined up on the target, and thumbed the trigger. A burst of machine-gun fire punctured the tailgate and left hindquarter of the pickup.

"Pull over!" Cody yelled again into the headset in the helmet.

The pickup swerved to the right! Cody followed and fired another blast. The right hindquarter of the pickup sprung a leak. In the fast and furious action, Cody saw F. Rank trying to stand up through the sunroof. He was holding a rifle. The driver was swinging back and forth, trying to get out of the line of fire. F. Rank couldn't get steady enough to aim. He hit himself three times in the eye with the rifle scope, and in one jarring arroyo the rifle barrel bounced off his forehead and jumped ship without firing a shot.

The driver was unable to see his pursuer and wound up swinging perpendicular to the motorcycle. Cody was three car-lengths away when he fingered the trigger and pulverized both front and rear tires on the left side. The truck listed like a sinking ship and drug itself to a stop.

Cody raced behind the truck and slid to a swooshing, ski slope, sand-and-gravel stop! Lick fell off sideways, flat on his back.

F. Rank staggered out of the truck toward the motorcycle, which now lay on its side. "What's goin' on? Have you lost your mind! Who's this?" he asked, pointing at Lick on the ground. "And what's the big idea!"

Lick reached out and jerked F. Rank's leg out from under him. He fell with an arm-flailing thump. Lick was on him like stink on a buzzard's bib.

"Remember me, Big Shot?" asked Lick, who was now sitting on F. Rank's chest, hands around his neck.

Realization came over F. Rank's face. "Where is she?" he asked.

"On her way, F. Rank, to make your day."

65

December 13: The Chase Continues

Two miles to the northeast, in section 29, a group of three rhinoceri stood munching on green alfalfa hay that had been scattered in a small clearing. The clearing also had a watering trough, a block of salt, and a couple of scraggly trees. Two of the rhinos were dark gray and the third was a lighter color and had a blunt horn. Two hundred yards away, parked on a small rise, were two custom-made Humvees. One had a machine-gun turret on the top. The other had a flying bridge. People were peering at the rhinos from the vehicles with binoculars.

"Miz Narong, we can move closer if you're not comfortable with this shot," the guide said to the sweet, grandmotherly woman by his side. "The lighter-colored male to the right of the group is the Sumatran rhinoceros, very rare. Only a few pockets exist in the wild. They are confined to southeast Asia. This one came from a business associate of Mr. de Crayon in Bangladesh.

"The two black rhinos are more common but still on the endangered-species list. These were acquired from exporters in Tanzania. The male to your left weighs fourteen hundred kilos and is estimated to be nineteen years old. In his prime. The female is thirty or so. These two have sired a calf but he is back at the facility. The horn is prized in the Orient for . . ." The guide paused, realizing Ms. Narong was probably aware of the value and use of powdered rhinoceros horn.

"Yes," she said politely, "but I plan to use it sparingly."

The guide wasn't sure if she was pushing his foot or not. Her smile was enigmatic, the Mona Lisa Thai.

"I think that this should be an easy shot," Ms. Narong said. "You have graciously provided me with a telescope to ensure me the greatest accuracy. I may rest the rifle over this windscreen, yes?"

"Certainly," assured the guide, eager to please. "Would you care to sight in on the animal so that you will have a feel for the rifle and the scope?"

"That would be very nice," she replied.

The guide handed her a Beretta double gun chambered for 470 Nitro Express ammunition. "It isn't loaded, Miz Narong. You may even dry-fire if you wish to gain a sense of the trigger pull."

As Ms. Narong, her guide, and her driver were making preparations, in the nearby Humvee Sheik Ryat Rokomon Fasasi, a member of the royal family from the sultanate of Yemen, was learning the fine points of a 50 mm machine gun. Riot Rock, as he was known to his classmates, was twenty-two years old, multilingual, and rich, and he had just graduated from Oxford with a degree in engineering. This hunt had been a graduation gift from his mother.

Ms. Narong's guide keyed the two-way radio and spoke into it. "With your permission, Sheik, we will allow Miz Narong the first shot. When her animal falls, the others will begin running. Your driver will be ready to follow. For generously giving her the first opportunity to shoot, you will be permitted, by the hospitable Ponce de Crayon, to shoot the other two," explained the guide. "You may start shooting as soon as you two clear her rhinoceros. We will follow the one that will be the hardest to kill first, then return for the other. Does that sound okay?"

The two-way clicked and came to life. "Bully!" shouted Riot Rock, with a strong British accent. He was standing in the pit behind the machine gun. A long cartridge belt snaked up from an ammo box. He crouched behind the gun and swung it side to side and up and down, testing its field of fire.

Meanwhile, Ms. Narong had loaded her gun with the two big cartridges and was steadying for the shot. The big black rhino male that was the object of her desire was filling her scope. He was chewing a mouthful of hay contentedly, his prehensile upper lip moving deftly like an enunciating finger. She was reminded of the antennae on the lobsters she used to bring up from the rocky shores of her native Thailand.

As she watched, the rhino turned his heavy head back to look over his shoulder. Ms. Narong panned left along the sight line of the rhino. Suddenly a blur swept across her circle of vision. It looked like a man on a horse!

Buster Montan, three times saddle-bronc top-ten finisher, originally from Broadus, Montana, was giving his horse the over and under! He was thundering across the sagebrush on a downhill glide toward the three rhinoceri that waited by the water tank. The wind was whistling through his hair, he had lost his hat, and he leaned over the horse's neck like Eddie

Arcaro! He felt his upper plate slide, his emphysema rattle, and the years slip away as if by magic. In his mind he was two days short of nineteen at the Cheyenne Frontier Days, forkin' a bronc in the final go, a girl in the grandstands, and his pocket bulging with a ticket to Fort Benning, Georgia, on a train that left in twenty-four hours. Ms. Narong panned back to her right to see her beautiful black rhino galloping off. She squeezed off a shot and missed the end of the magnificent rhino horn by inches. She swung her rifle back to the left, picked up Buster, and was trying to track him with the scope when the truck beneath her dipped and sank.

Suddenly five men were jumping off of horses and climbing onto her vehicle. The guide fought valiantly, but old men don't fight fair. Pickhandle Jerdon, onetime rodeo clown and bull rider, hefted an expensive Remington shotgun from the floor of the vehicle and clanged it up against the guide's head. The guide leaned sideways for a second, then toppled over. The driver had been allowed to escape. He was now running across the sagebrush like a jackrabbit.

Pickhandle stood face to face with Ms. Narong. She held the big rifle, pointing it up in the air, but it was her fierce look that made Pickhandle stop in his tracks.

"Don't shoot, ma'am, I ain't armed."

"Not very smaht, I would say." She held the rifle steady, although it was pointed slightly above his head. "Who are you?" she demanded.

"I'm Pickhandle Jerdon, but mostly . . . I'm with him." He gestured with his head to a man peeking his head up through the open back of the cab.

"Howdy, ma'am. Al's the name," spoke the old man.

Ms. Narong stepped quickly to the right to get a view of the head.

The old man took off his hat. "We are here," he said, "to save Nevada and make the world a better place to raise Brayford cattle. And, if that ain't enough, we do damsels in distress, which I might say, ma'am, meaning no offense, might be you. We also do lifeguarding, lighthouse watching, smoke jumping, steer roping, light MC, animal psychiatry, roadkill pickup, horn wrap, stirrup lettin' out, and . . . what am I leavin' out, Pickhandle?"

"Cabrito," said Pickhandle, honored to be included.

"Right!" said the old man. "Ka-BREE-toe!"

"So . . . what'll it be, a fight to the finish OR dinner tonight with Pickhandle Jerdon, world-famous rodeo clown, barrel man, and goat authority," the old man proffered.

"Mistah Owl, you have not mentioned the large amount of money I have invested in this hunting trip," Ms. Narong said, still holding the gun pointing slightly above Pickhandle's hat.

"That is something you may discuss with the owner of this grand facility, but for now I can guarantee you the hunt is off," spoke the old man.

"Off?" she asked, with a raised eyebrow.

"Over, discontinued, **adios, vaya con Dios,** blue smoke, fork in the steak, medium, well, and done! Fi-NEE-toe."

"Are you sure?"

"As I live and breathe. Apparently there is some illegality involved which could place participants, not unlike yourself, your majesty, in the direct path of a Fish and Game avalanche."

Ms. Narong looked at him quizzically.

"Hung from the yardarm, burned at the stake, stir-fried, wokked, and egg-rolled. We're talking time in the pokey," the old man concluded colorfully.

She considered the turn of events. "How would I get back to the, uh, hotel?" she asked.

"Can you ride double?" the old man asked. "It can be romantic. . . ."

"I think I would be willing. Does Mr. Jerdon still have any bullets in his gun?" she asked with a sideways glance.

"From what I hear, ma'am, he's loaded and ready for bear."

A round of machine-gun fire shattered the moment, blowing peace and quiet into a thousand pieces. The old man looked out his cab window at the modified Humvee with a machine gun mount less than a hundred yards away. The scene looked like a picture he remembered from the **National Geographic** wherein fourteen hyenas were attacking an elephant carcass.

Riot Rock, dressed like the Arabian knight he was, still had one long finger on the machine gun, which was pointed skyward and jerking his body like he was making a martini. At least three cowboys had a grip on his flowing white robe and were dragging him backwards off the rattling gun.

The old man couldn't see Riot's guide, but he could see a pile of cowboys that he assumed the poor fellow was under. The left front door was open and the driver was stumbling away from the rattling rocking vehicle.

Ms. Narong watched the activity placidly. When the big machine gun was finally silenced, she turned back to Pickhandle. "Mistah Pighandah, when is the next transportation to the hotel leaving?" she asked.

"Right away, ma'am. Right away!" he said.

The exuberant crowd applauded politely as Pickhandle helped Ms. Narong swing up behind him onto his horse. They started off in a slow walk toward the headquarters.

"May I call you Pig?" she asked as she reached around him and grasped his Clown of the Year belt buckle, worn smooth these last thirty years.

Why not, he thought. **Why not?**

66

December 13: T.A. Stops Qpid d'Art

Teddie Arizona had stopped her horse on a high ridge and was scanning the terrain ahead of her. Her horse was sweaty but still strong. She had to hold him back, he was dantsy. **Must have some Arabian blood in him,** she thought. He was a dark brown gelding with a long mane. Good horse for the job.

The weather was forty-five degrees, sky clear, a slight breeze out of the west. The matador's chaqueta under the long white lab coat was enough to keep T.A. warm, that and the cause that was now burning inside her. She was focused, in battle mode.

A good day for hunting, she thought. She saw at least three distant clouds of dust, but what drew her attention were two vehicles, dots really, at least a mile away. They were stationary. She thought she could detect activity around them. She turned to the two women and two men who were with her ahorseback.

"Whattya think, Sunny?" she asked.

"I can't see 'em, honey. They're too dang far away," Sunny Day said.

"There's a, shoot, it looks like a bus or an army truck, and a Suburban, maybe, and at least"—Posthole Jones, one of the men, stopped to count—"ten people."

"Gosh, I can't see anything but dark specks," said T.A. admiringly.

Posthole said, "I wore them durn glasses all my life, then my eyes went bad and I could see."

T.A. thought over the explanation but decided it was too complicated to absorb. "Here's the plan," she said. "We can't just charge 'em. Our horses would be worn out and they could see us coming for thirty minutes before we arrived. So, I'm gonna ride in alone."

"Sweetie, you can't do that. They could be some pretty mean men," said Sunny.

"Listen," said T.A. "Y'all know I'm just playing this by ear, but if I ride over there, they'll see me coming but they probably won't do anything. In the meantime, y'all spread out, sideways . . . a hundred yards apart, like a big fan behind me."

"Then what do we do when we get there?" asked the second man.

"I'm not sure," she said. "But we'll think of something."

"Don't sound like a great plan to me," said Posthole.

"You've done stupider things," harrumphed Sunny. "Like roping that big bull in the arena in Payson just as he was exiting the arena. Smacked your poor horse up against the gate and tore it off the hinges. How far did he drag the three of you—including the gate, I mean?"

They looked around and found that T.A. had already started across the open ground in the direction of the two dots. She stayed in a fast walk. **Should take about ten minutes to reach the vehicles,** she thought, time enough for them to notice her arrival. Sure enough, it wasn't long and she saw the crowd bunch up. Two bodies climbed on the vehicles and seemed to be using binoculars to look her way.

Qpid d'Art and her entourage of seven had turned away from the designated skeet-shooting range and joined the guide and two drivers who were watching the approach of the horsemen.

Teddie Arizona, with her white lab coat flowing out behind her, mounted on the Arab horse, looked like Lawrence of Arabia's nurse. Several yards behind her, in a thin company front, rode her companions.

"It's a girl!" said one of the drivers, lowering his binoculars.

"Is somebody else allowed to shoot at the eagles?" asked Lefty "Lime Green" Jefferson, one of Qpid's hulking bodyguards.

"No. We're not expecting anyone," said the guide. He looked at one of the drivers. "Check with car one, we're in section twenty, and see if there is a party on horseback that's supposed to be here." He turned back to see T.A. within a hundred yards.

"The eagles are fine," assured the guide. "We'll wait and see what's going on here, then we'll get back to the hunt. Everybody that Miz d'Art says will be able to take a shot. We've got eight of them altogether, plus some pygmy owls and koalas at the next stop."

"Oooh," said one of the girls in the entourage, "I've got a koala Beanie Baby! Now I'll have the real thing! I think I'll, like, stuff 'em, ya know, and maybe have a, you know, like, a family unit, ya know. Cool."

"Shut up, Azure Blue," said Qpid, without rancor. Qpid had chosen her hunting wear from the Neiman Marcus army-surplus department. Her fatigue pants with big pockets on the side were tucked inside combat boots that had gold lamé designs embossed on the toes and peppermint-stick shoelaces. The tails of the large polka-dot scarf tied around her head flapped in the breeze like streamers on a mainsail mast. But the pièce de résistance was the combination fur-lined pullover vest and hunting bodice with sewn-on bandoleras. It was as if Pancho Villa, Rambo, and Aretha Franklin had colluded to out-Cher Cher.

Teddie Arizona rode up on the group, signaling her backup riders to stop where they were.

"May I help you?" asked the guide politely. He was a handsome man in his thirties, wearing khaki short pants and a camouflage jacket with many pockets. He sported a Pharaoh's Casino baseball cap and aviator sunglasses. He was the kind of person you'd expect to see doing security at the Rocky Mountain Elk Club annual meeting.

"Yes. I am Mrs. F. Rank Pantaker and I have come to discuss the gravity of what you are doing."

"Mrs. Pantaker?" asked the guide.

The driver, also wearing a company ball cap,

leaned out of the Suburban window and said, "Nobody answers F. Rank's radio, and de Crayon told us he had a special shooter and would be out of contact. Let me see if—"

"She says she's Mrs. Pantaker," interrupted the guide.

"Well, I don't know. I just work here," said the driver. "Wait a minute, somebody's callin'."

Muffled radio transmission and a conversation could be heard coming from the dashboard. The driver stuck his head out the window and reported, "It's Valter, you know, that works for Pantaker. I think he went with one of the hunters. He says if it's Mrs. Pantaker then we should detain her immediately. And he is firm about it."

"What!" exclaimed the guide.

"Arrest her, he says!"

"Who says?" asked the guide.

"Valter!"

T.A. sat calmly on her horse during the conversation.

The guide started to raise his gun when he heard a shotgun shell ratchet into a chamber. It is a distinctive sound and will stop one in their gun-raising.

Qpid held her Mossberg 10-gauge full-choke level with her waist, but pointing in the direction of the guide.

"I think I'd like to hear what she has to say," said Qpid.

"Thank you," said T.A. "I'm sorry I don't recognize you, ma'am, but you seem to be in charge here. I assume you have paid my husband and Ponce de Crayon a million dollars to hunt endangered species."

Qpid scrutinized T.A.

T.A. continued, "Yes, I know all about it. I was there while they were planning this whole horrendous weekend. I have nothing against hunting, but what they're doing, and involving you in, is absolutely illegal, and not a very decent thing to be doing. I assume also that you have money to burn and you can afford to take your friends out for a good time. What are you shooting here?" she asked.

"Bald eagles, pygmy owls, and some kind of stork," answered Qpid.

"Whooping crane," interjected the guide.

"What are you going to do with the whooping crane once you shoot it?" asked T.A.

"Whoop it!" interjected one of her peanut gallery.

"What's it to you, and what business is it of yours, anyway?" asked Qpid.

T.A. was trying to think of a good reason that might connect with this hardened rock star in front of her. She resorted to the truth.

"It's nothing to me, really, and it's . . . everything at the same time."

Qpid looked at her, puzzled.

"She's a delusional paranoid schizophrenic," observed the hypochondriac in Qpid's entourage, with a giggle.

Qpid continued to look at T.A.

"I used to be like you," began T.A. "I had no core, I valued nothing, I took money for favors, I bought what I thought I needed. I partied hardy. But after a while I found that what I really needed couldn't be bought. So I changed my life and gave up everything I had that money could buy, and found what I really needed—self-respect. And you just happened to be caught in the middle of me taking my life back.

"Am I going to stop you from killing these endangered species? Yes, I am. I don't even know how, but I will, because this is the hill that I'm willing to die on. And I am betting that you won't shoot me. Am I wrong?"

The moment was pregnant with expectation.

"My gosh, that's about the best speech I've heard since Brigham kicked the domino players out of the temple," said Posthole Jones, recidivist Mormon.

"Lookie yonder comin'!" shouted one of the entourage.

A cloud of dust was heading in their direction at high speed.

T.A. never dropped Qpid's gaze. T.A. was quivering slightly.

Qpid slowly looked around at her entourage. She was a long way from her childhood in the backyard of Detroit. The only reason that her entourage, the dependents clinging to her shirt-tail, were here today, and not in jail for dealing drugs, prostitution, robbery, or car theft, was because she herself had fed their habits to keep them off the streets. Her mother was raising her two children, her managers were spending her money, her friends were smoking her pot, and her stud was two-timing her with her makeup girl. This madwoman on a horse had just shined the naked light of day into her soul, and found it empty. Not surprisingly, Qpid had known it all along. A fleeting consideration of the half million she'd laid out in down payment caused her a moment's pause. **People** magazine had estimated her worth at $160 million. She shook her head and grinned slightly. **Is this party worth takin' this crazy white chick out?** she wondered. **Not today, Sister, not today.**

"Back in the truck, everybody, we're done here," instructed Qpid.

A chorus of oohs and aws immediately rose from the group, as from children being told to go get ready for bed.

"Maybe you better give me that gun," Qpid said to the guide.

"You sure you don't want to shoot just one?" the guide asked her graciously. Then he noticed the shotgun she held was pointing below his belt buckle.

"Eagle, I mean!" he blurted, blushing.

"Positive," she said. Then she turned back to T.A. and said, "You go, girl!"

67

December 13: Lancel Lott and Dune Buggy Tiger

Meanwhile, in section 32, Lancel Lott, twenty-four-year-old number-three pro football draft pick from Rolling Hills, California, sat watching two guides unload a dune buggy with balloon tires, headers, a roll bar, and no windshield from the back of their one-ton flatbed.

"Man, that is cool," he said admiringly. He climbed into the single-seat cockpit, adjusted his safety helmet, and buckled up.

"Okay, Lancel, you remember the plan," said his guide. "You start out toward that flag down there in the swell. When you're within fifty feet of that blind, they'll release the tiger. It's the same one Ponce made disappear in his show—"

"I'll make him disappear for good, this time!" laughed Lancel.

"Right, just don't start shooting too soon. You'll have a level ride there for a good three minutes. And don't forget to wear your goggles. You might be shooting out the front, and the wind and sand can sure throw off your aim. The tiger shouldn't be able to run faster than thirty-five, and only for a couple minutes, and your buggy there will do sixty easy."

"I know. How 'bout this gun?" Lancel asked.

"A .357 Magnum, six shots. There's another in the holster attached to the dash. Get close enough to see his eye before you shoot. Get alongside and aim just behind his elbow. If by some chance you can't hit him, or change your mind, the grenades are in this box beside you. Reach through the rubber flap on top, grab one out, pull the pin with your teeth, just like we practiced with the dummies, and throw it at him. When you throw, immediately veer away from the grenade. Don't want to hurt that million-dollar throwin' arm, do we?"

"Ten million," smiled Lancel to his guide.

Within two minutes Lancel Lott, boy-wonder athlete, Southern California All-State

Everything, a future as bright as Prince William, was roaring across the cool Nevada high desert. A cirrus cloud of dust covered his tracks; the wind snapped at his cheeks and roared by his ears as he bore down on the target. The tiger burst from the blind in a spectacular leap and was running at full speed within five seconds!

Lancel was within field goal distance. He tried to hold the dune buggy steady with his left hand while readying the heavy pistol with his right. He swerved behind the racing tiger so that he could approach from the left rear quarter. He was close enough to throw a Hail Mary. He leveled the gun. He cocked the hammer. He could see the tiger's exhaust outlet. The dune buggy actually rared back like Trigger! The front wheels rose from the ground. All Lancel could see was blue sky! A shot rang out! A hole appeared in the chrome-plated bumper guard. He was out of control!

He heard a roar. Not like a tiger's roar, which he assumed was like a lion's roar, which he was familiar with because he'd watched the MGM trademark lion at least a thousand times as a youth and had practiced roaring. No, this was more like the roar of a drag racer leaving the starting line, or at least a bus passing through the Eisenhower Tunnel. It was as if they'd poured two hundred pounds of tyrannosaurus roar into a five-gallon bucket and pulled it down over his ears. He looked back over his shoulder and the sight he saw caused him to add a monarch butterfly silhouette to the design on his Calvin Kleins.

An old man with his hat pulled down over his ears was standing at a rakish angle behind a 50 mm machine gun mounted on top of a Humvee. He was grinning wildly and pointing it at Lancel. It was Al Bean, senior important character. His accompanist, Hubie McCormick, ex-Almost World Champion Bronc Rider, veteran of the early days, now a resident of Mesquite Thicket Adult Care, Pomerene, Arizona, was behind the wheel, so to speak. The Humvee was cockeyed because his right front tire was still up on the rolled steel bumper of the dune buggy, which was now moving across the terrain at 40 mph tail down, like a dog scooting across the carpet.

Lancel had a brief thought that he might shoot back over his shoulder, but the menacing gun barrel and the old man's maniacal smile gave him pause. He'd seen that same look on a mentally deranged linebacker just before he was dropped for a ten-yard loss in a game where his high school had played the local halfway house in a scrimmage. He threw the pistol out the right-hand side. The dune buggy crashed back down when the Humvee backed off. It swerved to the right.

The old man saw his chance and pulled the trigger. A blast of gunfire exploded the dune buggy's right rear tire. The buggy rolled over in a lefterly direction and settled on its back. Lancel Lott hung from the seat like a fruit bat waiting for a new idea.

The old man leaned down into the cab and shouted to Hubie. Hubie stepped on the gas, swerved to his right, and drew a bead on Lancel's guides, who were now headed toward them in their fancy Ponce Park truck.

As the Humvee drew near them at an alarming pace, the guides in the approaching pickup began to doubt the wisdom of their decision. They could see the old man crouch down behind the machine gun.

"Surely he wouldn't," said one of the guides. At that very moment, their radiator blew up in spectacular fashion, steam and steel flying away in whiffs and bits.

The guides wheeled around and hightailed it back south. They made it a mile and a half before the engine froze up. They jumped out and discovered, to their great relief, that they had not been followed.

68

December 13: Busby and the Condor

Ponce and F. Rank had gone to great lengths to accommodate their guest from South America, one Matís Poblano Coctil, or, as he was known to his illicit pharmaceutical friends and enemies, Lagarto. When F. Rank Pantaker had solicited Lagarto through his father's contacts at the American Embassy in Colombia, Señor Coctil had expressed interest in the hunt. He had a specific request. Since he already had an Andean condor stuffed and hanging from the sixteen-foot ceiling in his den, he would like to have the American counterpart. F. Rank had checked with Ponce to see if that particular endangered species was available. Ponce said, in so many words, "for a price." It turned out to be an additional two million.

"Cheeken feet," said Lagarto, using the movie-rental slang he was acquiring from his continuing education courses.

The guide that Ponce had chosen to escort Lagarto was an actor named Esubio Martinez from Los Angeles who had done a quick study of condorology and was passing himself off as a college professor of ornithology. Lagarto and Esubio sat in the plush backseat of F. Rank's personal Humvee stretch limo.

The actor's voice was as smooth as rich Corinthian leather. "This bird is as magnificent a creature as I have ever seen. It is almost prehistoric. The wingspan is nine feet, six inches. There are only a couple of hundred of these babies in the world. This one is as black as . . ." He started to say "a drug dealer's heart," but changed it to "the inside of a snake."

"When I get him, I will cut out his heart and feed it to my anaconda," said Lagarto, grinning. Lagarto was not your stereotypical South American contrabandista. He was a large balding man with a florid face and small round glasses with dark lenses. He was dressed to hunt: mud-and-snow-grip work boots, a beautiful red wool serape hunting jacket with appropriate patches, and a baseball cap that said MARY KAY, in pink letters.

Esubio thought his job was to appeal to Lagarto's love of birds, but it seemed Lagarto's only interest was in hanging one on the wall. He quickly switched tacks. "As we discussed last night, you will be using an AK-47. A shotgun simply would not be powerful enough. The machine gun will allow you to scatter shot and still penetrate."

"I don't understand exactly how you were going to release the **zopilote,**" said Lagarto.

"In truth, my fine amigo," answered Esubio, warming to the role and recalling with glee the Zopilotes, a bicycle gang of pachucos in his grade school that had tee shirts with a one-eyed vulture as their symbol, "the bird will never actually be released. It would be too big a chance to take. If he ever got away he would go back to California, I guess, and we would lose him," **and my job,** he thought. "But! . . . Señor Ponce has devised a wonderful plan. He has arranged to have the condor tethered to an ultralight. We simply fly around over you until you shoot him. Simple."

"What is ulterlight?" asked Lagarto.

"It's a small plane," answered Esubio, "not really an airplane, more like a flying go-cart—"

"Go card?" said Lagarto, thinking it was a variation of a green card, which he manufactured by the hundreds of thousands and sold to exchange students planning to cross the U.S. border in the dark of night.

"No, no, go-CART! A flying go-CART," said Esubio.

"Will I be in the go-cart?"

"No. No one will be in the go-cart. It's an ultra-light. Ultralight. And you will not be in it either."

"Then where will I be?" asked Lagarto.

"You, my esteemed **cazador** (Esubio remembered the word because he was familiar with the tequila of that brand name and knew that it meant "hunter"), will be on the ground, shooting up at the **muy grande** California condor."

Five hundred feet above Stinkwater Meadow, chief pilot and part-time buzzard walker Charles Lindbergh Busby was freezing his buns. He crouched behind the controls of a single-seat, fixed-wing, 15-horsepower, propeller-driven ultralight aircraft, which was attached by a leash to a twenty-five-pound condor.

Busby wasn't a risk taker. He was a pilot, a careful pilot who didn't drink the night before, had his annual physical annually, and always did his preflight check with the meticulousness of an astronaut. He was certain there was nothing in the manual that covered this situation.

After three unsuccessful attempts at taking off simultaneously with the tethered bird, during which the condor bounced and drug like a bone tied behind a wedding car, he loaded the condor in the seat with him and went aloft. That wasn't a pleasant task either. The condor was difficult to hold and very powerful. It also smelled like rotten meat.

Ponce's crew had built a harness that fitted around the bird's body but did not interfere with wing movement. The hundred-yard leash was attached to a self-winding reel and strung with 200-pound-test fishing line strong enough to hold a breaching marlin on an automatic reel. It hooked to an eyelet on the back of the condor's harness.

When Busby reached his assigned altitude, he tossed the bird overboard, allowing the line to play out. The condor dropped like a rock! Busby pointed the ultralight down to prevent the sudden snap. It was masterful flying on his part. He managed to stop the descent gently and slowly climb aloft. The condor began to flap and eventually got his sea legs, so to speak.

Busby practiced flying around with the condor attached. He had to let it fly on its own and guide it like Ganymede goes around Jupiter. Each in a separate orbit.

It was 10:45 a.m. Pacific Standard Time by Busby's chronometer. The hunters should be here anytime, he reassured himself.

At 10:49 a.m. the Humvee stretch limo drove into section 43.

"Stop the car, Santiago!" said Esubio to his driver. He invited Lagarto to step out and see the lay of the land.

"There he is!" exclaimed Esubio, as if he had found Dr. Livingstone.

"**¡Ijuela!**" exclaimed Lagarto. "Yus' like you said."

They were a quarter mile away from the predetermined shooting spot in a small meadow. Beyond, the terrain sloped up toward some barren foothills. The buzzing noise of the prop and motor could be heard on this quiet morning. The ultralight itself seemed to be chasing the condor in a big circle. The men on the ground could not see the tether from their distance.

"**¡Ándale!**" said Lagarto.

"Walk on, brother!" said Esubio. "**¡Ándale, pues!**"

Busby was relieved to see the arrival of the vehicles. It was getting progressively more difficult to control the situation. The condor was getting stronger and was dragging the ultralight, instead of the other way around. It was a battle to stay over the designated area.

He could see the guide and a big man in a red coat getting out guns and talking to each other as they walked off the ridge down into the meadow. They were accompanied by another man, either a driver or a bodyguard, Busby guessed, and all three were looking up at him. He was still a hundred yards up and away.

Suddenly he heard a staccato volley of shots and the whine of bullets close enough to make him jump! Looking down, Busby saw the guide pointing excitedly at the condor. He pulled back on the stick and went into a maneuver to circle the condor back across the hunter. As he swung around slowly, he noticed a dust storm sweeping across the Nevada desert from the south, heading his way.

Lick and Cody had commandeered a brand-new ¾ T four-wheel-drive pickup that had been abandoned by Ponce's retreating army. They were approaching section 43, the location of Busby's Last Stand, from the southwest. Behind them were three older pickups, two Humvees, one dirt bike, and nine mounted cowboys they'd found along the way. They were in radio contact with the old man, who was riding shotgun with Hubie McCormick in one of the Humvees.

The old man and Hubie were coming directly out of the south in the direction of section 43. They were being followed by a jeep, two pickups, and thirteen mounted cowboys. To the east of the old man's group came eight horsemen, Teddie Arizona in the lead. They were accompanied by a two-ton army-surplus water truck driven by Pike and the darling Chrisantha. In the back of the truck were a full-grown panda and F. Rank Pantaker, both tied up.

The three platoons of cowboys had cleared

the area of all the invited guests and their sherpas, save this last group.

"My gosh," said Busby out loud . . . to himself, "the entire hunting party is coming to watch." It was not the best news. Busby felt a small bubble of panic rise in his stomach. The condor was leading him farther away from the target area. Busby had the little gas-powered 15-horsepower engine at full throttle and was losing ground with every circle. The condor was migrating to Bakersfield.

One by one, the trucks, Humvees, pickups, armored cars, motorcycles, and mounted cavalry began to line up along the ridge looking down over Stinkwater Meadow. The passengers debouched or stood on the vehicles. The riders stayed mounted.

The old man and Hubie drove up beside Lick and Cody. They all got out. Cody had found a set of binoculars in their truck and he was sighted in on the airborne contraption. "It looks like one of those ultralight airplanes but there's a big bird flying along with it," reported Cody.

"Lemme see there, Cody," said the old man, taking the binocs. "I believe he's takin' the bird for a walk. I can't see no leash but they're flyin' like they was connected." He aimed the binoculars down to the three men in the meadow. They were loping across it, stopping occasionally to point their rifles to the sky and shoot. The ultralight kept moving farther away.

Busby heard bullets tear through the cloth fabric of the wing. He was in full panic now. The condor had caught an updraft with his ten-foot wingspan and they were climbing. Either those guys on the ground were bad shots or they were shooting at him!

F. Rank had explained to Busby that this part of the hunt was very important, since the hunter had paid an additional two million dollars to shoot the condor and there was a significant bonus to the pilot if all went well. Ponce had added that there would also be a significant equal and opposite reaction, should the job be flummoxed.

Busby was nearing the point where neither offer was going to matter. He made one last attempt to circle, but the condor was now above his nose and rising, always drifting westerly. Bullets whizzed by. One richocheted off the aluminum engine housing. Making the decision to "cut bait," Busby dug his Leatherman out of his pocket. He clumsily retracted the scissors appendage from the knife. Then, grasping the fishing line that connected him to the condor, he reached forward to snip it.

Lagarto had been aiming at the pilot. When

Busby leaned forward, the bullet zinged through the tangle of wire, aluminum pipe, rubber hoses, and cloth skin, just missing his helmet. He dropped the handy-dandy pocketknife.

One thousand feet below, Lagarto was still firing into the sky. "Shoot the——" (he made an adjectival reference in Spanish to the lineage of the pilot, insinuating bestiality had played a part). "Blow the——" (this time it was a Spanish noun inferring the pilot was the product of the coupling of small vermin). **"¡Traigame el Uzi! ¡Voy a disparar éste** (he inserted a brief description of a carrion eater) **del cielo! ¡Ándele, ellos se fue!** "

"¡Como esta usted!" shouted Esubio, enthusiastically injecting some phrases from his limited second-language vocabulary. **"¡Muy bien, gracias!"** he yelled at the top of his lungs. He was smiling and urging Lagarto on.

Lagarto's rifle emptied. He turned a cold eye on Esubio.

"Keep shooting!" urged Esubio.

"Too far, you goat offspring, you slobber of a baby. Even if I had more bullets he has **quito de aqui.** But if I had one more bullet, I would save it to make chure I would get my moneys back."

The army of cowboys lined up on the ridge, watching the play unfold before them. They could hear the shouted conversation and the gunshots, but only dimly; the wind had dispersed the words. They could no longer hear the buzzing of the ultralight. Matter of fact, it was getting harder to see it and its bird-on-a-leash. They were no longer circling, but gaining altitude and heading in the direction of eleven-thousand-foot Charleston Peak in the Spring Mountains.

"Guess the show's over," said Lick. They climbed in the pickup, with Cody behind the wheel. Teddie Arizona rode up beside them on a horse.

"I don't know," worried Lick. "Nobody's seen Ponce."

One hour later the airport controllers in Las Vegas received a report of a strange sighting from a commuter-airline pilot on a flight between Las Vegas and Reno. When pressed for a description, they said it looked like a big bird had gotten tangled in some kite string.

69

December 13: Hafiz and the Gorilla

"I have killed many men in my life . . . in the line of duty, but rarely has it been a fair fight," explained Hafiz I. Coca, former assassin for the Iraqi secret police. "That is why it has been my dream to fight an equal. It does my heart good work that you can furnish of me this opportunity. You were able to locate such a beast, I am glad to hear."

"Absolutely," affirmed Ponce in his best Middle Eastern accent, which sounded more like a Hindu graduate student. "I have spared no expenses to deliver you the dream you wish to attain. He is a twenty-five-year-old silverback weighing three hundred ninety-five pounds. He was captured only recently, with great difficulty. Secrecy to secure such a beast so rare and magnificent is very hard to guarantee. He is everything you can imagine. I know you will be pleased. I also understood that you don't want to see him until you meet him in the ring."

"In the cage," corrected Hafiz. "The fight should take place in a cage so that he may not get away. Hand-to-hand combat. I shall meet him carrying the sword and sacred dagger of my father's father."

"Mano a mano, as you say. It is all prepared as you asked," said Ponce. "May I say you are a man of great courage and honor, Sayyed I. Coca. I, too, understand the need to prove oneself. It is part of the reason that I continue to stay in the cages. It is the ultimate affirmation of one's character. Very few would understand your desire to battle a gorilla barehanded, but I do. You have brought the additional two million?"

"It will be delivered when you open the door to the cage when I meet the true king of the jungle, my worthy foe. Please show me to my dressing room."

Ponce and I. Coca had reached the door to the Big Cat House beneath the tower. He opened it, allowing I. to enter first, then followed him in.

70

December 13: Guinevere's Final Ride

They'd left a battlefield of disrupted hunts in their wake. In addition to Cody's surreptitious substitution and derailing of mysterious financier Anakra Nizm's nefarious intentions, the old man's one-two punch knocking out the sweet Ms. Narong and Sheik Number One, aka Riot Rock, then running Lancel Lott, the ath-elite, off the road, and T.A.'s intercession with Qpid d'Art (not to mention the self-disintegration of the sleek contrabandista Lagarto, shooting himself in the foot, so to speak), the remaining Old Timer Rodeo Reunioneers had also distinguished themselves.

They swept across the hunting preserve like a swarm of arthritic locusts. This geriatric tornado struck with the ferocity of a rock slide. Trucks rolled over, names were called, horses went down, and nitroglycerin was taken. Casualties were loaded in the pickups. Enemy transportation was commandeered and enemy arms were expropriated.

The Texas Oil Man had been afoot stalking a black panther when he was descended upon. The cowboys roped him, then tied him across the hood of a repossessed Humvee like a mule deer in hunting camp. When they caught up with the second Saudi sheik and he saw the trussed Texan, he threw his gun down, jumped from his vehicle, and ran for the far hills! The cowboys let him go.

T. Rex Bunting, attorney to the celebrities and famous in his own right, had actually bagged his tiger. He had left his guides to do the skinning and was motorcycling the two miles back to headquarters. He would have made it scot-free except that both Leo Don Autry and Wildcat Willcox had taken a little longer in the men's room and were left behind by the Old Timers' army.

The two departed camp to join the fray in a 1947 Willys Jeep CJ2, with a shovel and a thirty-five-foot rope Leo Don had won at Pharaoh's yesterday as a door prize. They were puttering down the trail trying to see, steer, and talk simultaneously. Coming down the dusty track in their direction at a leisurely pace was T. Rex, who pulled up beside them.

"Huntin', are ye?" asked Wildcat.

"Yessir, my fine gentlemen," answered T. Rex expansively. "A Siberian tiger. Verry rare . . . verry, verry, rare. And what, might I ask, would you fine septuagenarians be doing out on such a brisk morning? Getting your exercise?" he joshed them a bit, nodding at the jeep.

"Actually," said Wildcat, "we were just fixin' to have a nip." He produced a bottle of Black Velvet blended whiskey from the floor of the jeep. "Care for a snap?"

"How colloquial. How quaint. And why not! We could drink a toast to me and the conclusion of my great hunt!" T. Rex reached over, taking the bottle from Wildcat.

"You got anything to dally to?" Wildcat asked Leo Don in a conversational tone.

"I'll find sumpthin'," he said, and threw a loop that caught T. Rex and his handlebars around the waist. Leo Don popped the clutch, the rope tightened around T. Rex and his cycle, and off they went down the road just fast enough to keep T. Rex's towrope tight and his cycle upright.

Every time he shouted "I'll sue, you old ba—" they would speed up and he would crash. After the third time he shut up.

Meanwhile, out on the savannah, vehicles were burning and endangered wild animals were running loose. A cavalry of horsemen and assorted vehicles were mopping up the condor mess.

"They said Ponce never left the headquarters. That he had a special client and was taking care of him personally," said T.A. She spoke slowly but with intensity. "That's something I would like to do. Take care of Ponce . . . personally."

T.A. was ahorseback looking down at Lick and Cody, who were in the front seat of the fancy pickup. They could tell something had come over her. Cody could only read confidence, but Lick read valor. A wave of pride in her rolled down his spine.

"Are you coming with me?" she asked.

Cody glanced over at Lick, then turned back to look up at T.A. "I didn't come all this way to leave without cutting the head off the snake."

She looked down at the two cowboys in the pickup cab and a big grin smiled across her face. Lick caught her eye. He smiled up and asked with a theatrical leer, "Hey, Cowgirl, need a ride?"

T.A. eased her horse over next to the vehicle and stepped off into the bed of the pickup. She slid down through the rear window and over onto Lick's lap. T.A. was burning with the cause. She was so full of accomplishment she couldn't speak. **Just one more mountain,** she thought. **I can't lose.**

She held Lick in a hammerlock. She could feel the blood pumping through her veins. Her body was humming next to his. Every place their bodies touched it felt like she was being recharged. Her energy went through him, too, like an electric current. She was warm to the touch. She was Seattle Slew in the last furlong, Sir Edmund Hillary ten feet from the top, Babe Ruth in the bottom of the ninth.

It took him right back to the tenth performance of the National Finals Rodeo two years ago, when he virtually blew into the arena like a rocket and wired himself to his destiny. Whatever he'd lost these last two years came back with a surprising intensity. He was with her. Oh, it felt good.

He leaned in quickly and kissed the side of her face. She gave him a sideways look with a sharp-eyed twinkle and squeezed his neck harder. Then she turned to face him, pulled him to her, and planted a deep firm muscular kiss on his lips.

Cody grabbed second high gear and the huge tires bit into the rocky ground. Guinevere rode off to slay the dragon.

71

December 13: Gorilla Showdown

Ponce had done a little redecorating at the tiger-training cage in preparation for this particular endangered-species hunter. The room was well lit by the late-morning sun shining through the high windows. He'd arranged to have a jungleful of potted palms, ferns, and plants from Pharaoh's Casino spaced around the twelve-foot-high cage, the same one where he'd threatened T.A. with the tiger. A professional soundman was prepared to pipe in a tape of jungle sounds—birds calling, monkeys screeching, bugs buzzing, and the occasional distant growl—while a cameraman stood by to video-tape the action. Hafiz I. Coca had insisted that no standby medical people would be necessary. Ponce had engaged a doctor anyway, but had him stationed over in the hotel, two build-ings away.

The moment had arrived. Ponce signaled the

soundman, and he began with the theme song from **Chariots of Fire.** Hafiz I. Coca strode in alone. He was wearing a tight red doo-rag around his head, loose white pants that came to midcalf, and a black-and-gold sash around his waist. His black moustache glistened. He was bare-chested and barefoot. He looked like an orange-skinned pirate.

Hafiz was powerfully built, his shoulders grown massive from regular exercise. He tried to keep in shape, getting in at least a hundred lashes a day when prisoners would cooperate. He'd lift prisoners by a rope tied to their ankles over a smooth beam and drop them, doing three sets of twelve reps each three days a week. He practiced throwing knives at cats and rats in the prison yard. He decapitated sheep and goats with his scimitar at picnics and religious ceremonies. He practiced holding a dog's attention with his mesmerizing stare by using intense concentration and a shock collar. He could go in and out of a Zen state as easily as most people can slam on the brakes. He often took hot baths in rusty water, thinking it would put iron in his skin. This explained his icteric appearance.

Ponce grandly opened the door to the cage and spoke. "You, Hafiz I. Coca the Brave, have reached your apogee, your pinnacle, your peak, the height of your magnificence, the apex of your dominance, the climax of your life's preparation—discipline, strength, self-esteem, determination, all seething to a white-hot point at the end of your warhead. You have become one with the blade, you are Orion personified!" Ponce took a breath. "Bring on the Challenger!"

The back cage door that connected to the tiger tunnel slid up and the worthy opponent peeked up from his crouching position and knuckle-walked into the cage.

"And in this corner," bellowed Ponce, "weighing three hundred and ninety-five pounds, standing five feet four inches on his knuckles, twenty-four years old, with a reach of forty-seven inches, originally of Equatorial New Guinea, the pride of the Lowland, the Prince of Primates, undefeated in two hundred and forty bluffs, bellows, and skirmishes for food, females, and territory, Ponce Park's own **Gorilla gorilla,** the one and only GAR-GAN-ZO!"

The soundman affected wild applause with trumpets blaring. He then pulled it down to a percussive tension-making timbre.

Hafiz slowly approached Garganzo. Garganzo watched him warily. There was something in his bearing that set the gorilla's warning bells off.

When Hafiz was within six feet of the beast, he drew his sword. Garganzo had not moved. His coal black eyes followed the sword as it slowly withdrew from the black-and-gold sash. The silver glistened. Garganzo furrowed his brow.

The tip of the sword slowly reached out like a lethargic snake. Garganzo looked down at it, then back up at Hafiz. Hafiz applied his stare. The gorilla would not hold his gaze. He was intimidated.

Hafiz could tell. He had seen thousands of men look away. He knew what it meant. With the flick of his wrist, he thrust with the sword and nicked Garganzo's chest.

What happened next could never be properly explained, even with the video replays, but literally one second later Hafiz was standing there holding half a sword and wearing no pants. His sash hung like a tattered loincloth. It fluttered briefly, then sagged limp.

For disbelievers who think I simply fabricated this debriefing of Hafiz I. Coca to further test the gullibility of the naive reader, allow me to repeat a similar harrowing incident that was told to me by a witness and related in that wonderful collection of tall tales, *Horseshoes, Cowsocks & Duckfeet,* Crown Publishers, copyright 2002 by Baxter Black. The names I use could be fictitious to protect the innocent.

Del decided to build a fence in the spring but finally got around to it in December. He enlisted the aid of two friends, Chappy and Filbert. They all dressed warmly since it was twenty degrees that day in west Tennessee. The boys were havin' trouble diggin' one of the holes. It was close to the paved road, and the ground was hard.

Del backed his tractor up to the future hole and poised the posthole auger over the designated spot like an ovipositing wasp. The auger spun on the surface of the frozen ground. Chappy, who's big as a skinned mule, pulled down on the gearbox. No luck. So Filbert stepped between the auger and the tractor and leaned his weight on the horizontal arm supporting the auger.

Now, Filbert had come prepared to work in the cold. He had on his hat with Elmer Fudd earflaps, mud boots, socks, undies, long johns, jeans, undershirt, wool shirt, and Carhartts™ (coveralls made of canvas and tough as carpet in a tugboat).

Filbert gave Del the go-ahead. Del engaged the power takeoff. The auger clanked and started to turn. Suddenly Filbert seemed to explode before Del's eyes!

Del engaged the clutch immediately, and everything stopped. Filbert stood before them . . . naked.

I said naked. Not quite. He had on his boots and his belt, still snug through the belt loops. The jeans had been ripped off his body from the pockets down, leaving only a small piece containing the fly. Other than that he was immodestly clad.

Delbert's explanation for his friend's near denuding was that Filbert's pant leg had brushed up against the extended arm of the PTO. In a split second, as fast as Superman could skin a grapefruit, the PTO had torn all the clothes off Filbert's body. In less than three minutes, his body turned blue. Nothing was broken, but he was as bruised as the top avocado at the supermarket. Chappy commented later that he looked like he'd been run through a hay conditioner.

Delbert figgered he was a blazing example of that expression "He looks like he's been drug through a knothole."

Back to Hafiz I. "Mano a Mano" Coca, who's got the next move. Garganzo was still resting on his knuckles in the same position he had maintained during the face-off. The torn pair of white pants lay ten feet away and the first eighteen inches of the sword of Hafiz's ancestors was embedded in a sign reading NO FEAR that hung on the cinder-block wall outside the cage.

The gorilla was now looking Hafiz right in the eye. The four muscular cheeks of Hafiz were trembling.

"Ayatollah, Sayyed, Monsieur, Señor, Capitan," Ponce said urgently, "are you all right?" Hafiz I. Coca neither turned nor spoke. His right arm was still crooked at the elbow and holding the broken end of his sword. His left arm was posed stiffly at his hip as if he were waiting for a gunfight.

Ponce opened the catch on the cage door and slowly entered. He was holding a whip in his right hand and a pistol in his left as he worked his way around until he could see Hafiz's face. It was blank, in a trance, the lips slightly parted. Hafiz's eyes were dull, catatonic. You see that same look on the audience, old and young alike, halfway through **Barney & Friends.**

Garganzo was staring at Hafiz, at the ready, or so it appeared to Ponce.

"Hafiz, you need to relax. Just relax, turn around quietly, and walk out the door," Ponce encouraged. "Nothing will happen, you'll be fine."

"Unless, of course," a quiet voice said, "someone makes a threatening gesture, or fires a gun, or rattles the gorilla's cage. Then the King of the Jungle might attack the naked Shah and bite a huge hole in his pride—and your pocket-book. How would it look to his influential friends if he went home circumcised?"

Ponce gently swiveled his head to the sound of the voice, careful not to make any sudden moves.

Teddie Arizona, the kept woman of Pharaoh's Casino, demolisher of diabolic dreams and poi flinger, stood there boldly, like the Avenging Angel.

72

December 13: Ponce Gets His

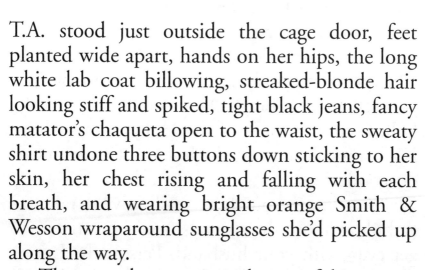

T.A. stood just outside the cage door, feet planted wide apart, hands on her hips, the long white lab coat billowing, streaked-blonde hair looking stiff and spiked, tight black jeans, fancy matator's chaqueta open to the waist, the sweaty shirt undone three buttons down sticking to her skin, her chest rising and falling with each breath, and wearing bright orange Smith & Wesson wraparound sunglasses she'd picked up along the way.

The soundman snapped out of his trance

and cued up the theme song from **The Good, the Bad, and the Ugly.**

T.A. drew a large-barreled pistol from her waistband and aimed it at Ponce. "You're done, Ponce. You've cooked your last goose," she announced.

He studied her. He was a superb judge of animal behavior and reader of the mammalian psychology. He slowly raised the pistol in his left hand and pointed it at the gorilla. His aim was steady. He had called her bluff.

"It has come to this, my fine, spirited lady," he said in his best Sheriff of Nottingham accent. "You, who are willing to give up everything to save these endangered beasts, have the choice. Submit to me or I will kill this grand specimen of the eastern lowland gorilla. A silverback in the prime of life. One of less than four thousand on the face of the earth.

"I know you do not doubt that I will do it. The question is only, Are you willing to sacrifice yourself to save him? Or is your quest just the hollow commitment of the Hollywood shallow. Is all your bluster just the hot air of an armchair do-gooder?

"You know you don't really give a rat's acetabulum about the animals. You're just trying to get even with your husband. Personally, I don't blame you. You could do a lot better than F.

Rank. Matter of fact, I'm beginning to think, if you could be house-trained, you'd be good company. Think what you could achieve if I took you under my tutelage. With your spirit, you could actually be good in the lion's cage. Or we could create an act with Garganzo here. Call it "The King of Kong." Granted, I would expect certain favors—a grape peeled now and then, a shirt washed, a tension relieved. You would come to love me, I suspect. It has happened before, or are you really just a sophomore coed out for adventure who got in over her head, a clever country bumpkin who conned a conniving but gullible rich Texan?"

Ponce's eye narrowed and his voice assumed a new malevolence. "The time for make-believe is over. Drop your gun and walk into the cage or I will kill the gorilla." He cocked the hammer.

T.A. lowered her pistol, tucked her chin submissively, and stepped sideways into the cage. For a split second Ponce was partially hidden by the frozen Hafiz. T.A. dove back to her left, pointing the pistol at Ponce, and fired as she hit the ground and rolled!

She hit him right between the eyes. She fired again! **Thwoot! Thump!** The second shot hit him just below the collar. Balloons of color blossomed on his forehead and his chest. Odd, she thought, the color that blossomed was green.

Simultaneously Hafiz I. Coca came to, whirled, waving his arms, and ran screaming from the cage, slamming the door behind him! Garganzo roared to life with a thunderous boom and ran after Hafiz! The door latch slammed closed right in front of the silverback, who grabbed the bars on either side and bent them like paper clips. The next time that door would be opened would be with the Jaws of Life.

Ponce thought he'd been killed. He dropped his gun and began reeling about like a bad guy in a B Western movie who was allowed twelve seconds in the scene in which to die. Blinded by the shot between the eyes, he staggered, clutching his face.

"I had always hoped to die in the cage with my tigers. The death of a true warrior. Quick, where's my whip? I want to die with my whip in my hand!" He dropped to his knees. "There is no pain, everything is crystal clear, I can see a long, dark tunnel with a light at the end. It is so beautiful, so peaceful."

T.A. looked at her gun curiously. Without thinking, she shot Ponce again, this time in the pant leg. A bright yellow blotch appeared where she hit him. She fired again. The result was a fluorescent orange blotch on his white shirt.

Her first thought was that Ponce was an alien bleeding Technicolor blood; then she tipped the pistol and a blue paintball rolled out of the barrel.

Ponce's tiger-tamer pistol was lying in the sawdust less than ten feet from her. She rolled sideways in Ponce's direction and snagged it.

By now Ponce had lain down on his side and was trying to remember Hamlet's last words.

"Shoot him!" a voice shouted.

T.A. raised her eyes and saw the gorilla advancing on Ponce. Lick stood outside the cage shaking the jammed door.

"Shoot him, Teddie!" Lick shouted again.

Ponce looked up. His mind cleared quickly. "Shoot him!" he, too, shouted.

The gun was shaking in her hand. In three quick steps she placed herself between the gorilla and Ponce. The gorilla stopped less than four feet from her. T.A. lowered the pistol and looked down.

The gorilla was very agitated. He stood to his full height, opened his fearsome mouth, displaying a set of saber-toothed tusks, and let out a locomotive roar! Ponce, still behind T.A., lunged and grabbed the gun from her hand and fell back. The gorilla, with a strong backhand, swept T.A. off her feet and knocked her eight feet away. Then he was on Ponce like a mink on Marilyn Monroe. He picked him up by one ankle and swung him around his head like a helicopter blade. On one particularly painful revolution, Garganzo leaned a fraction too close to the cage and Ponce's head rattled the bars like the two of clubs pinned to a bicycle spoke.

Finally Garganzo stopped spinning and tossed Ponce straight up in the air. Ponce grabbed the steel bars at the top of the cage and managed to get a leg wrapped around one. There he clung like a three-toed sloth. Garganzo stared up at him, took a lazy swat at Ponce's hanging leg, but missed. It was too high to reach. He turned his attention back to the inert body in the sawdust on the floor.

"Who's got a gun?" yelled Lick as he shook the hopelessly twisted door.

"I'll find one," said Cody, and he disappeared through the gathering crowd. He was about to head back outside when he practically knocked down Al, who was just stepping inside the room.

"What's the problem here, Pilgrim?" asked the old man pleasantly.

"Al! Where you been?" screamed Lick. "Teddie's in this cage with that gorilla! Get a gun! We've got to stop him before he kills her!"

"Now hold up, young Lick. Get a grip. He's just lookin' at her," said the old man.

Lick stopped and looked into the cage. The gorilla was standing over an inert T.A. Unconscious, maybe; hurt, probably; in danger, no doubt.

The old man started playing a little rhythm on the bars and whistling.

"What the—" Lick started to say. Then he saw the gorilla turn his gaze back toward them.

The old man started singing along with his gorilla rap:

"See that sweet girl on the floor, oompa,
    oompa, oompa, oom,
Right there by that other door, poompa,
    poompa, poompa, poom.
It don't take no wise old sage, roompa,
    roompa, roompa, room,
To get through the backdoor cage,
    stoompa, stoompa, stoompa, stoom."

Garganzo had now turned around to get a good view of the old man and his mesmerizing percussion act.

The old man's plan sank into Lick's over-loaded brain. "Okay," he said, nodding his head. "I get it. Keep him busy, Al, I'm comin' in the back way."

Teddie Arizona had blacked out for less than thirty seconds. When she became groggily aware of her surroundings, she found herself looking up at the massive gorilla in his knuckle-dragging stance above her. She willed herself to remain motionless.

A plaintive whimpering from high above her carried on the air like a squeaking swamp cooler. Lick was yelling excitedly. She heard a rhythmic banging on the bars accompanied by whistling, then singing.

"Would somebody send out for a banana, please," asked the old man politely. Then he returned to his gorilla rap.

"Pay no mind to Teddie A., toompa,
   toompa, toompa, toom,
She'll only make your hair turn gray,
   voompa, voompa, voompa, voom.
We will rescue her right quick,
   whoompa, whoompa, whoompa,
   whoom.
Look behind you, here comes Lick!
   Zoompa, zoompa, zoompa, zoom."

"Dadgummit, Al," said Pickhandle, "you'll give it away! Be careful what you say."

"Right," said Al, realizing that if Pickhandle could comprehend his coded rap message, it was entirely possible the gorilla could as well. But Garganzo, swaying gently to the beat, simply continued staring at Al.

T.A. slowly rolled her head to the side and

spied Lick crawling down the tiger tunnel that connected to the cage. She managed a weak smile as Lick silently reached the back entrance to the cage. He was now six feet from her.

Lick quietly raised the sliding back door and eased into the cage on his hands and knees. He reached for her hand.

Suddenly, the old man sneezed! The crowd gasped! Garganzo shook himself out of his trance and lifted T.A. off the sawdust floor so quick her head snapped back. He roared, then lifted her over his head as if he was going to throw her across the cage.

Lick pushed off the cage wall and hit the gorilla with a shoulder-crunching body block to the stomach. Lick bounced backwards just as T.A. tumbled from Garganzo's grasp. T.A. fell on top of him like a slamming car trunk just as Ponce lost his grip and fell from the ceiling into Garganzo's open arms.

T.A. had had enough. She whirled on Garganzo and picked up the whip Ponce had dropped. Using the heavy, blunt handle end, she took a swing at him.

"I'm trying to save you, you ungrateful thickheaded pie-faced primate! It's no wonder you're becoming extinct! I've put myself through humiliation, heartbreak, heartburn, and horrific horrible hazards to save you and your unrelated, unthinking, unable, Feed-Me-I'm-Yours, moronic, mentally unsophisticated mammalian mothers of the Endangered Species Club! Get your act together, I can't do it alone!"

Each expostulation was accompanied by a resounding thunk or whack of the whip. Garganzo used Ponce to block each blow. Finally T.A. ran out of steam. Garganzo was backed up against the bars, Ponce cringing in his arms. Lick was sitting upright in the sawdust out of the line of hellfire.

T.A. took a deep breath. Her shoulders fell. The white lab coat was ripped in two down the back and draped off her arms like angel wings. Pieces of sawdust speckled her wild hair. Her lip was bleeding. She stared at Garganzo, trying to regain her composure.

"It's all right, boy. I just got carried away," she said in a calm voice. Then to Ponce she said, "From you, I don't want much."

Ponce mustered a moment of bravado. "You won't get out of here alive, you little—"

T.A. screamed at the top of her lungs. A collective chill ran down the multiple spines gathered in earshot, including that of **Gorilla gorilla.** Garganzo thrust Ponce out in front of him in self-defense, holding the tiger tamer by the neck and thigh. T.A. brought the butt of the whip down hard on Ponce's presented rear end. Ponce stifled his scream. His eyes were bulging and he was making gagging sounds.

"It's okay, gorilla," T.A. said, breathing heavily. "It's okay." Then to Ponce, "It is okay, isn't it?" She looked at him quizzically.

Ponce gagged again.

"What?" she asked. "I can't understand you."

Ponce gagged again, his face turning redder.

"Maybe if you'd nod your head, I'd know you understood," she suggested.

Ponce struggled to nod his head. Garganzo didn't like that, so he shook him fiercely, causing Ponce's head to bob.

"I'll take that as a yes," she said. "All right, gorilla, relax."

Garganzo did. He released his chokehold on Ponce, dangling the tiger tamer by one foot like a doll.

T.A. slowly squatted down so she could speak to Ponce. "From you I would like a promise that you will never keep endangered species again. Since your promise is worth nothing, being as how you are a dishonorable man, in one month I am calling the FBI, the CIA, the Humane Society, the Rotary Club, whoever is in charge of the Endangered Species Act. I will tell them that there are reports that you're holding these animals captive. You will return the millions you have already taken from these high-dollar scumbags you suckered into the hunt."

"What about the money you took?" he gasped out.

"That money will be my insurance. For now you'll have to cover the debit from your own account. You stay clean and out of the endangered-species business, and I'll give you all your money back in ten years. You come after me or the animals in any way, and letters go out to every major newspaper and every animal rights organization you can shake a stick at. That's my deal. Take it or leave it—and all your money.

"Anything else?" asked T.A., looking around at Lick and then at the old man, who still stood outside the bars.

"Looks like you've said it pretty well, darlin'," said the old man. "Except maybe these good folks would like to have a word with Mr. Pantaker and the lion tamer there."

With that Cody pushed F. Rank up to the cage door, then stepped back. "Cowboys," he said, "stand back and let those good folks through!"

Two Arabian sheiks (the deserter had found his way back), the Asian grandmother, Southern California baseball player, Colombian drug dealer, Texas oilman, lady rock singer, and a scraped-up and bruised trial lawyer crowded into the area.

Qpid d'Art pushed her way to the front. She was carrying a beautiful hand-carved 12-gauge shotgun. It was a souvenir of the brace of bald eagles she signed up to gun down before Teddie Arizona intercepted her hunt. She stood in front of F. Rank Pantaker, who was a foot taller than she.

Qpid spoke: "When you first approached me about this exotic hunt, I saw it as expanding my horizon. After all, lots of money can help you look beyond what normal people can see. I thought I'd be testing the limits of what I could do if there were no restrictions, if no rules applied to me—if I were above the law.

"I cannot speak for that poor orange man in the corner wearing the black-and-gold loincloth and blubbering uncontrollably. Nor for these practitioners of excess gathered behind me in various states of denial and disappointment. But as for me, this woman before me, this Princess Di without Chuck, this Rosa Parks without Jesse, this Cher without Sonny, this Harley without Training Wheels, has shown me the Power, the Eloquence, the Infinity, and the Roar of Righteousness!

"She has not only stood up to your organized army of Park Avenue thugs who would destroy without remorse, she went to war without a gun, a banner, or a chance. Except, my fellow wayward sheep, she had right on her side! She has shined the light of Truth, Justice, and the American Way into this Rock and Roll heart!"

Qpid d'Art was now standing on tiptoes and breathing in F. Rank's face. Her two large offensive guards stood behind her, one over each shoulder. Both were scowling at F. Rank.

"As for you," she said, glaring up at him, "I want my money back. All five hundred—count-it-friends-in-cash—thousand smackeroos." She paused, holding his gaze through his fluttering eyelids. "GOT IT?!" she screamed.

There was a roar from the crowd, clapping and cheering. Qpid turned to the other hunters and asked, "Who would also like their money back?"

It was like an octopus wedding. All eight said, "I do."

"May I have a word with you?" T.A. asked Qpid.

"Girl, you have my undivided attention."

T.A. took Qpid aside for a short private conversation. At its conclusion Qpid returned to speak directly to F. Rank.

"I have been asked to provide an affidavit for your ex-wife that you and your nasty little circus friend deliberately tried to induce me into committing multiple felonies for your personal gain. I will gladly, and I do mean gladly, do it, and testify on her behalf should you attempt to cause her harm in any way. It is possible that I could get Golden Boy and that tall Texan each to sign one, too. They seem to have at least a spark of decency left in them. This threat, which you better believe is a threat, should help keep your relationship with your ex-wife cordial until her warrant expires, if you get my drift."

F. Rank resigned himself to making the best of a bad situation. "I get yer drift," he said. "She'll get no trouble from me."

When the attention was finally returned to Ponce de Crayon, he was on his hands and knees in the sawdust gasping for breath. His brilliant suit was in tatters and he was barefoot. The gorilla was chewing on one of his shoes.

"Am I going to have any trouble with you, Ponce?" asked T.A.

He gagged and coughed.

"I need to know now, while Godzilla here can be my witness," she said.

"Why you—!" Ponce screeched. The gorilla reached out and whacked him upside the head with the shoe.

"Okay, okay," he said, cringing. "I'll refund the money. Not because of you—" THWACK! T.A. had signaled the gorilla, who shoe-slapped him sideways again. "Well, yes, because of you. But"—he resorted to a whine—"as for the endangered species, you're making a mistake. I was doing a lot to preserve the animals, special breeding programs and—"

She cut him off with, "Tell someone else. You just do what I say or I'll be siccing the Endangered Species dogs on you. Your career will be blue smoke quick as you can say 'Lock me up!'"

"It's not over," he ventured bravely.

"You lost, Ponce," she said. "Get used to it. Lick, take me out of here."

73

December 13: The National Finals Rodeo

At 8:00 p.m. that night, Teddie Arizona was sitting in the block of seats reserved for the Old Timers Reunioneers during the ninth performance of the National Finals Rodeo at Thomas & Mack Arena in Las Vegas, Nevada.

She sat with her shoulders slumped. A shower and a change of clothes hadn't done much to restore her energy. Even her bone marrow was exhausted. She should have been Mount Everest–exhilarated but the most she could stir up was a sea-level satisfaction. Looking in the hotel room bathroom mirror, she'd been shocked at how thin she looked. **Down fifteen pounds, at least,** she thought. Numb, jittery, she had a bad case of winding down.

The announcer's animated voice seemed far away, metallic, echoing. T.A.'s meltdown continued. She'd barely noticed when an officious cowboy had come and taken Lick and Cody away during the calf roping. The old man sat on her left in conversation with whoever would listen to him. At present it wasn't her. She closed her eyes and seemed to collapse inside herself.

Earlier in the evening when they arrived at the arena, Lick, Cody, T.A., the old man, and all the Old Timers had gone directly to the Gold Card Room as guests of the Old Timers Rodeo and Reunion.

The Gold Card Room was a living Rodeo Hall of Fame. A painting-in-progress of the sport. A buckin' and ropin' buffet. Eavesdroppers could hear history being rewritten between slaps on the back, drinks served, and rides rerode and reroped.

The nightly party was sponsored by those companies that sponsor everything rodeo does. The companies pay dearly to be part of the sport. They make sure those professional rodeo cowboys and cowgirls who qualify as Gold Card members are treated like royalty. Of course, since even rodeo royalty aren't always that well behaved, the stories can get raucous and the bull manure knee-deep. Matter of fact, just havin' the old man in attendance brings it up to your ankles.

"Why, Pickhandle here jumped off the back of a moving army tank onto a Benedictine tiger!" he told a circle of groupies who'd already heard about the morning's endangered-species hunt. "Threw him to the ground! Last time I saw him move that fast was when them two big ol' boys threw him headfirst out the door of that cantina in Juárez the night Benny won bronc ridin' and broke the heels off his boots!" Et cetera, et cetera, ad infinitum or closing time, whichever comes first.

Pike and Chrisantha had come along as guests at the old man's insistence.

Cody became boisterous. He was not necessarily prone to wearing the lampshade but tonight he tried it on. The old man made sure it fit. To his credit, Cody had maintained good behavior for these first two years of his marriage. Tonight was also his anniversary, with his first child due in January, whom he planned to name Lick if it was a boy, and he was wishing his darlin' Lilac was with him.

Lick was unnaturally subdued. It was good to be back among his rodeo peers. In that small

Gold Card Room everyone knew about his spectacular ride at the National Finals two years ago on the unridden bull Kamikaze. But they also all knew of his poor performance the following year and his departure from rodeo shortly after. He was, in his own mind, and he supposed in theirs, a One-Ride Wonder. Whether he considered his condition out on Pandora's Thumb to be the bottom of his fall, or the mountain he had to climb to find himself, is moot. Up until this last month or so, all he knew was that life was shooting at him and he was layin' low.

Then Teddie Arizona had parachuted into his self-imposed mental monasticism and tangled him in the lines. It was not until he'd lost her in Mountain City that the love bug had burst like a leaky dam inside his heart, releasing a torrent of urgent fingerling feelings all swimming upstream through the rivers of his body desperately seeking some validation that he was worth more than the algae that grew on the rocks at the bottom of Bruneau Canyon.

Teddie Arizona had moved from a basic urge in his loins into the cerebral part of his mind, and then deeper, into the bedrock of his being. Without knowing it, she had staked a claim on the mineral rights of his soul. She went from being something he could manage to something that could squeeze his heart, make him cry, and give him wings.

Love comes without a warning and proves that the intellect of man, in all its brilliance, is no match for the magic of pheromonic pollen that has guided creation before the time the apple evolved into a dumpling.

Lick had stayed close by Teddie in the Gold Card Room, protecting her in his own way. She seemed to appreciate his nearness, and though she wasn't giddy or vociferous, relief shone from her eyes.

Now Teddie was back in the rodeo bleachers, the Women's Barrel Racing being played out in front of her. It was fast and furious, the loud music fitting the frenetic pace of the horses. Teddie Arizona watched them mechanically, her mind a blank. At the conclusion of the barrel racing, the announcer, the ubiquitous Emerald Dune, spoke to the full house. "Ladies and gentlemen, we have a special presentation and would like your attention before we start the bull riding!

"As you know, the cowboys couldn't show their skills and talent without the animals to make them look good: the calves, the steers, the broncs, the barebacks, and the bulls. What you see performing here at the National Finals are the best our stock contractors are able to produce. Some of these horses and cattle are bred, selected for desirable traits, and others are discovered at smaller rodeos, on ranches, or in somebody's backyard.

"Every year we honor the Best Bareback, Best Saddle Bronc, and Best Bull. We did that last night, as many of you know. But even among such outstanding animals there are standouts. Once in a generation a giant comes on the scene that makes us step back in awe. The best of the best, the epitome, the pinnacle, the peak, a single beast that reminds us that no matter how good we cowboys get, there will always be some lone lion that can put us in our place. Tonight we are going to honor one such animal, who will be the first animal to actually be inducted into the Pro Rodeo Cowboy Hall of Fame."

T.A. sat bolt upright.

"This is such an unusual presentation that I'm not sure it will ever happen again," Emerald Dune went on. "Without further fanfare, if you will turn your eyes to chute number four!"

The lights in the arena went dark. Music reminiscent of the theme from **Jaws** began to pound. A spotlight began to pulse along with the music, getting brighter with each deep throb. The strobing light found chute number 4.

A lone cowboy stood behind the chute, up on the catwalk, holding a bull rope. The crowd could see a bull in the chute beneath him. A sonic crescendo rose to the occasion, then dropped to white noise. The sudden silence caused the crowd to still.

Emerald Dune broke the silence in reverent tones: "Ladies and gentlemen, after only six years in rodeo, during which he won Bull of the Year three times, Maid Brothers Rodeo Company is retiring the great KA-MA-KA-ZEEEEE!"

The cheering tickled the rafters!

Hard-core rodeo fans in the stands knew why such a spectacular bull was being turned out to pasture long before most others in his business would be. He was simply too danger-ous. Kamikaze had shown his single-minded in-tent to rule by deliberately attempting to pulverize any riders who attempted to conquer him. His legacy was littered with broken bones, broken spirits, and at least one corpse.

In real life there are animals that cannot be dominated. Horses, dogs, bulls, rams, maybe boars and tomcats, too. They may be of domesticated stock, but they are a throw-back to the fight-to-the-death instinct.

Whenever man is forced to deal with these special creatures, he assumes the position of just another challenger in the pecking order.

To these animals, life is not a game.

The chute boss pulled open the gate on chute number 4. One thousand eight hundred and ninety-five pounds of muscle and blood, skin and bone stood quietly inside. Kamikaze slowly swung his massive head so that he could look straight out into the arena. The dark stripes above his eyes looked like eyebrows on a gargoyle. The horns as big around as a man's calf spread their wings like an evangelist at the altar call.

The announcer continued to elucidate the bull's background, while Kamikaze continued to stand inside the chute even though the gate was wide open. He was confused. The gate wasn't supposed to open until a victim had sat down on his back. If you could read his bovine mind, it would have said, "?"

It was then that Kamikaze recognized the scent of the cowboy standing above him behind the chute.

One could forgive Kamikaze for not identifying the atoms of Lick right away. After all, there had been hundreds of cowboys on his back. But this particular olfactory signal brought back a bad memory. Camel hair was somehow involved?

Rage or revenge is not something a bull would know anything about. Bulls have no motive to fight, save to protect their territory. And in Kamikaze's case, his territory was . . . wherever he was. But his ponderous mind began to sift back through the mental Rolodex and it located Lick's scent. It was, to him, as specific as the track of a crippled gnu to a hungry cheetah. The memory of their battle sluiced through his mind. Resentment stirred inside him. The competitive need to reassert his dominance rumbled to the surface like a tidal wave. He focused the feeling. Then he swung his two-hundred-pound head to the left far enough so that one big eye could see the cowboy on the catwalk behind him. Lick returned his gaze. For a supernatural moment, they entered each other's consciousness.

After an eternal second, the bull squinted his eye to a glare. He dared into the space between them, "FEELIN' LUCKY?"

Lick had this terrible urge to jump on Kamikaze's back.

There are moments in everyone's life, or at least in mine, when you become extraterrestrial. I remember hanging from a windmill twenty feet off the ground and thinking, I can fly. I can make that green light, I can eat that seventy-five-ounce steak, I can swim to shore, I can ride that horse.

Add into the mix the thrill, an audience,

alcohol, a fair damsel to impress, the feeling of invincibility, and the siren that calls to people who live on the edge, and you have the formula for greatness or disaster, Apollo 13 or Little Bighorn.

My doctor once said to me, "You know how some people will have a drink to reduce their inhibitions?"

"Yes," I replied.

He said, "You need yours."

The sparrow of sanity fluttered in and lit on Lick's shoulder, breaking his concentration. His head cleared and he slid slowly back to earth. Cody was standing beside him, holding on to his arm with both hands. Lick had his hands on the top board and one leg over the board into the chute.

"Come on back, Lick," said Cody, gently. "You don't have to ride Kamikaze . . . twice."

The crowd had watched the exchange between the cowboy and the bull. They all sat forward when he started to climb into the chute, then slipped back into their seats in relief when his partner stopped him. Most didn't understand what had happened. Matter of fact, maybe only Cody had an inkling. But it was nothing he could explain to anyone.

Teddie Arizona recognized Cody as the other

cowboy behind the chute. She grabbed the old man's arm when Lick swung his leg over the back of the chute.

"Al! What's he doing!" she cried.

"Jis' playin' with him, darlin'," said the old man, admiringly. "Jis' playin' with him."

"Ladies and gentlemen," the announcer intoned, "that cowboy scratching Kamikaze's back is none other than the one and only cowboy in the whole wide world to ever make a qualified eight-second ride on the otherwise unridden bull. Two years ago at the National Finals, in the tenth go, he came out of nowhere, literally," he added for the benefit of those who had been there, "and made a ninety-nine-point ride to win the average. Their names will forever be tied together and remembered by millions of rodeo fans."

The people in the audience rose in a standing ovation.

"Raise the roof for Kamikaze and Lick—" But by then the roar of the crowd had drowned out the announcer's voice.

Kamikaze strolled out into the arena. Lick dropped down into the chute dirt and stepped out there as well. Man and beast accepted the loving reception of a home-team crowd. It was a moment to die for, for the players and everyone in the bleachers.

We pick our heroes. It is a personal acco-
lade dispensed often in private to someone
who has affected only you. It is uncommon to
find a man or beast that stirs the same adula-
tion in a multitude.

Sports heroes are unique. They've saved no
lives, written no constitutions, built no coun-
tries. They simply inspire us. Let us rise vi-
cariously above the nuts and bolts of life's
day-to-day maintenance and show us a facet
of what our very own human race can do with
the right physical gifts, perseverance, and will
to achieve.

The audience's applause was recognition
of the effort two competitors gave to a sport
that sometimes lifts the cowboy way of life
above Louis L'Amour and ridin' pens at
Hitch's Feedlot in Guymon, and they poured
it on.

The big bull sniffed the air and smelled the
adoration. Lick did, too. Glory has its own
scent. The applause died down, the exit gate was
opened, and Kamikaze walked out of the dirt
arena without so much as a look back.

The lights suddenly came up and Lick was
swept off to the side as the ceremony came to a
close.

Lick and Cody were escorted back to their

seats in time to watch the last of the bull riding. Lick sat next to T.A. at the end of the row while Cody found a seat on the other side of the old man.

T.A. put her arm through Lick's and squeezed it. After the lights came up, they all remained seated for a while to let the crowd disperse. As they walked up the concourse toward the exit, everybody and their dog wanted to visit with Lick.

Representatives of one of the major sponsors invited him into their skybox for a soda. Lick was introduced to a marketing man, who asked about his availability for endorsement of their product. Lick told them he'd quit chewing tobacco. They said it didn't make any difference. Could he leave them his card?

Lick didn't have a card. He didn't have a phone number. Lick didn't even have an address. "I'll call you," he said, not the least bit embarrassed, and they gave him their card.

Cody and the old man had joined the Old Timers and gone with them to Pharaoh's for a nightcap. The marketing man turned to Lick and T.A. "Can I drop you two somewhere?"

Teddie Arizona knew just the place. After all, this was her town. Soon she and Lick were seated in a luxurious private booth in an alcove at one of Las Vegas's finest restaurants.

They ordered. Lick ate heartily while T.A. picked at her food. They both were mentally and physically exhausted.

Finally, after T.A.'s third glass of wine and Lick's second tequila and soda, the time had come. She waited until the waiter had cleared the entrée plates. Then she stared at Lick until he paid attention.

"What," she asked, when she had his eye, "do I do with you?"

Lick looked at her with a silly grin. Then he set his glass down and leaned back in his chair. "Well, I've got some good news for you and some bad news. The good news is . . . I think— no, I know—I love you."

She looked at him without changing expression. "And the bad news?" she asked.

"And, the bad news is," he continued, "I love you."

She had known what he was going to say before he said it. She knew, because females know. But knowing it didn't lessen her inability to deal with it. She was an emotional wreck. All she wanted was a good night's sleep, a week at Tenkiller, and a hot fudge sundae from Braham's.

Lick, on the other hand, had spilled the beans, placed his life in her hands, and confessed his heart's desire. He wanted to catch a cab, marry her, and get her in bed, not necessarily in that order.

* *   *

☾   Half an hour later, he was standing at the door of her hotel room, literally smothering her in kisses until they both were breathless.

She could feel the flat of his hand against the naked skin of her back. She could smell his outdoor maleness, a mixture of testosterone and sagebrush, which took her right back to Pandora's Thumb and the cow camp. His muscles were hard, his hands rough, his fingers gentle. He pressed against her and whispered his request in her ear: "Can I come in?"

Her conscience rose through the steam and said, "Yes. Yes, but I need your help to keep my vow. For the sake of all we've been through, and the new person I want to become, I'm not going all the way."

He kissed her neck and promised he'd try.

X

About the Author

BAXTER BLACK is one of the bestselling poets in American history. In the tradition of humorists like Robert Service, Mark Twain, and Will Rogers, he examines his corner of Americana and sheds light on the whys and the why-nots of humanity.

His job, as he describes it, is to "turn over our sanctimonious stones, locate our flaws and foibles, and wrap them in hunter's fluorescent orange. To nudge that fine line between good taste and throwing up in your hat."

Baxter can be seen "on the road" entertaining the agricultural masses, heard on National Pubic Radio amusing the urban intelligentsia, or found in the company of interesting domestic and nondomestic beasts.

He lives in Cochise County, Arizona, amid the cactus and Gila monsters, and runs a few cows. It's not a bad life.

If your curiosity is not yet slaked, find out more on www.baxterblack.com.